MURDER
IN PARK LANE

ALSO BY KAREN CHARLTON

The Detective Lavender Mysteries

The Heiress of Linn Hagh

The Sans Pareil Mystery

The Sculthorpe Murder

Plague Pits & River Bones

Individual Works

Catching the Eagle

Seeking Our Eagle (non-fiction)

The Mystery of the Skelton Diamonds (short story)

The Piccadilly Pickpocket (short story)

Life After Men (short story)

KAREN CHARLTON

MURDER
IN PARK LANE

THE DETECTIVE LAVENDER MYSTERIES

THOMAS & MERCER

Published by Thomas & Mercer, Seattle

www.apub.com

Amazon, the Amazon logo, and Thomas & Mercer are trademarks of Amazon.com, Inc., or its affiliates.

ISBN-13: 9781503955622
ISBN-10: 1503955621

Cover design and illustration by Lisa Horton

Printed in the United States of America

Dedicated to my good friends,
Kath Thomas and Eirwen Appleby.
Enjoy your book, ladies. xxx

Chapter One

Monday 21st September, 1812
Bow Street Magistrates Court & Police Office, London

The tall, athletic figure of Detective Stephen Lavender, a Principal Officer with the Bow Street Police Office, strode across the cobbled yard towards the stables, where his constable, Ned Woods, waited with their saddled horses. Woods was chatting with his fourteen-year-old son, Eddie, Bow Street's newest stable hand. Lavender had left father and son together while he sought out Magistrate Read for new instructions.

Woods must have noticed the spring in Lavender's step and the gleam in his eyes, because a wide grin spread across his broad moon of a face. 'Do we have a new case?' he asked.

'Yes, we have a suspected murder in Mayfair.'

Lavender took a set of reins from Woods' hand, pulled his black hat firmly down over his dark, wavy hair, then swung himself up on to the back of his mare.

Woods' greying eyebrows rose in surprise. 'Mayfair, eh? This seems a funny place for a suspicious death. We're used to the ragtag and scum of the Seven Dials murderin' each other but don't often find the toffs doin' it.'

'Sir Richard Allison, the surgeon, has requested our assistance,' Lavender explained. 'He's been called out to a dead body in a house on Park Lane. He believes the circumstances of the man's sudden death are suspicious.'

Woods' broad face contorted into an uncharacteristic frown. 'Huh! That's what the wheedlin' sawbones would have us believe.' He yanked the girth of his saddle a little too tight. His horse snorted in protest and stepped away from him.

Eddie frowned. 'Careful, Da.'

The experienced patrol officer ignored his son, raised his big hand and stroked the animal's neck in a soothing gesture.

Lavender fought back the urge to smile. 'I see your prejudice against Sir Richard hasn't abated with time, Ned.'

Sir Richard Allison expected to be treated like royalty whenever he deigned to assist the Bow Street constables with their investigations and his condescending arrogance made him unpopular with most of the officers. But with Woods it went deeper; he disliked Sir Richard with a vengeance and always had. Earlier that year, Sir Richard had removed a pistol shot from Woods' shoulder and saved his arm from amputation but the incident had done little to soften Woods' attitude towards the surgeon. In fact, it seemed to have made things worse; Woods hated to be beholden to anyone or anything.

For his own part, Lavender tried to remain professional in the surgeon's presence and recognised the man's brilliant medical expertise. But Allison had a vigorous enthusiasm for carving up dead bodies that even Lavender found slightly repulsive.

'He's probably killed one of his patients in a vile experiment and now he looks to us to cover up his mistake,' Woods grumbled as he heaved himself up into the saddle.

Lavender noticed the difficulty his constable had mounting the horse. Woods' shoulder injury made riding difficult and had meant the end of his distinguished career with the horse patrol. Following this, Magistrate Read had assigned Woods as Lavender's permanent assistant. The crime rate in the capital had grown alarmingly in recent years and Lavender was relieved and grateful for the extra help; besides which, there was no other man in the country whom Lavender trusted as much as Ned Woods.

Lavender gathered up his reins in his gloved hands and dug his heels into his horse's flank but Woods was already ahead of him.

'Park Lane, you said?' Woods asked as he led the way across the dung-strewn stable yard.

'Yes, number ninety-three.'

'I suppose we'd better go and see what that sly fox of a surgeon wants. See you later, son.' Woods' broad shoulders were rigid with disapproval beneath the blue greatcoat of his uniform. As they rode out of the stable yard beneath the arched entrance, he turned and added to Lavender: 'Sir Richard were probably extractin' the poor fellah's organs while he were still breathin'.'

Lavender grinned and followed him out into the heaving streets of Covent Garden.

They made slow progress through the heavy traffic. Hackney carriages were nose to tail, with a long, rumbling line of empty wagons returning from Covent Garden's fruit and vegetable market. Stalls blocked the pavements on both sides of the Strand, selling everything from ladies' bonnets to quack cures for arthritis, dropsy and gout. The shoppers jostled for space and were forced out on to the road by the stalls, further slowing the traffic. The rumble and clatter of wheels over the stones and cobbles and the shouts of the traders, hawkers and frustrated wagon drivers filled the air.

The roads were wider in the quieter, leafier streets of the burgeoning West End of London, and better maintained. Hyde Park, too, was quiet this morning. A few liveried grooms on thoroughbreds thundered up and down the loose gravel bridle path known as Rotten Row but it was still too early in the day for the promenading gentry in their gleaming carriages and elegant finery.

The houses on Park Lane were mostly five or six storeys high, colonnaded and topped with ornate and exaggerated chimneys, displaying the wealth of their owners. A plain, flat-fronted house in a short, narrow terrace, number ninety-three was modest in comparison with its elaborate and stuccoed neighbours.

Lavender and Woods dismounted and tied their horses to the park railings opposite the property.

A small, grubby boy with a broom was sweeping away the horse dung from the paved street. Woods beckoned him over. The boy scowled with distrust at the sight of Woods' distinctive uniform but his eyes widened with delight when he saw the penny in the officer's palm.

'What's your name, son?'

'It's Will, guvnor.'

'It looks like you do a good job on the road with your broom, Will.'

The boy was undernourished and dressed in rags but he pulled himself up to his full height and bristled with pride. 'I'm paid by the Kensington Turnpike Trust to sweep 'er clean every day.'

Woods glanced up and down the street and nodded approvingly. 'I can see you keep her very clean, son.'

The dirty little face below the greasy fringe beamed. 'I do me best. It's the 'aycarts that's the worst. Wisps of the stuff just float down everywhere. And what wi' the black dust from them coal carts and trails o' gravel from the stone wagons, it can be an 'ard job sometimes.'

Woods wiggled the penny. 'It sounds like a hard job, but do you think you can work and keep an eye on our horses at the same time, son?'

'I can, guvnor.'

'Good lad,' Woods said. 'You keep them safe and I'll give you this penny when we come back.'

The boy beamed and touched the ragged brim of his filthy cap.

Lavender smiled. This was why he and Woods worked so well together. Ned had the common touch, a quality Lavender knew he lacked himself. His constable's help was invaluable whenever they had to seek the trust or support of ordinary working folks.

Not that there would be many working men and women involved in this case. Park Lane was one of London's most desirable areas and the houses tended to be inhabited by wealthy aristocrats and ambassadors. Sir Richard's involvement in the case also suggested the dead man wasn't an ordinary citizen of London; the surgeon charged a hefty fee for private medical treatment.

Beside him, Woods shook his head gently and said again: 'This seems an odd place for a suspicious death.'

The maid showed them into the parlour on the ground floor. The narrow room was modestly furnished, with just a hint of old-fashioned grandeur. The wood-panelled walls had been painted white to reflect back the weak light filtering through the heavy drapes around the window. The floral upholstery, cushion covers and Meissen ornaments on the mantelpiece softened the starkness of the room.

Sir Richard Allison and a pale but dignified woman aged about fifty sat by the fireplace in a pair of faded Queen Anne armchairs. The woman wore a long-sleeved, high-necked black dress with a woollen shawl draped over her narrow shoulders and a simple white lace cap on her silver hair.

Sir Richard was leaning forward, holding the woman's hand, his face etched with concern above his spotless cravat. He sat back hastily when the maid announced their arrival. 'Lavender! Woods! Thank goodness you were able to get here so promptly!' He brushed back his thick mop of grey, curly hair from his face and rose to his feet. His cheeks were flushed and matched the dark red damask of the silk waistcoat he wore beneath his beige cut-away coat. 'This is Mrs Palmer, the owner of the property. The deceased is Mr David MacAdam. Come! Let me take you straight to the body.'

Lavender and Woods nodded politely to Mrs Palmer while Sir Richard ushered them out of the room.

'This is your kind of case, Lavender – a mystery of the greatest magnitude,' Sir Richard said over his shoulder as they mounted the stairs. 'A man stabbed to death in a locked bedchamber, with no murder weapon or murderer to be found! Come! The body is on the top floor.'

Lavender was about to protest that no such thing was possible but decided to save his breath for the climb up the stairs. The surgeon was right; Lavender's interest was piqued. This was exactly the kind of mystery he most enjoyed.

'MacAdam was a businessman and a lodger in this house. When he didn't come downstairs for breakfast, Mrs Palmer came up here and found the door locked from the inside.'

'But if he were found dead inside a locked room, it must be a case of suicide, surely?' Woods said.

'Those were my first thoughts, too, Constable. But how is a man to stab himself to death when he has no sharp implement?'

Woods frowned. 'How did Mrs Palmer gain entry if the room were locked?'

Sir Richard paused for a moment on one of the landings. Unlike many of London's lodging houses, which stank of kippers and boiled cabbage, this establishment smelt pleasantly of beeswax polish. 'When Mrs Palmer received no response to her calls, she used her spare key to force the other key from the lock inside the room. She found MacAdam on the bed in a pool of blood. She's very distressed, the poor woman – this is a respectable house – but she'd the presence of mind to send for me immediately. I found him dead on my arrival – quite dead. In fact, I suspect he'd been dead for some hours. Rigor mortis has already set in on the corpse.'

Lavender's eyebrow twitched with surprise at the surgeon's uncharacteristic display of empathy for the woman. 'Was there . . .' He broke off when a door opened on to the landing and a pale-faced young man appeared. He had fine, chiselled features and vivid blue eyes, fringed with long, dark lashes. Alarm flashed in those eyes.

'Sir Richard.'

'Mr Bentley.'

The surgeon and the stranger nodded politely to each other before the younger man moved past them to descend the stairs.

'How many people live here?' Lavender asked.

'I knew you would be interested in the household, Lavender, so I took the time to acquaint myself with the occupants before you arrived. There's Mrs Palmer, her maid and three lodgers: Messrs Bentley, MacAdam and Collins. Mr Collins is away on business in Yorkshire and Mr Alfred Bentley, whom you've just seen, is a clerk at the Grosvenor Estate office.'

'Why isn't he at work now?' Woods asked.

'I've no idea,' Sir Richard replied. 'You can't expect me to do all of your job for you, Constable. You'll have to ask him yourself if you think it's pertinent to the case.'

'Does Bentley know MacAdam is dead?' Lavender asked.

Sir Richard nodded. 'Mrs Palmer's cries of horror brought Bentley and the maid running when she discovered the body. Mrs Palmer is the widow of Colonel Palmer of the 53rd. Sadly, he left her in straitened circumstances when he died. She takes in lodgers to make ends meet. This . . . this *incident* is a great blow to her; she's always run a respectable house and is fearful of the scandal it might invoke.'

'Who was the last person to see MacAdam alive?'

'Mrs Palmer. She heard him come home around half past nine last night and met him on the landing when he came up to his bedchamber.'

'Did they talk? Was he in good health?'

'He wasn't bleeding to death if that's what you mean, Lavender. I understand they wished each other goodnight, then went to their rooms.'

'How is it you're so well acquainted with Mrs Palmer?' Lavender asked.

But Sir Richard didn't reply. They'd reached the top landing and were all breathless – especially Woods. The surgeon pointed to one of the doors and said: 'I've asked the undertaker to come this afternoon.'

Lavender made a mental note of Sir Richard's evasion then braced himself for what lay within the room.

Chapter Two

Lavender's sense of smell was the first thing to be assaulted by the stuffy death chamber. Stale alcohol mingled with male body odour and the ferrous tinge of congealing blood. Lavender wrinkled his nose and breathed through his mouth; the smell of blood always made him feel nauseous.

The bedchamber was another long, narrow room, darker than the parlour below because of the smaller window. But they didn't need much light to make out the grisly sight on the bed pushed next to the wall. Lavender felt Woods recoil then stiffen beside him.

MacAdam lay on his back in his undergarments on top of the crumpled and stained bedsheets. The corpse's eyes were partially closed and his firm, square jawline was slack. His abdomen was a bloodied mess. A limp, crimson arm trailed over the edge of the bed. It looked as if he'd tried to use his hands to stem the bleeding. MacAdam's clothes and the blankets were scattered around the bed in heaps on the floor.

For a moment, the three men stood and stared in grim silence, then Sir Richard moved over to the bedside and Woods turned to examine the door lock.

'We need some fresh air.' Lavender walked to the window and tried to open it.

'The wood's warped and the window's jammed,' Sir Richard said behind him. 'Mrs Palmer has meant to call a carpenter for some time.'

Lavender paused. His sharp ears caught the dull thud from several floors below as the front door shut. He glanced down to the street and watched the athletic figure of young Mr Bentley stride across Park Lane and climb into a waiting carriage. Lavender made a mental note of the coat of arms, with its pair of rampant stags, emblazoned on the gleaming veneer of the mahogany door.

The washstand stood beside the window. MacAdam's razor and shaving cream stood beside the bowl, along with an unlabelled dark brown glass bottle. Lavender unscrewed the lid and sniffed but recoiled at the biting odour of the lye. Hair dye. He glanced back at the bed and MacAdam's healthy head of thick, fair hair fanning out behind him on the pillow.

'The lock hasn't been forced, sir.' Woods stooped and retrieved an iron key from the floor. 'I reckon this is the key used to lock the door from the inside – the one Mrs Palmer claims she forced out of the lock with her own.'

Sir Richard bristled. 'Claims? Surely you've no reason to doubt the good lady's account, Constable?'

Lavender ignored him. 'Please give this room a thorough search, Ned. We need to find the knife.' Woods nodded and moved across to examine behind a row of books and papers stacked neatly on a shelf.

'You're wasting your time, Lavender,' Sir Richard said. 'It's not here. I've already looked.'

'We have to check again.' Lavender joined Sir Richard by the bed. He placed his hand on the dead man's head and parted MacAdam's fair hair. The scalp was burned red from the dye. Parallel lines of grey ran close to the roots down the parting.

David MacAdam had been what Lavender's mother would have called a 'fine figure of a man'. Probably in his mid- or late thirties, he would be as tall as Woods in his stockinged feet; nearly six feet tall. The dead businessman had well-proportioned shoulders and a broad chest but beneath the gaping crimson slash on his stomach an extra layer of fat snaked around his middle – the thickening waistline of middle age.

Despite his chubbiness and the greying hair, MacAdam had been a good-looking man with evenly spaced features. The blood had drained away from his face, leaving a deathly pallor, but apart from a trickle of blood beneath his nose, his complexion was clear of pock-marks and blemishes. He looked peaceful in death.

Lavender's eyes followed the dried rivers of blood snaking down the man's generous girth to the crumpled sheet and he frowned. Why did the man just lie there and let himself bleed to death? This must be a suicide. There was no other explanation for such passivity in the face of death. If he'd been attacked, surely he would have sought help?

'What happened here, Sir Richard?' he asked.

Sir Richard cleared his throat, removed his coat and rolled up his sleeves. His medical bag was already in the room on the bedside table. 'Well, as far as I can establish without an *autopsia cadaverum*, the fellow died from a single stab wound to the stomach. There are no other visible marks of injury or assault on his body.'

Lavender glanced at the dried lake of blood beneath the corpse. 'What about on his back?'

Sir Richard's eyes narrowed. 'Ha! So, you think I've left the stone unturned, do you, Detective? No. I turned him over earlier – there's no injury on his back. This is the only one. The blood from his nose is the direct result of internal haemorrhaging and not a separate injury.'

'Can you tell us about the weapon we're searching for?'

'The blade was narrow, about half an inch wide and . . .' The surgeon straightened and reached for his bag. He pulled out a long, thin metal object, which he gently inserted inside the wound on MacAdam's stomach, pushing it in as far as it would go. Despite his revulsion, Lavender leaned forward to get a better look.

Sir Richard frowned and jerked the implement backwards and forwards against MacAdam's flesh. He pulled it out, cast it aside and returned to his bag for another probe. This one had a slight curve to the blade and slid easily into the corpse. Finally satisfied, Sir Richard pulled out the implement and examined the dark stains mottling its surface.

'The blade penetrated about four inches – and it was curved.'

'Curved? What kind of street knife is narrow and curved?' Lavender exclaimed.

Sir Richard shrugged. 'It's your job to answer that question. I can only give you the facts.'

'Are those four inches right up to the hilt?' Woods asked. 'Were it jammed right inside of him?' He'd finished his examination of the cold fireplace and chimney and was now on his knees by the bed, rummaging amongst the pile of discarded clothes and blankets.

'I can't tell.' Sir Richard scooped up MacAdam's discarded cravat from the floor and wiped his implements clean on the fine linen. 'The weapon may have been longer and only partially inserted. Either way, it stabbed him in the liver, a solid organ that bleeds profusely. He was unfortunate. If the knife had penetrated him an inch or so lower and gone into the hollower organs, the stomach or the intestines, he may have survived.'

'Gawd's teeth! What devilish contraption is this?' Woods pulled a large, sweat-stained garment made of strong linen from the bottom of the pile of discarded clothing on the floor. Rigid with whalebone stays, it trailed a line of discoloured laces behind it.

Sir Richard laughed. 'Haven't you seen a man's corset before?'

Woods looked revolted. 'Men wear these as well as women?'

Lavender smiled. 'Some men do, especially those popinjays who've gained weight and are vain about their appearance – like MacAdam. I found a bottle of hair dye on the dresser, too.'

'Does this knowledge about his vanity help us find out how he died?' Sir Richard's tone was sceptical.

'No, but it gives us a better understanding of the living man.'

Woods continued to hold the corset at arm's length. 'This looks like a torturous contraption to me.'

'I think you should try one, Constable,' Sir Richard said, smiling. 'It would suit you.'

Woods sucked in his belly and glared at the surgeon. 'Are you sayin' I'm fat?' He patted his stomach. 'I'll have you know, this is all brawn and muscle.'

Sir Richard grinned. 'All brawn and no brains, eh, Woods? Yes, I've thought that for a while.'

Woods threw down the corset, rose to his feet and stomped across to the closet. He yanked open the door and rummaged through MacAdam's clothes.

'How long would it have taken MacAdam to die after he was stabbed?' Lavender asked hastily. Woods' shoulders were rigid with anger.

Sir Richard went to the washstand and poured water out of the jug into the bowl to wash his hands. 'The effects of internal haemorrhaging are always difficult to gauge. It depends on the severity of the injury. The victim would have been blinded with headaches, quickly become disorientated and lost consciousness within twenty or thirty minutes.' He picked up a thin towel and dried his hands. 'That's all the help I can give you, Lavender. It's up to you now to make sense of this infernal mess.'

Woods slammed the door of the closet shut. 'There's definitely no knife or weapon of any kind in this damned room. There's long-handled combs on the mantelpiece and there's no blood on them.'

'I told you so,' Sir Richard grinned. 'So, what do you think, Lavender? It's quite a mystery, isn't it?'

'Yes,' Lavender agreed. 'On the surface, it looks like our victim either stabbed himself with an invisible knife and lay back on his bed to die – or an unknown person assaulted him then walked out of this room through a locked door and took the weapon with him.'

'Exactly what I thought!' Sir Richard exclaimed.

'And both scenarios are fantastical,' Lavender replied. 'MacAdam was obviously injured on the other side of his bedchamber door but came back here and died.'

'But how is that possible?' Sir Richard argued. 'Mrs Palmer saw him on the stairs and he wasn't haemorrhaging or complaining of any injury.'

'He may have been too addled to notice,' Woods said. 'This room and the corpse reek of stale brandy.'

'I've an idea.' Lavender pointed to the soiled undergarment on the floor. 'Ned, pass me the corset.'

Woods handed it over with disgust. Lavender soon found what he was looking for: a small, brown stain around a short tear in the cloth. He walked across to the better light at the window. 'Check his shirt and waistcoat for rips and bloodstains.'

Woods bent down to scoop up the clothing. 'I didn't see any before . . .'

'There might not be any blood. Look out for a straight, half-inch tear.'

Sir Richard watched curiously while the two men examined the clothes.

Woods' fingers explored the fine linen of MacAdam's shirt. He pointed to a faint mark. 'It's ripped like you said and there's a stain – but I think it's just dirt.'

'There's another tear in his waistcoat,' Lavender said, 'but no signs of any blood.' He removed the jug and bowl and laid down the corset on the washstand. Next, he took the shirt and the dark-blue silk waistcoat and positioned them on top of the corset, trying to replicate how he imagined they were draped across MacAdam's body. The tears in each garment lined up almost exactly but only the corset and the shirt had the tiniest specks of blood.

'What does this mean, sir?' Woods asked.

'It means, Ned,' Lavender said, 'that MacAdam was stabbed when he was fully clothed and outside this room – but the wound didn't bleed.'

Sir Richard frowned. 'But an injury like this would have haemorrhaged profusely!' the surgeon said. 'You saw the state of the bed. These clothes should be covered in blood – and Mrs Palmer said he looked fine when she met him on the stairs.'

'Is it possible,' Lavender asked slowly, 'that the constriction of the abdomen caused by the tight corset may have stemmed the external flow of the blood?'

Woods' eyes widened. 'What? You mean he were laced that tight he didn't bleed?'

Sir Richard reddened with frustration. 'A highly improbable theory, Lavender, but, yes – I suppose it's possible. For a while, the bleeding may have been internal – but the pain would have been intense. He'd have known something was wrong.'

'The lack of blood might have confused him. MacAdam may not have realised he'd been stabbed and had a life-threatening injury.'

'He had been drinkin' heavily,' Woods said thoughtfully.

Lavender glanced back at the lifeless corpse on the bloodstained bed. 'Gentlemen, I think we've just solved the first mystery of what happened to MacAdam. Now we need to talk to Mrs Palmer.'

Chapter Three

O n their way back down the stairs, Sir Richard warned Lavender not to press Mrs Palmer too hard with his questions, claiming she was of a delicate disposition. Lavender frowned and didn't respond. *Delicate* or not, Mrs Palmer was the last person to see MacAdam alive and – however improbable it may seem – she was now a suspect in this murder case.

A plain, silver-haired woman with pale, almost lashless eyes and a slightly bulbous nose, Mrs Palmer wore a black gown, which emphasised the whiteness of her skin. She put her needlework to one side when they entered the parlour and Lavender was struck with the elegance and grace of her long hands.

Shock flashed across her face and her hand fluttered to her mouth when Lavender explained what had happened to MacAdam. Sir Richard asked her if she needed a cup of tea to calm her nerves but the lady blinked back her tears and regained her composure.

'Oh no, Sir Richard. No tea, thank you.' Her voice was refined and gentle. She turned to Lavender. 'Please don't worry, Detective, I'm not as fragile as Sir Richard believes. I travelled the world with the British Army when my husband, Colonel Palmer, was alive. I've seen many sights in India that would give most young women the vapours – but I've always managed to remain conscious and calm.' Her eyes flicked towards an oval miniature on the mantelpiece of a proud, whiskered man in army uniform.

'Is that your late husband, ma'am?' Woods asked sympathetically.

'Yes, that was George.'

'He looks a fine figure of a man.'

'Yes, he was.' For a moment, she seemed to be lost in her memories.

Sir Richard sat down opposite Mrs Palmer. He hadn't put his coat back on and lounged casually in his shirt sleeves.

Mrs Palmer managed a sad smile and turned to Lavender. 'I always thought Mr MacAdam was a very handsome man, too. I never realised he needed the aid of a corset to sculpture his figure. This is almost as big a shock as his death. I can't believe he was mortally wounded when I saw him last night. I suspected nothing.'

'Were he in his cups, ma'am?' Woods asked. 'Had he been drinkin'?'

'Yes, I believe he was. He grunted when I wished him goodnight and he stumbled up the steps when he left me.'

'Do you know where he went last night?' Lavender asked.

She shook her head and her white lace cap wobbled on her silvery head. 'I don't. He left about seven o'clock and returned here at half past nine.'

Lavender nodded. 'Whereabouts on the staircase did you meet him?'

'On the floor above this room, just outside my own bedchamber.'

'Isn't that the floor below Mr Bentley's room?' Woods asked, voicing the question that leapt into Lavender's own mind.

'Yes.'

'Was Mr Bentley in his room?'

'Yes.'

'How long has David MacAdam lodged with you?' Lavender enquired.

'For nearly a year.'

'Was he a troublesome guest? Had he fallen behind with his rent?'

17

'No, certainly not. He was a perfect gentleman and always paid me on time, although he's a week or two behind at the moment. He was a most genial and charming man, very courteous.'

'Were his heavy drinkin' a problem?' Woods asked.

She shook her head and smiled gently. 'He wasn't a heavy drinker, Constable. He occasionally imbibed, yes, but he seemed to handle his liquor well. I've had many gentlemen tenants over the years and Mr MacAdam was one of my favourites. Such a cheerful, pleasant man.'

'Do you know which taverns or gentlemen's clubs he frequented?' Lavender asked. She shook her head again.

'Did he ever talk with you about his family? We need to notify his relatives of his death.'

A slight pause followed and something indiscernible flickered across Mrs Palmer's face. 'Oh, of course you will, yes. Mr MacAdam was unmarried and never talked about any other family, although I believe his relatives own a textile business in Chelmsford in Essex.' She dabbed her eyes with a lawn handkerchief. 'He worked for the family business.'

'What was it called, ma'am?'

'I'm afraid I can't remember the name . . .' She paused, perplexed. 'He used to stay here for short periods. He moved permanently to London about six months ago. He seemed to have plenty of money and was always smartly dressed.'

'We need to know the name and address of this family business in Chelmsford,' Lavender said. 'His parents may still be alive or there may be other relatives, siblings perhaps, who work within the company. I'm sure they'd want to know about his demise.'

Tears welled up in her pale eyes and slid down her cheeks. She dabbed them hastily with her handkerchief. 'Oh, those poor people! How sad they'll be. I'm sure he was well loved by his family. Everyone who knew him in London liked him.'

'Who were his acquaintances, Mrs Palmer? Can you supply me any names and addresses?'

Sir Richard shuffled uncomfortably in his chair and intervened. 'I think that's enough questions for now, Lavender. We don't want to distress Mrs Palmer any further.'

Woods turned to face Lavender and lowered his voice. 'I saw a pile of personal papers in the bookcase in MacAdam's room – and I think a company ledger is amongst them. It might give us a clue about the textile business, sir.'

Lavender nodded. 'Well done, Ned. I apologise for any distress I've caused you, Mrs Palmer, and I'll need to talk to you again, but you've been most helpful.'

Now weeping profusely, Mrs Palmer could only nod her head.

Lavender and Woods backed out of the parlour. Sir Richard leaned forwards and took the distressed woman's hand in his own when they left the room. Lavender closed the door gently behind them.

The hallway was refreshingly cool after the heightened emotion in the parlour.

'I'll go back up to the room and find that ledger,' Lavender said quietly. 'I need you to interview the maid, Ned. Find out what she saw and heard this morning and last night and check her account matches with that of her mistress.'

Woods' grey eyebrows rose in surprise. 'Do you think she may be lyin', sir? She seemed a pleasant lady to me, genuinely upset.'

Lavender frowned and he wrestled with his instinct to agree with Woods against the nagging seed of suspicion that niggled in his logical brain. 'I think there's something she's not told us about MacAdam. As far as we know, she was the last person to see MacAdam alive. She may have administered the fatal stab wound.'

Woods gasped. 'But what would be her motive?'

'I don't know. It's early days yet in this investigation and we must treat her exactly the same way we would any other suspect.'

'What about young Bentley? Maybe MacAdam met him on the next floor after he'd left Mrs Palmer outside her room.'

Lavender nodded and thought back to the coat of arms on the gleaming carriage door. 'We'll leave him until later. There's something I need to find out before we interview Bentley – and I suspect we need to travel to Essex this afternoon. Notifying MacAdam's next of kin of his death must be our priority today.'

Woods nodded and turned towards the kitchen door at the rear of the hallway, but he turned back and looked over his shoulder. 'And what about him?' The tone of his voice and the angry jerk of his thumb left Lavender in no doubt that Woods referred to Sir Richard. 'If you suspect her, then you can't rule out that he's involved. I've never known him so helpful in one of our investigations – or so carin' about a livin', breathin' woman.'

Lavender agreed with him but conscious of the couple on the other side of the parlour door, he held up his hand. 'We'll discuss this later.'

Chapter Four

B ack up in MacAdam's bedchamber, Lavender wedged open the door to air the stinking room. He avoided looking at the silent, bloodied corpse on the bed and caught sight of his own reflection in the mirror hanging above the mantelpiece. His brown, slightly hooded eyes were frowning with concentration. He brushed back a lock of dark, wavy hair from his high forehead and focused his attention on the shelf of books and papers.

Most of the books were borrowed from circulating libraries. They were a mix of sentimental melodramas, visitor guides to London attractions and a well-thumbed volume entitled *The Manners and Conduct of an English Gentleman*.

There was also a receipt from the bank of Messrs Down, Thornton and Gill, acknowledging a deposit of fifty pounds. He pocketed the receipt and turned back to the shelf.

The battered, dark-red company ledger was at the bottom of the pile and was the property of 'Drake's Tailors, a maker of gentlemen's clothing' on Moulsham Street in Chelmsford. The ledger was almost empty, apart from a few handwritten entries of sales to various establishments in London and the home counties. Lavender recognised the name of one of the establishments on Oxford Street; he'd purchased a new cravat from there recently. The sales recorded included greatcoats and waistcoats, with the odd batch of pantaloons and linen shirts. There was nothing to connect the ledger to MacAdam and the dates of the sales were several years old.

A small rectangular box at the end of the shelf caught Lavender's eye. Light ebony stripes and tiny beads patterned the glossy veneer, underlining the elegant forms of the body and lid. Too small to hold a weapon and therefore to attract Woods' interest, the box had passed unnoticed in their earlier search of the room. Lavender picked it up and tried to prise open the lid. It was locked. He glanced around at MacAdam's discarded clothes and wondered where the man kept the key that would open the tiny iron lock.

Returning to the washstand, he picked up MacAdam's dark-blue silk waistcoat and checked the pockets. Nothing. He found over three guineas and an expensive silver pocket watch in the dead man's black coat. He fingered the watch and its heavy chain for a moment. Robbery was clearly not the motive for the attack on MacAdam; no thief would leave something this valuable behind. But there was no sign of the key for the box in his coat pockets. Nor was it in the pockets of his smart kerseymere pantaloons.

He examined MacAdam's clothes. Made from good-quality materials and well tailored, they were the sort of garments Lavender himself would have happily worn – the clothes of professional and wealthy businessmen.

A long, silky, burnished copper hair was caught on the coarser material of the pantaloons. There were other chestnut-red hairs on the cuffs of a coat. *A clue to the female company MacAdam kept, perhaps?*

The silk label on the inside of the coat caught his eye: 'Drake's Tailors, established Chelmsford, 1777'. A quick examination of the labels in MacAdam's shirt, waistcoat and pantaloons revealed they were also made by the Chelmsford company. In fact, when he opened the closet and rummaged through the clothes, he found that nearly every item came from Drake's. Mrs Palmer had been right about MacAdam's connection with the clothing manufacturer; the man had been a walking advertisement for his family business.

He eventually found a small key in the pocket of MacAdam's spare coat in the closet and he returned to the bookshelf and the wooden box. The interior of the box was lined with white silk and a latticework of thin ribbons. It contained a pile of folded handwritten letters.

Lavender moved to the better light at the window to read.

> *My deerest, deerest David, I cannot but wait but until I see*
> *you again tomorrow . . .*

These were billet-doux, private love letters. Each one was recently dated and written by a devoted woman called Amelia Howard to MacAdam. Judging by her lapses in grammar and spelling, Miss Howard was either very young or had been poorly educated. He noted with surprise the expensive Mayfair address printed on the letterhead and wondered if she was a servant at the house. The next sentence cast doubt on that thought:

> *. . . it is my most ardint joy and pleasure to ride carriage with*
> *you on the Row . . .*

Servants didn't promenade with the gentry on Rotten Row through Hyde Park. Concluding that Miss Howard must have badly neglected her studies with her governess, he arranged the letters into chronological order and scanned their contents.

> *. . . kind Granpapa say he see no impediment to calling the*
> *bans in churches . . . my sister is so jelus of us . . . I miss you so*
> *much alredy and want to laff with you again . . . I send you*
> *precius box from India to keep letters in from me. I have its*
> *match for yours . . . write again today, deerest David . . . my*
> *heart leaps for your letters . . .*

The sound of Woods' heavy step on the stairs was a welcome relief from Miss Howard's passionate declarations of love for MacAdam. Lavender put the letters back in the box and looked up expectantly when his constable entered the room.

Woods shook his head. 'I've found out nothin' new. The maid slept through MacAdam's return last night. She were busy in the kitchen this mornin' when she heard Mrs Palmer scream. She found her mistress and Bentley in great distress on the landing. They sent her to fetch Sir Richard. She's only worked here for five weeks but tells me our sly fox of a surgeon is a regular visitor to this house.' He narrowed his eyes and looked challengingly at Lavender.

Lavender smiled. 'There could be several explanations for this, Ned. Mrs Palmer is probably one of Sir Richard's patients and has a malingering condition that is not obvious to our eyes.'

'Or she might be his mistress.'

'His what? Oh, for heaven's sake, Ned, that's a fanciful leap of the imagination. She must be ten or fifteen years older than he, at least.'

'There's no accountin' for a man's taste,' Woods growled. 'And he were holdin' her hand when we walked in . . .'

'Probably offering comfort. The woman has had a great shock.'

'When did your doctor last hold your hand?' Woods demanded. 'And when did either of us ever see that wheedlin' sawbones touch a woman before except with a scalpel?'

Lavender was almost lost for words in the face of Woods' indignant tirade, but his constable hadn't finished yet. 'And when did he ever take it upon himself to interview our witnesses for us? He's mightily concerned with this case. Overly concerned, in my view.'

'Ned, yes, Sir Richard does seem to be very protective of Mrs Palmer, but that doesn't make him her lover – or a suspect in MacAdam's murder. Sir Richard is Guy's Hospital's most eminent surgeon and he's married. I've never heard any rumours that he and Lady Allison aren't happy together.'

His words only partially mollified Woods. 'All men have their secrets. He's a dark horse, he is. I wouldn't be surprised if he weren't a rake in his youth. There's more to this than meets the eye, you mark my words.'

Lavender jammed the box of billet-doux into his greatcoat pocket and turned for the door. 'Come on, I've found some clues about MacAdam's family business and some letters from his sweetheart. We need to pay the young lady a visit then take a coach to Essex to find his family. Let's stop speculating and follow the evidence, Ned.'

But Woods still grumbled about slyboots and surgeons while he followed him down the stairs.

Sir Richard was waiting for them in the hallway when they reached the ground floor. 'Any luck up there, Lavender?'

'Yes, I've found a name and address for MacAdam's family business in Chelmsford. We'll go there this afternoon. We've finished with the scene of the crime. The undertaker may remove the body. Ask him to bring it to the Bow Street morgue. I'll try to find someone to claim it in Essex and pay for the funeral.'

'But what about the murderer? This fellow must be caught and hanged as soon as possible.'

'What makes you think it's a fellah?' Woods growled.

'Notifying the next of kin of the death is always our first priority in a murder case,' Lavender said. 'Sometimes the family can be very helpful. They might know the enemies of the deceased: disappointed business partners, scorned lovers, creditors, etcetera. We must also try to establish MacAdam's movements last night and find out where he went and whom he met.'

'Good, good . . . you seem to know what to do. By the way, I can rely on your discretion in this case, can't I, Lavender?'

Lavender stiffened and his eyes narrowed.

'You won't talk to the news-sheet reporters and will conduct your inquiries quietly, won't you?' There was a fine sheen of sweat on Sir

Richard's high forehead and the gleam of desperation in his pale, shifty eyes. 'The scandal of a murder in Mrs Palmer's house will be detrimental to both her business and her reputation.'

'I've no intention of speaking to journalists at the moment but this is a murder inquiry. The coroner will have to be informed and Magistrate Read will open an inquest. There'll be newspaper interest in this.'

'Yes, yes, I know the procedure. We'll cross that bridge when we come to it. But let's practise discretion where we can, shall we?'

Lavender said nothing and Sir Richard continued, 'Is there anything I can do to help? The sooner this ghastly business is resolved, the better.'

Lavender paused before he replied. 'I also came upon some personal correspondence from a Miss Amelia Howard to MacAdam. Perhaps you can ask Mrs Palmer what she knows about the young woman? It would also help if she can draw up a list of any other friends and acquaintances of MacAdam.'

'Yes, yes, you mentioned this before. Good luck in Essex.' Sir Richard turned back towards the parlour, opened the door and disappeared inside.

A man with a scythe was mowing the grass in Hyde Park close to their patient horses. The smell of fresh cut grass was a welcome relief from the stench of MacAdam's death chamber.

'What did I tell you?' Woods said when they walked out into the sunshine. 'Sir Slyboots Allison just offered to *help* us – and wished us luck? Don't try and tell me he's behavin' normally.'

Lavender paused for a moment beside his horse to think. Woods was right, of course – Sir Richard's behaviour was out of character, but they couldn't let that distract them in their hunt for the murderer.

Young Will, the road sweeper, scampered across to claim his penny from Woods. Lavender stroked the smooth neck of his horse and watched while Woods teased the boy for a moment or two before handing over the coin. He glanced up and down Park Lane thoughtfully. A uniformed nursemaid walked beneath one of the modern gas lamps, holding two small, well-dressed children by the hand. Birds warbled in the trees overhead and another carriage emblazoned with a coat of arms rumbled slowly down the tranquil street.

Woods came to his side and looked at him expectantly. 'Where to first, sir?'

'I think we need to split up. I'll go to Bruton Street and interview Miss Howard but I want you to visit some of the neighbours. Tell the occupants there's been a nasty murder at number ninety-three and tell them Bow Street officers are investigating the case and need information. Give them MacAdam's description and ask them to question everyone else in the household about anything suspicious they may have seen or heard last night.'

'It would have been dark by then,' Woods said.

'Yes, but look at those lamp posts, Ned. This street is well lit and if MacAdam was on foot when he was attacked, someone may have seen or heard something unusual.'

'He may have come home by hackney carriage.'

Lavender frowned. 'Yes, perhaps he did, but he would have been in terrible pain and if he was in a cab, why not ask the driver to take him straight to the nearest doctor? No. I think he was on foot – and the stabbing happened not far from here. He staggered home to examine his wound.'

'Perhaps he intended to ask Mrs Palmer to send for a doctor?' Woods suggested.

Lavender nodded and paused for a moment, his mind lost in speculation. 'Sir Richard was quite clear MacAdam would have only had about half an hour after the attack before he lost consciousness.

27

MacAdam needed at least five minutes to get into the house, up to his room and undress.'

'So you reckon the attack took place within a twenty-five-minute walk of here?' Woods glanced up and down the street. 'That's a lot of fancy households to visit – and it'll cause quite a commotion on a respectable street like this.' A wide grin stretched across his round face. 'And I don't think it'll meet Sir Slyboots' notion of "discretion".'

Lavender shrugged and untied the reins of his horse from the railings. 'It's impossible to conduct a murder inquiry quietly. Sir Richard has worked with us long enough to realise this. You make inquiries here and meet me back in Bow Street in two hours. Word of the murder will spread rapidly. Make sure everyone knows that any information pertaining to the attack on MacAdam is to go straight to the Bow Street Police Office. We'll come back tomorrow afternoon and visit more houses if we have to.'

'Are we still goin' to Essex?'

Lavender nodded and began to lead his horse in the direction of Berkeley Square. 'We'll take the two o'clock coach to Chelmsford. We may need to stay overnight.' The horse clopped steadily behind him.

'Why are you walkin'?' Woods called after him.

'I want to see if Miss Howard lives within a twenty-five-minute walk from here.'

Chapter Five

I t took Lavender about fifteen minutes to lead his horse through the traffic to Bruton Street, the home of Miss Howard. The road ran off Berkeley Square, one of the most famous and desirable residential locations in all of London.

Personally, Lavender thought the towering houses in this part of London were rather ponderous and heavy, but the five acres of parkland in the centre of the square, with its statues and shady plane trees, added a touch of elegance. The neighbourhood was also haunted by footpads, who waited to pounce on unwary pedestrians on the unlit steps of some of the small alleys that ran off from the square. Most of the Berkeley Square inhabitants only left home in their carriages, accompanied by burly servants for protection, but Bow Street Police Office had dealt with several cases of robbery and assault in this vicinity.

Bruton Street consisted of two long terraces of five- and six-storey houses, similar to the ones he'd just passed in the square. They had gardens at the rear and behind them a row of mews houses provided stabling for horses and carriages. Lavender knew he should take his horse around to the stables but a spectacular sight drew him down the street to the front door of the Howards' home.

A gleaming ebony phaeton, with highly polished brass trimmings and lanterns, stood in front of the house, harnessed to a magnificent pair of black stallions. The soft hood was pulled back, revealing its luxurious red leather interior. A dark-skinned and turbaned Indian groom was mounted on one of the drawing horses, waiting for his passengers. He wore a livery of billowing crimson silk, which matched the plump red cushions of the vehicle. A white ostrich feather was pinned to his turban with a glistening spinel, which contained a bright red stone surrounded by imitation diamonds.

Suddenly, the door of the house opened and a well-dressed, dark-skinned young woman skipped down the steps with her maidservant and another turbaned footman. The young woman's muslin dress with its empire waist, her trimmed bonnet and matching little jacket were the height of English fashion, but her caramel skin tones and glossy raven ringlets suggested an Indian ancestry. The burnished red hair he'd found on MacAdam's trousers certainly didn't belong to her.

She was a pretty little thing and chatted amicably in a foreign tongue to her ayah as they climbed into the carriage with the assistance of the footman. Her sleek ebony hair briefly reminded him of the dark beauty who waited for him at home, his Spanish wife, Magdalena.

The women only had enough time to settle back into the seats and smooth their skirts before the postilion driver urged the impatient horses forward and the phaeton set off down the street at a smart pace.

Lavender tied his own horse to the railings at the front of the house, mounted the steps and knocked at the door. If the footman was surprised by a Bow Street officer's request to see Mr Howard, it didn't register on his dark, impassive features. He left Lavender standing in the spacious marble hallway, filled with a dazzling display of Mughal artefacts, while he delivered his request for an interview to Mr Howard.

A glittering arsenal of Indian armoury swept across the white plastered walls and up the side of the elegant curved staircase. Elaborate patterns formed from round, burnished gold shields surrounded with dozens of curved, silver-hilted sabres filled the entire wall. Jewelled daggers set with yellow topaz or rubies the colour of pigeon's blood and exquisitely carved wooden arrows fanned out above the doorways. To have amassed such a collection, Mr Howard must have spent many years on the Asian subcontinent and no doubt had amassed a vast amount of wealth too.

Lavender examined these blades closely but nothing appeared to be missing from the display and none of the knives matched the description given to him by Sir Richard of the murder weapon.

The footman returned and took him into Mr Howard's study.

This room was a mixture of traditional British furnishings and exotic artefacts from India. Bookcases full of leather-bound tomes towered to the ceiling on either side of the rosy marble fireplace. A large oak Chippendale desk, which gleamed with inlaid brass ornaments and the glossy veneer of rosewood, stood between the tall double windows. Against another wall stood a pair of ornate silver tables, embellished with mother-of-pearl and a glittering mosaic of tiny round mirrors. On one stood crystal decanters and glasses, on the other a gilt statue of a Hindu god, who glared back at Lavender with its lizard-green emerald eyes.

Howard himself was a small, grey-haired man of about sixty. His white complexion had long ago been burned to dark leather by the tropical sun. He wore a tasselled hat and a jade-green silk banyan, which enveloped his wiry frame. He lounged back in a fireside chair, smoking from the pipe of a hookah of burnished gold inlaid with empurpled ebony, which stood on the small table beside him. The air was thick with the aroma of tobacco and spices.

Opposite Howard sat another grey-haired man in a plain dark coat and waistcoat, whom, from his sober attire, Lavender assumed to be a secretary or steward. His pale complexion had never seen a tropical sun. Broken blood vessels had formed a mesh of red lines on the skin stretched over his cheekbones. It gave him a childlike, pinkish glow.

Lavender cleared his throat. 'Thank you for seeing me, Mr Howard.'

Howard regarded him curiously and in silence for a moment. 'So, you're a Bow Street Runner, are you?' His voice bore the faint trace of a northern accent.

'I'm a Principal Officer with their police office, yes.'

Howard gave a little laugh, inhaled from the pipe and exhaled a billowing cloud of white smoke. The joints in the hand that held the tube to his mouth were swollen with arthritis. 'I believe one of the Fielding brothers was the magistrate at Bow Street when I left England forty years ago.'

'That would have been Sir John Fielding, sir. He was an excellent magistrate – and blind.'

'Yes, they called him "The Blind Beak of Bow Street", didn't they? This is Jackson,' – he pointed a knobbly finger towards his companion – 'he's my secretary and is charged with easing me back into genteel English society after my long absence on the subcontinent.'

Lavender nodded politely to Jackson before turning back to Howard. 'You worked for the East India Company, sir?'

'Yes, but I've retired now. Jackson tells me the Bow Street Police Office has a good reputation for solving crimes and that you're one of their most respected officers.'

'Thank you, sir.'

'So, what brings you to Bruton Street, Detective?' He replaced the hookah pipe on the table and stretched out his knobbly fingers.

'I've come about a man called David MacAdam, sir. I understand you and your daughter were acquainted with him.'

'MacAdam? What of him?'

'I'm sorry to inform you he was stabbed to death last night. He died at his lodgings on Park Lane.'

'What?' Howard sat up straight, pulling his voluminous gown from beneath him in agitation. Beside him, Mr Jackson turned pale and gasped.

'How so?' Howard demanded. 'How is this possible? Was it robbery? The footpads in London are a disgrace . . .'

'We're still trying to establish exactly what occurred, sir, but we don't believe the attack was part of a robbery. MacAdam still had his pocketbook and watch in his greatcoat when we found him.'

Howard's shocked face crumpled when another thought hit him. 'Oh my God – poor Amelia! She'll be devastated, the poor girl.'

'I understand Miss Howard and MacAdam . . . were close,' Lavender said gently.

'Close? No, far more than that – they were betrothed, for heaven's sake! Jackson was just about to tell the vicar to post the banns in the church and send an announcement to *The Times*. Jackson, fetch me a brandy.'

Lavender waited patiently while the secretary hurried to the decanter on the silver side table. Both men seemed in genuine shock at the news of MacAdam's death and would need a moment to recover. Jackson poured out a generous measure of the amber liquid into a crystal glass and gave it to his master before slumping back down into his own seat. His face, too, had turned grey.

Howard took a generous gulp of the drink before turning back to Lavender. 'But how did this happen? MacAdam was here last night – he drank a glass of brandy or two with me after Amelia had retired for the night. I can't believe he's now dead!'

Lavender felt a surge of excitement shoot through his body. 'MacAdam was here last night? What time did he leave?'

'He left in his carriage at his usual time of just after nine o'clock. What happened to the poor fellow, Lavender?'

His carriage? Mrs Palmer hadn't mentioned that MacAdam kept a carriage and horses.

'We believe he was attacked on his way home. For some reason, he didn't seek assistance and bled to death in his bedchamber. He was found by his landlady this morning. I've ruled out both suicide and robbery as a motive. We're investigating this as a murder.'

Howard and Jackson stared at him, aghast.

'Good god,' Howard murmured.

'How . . . how can we assist you, Detective?' Jackson's voice cracked when he spoke.

'I need to tell MacAdam's family of his death and I understand MacAdam was from Essex. It would be a great help if you can tell me what you know about him and his family.'

Howard put down his glass and sank back into his chair. 'Well, he's a gentleman, of course – the second son of a baronet. I understand the MacAdams are a respected family in Essex, with business interests in textiles and coal mines.'

'That will be Drake's Tailors, perhaps?'

Howard looked confused and shook his head. 'No, he said the family business was called MacAdams'. They're not as wealthy as us, of course.' He waved his hand languidly to draw attention to the fine furnishings of the room. 'But he was a decent fellow, devoted to Amelia, and I'm happy to overlook the discrepancy in fortune if it makes Amelia happy. It's my greatest ambition in life to see my granddaughters happily settled in marriage.'

'Miss Howard is your granddaughter?' Lavender already knew the answer but he asked anyway. Howard had stopped talking and was staring miserably at the expensive Turkey carpet. Lavender's question made him loquacious again.

'I've two granddaughters – both the progeny of my romantic son and his beautiful Indian wife.' His eyes suddenly narrowed and he scrutinised Lavender's face. 'Are you shocked, Detective, at the thought of a white man's marriage with a foreign, coloured woman?'

'No, sir. I could never judge another man harshly for falling in love, whatever the woman's race, colour or religion. My own wife is a Spanish Catholic.'

'Love?' Howard said with a tinge of sarcasm. Then he shook his head. 'Yes, it was love, I suppose. I tried to persuade my son to keep his woman as his mistress but she was high caste and a distant relative of a maharaja. After she converted to Christianity for him, I had no more objections.'

'Why do their children live with you?'

'Sadly, my son and his wife were killed in a coaching accident in Bengal six years ago, leaving me to care for their girls.'

'You know you adore them, sir,' Jackson said quietly. 'They're such a comfort to you.'

'I'm sorry for your loss, sir,' Lavender said.

Howard dismissed Lavender's sympathy with a wave of his gnarled hand and his tone hardened. 'Fortunately, I've amassed enough wealth during my time with the company to provide for my chee-chee grand-daughters and buy them good husbands.' Sadness washed over his features again. 'Amelia is the elder. Poor Amelia suffered greatly after the loss of her parents. I dread to think how she will take the news of the death of her fiancé.'

'Is Miss Howard at home now?' Lavender asked, although he suspected he already knew the answer to this question.

'No, she left to go shopping on Oxford Street just before you arrived,' Jackson said. 'Perhaps you saw them leave in a black phaeton?'

Lavender nodded. 'How did Miss Howard meet Mr MacAdam?'

'Riding on Rotten Row back in May. One of the horses became skittish and MacAdam went to the driver's assistance. Amelia and he fell into conversation and before we knew it, MacAdam was a regular caller at the house and a most attentive suitor. He asked my permission to approach Amelia and proposed to her last week. Sometimes he would drive her in the phaeton to the park. In fact, I suspect the man has been out more in my expensive new toy than I have. He was an excellent horseman.'

'But you said he kept his own carriage?'

'Yes, an ancient bone-rattler of a thing. It had the family crest painted on the side, of course, but I got the impression MacAdam preferred to be seen in our phaeton.'

'Family crest? Can you describe it, please?'

Howard and Jackson looked at each other in confusion.

'Was it a red shield with a coronet, supported by two rampant black stallions?' Jackson suggested.

'I've no idea,' Howard replied. 'Is this relevant, Detective? Surely you can find this out from his family?'

'Yes, of course, sir. Can you tell me the name of his family seat in Chelmsford?'

'Chelmsford?' Howard frowned. 'I thought the man said he was from Colchester? Either way, I'm afraid I can't remember the name of their family estate. I'm sure you'll find it easily enough – there can't be many Baron MacAdams living in Essex. Failing that, you'll have to come back later and ask Amelia.'

'With your permission, sir, I'll return tomorrow to talk to Miss Howard.'

Howard's chin sank to his chest and he nodded glumly. Lavender knew he was dreading the moment he would have to tell his grand-daughter about the death of her fiancé.

Jackson rose to his feet. 'I'll show you out, Detective.' The two men walked quietly out into the dazzling hallway, leaving Howard lost in his own thoughts. Jackson closed the door behind him, frowning.

'Have you something you want to tell me about MacAdam?' Lavender asked intuitively.

The older man nodded and they walked a few steps away from the study door. 'I don't want to add to Mr Howard's distress at the moment, but something you've said doesn't make sense.'

'What's that?'

'You've mentioned "lodgings" – and a "landlady". MacAdam always claimed he lived with his elderly aunt in a big mansion on Park Lane when he stayed in London. We assumed it was the family's London residence – not "lodgings".'

Lavender regarded the secretary shrewdly, his mind churning with this new information. 'You didn't trust MacAdam, did you?'

The mesh of broken red blood vessels on Jackson's face flushed brighter. 'I'd never be so impertinent as to voice my suspicions to the family . . .'

'But?'

'But MacAdam always seemed a little too keen to please.'

'How do you mean?'

'Miss Howard is a beautiful young woman, of course, despite . . .' Jackson paused, unsure how to finish his sentence.

'Despite her dark skin and racial background?'

Jackson flushed. 'Mr Howard was a powerful and ruthless man on the Indian subcontinent,' he continued quickly, 'few men were able to deceive him – though many tried. But he's grown softer and more affectionate in his old age, especially around his granddaughters. The rest of his family are dead and the young ladies are all he has. He should have stayed in India and found husbands for the girls there but he was desperate to return to England, to show off his wealth to his fellow countrymen and live out his final years in London.'

'Do you suspect MacAdam's motives in his pursuit of Miss Howard?'

Jackson nodded sadly. 'It's a long time since Mr Howard has lived in England and he was never part of the gentry back then. His family were merchants from Bradford. They had the connections to get him his lucrative position with the East India Company. I think that the subtle mores and codes of high society elude him. He's blind to the prejudice in London society and doesn't notice when the aristocracy patronise him. It seems improbable to me that a baronet's son would fall so quickly and passionately in love with a foreign, dark-skinned young woman . . .'

'. . . unless he was after her fortune.' Lavender completed the sentence for him.

Jackson looked miserable. 'A fortune hunter, yes. The two girls have been poorly educated,' he added. 'They don't have the accomplishments required for an English drawing room and they're barely literate. Without their future inheritance, I doubt most English young men would consider them as wives.'

'You've been most helpful, Mr Jackson, thank you.' Lavender bowed and took his leave.

Chapter Six

Woods received a mixed welcome from Mrs Palmer's neighbours. He left his horse tied to the park railings under the watchful eye of young Will and went down a narrow road called King's Street Mews, lined with stables and coach houses, to the back of the Park Lane houses. Ducking beneath lines of flapping laundry in the cobbled yards, he knocked at the servants' entrance of each home.

Depending on the size and status of each house, the doors were answered by a variety of wary cooks, housemaids and butlers, most of whom greeted the news of MacAdam's murder with a mixture of shock and disbelief. They treated Woods as if he were the diseased harbinger of bad luck and were quick to close the door on him after he'd delivered his message and asked a few questions. One or two wide-eyed servants lingered on their doorsteps and pressed him for gory details of the stabbing.

'Were there a lot of blood spilling out o' his guts?' asked one footman.

'Did 'e foam at the mouth and gurgle?' enquired a cook.

It never ceased to amaze Woods how bloodthirsty his fellow Londoners could be.

No one had seen or heard anything unusual the night before but everyone promised to alert the rest of their households to the crime and encourage witnesses to come forward.

''E were that good-looking blond fellah, weren't he?' asked one curious housemaid. 'Nice chap, 'e were. Sorry to 'ear 'e's dead. 'E sometimes passed the time of day wi' me out 'ere in the back yard.'

Woods' grey eyebrows knitted together. 'Did he come and go through the rear entrance of the house?'

'Yes, 'e must 'ave. Sometimes I'd see 'im pass by on 'is way to the mews.'

Woods thanked the housemaid for her information and moved on to the next property.

He received the best welcome of the morning from a large house four doors away from Mrs Palmer's home. The shocked butler stood back from the doorway and waved him inside. 'I think you'd better speak with the mistress. She'll want to hear this herself.'

'Who's your mistress?'

'Lady Tyndall. She's a friend of Mrs Palmer's. The two ladies have known each other for years.'

Woods hesitated but the stiff-backed butler had already shut the door behind him. He led Woods through a steamy kitchen, which smelt tantalisingly of roast beef, and up two flights of a dark, narrow, back staircase to the first floor of the property. The climb left Woods out of breath.

'Wait here.' The butler left Woods on the spacious landing and disappeared inside one of the rooms at the front of the house.

Woods smoothed down his creased coat, glanced around at the gilt-framed portraits hanging on the plastered walls and wished his riding boots weren't quite so muddy. He was never as comfortable as Lavender when it came to dealing with the nobs. The butler soon returned and gestured for him to enter the drawing room. 'Constable Woods, ma'am.'

Woods' muddy boots sank into a thick Turkey carpet and he had to blink to protect his eyes from the brilliance of the light pouring in through the tall arched windows. Decorated with pale yellow silk wall hangings, Lady Tyndall's drawing room was sunny in every sense of the word. Light bounced around the lemon walls, towering gilt mirrors and crystal chandeliers of the elegant and spacious chamber.

Her ladyship was dressed in a dove-grey silk gown that matched the grey ringlets peeping beneath her white lace cap. She sat on a yellow sofa upholstered with the same patterned silk as the wall hangings. A discarded news-sheet lay on the seat beside her. She had her back to the windows and regarded Woods coldly through a tortoiseshell lorgnette. The hand holding it shook slightly but he was relieved to see that although she looked pale and distressed, she was dry-eyed.

'Good mornin', ma'am.'

'Good morning, Constable.' Her voice was like ice. 'My butler tells me there's been a terrible incident at Mrs Palmer's house. Is this true? Has Mr MacAdam been found dead – and is Lavender investigating?'

'You know of Detective Lavender?'

'Of course!' she said quickly. 'Most of London knows of Lavender.' She patted the copy of *The Morning Chronicle* by her side. 'The news-sheets are full of his exploits and his success in solving crimes.' This fact didn't seem to give her any pleasure.

'Yes, ma'am,' Woods said hastily. 'Detective Lavender is investigatin'. We believe Mr MacAdam were stabbed on his way home last night. Mrs Palmer found him dead in his room this mornin'.'

She winced. 'Good grief! Poor Sylvia! I must go to her at once. What a dreadful thing to happen.' She turned to the butler, who stood behind Woods, and instructed him to ask her maid to fetch her cloak and bonnet. The servant nodded and backed out, closing the door behind him.

'Now, tell me everything, Constable,' she demanded. 'Mrs Palmer and I – and our late husbands – were friends for many years. What on earth happened to poor Mr MacAdam and what have you uncovered so far?'

Woods paused and narrowed his eyes against the fierce glare of the woman before him. He was an experienced police officer and unaccustomed to being browbeaten by a member of the public, no matter how aristocratic she may be. He asked the questions and did the interrogating, not the other way around.

'How well did you know the deceased, ma'am?' he asked.

Frustration flashed across Lady Tyndall's features. 'Why, I barely knew him! Mr MacAdam was Mrs Palmer's lodger, that's all. What have you learned about the events of last night so far?'

'It's early days in the course of our investigation yet.'

'But you must have some notion!'

'How did you find him, ma'am?'

'How did I find him?'

'Yes, what manner of man was MacAdam?'

She shook her head in irritated confusion and her grey curls quivered like fat sausages beneath her cap. 'I had only a brief acquaintance with Mr MacAdam but from what I saw of him, he seemed the perfect gentleman. But you haven't answered my question, Constable.'

'We believe the attack took place on, or around, Park Lane about nine o'clock last night.'

'That's very vague.'

'It's the best we can do at the moment, your ladyship. I'm enquirin' along the street. Detective Lavender and I hope to find some witnesses to the incident that killed MacAdam.'

'And have you?'

'I beg your pardon, ma'am?'

'Have you found any witnesses?'

'Not yet.'

'Well, you won't find any here,' she said firmly. 'I myself always retire to bed and read before nine o'clock and so does my household.'

'Very good, ma'am, but if anyone remembers that they saw or heard anythin' unusual outside the house last night, please ask them to inform us at Bow Street Police Office . . .' The maid appeared with Lady Tyndall's cloak and bonnet and Woods' voice trailed away.

Lady Tyndall rose to her feet. The young girl helped her into her cloak and tied the ribbons of her bonnet. The young girl was of African descent and she seemed a nervous little thing. Her frizzy hair was scraped into a bun but wiry black curls escaped from beneath her cap.

'Not so tight, Harriet!' the old harridan complained. The girl murmured an apology. 'And before we leave, go and tidy your own hair – you look like a tavern slut.'

Woods shuffled uncomfortably from foot to foot and decided there was nothing further to be gained by staying any longer. 'If you don't mind, ma'am, I'll leave you to your visit.'

'Yes, you may go.' She dismissed him with a short wave of her hand. 'Make sure you return when you've more information about the case. I need to be informed.'

Woods bit his lip and backed out of the room, silently cursing the imperious old woman. The butler showed him out through the servants' entrance.

Woods was glad to be back out in the fresh air and sunshine. He pulled out his pocket watch and realised with relief that it was time to join Lavender at Bow Street. He retrieved his horse from the watchful care of young Will, tossed the ragged little road sweeper another halfpenny for his trouble and pulled himself up into the saddle. The exertion pained his injured shoulder and left him breathing heavily again.

Gathering the reins into his hands, another thought crossed his mind. 'Will? What time do you go home in an evenin'? Were you here about nine o'clock last night?'

The boy looked up, surprised. 'No, guvnor, that's too late for me.'

Woods nodded and tried another line of questioning. 'Did you see much of the man who lived at number ninety-three? Did you know him?'

'Which geezer were that? There's several of 'em lives there.'

'Mr MacAdam – a tall fellah, fair-haired.'

'What, the fat geezer like you?'

Woods' mouth opened wide in protest but he froze, bit back the sharp retort that sprang to his lips and said coldly: 'D'you know what, son? Forget I asked. It don't matter.'

Digging his heels in the flank of his horse, he mustered as much dignity as he could and set off at a brisk trot down the street.

Magdalena Lavender was resting on the blue velvet sofa in their sunny drawing room when her husband unexpectedly arrived. She twisted round awkwardly towards the door and smiled. 'Stephen! You're home for luncheon again – how lovely.'

He kissed the sleek raven hair on the top of her head and his hand reached out to stroke her stomach gently. The baby was just beginning to show. 'Are you both well?'

'Very well,' she said. 'I felt her move this morning. It was only the faintest flutter but it was definitely her, stretching and wriggling.'

He froze in surprise, his hand still resting on the red, patterned dimity of the gown over her stomach. 'Her?'

'Yes, "her". I dreamed about her last night. It's definitely a girl – and a beautiful one too.'

A slow smile crept across his handsome face. She knew he secretly hoped for a daughter to complete their family. He looked far younger than his thirty-three years when he smiled. She loved to see him smile.

But it didn't take long for the rational part of Stephen's mind to come to the fore. 'Dreaming of your child? This is a pregnant woman's superstition, surely?' He sat down in the chair opposite hers and brushed a speck of dust from his breeches.

'Ah, you English have no imagination. I dreamed of Sebastián when I carried him and he turned out to be exactly as I'd imagined.'

'I shall have to take more notice of my dreams,' he said. 'If they can predict the future with such accuracy, they may help me with this latest murder investigation.'

'You have a new mystery to solve?'

'Yes, I have to go to Chelmsford this afternoon and may need to stay there overnight. I came home to collect a few things and to get a book about heraldry from my study.'

She pouted, tossed her head until her ringlets wobbled and pretended to be cross. 'Hmmph! And I thought you'd come home to enjoy my dazzling company!'

'That was my main reason, of course,' he said, smiling. 'I need little excuse to rush back to the side of my beautiful wife.'

'Your fat wife,' she corrected him, patting her stomach.

'You're barely showing.'

'My waistline is thickening. I have already asked Teresa to start letting out my gowns.'

He stood up. 'Come. I'll tell you about my latest perplexing case over lunch. I came in through the kitchen and Mrs Hobart has prepared us a cold collation.' He held out his hand to help Magdalena up from the sofa. 'Shall we go through?'

She eased herself to her feet, took his arm and walked with him to the dining room, enjoying the warmth and the firmness of the muscles beneath his coat sleeve. Despite his slender frame, Stephen was surprisingly strong. His dark eyes were frowning with concentration and she recognised this sombre expression. It was the look of intensity he often wore when he pondered an intriguing new murder case.

Mrs Hobart had left them a simple meal of cheese, cold meats, game pie and blancmange left over from their dinner the night before. Magdalena picked at her food and sipped a small glass of Madeira while Stephen recounted the morning's events in Mayfair.

The early months of her pregnancy had been dominated by appall- ing nausea and although it had now eased, she still hadn't regained her full appetite, nor her energy. It was twelve years since her last pregnancy but she'd been startled by how exhausted she felt all the time – and frustrated. An energetic and passionate woman, she now napped more than a household cat. With Sebastián away at school and not here to distract her, she sometimes felt she was living vicariously through Stephen's life because she was too exhausted to have one of her own. But it was a small price to pay for the child they both desperately wanted.

The murder of David MacAdam certainly sounded unusual. She was always saddened to hear of a man struck down in the prime of his life but she giggled when Stephen told her about MacAdam's corset and Sir Richard's suggestion that Ned Woods needed one too.

'Ned was deeply offended.'

'I'm not surprised,' she replied. 'Betsy tells me Ned's very conscious of his weight at the moment. He's gained quite a few stone.'

Stephen shrugged. 'It's middle age. Everything about the body slows down when we age, including the digestive tract. He's still the fittest, strongest man in the horse patrol and has the strength and energy of a man half his age.'

'Betsy has tried feeding him smaller portions and watering down his ale,' she said, 'but it doesn't work. When Ned gets hungry he simply raids her larder – and complains loudly if she feeds their sons larger portions than his.'

Stephen smiled. 'Ned feels insulted by Sir Richard's comment about his weight and is now after his blood.'

Magdalena nodded. 'It doesn't take much to ignite Ned's prejudice against Sir Richard.'

'He's sure our eminent surgeon is connected to MacAdam's murder in some way,' Stephen continued. 'He even suggested Mrs Palmer is Sir Richard's mistress.'

Magdalena dropped her spoon in her blancmange dish and laughed. 'Sir Richard Allison is the last man I would expect to keep a mistress. He's so enthusiastic and revolting about his work, I can't imagine any woman would want him to come near her.'

'Well, Lady Allison obviously doesn't mind. It would help if I knew a little more about them. While Ned is distracted with this suspicion, he won't think clearly and I need him to be more objective. He behaved strangely today . . .'

She held up her hand to interrupt him. 'Was that Ned or Sir Richard?'

'Sir Richard. He even sat down in the woman's parlour in his shirt sleeves.'

Magdalena's eyebrows rose in surprise.

'I need to eliminate him from any involvement in the case, in order to focus Ned's attention on the evidence,' Stephen continued.

'I may be able to help you with this,' she said. 'I'm visiting Charity Read this afternoon and she knows everything about everyone in London and is an incurable gossip. I can make discreet enquiries about Sir Richard and Lady Allison, if you would like me to?'

Stephen hesitated while he thought over her suggestion. She knew he was pleased about her recent friendship with the wife of his employer, Magistrate John Read. Staunch Anglicans, the Reads had initially been wary of forming a close acquaintance with her because of her religion, but things had changed over the last few months and her friendship with Charity Read had blossomed. Magdalena suspected Stephen was battling with his conscience over her suggestion that she should fish for scandal about the surgeon and his marriage. Despite the occasional bout of friction, there was a close bond between all of the lawmen who worked through Bow Street Police Office, including Sir Richard. It was essential for their jobs – and sometimes for their lives – that they trusted each other.

Eventually he nodded: 'Very well, but please be as discreet as possible – and take care of yourself while you're out of the house. Make sure you take Teresa with you. I think sometimes you forget your condition, my darling. I do wonder if you should go out so often?' The concern in his eyes was genuine.

She smiled. 'You forget, Stephen – this is my second child. I know what to do.'

'Magdalena, please take care – I worry about you when I'm not here and you're out in the city – or alone in the house.'

'But I'm never alone! I have my maid, Teresa, and Mrs Hobart. And Lady Caroline visits almost daily.'

'None of whom have ever had a child.'

She leaned forward, smiled and covered his hand with her own. 'And neither have you, my darling – until now. Do you really think it would help me to stay cooped up in the house, with three or four childless people fussing around me? I would go insane and you would have to admit me to Bedlam.' She squeezed his hand and let it go. 'You must trust me to take care of myself and our baby. There will be plenty of time for me to sit like a fat sow on the sofa when I enter my confinement. Now, hurry along. You mustn't be late for your coach to Essex. Ned will wonder where you've got to.'

He wiped his chin with his napkin and pushed back his chair. Reassured by her words, his mind returned to his case. 'To be honest,' he said when he bent down to kiss her goodbye, 'MacAdam is an enigma. I don't know where we're going in Essex. Do we seek the family of a baronet's son in Colchester? Or look for a tradesman from Chelmsford?'

'Do what you always do, Stephen,' she said as she returned his kiss. 'Follow the evidence you have in your hands.'

Chapter Seven

L avender and Woods walked to The Saracen's Head in Holborn to board their coach. They exchanged information about their separate inquiries while they pushed through the crowds of pedestrians on Snow Hill.

'Lady Tyndall is a tart old harridan,' Woods complained. 'By now, she'll have told Mrs Palmer and that sly fox, Allison, that we've alerted all their neighbours to the murder.'

Lavender nodded in sympathy but Sir Richard Allison's outrage was the least of his worries right now. 'And you said MacAdam was in the habit of using the back door of the house?'

'Yes. It's the quickest route to the carriage house and mews.'

'Maybe he was stabbed round the back of the house,' Lavender said thoughtfully.

'The mews may be where he kept that bone-rattlin' old carriage the nabob, Mr Howard, told you about,' Woods suggested.

They approached the spacious arched gateway of the coaching inn. A pair of menacing and turbaned Saracens were painted on large boards that projected from the walls, swinging gently in the breeze. The inn stood next to the Newgate gaol, one of many mean buildings that crowded around and dwarfed the historic spire of St Sepulchre's church.

'So where are we goin' to search for MacAdam's family?' Woods asked. 'Chelmsford or Colchester?'

'Chelmsford,' Lavender said. 'Magdalena has advised me to follow the evidence in my hands. At the moment, this consists of a ledger and a set of clothing labels that link MacAdam to a company called Drake's Tailors in Chelmsford. If we've no luck there, we'll take the next coach on to Colchester and try to track down the family of this mysterious Baron MacAdam.'

The gateway opened into a large, cobbled courtyard full of sweating horses harnessed to dusty coaches. The carriages swayed as the passengers clambered out. Blinking against the strong sunlight, many wrinkled their noses in disgust against the rank smell of the nearby gaol, which mingled with the stink of blood and offal wafting on the breeze from Smithfield meat market. The inn towered four storeys high around them, with external wooden staircases and long balconies leading to the bedchambers.

'We may have a long day ahead of us,' Lavender continued. 'To be honest, it would help if I had a copy of *Debrett's Peerage*. I wonder if there's a circulating or subscription library in Chelmsford? Did you manage to get something to eat?'

'No,' Woods said abruptly.

They bought tickets for the two o'clock coach but Woods gave up his seat for a young woman with a child. 'It'll get stiflin' inside soon,' he said as he disappeared to travel on the outside of the vehicle.

Crammed between the window and a buxom housewife with a large, scratchy wicker basket full of groceries on her lap, Lavender silently agreed with him. On the seat opposite, a corpulent gentleman ran his finger around his neck to loosen his cravat and mopped his brow with his handkerchief. Following one of the wettest springs and summers England had ever known, the capricious British weather had given them a gloriously balmy September in which to harvest their ruined crops. Once the coach began its ponderous journey through the crowded streets out of the city, Lavender forced open the stiff sash window to let in a breeze.

He settled back in his seat and took out his notebook and a pencil. He searched his memory and did a rough sketch of the coat of arms with the rampant stags he'd seen on the side of the coach that had whisked Bentley away from the house on Park Lane. Next to it, he drew another coat of arms with the shield, coronet and stallions that, according to Mr Jackson, belonged to MacAdam's titled family. Then he pulled out the book on heraldry he'd taken from his library and spent a frustrating half hour reading about mottos, shield elements, crests and supporters. The book confirmed his suspicion that there were thousands of families in England with coats of arms but it gave him no clue about who had the hereditary right to use either of the crude drawings in his notebook. It did, however, confirm that the coronet on MacAdam's coach signified that the vehicle was owned by a baronet.

They picked up speed when the coach left the city and flew through the gently rolling and fertile Essex countryside. Chickens flew squawking off the dusty road as the hooves of the horses thundered through tiny hamlets of thatched cottages. Fattened pigs rooted amongst the stubble in the harvested fields while hundreds of migrating birds gathered and wheeled in the sky above.

Finally, they crossed the elegant arched stone bridge over the River Can and reached The Great Black Boy coaching inn in Chelmsford. The broad, paved High Street bustled with shoppers, a flock of sheep and red-coated officers from the local barracks. The smell of hops from the riverside brewery sweetened the stench of manure that lingered in the air close to the penned livestock. On the way to Moulsham Street, they passed tallow chandlers and soap boilers, bootmakers and clockmakers, glovers and hatters. The market town's close proximity to London and the Essex ports had ignited an explosion in manufacturing.

Drake's Tailors was a large flat-fronted two-storey building with tall windows. A smart selection of creamy white shirts, men's coats and silk waistcoats were displayed in one of the windows at street level. One waistcoat, exquisitely sewn, with thin, pale gold and white stripes, caught Lavender's eye in particular.

Was it too ostentatious, he wondered, to wear at his child's baptism? His little infant stranger would need carrying to the christening font and all eyes would be on the proud father. A new waistcoat would probably be needed . . .

But he dismissed the idea as soon as it entered his mind. Ever since the death of his former fiancée, Vivienne, he'd refused to tempt fate with wild dreams and hopes. Childbirth was dangerous for both a woman and a child and his future happiness was once again in the hands of God. It was best not to tempt fate.

He still couldn't believe he'd managed to attract a wife as vivacious, accomplished and beautiful as Magdalena. In the early months of their marriage, he'd harboured an irrational fear that she and Sebastián would leave him to return to their estates in Spain once Wellington had finally ejected the French from her homeland. He'd been less fearful of that since her pregnancy; he knew the child would bind her to him for life. Madrid had been liberated in August but the French still held out in isolated pockets in the rest of Spain and the fighting dragged on. Magdalena had been unable to find out any news about the fate of their former home. Sooner or later, they would have to travel to Spain to reclaim Sebastián's inheritance – but not yet. Not until the baby was old enough to travel.

He glanced at the waistcoat again and despite himself, a tingle of excitement and pride fluttered in his heart when he thought of the baby once more. Was it so wrong, he wondered, to allow himself to hope?

'Have you got indigestion again?' Woods' voice cut through his daydream.

'No.'

'Well, you've got a funny look on your face. Come on.'

A short flight of steps took them into the wood-panelled shop and a jingling bell announced their arrival. They were greeted by a white-haired man with round spectacles and a measuring tape draped around his shoulders. He left them to wait while he took their request for an interview to the proprietor of the company.

The interior doors of the shop had been left ajar to allow for the circulation of air and they had a good view of the bright workroom full of tailors and apprentices. Compared to some of the poor half-starved wretches who strained over their sewing in the poorly lit sweatshops of London, these men and boys seemed healthy and well fed and were diligently bent over their tasks. Some used paper patterns and scissors to cut out pieces from long rolls of wool, tweed and cotton. Others sat with their heads bowed over their sewing, swiftly dipping and raising their needles and thread. The tables before them were littered with skeins of colourful silk and bowls of glittering metal and bone buttons. Finished and half-finished coats, shirts and waistcoats were lined up on racks or hung on hooks on the walls.

Lavender flicked through one of the illustrated company catalogues of men's clothing he found lying on top of the wooden counter. Woods poked around in a bowl of shiny military buttons.

The shopkeeper returned. 'Mr Drachmann will see you now, Detective.' They followed him through the back of the shop and up a flight of stairs.

'Drachmann?' Woods said. 'Isn't that a Hebrew name?'

The shopkeeper glanced over his shoulder, frowning. 'Yes, it is – and it's a respected name in these 'ere parts, so mind yer manners with Mr Drachmann. The company name were changed to Drake's ten years ago.'

Woods winked at Lavender behind the man's back.

They were led into a small office dominated by a solid desk piled high with papers and catalogues. Behind the desk, twirling a quill in his inky fingers, was a swarthy-skinned man in his mid-thirties with a prominent hooked nose. His intelligent dark eyes gleamed with amusement at their arrival. Lavender sensed the man's restless energy from across the room.

Drachmann wore a dark green velvet yarmulke on his head. Beneath the exquisite tailoring of his matching coat, he wore an identical pale gold and white striped waistcoat to the one Lavender had admired in the shop window.

'Good evening, gentlemen. I'm Saul Drachmann, owner of Drake's Tailors. I don't often get visits from police officers to brighten up my dull days in the office. How can I assist you?' His eyes scanned the smart cut of Lavender's black coat with approval but he seemed to recoil at the sight of Woods' heavy blue greatcoat and his bright red waistcoat. 'Does Bow Street require a new uniform for its horse patrol, perhaps?'

Despite the seriousness of their mission, Lavender allowed himself a small smile. 'No thank you, Mr Drachmann.'

'That's a shame,' Drachmann replied, smiling. 'I can understand now why Londoners refer to the constables of the horse patrol as "Robin Redbreasts". The criminals must be able to see you officers coming from several miles away.' Woods stiffened with indignation.

'We're here on more serious police business, I'm afraid,' Lavender said.

Drachmann waved his quill towards the pair of wooden chairs on the opposite side of his desk. 'Oh well, you'd better sit down then.'

They lowered themselves into the seats and Lavender cleared his throat. 'Early this morning, the body of Mr David MacAdam was found stabbed to death in his lodgings in London. We've reason to believe MacAdam had some connection with your company.'

Shock flashed across Drachmann's face and all traces of amusement vanished. 'MacAdam? Big fellow, fair-haired?' Lavender nodded. 'Good grief – yes, I knew him. I haven't seen him for months, though. Stabbed, you say? Murdered?' Lavender nodded again. 'That's disgraceful. No man should die like that.'

'May I ask in what capacity you knew him, sir?' Lavender asked. 'We're trying to locate MacAdam's family to notify them of his death. What was MacAdam's connection with your company?'

'He worked for me.'

Even though he was prepared for a surprise, the news still shocked Lavender. 'MacAdam worked for *you*?'

'Yes, he was what you would call a commercial traveller – and when he could be bothered to work on our behalf, he was a damned good salesman. MacAdam would charm the birds down from the trees if they had something he wanted.'

'He were a hawker?' Lavender heard the surprise in Woods' voice.

'Oh, it's a little more than a mere hawker and peddler of goods, Constable,' Drachmann replied, smiling. 'This company was founded by my grandfather over thirty years ago. It always had a good reputation in the local area but I decided to expand the business about ten years ago. The tailors in London can barely keep up with the burgeoning demand for high-quality gentlemen's clothing in the capital and they often don't have the space or the workforce to do so. Many establishments welcomed my idea to provide ready-made garments for them to sell through their shops. Thanks to the endeavours of my small group of commercial travellers and my illustrated catalogues, Drake's' menswear is now sold all over southern-eastern England from Cambridge to Brighton.'

'How long was he in your employment?' Lavender asked. 'And why haven't you seen him for several months?'

'I haven't seen him, Detective, because in May he left my company for another, more lucrative job in London, or so he said. He joined us about eight years ago and was an excellent salesman. Unfortunately, the orders he placed dwindled this spring and his accounts became – how shall I put it? – muddled? I was relieved when he departed, to be honest with you.'

'Were he stealin'?' Woods asked.

Drachmann waved his hand in the air. 'Nothing I could prove. He ordered lots of samples of our coats in his size – which we never saw again. But I was happy to cut our losses and employ someone else. Before us, MacAdam worked for a local horse dealer, buying and selling the animals at market. But he had ambition and was desperate for an opportunity to move to the capital.'

Woods laughed. 'So, he were a horse courser!'

Drachmann glanced between them curiously. 'Does this information surprise you, gentlemen?'

'I'll say it does!' Woods laughed again. 'MacAdam made himself out to be a grand swell down in London and most folks had swallowed his lies.'

Drachmann smiled. 'Like I said, the man was very charming and ambitious. He even took lessons from the local vicar to round off the rough burr of his country accent. He said talking like a gentleman helped him to sell more garments.'

Elocution lessons? Then Lavender remembered the well-thumbed copy of *The Manners and Conduct of an English Gentleman* in MacAdam's bedchamber. Things were beginning to make sense. MacAdam had perpetuated a fraud; he'd pretended to be an English gentleman – and everyone from Mrs Palmer to the Howards had fallen for his deception. 'Do you happen to know anything about his family?' he asked. 'I assume he was from Chelmsford and he has relatives in the town.'

'Yes, they live in the town, near the riverside.' Drachmann rose to his feet and moved across to a shelf stacked with old ledgers and files. 'I think I still have the address.' He pulled a ledger down and flicked through its pages. 'Yes, here it is.' He brought the book back to his desk and sat down. 'I saw his wife at the market a few weeks ago. She always was a sharp, humourless woman but I feel sorry for her today. No doubt your news will distress her.'

'Wife?'

Drachmann paused and smiled at the shock on Lavender's face. 'Let me guess,' he said slowly. 'That silver-tongued rogue MacAdam forgot to mention to anyone in London he was married?'

Lavender nodded, made a note of the address and rose to his feet. 'You've been very helpful, Mr Drachmann. Thank you.'

Drachmann gave them instructions about how to reach Mrs MacAdam's house and they hurriedly left the building.

Lavender was grateful for the fresh air in the street. His mind reeled with these latest revelations and he needed to make sense of it. He pointed to the tavern across the road. 'Are you hungry? Shall we get some food and a tankard of ale?'

'No, let's visit Mrs MacAdam and get to the bottom of this puzzle,' Woods said. 'It looks like our victim were livin' a false life and were a sharper and a cheat as well as a lothario.'

'Yes,' Lavender replied grimly, 'and if he'd lived a few more weeks, he would also have been a bigamist. Miss Howard has had a lucky escape – although I doubt she'll see it that way.' They waited for a gap in the traffic, crossed the road and ducked down a narrow, damp alley that led to the riverside cottages. Their boots slipped on the slimy cobbles.

Woods frowned. 'I can't believe that nabob didn't make a few more enquiries about MacAdam before consentin' to his marriage with his granddaughter.'

'MacAdam's wife and Miss Howard may not be the only women in our victim's life,' Lavender said. 'I found several long auburn hairs on the clothes in his room. Unless Mrs MacAdam is a redhead, I suspect there's another woman. Your description of MacAdam as a lothario may turn out to be accurate.'

'No fellah will marry my little girls until I've seen his baptismal record and know all his bad habits and the amount of his savin's.'

Despite his preoccupation with this startling new development in the case, Lavender managed a small smile. 'I pity the suitors of little Rachel and Tabitha.'

'But what about Howard, eh?' Woods persisted. 'Do you think he were negligent? His granddaughters are young gals and helpless against scoundrels like MacAdam who come danglin' after their fortunes.'

'I think Howard is aware that his granddaughters' best asset in the marriage market is their fortune but he's ill-prepared for his role as their guardian. His secretary, Jackson, hinted as much. Despite his incredible wealth, Mr Howard is not from the gentry himself and is blinded by titles. He's as much at risk from the lies of a swindler as the young ladies are themselves. We need to know how MacAdam supported himself since he left his employment with Drake's in May – and more about that damned carriage he owned.'

They turned down a dark, muddy path between two rows of ancient timber-framed cottages, whose plastered walls flaked with damp. The smell of roasting meat suppers drifting down from their smoking chimneys did little to mask the sharp stench from the nearby tannery.

'Well, Drachmann's comments explained one thing, anyway,' Woods said, as they arrived at the low door of Mrs MacAdam's home.

'What's that?'

'We now know why MacAdam were so good with horses – a horse dealer, indeed!'

Lavender rapped on the peeling wood and after a few minutes the door opened to reveal a small, sharp-featured woman with a sallow complexion and dark, greying hair. She wiped her hands on the stained apron she wore over her plain black gown. 'Yes?'

'Are you Mrs David MacAdam?' Lavender asked.

'Yes, what do you want?'

'I'm Detective Stephen Lavender from Bow Street Police Office in London, ma'am. I'm sorry to inform you your husband, David, is dead.'

She jerked and emitted a loud gasp. Her thin lips slammed shut. Then she recovered from her shock and bristled. 'I should 'ope so, Detective,' she snapped, 'because I buried 'im three months ago.'

Chapter Eight

I t took several minutes for Lavender to persuade the indignant Mrs MacAdam that he and Woods weren't a pair of heartless tricksters. The little woman was outraged by their suggestion that her husband had still been alive the previous day and railed at them loudly on the doorstep, cursing them for their cruelty.

A tall, grey-bearded man with long shaggy hair suddenly appeared behind her. 'Let 'em come in, Winnie,' he suggested quietly. 'We need to 'ear what they 'ave to say.' Grudgingly, the woman stepped back and opened the door wider. The slow-moving man, with his deep voice and strong country burr, seemed to have a calming influence on her.

They ducked below the lintel and entered a warm room dominated by the stone fireplace and a large pine table. A shabby padded armchair and an ancient settle faced each other across the hearth, scattered with crudely made cushions. Along the back wall stood a battered oak dresser crammed and cluttered with pots, pans, baking ingredients, sewing equipment and just about everything else the family owned. Two doors led out of the room: one into a small scullery and the other into a bedroom.

A pair of wide-eyed, fair-haired young boys sat at the table, their spoons paused above their bowls of thin stew in alarm. They were miniature versions of MacAdam. Their mother told them to leave their meal unfinished and go up to their bedchamber. Grumbling, they grabbed handfuls of bread from a bowl on the table and scampered up the wooden ladder into the chamber in the eaves of the roof. Lavender had no doubt they'd have their ears glued to the floorboards as soon as they disappeared from sight.

The grey-whiskered fellow sat down in the armchair by the fire, calmly picked up his bowl of food and resumed his meal. 'This sounds a real mystery, Detective,' he said between mouthfuls. 'Perhaps you should start at the beginnin'?'

'Thank you, sir. What's your name?'

'I'm Ike Rawlings.'

''E's a neighbour who eats with us sometimes.'

Lavender's eyebrow twitched cynically. Mrs MacAdam didn't strike him as the kind of woman who offered charity. She sat down on the settle opposite Rawlings but was too agitated to take up her own supper bowl and finish her meal. She continued to glower at Lavender and Woods while they stood awkwardly by the table.

Lavender cleared his throat. 'This morning, we were called to a lodging house in Park Lane where we found the body of a man called David MacAdam who'd been stabbed to death.'

'Well, it must have been another 'un!' Mrs MacAdam exclaimed. 'Another Davy MacAdam.'

For a second, Lavender hesitated and weighed up her suggestion. Then he dismissed the notion and carefully described the facial features and stature of the dead man.

Rawlings nodded, put down his empty plate and reached for his pipe and tobacco pouch from the mantelpiece. 'That sounds like Davy, all right,' he said.

'I can see the resemblance between your sons and the man who died in London last night, ma'am,' Lavender said.

Mrs MacAdam didn't comment.

Lavender then explained how the ledger book for Drake's Tailors had brought him to Chelmsford and how they'd sought assistance from Mr Drachmann to locate MacAdam's family. 'Your husband worked for Mr Drachmann, didn't he?'

'Yes, but that's not the point,' she persisted. 'It can't 'ave been 'im that's died in London. Davy were sent 'ome to me in a coffin in June. We've buried 'im already in St Mary's.'

'Who brought you this coffin?' Lavender asked.

'It were a friend of 'is. A nice man. Said 'e were sorry for me loss and that 'e and Davy had been good pals. 'E said Davy had died of smallpox two days before and that 'e'd bin ravaged by the disease.' She twisted her filthy apron in her hands in distress.

Woods stepped forward during the embarrassed pause that followed. 'Can you remember this man's name, ma'am? I know it's upsettin' for you but it would help us to get to the bottom of this puzzle, if you can. The detective and I are as bewildered as you about all of this.'

Her face puckered up and for the first time she looked like she was about to dissolve into tears. 'No, I can't remember 'is name.'

Rawlings leaned forward and patted her hand. 'I may be able to 'elp, Winnie.' He turned to Lavender. 'I think 'e said 'is name were Collins. Yes, that were it: Collins.'

Collins? Mrs Palmer's third lodger? The man currently away in Yorkshire on business?

'Did he mention where he lived or how he came to know Mr MacAdam?' Lavender asked.

Rawlings shook his head and lit his pipe with a splint dipped into the fire in the hearth. Clouds of smoke billowed up around him. 'I don't remember much about what that Collins fellah said. We were upset and Winnie were distracted wi' findin' the money for the funeral and worryin' about her future and the boys.'

'Did he bring any documentation with him, a letter from the doctor who'd attended him and witnessed the death, perhaps?'

Rawlings and Mrs MacAdam looked at each other and shook their heads.

'What did this Mr Collins look like?' Lavender asked.

Rawlings paused and scratched his beard. 'I remember 'im as a young, dark-'aired fellah.'

''E were a smart dresser and educated,' Mrs MacAdam added.

'I'm sorry to have to ask this, ma'am,' Lavender said, 'but did you open the coffin and look inside?'

She looked horrified at the suggestion. 'I didn't! It were sealed shut and the last thing I wanted to do was see my Davy stiff and ravaged wi' disease. 'E were a good-lookin' man, my husband. That's 'ow I wanted to remember 'im.'

'So how did you know for sure there were a body in the coffin if you didn't look?' Woods asked.

Rawlings leaned forward and took Mrs MacAdam's hand again. 'Because it was 'eavy and took four of us – me and 'er brothers – to carry it to St Mary's. That's 'ow we knew there were a body in it. I'll show you where 'e's buried if you want. You didn't do anythin' wrong, Winnie,' he added.

There was another embarrassed pause. Lavender considered their next move. 'Mr Rawlings is right,' he said to the widow, 'you didn't do anything wrong. But I do believe you've been the victim of a most terrible hoax.'

Woods nodded sympathetically. 'Most folks would have done the same if they were in your shoes, ma'am. I know I would. It addles my poor noddle to think someone may have played such a cruel trick and caused you so much grief and sufferin'.'

'But if it weren't 'im . . .' Confusion flooded over Mrs MacAdam's face and Lavender felt a stab of sympathy for her. He braced himself for her next question.

'If it weren't Davy in the coffin . . . why did that Collins fellah say it were 'im? And where's Davy been for the last three months if 'e were still alive?'

Lavender ignored her question. He knew exactly where MacAdam had been for the last three months and what he'd been doing, but he didn't want to add to her distress by revealing the truth. 'I'm afraid there's only one way to sort out this mystery, Mrs MacAdam. I need you to come to London as soon as possible and see the dead man in the Bow Street morgue. It's the only way we can know for sure if our murder victim was your husband.'

Her hands fluttered to cover her mouth. 'London? I can't go to London!'

Once again, Rawlings patted her hand. 'Course you can, Winnie. I'll take you tomorrow, if you like. Get your sister to take care of the boys for a day.'

'In the meantime, Mr Rawlings, I'd appreciate it if you took us to the grave.'

Rawlings nodded and stood up. 'I'll just get me coat.' He disappeared into the bedchamber off the kitchen.

'You said 'e were murdered?' Mrs MacAdam asked. She was still struggling to understand.

'Yes, ma'am. He was stabbed.'

'Ha!' Her face darkened with anger. 'It's a bloody good job 'e is dead, Detective, because I tell you this: if I'd found out Davy were lyin' to us in June and only pretendin' to be dead – then I'd 'ave bloody stabbed 'im myself!'

It was a relief to be outside in the breeze again even if it did carry with it the acrid stench of the tannery. Lavender needed fresh air, peace and quiet, with Woods by his side, to try to make sense of this extraordinary and gruesome horror forced upon the MacAdam family.

Woods echoed his thought. 'Well, she isn't your mysterious red-head. This case has more twists and turns than the back alleys in the rookery of St Giles.'

They fell into step behind the tall, gangly figure of Rawlings and his billowing cloud of tobacco smoke. He led them towards the towering medieval church of St Mary's. The daylight was waning now and the sunset draped itself over the rooftops and smoking chimneys of the town like a soft pink blanket. It illuminated their path with a rosy glow as they picked their way through stagnant puddles and the indiscernible piles of rubbish that littered the street. Lavender imagined the sad funeral cortège of David MacAdam making this journey and shook his head at the extent of the man's cruel deception.

'Who do you suppose is in that coffin?' Woods asked.

'It might just be a pile of rubble,' Lavender conceded. Unless we can find Collins quickly – there's only one way to find out for sure.'

Woods' eyes widened with shock. 'Exhumation? You'd ask for an exhumation?'

Lavender nodded grimly.

They quickened their step to keep up with Rawlings' long stride.

'Do you often travel down to London, Mr Rawlings?' Woods asked.

The pipe bobbed up and down in his clenched teeth when the tall man nodded. 'I'm a carrier for a local quarry and stonemason. I only got back late last night and I've another load to take down to town tomorrow. Ye've got a lot of building work goin' on in London. I'll bring Winnie. We'll be at Bow Street about two o' clock.'

'That's helpful, thank you,' Lavender said.

'I'm happy to 'elp poor Winnie,' Rawlings replied. ''Tis a real puzzle, this mystery about Davy. The poor woman has never had an easy life bein' wed to 'im – 'e often left 'er alone for months at a time. 'E swanned around the city in 'is fancy clothes, while she and the boys were always short of money.'

'It sounds like you've known the family for a long time,' Woods said.

'Aye, that I 'ave. I knew Winnie as a young girl.'

'Was their union ever a happy one?' Lavender asked.

Rawlings shook his shaggy head. 'They argued a lot.'

Lavender thought back to another case he'd worked on earlier that year when he'd tracked down and arrested a man for deserting his wife and family. While he stood in the dock, the errant husband declared that he might as well serve time in gaol as his own marriage was a foul prison and his wife a vicious turnkey. The courts were full of such unhappy cases and the workhouses full of impoverished and abandoned wives and children. A miserable marriage led to desperation. Bigamy was common. But this was the first time he'd come across someone who'd faked his own death to escape his marriage. He wondered how the 'widowed' Mrs MacAdam had managed to support herself and her children throughout the summer. No doubt Rawlings had helped her. His thoughts returned to the grisly practicalities of the impending exhumation.

They reached the low wall topped with iron railings that skirted the churchyard of St Mary's. Rawlings lifted the latch of the creaking wooden gate and led them across the damp grass between the crumbling gravestones. Their boots sank into the soft, muddy ground. A few birds still chirped sleepily in the boughs of the yew trees above their heads but most had settled down to roost now.

MacAdam's tombstone was plain, cheap sandstone and simply gave the year of his birth and the date of his death, 13th June, 1812. A dead posy of hedgerow flowers lay across the grave. Lavender glanced uneasily at the nearby road. Exhumations were a nasty business, often carried out at dawn to deter gawkers and protect the sensibilities of the local residents and the mourners at other funerals.

'Who oversaw the funeral service?' Lavender asked.

'The vicar. The Reverend Calvin.'

Lavender glanced back at the solid rectangular building of the church. 'He needs to be told that he's probably buried the wrong man.' The arched wooden door on the two-storeyed porch was open but the windows were black, with no glimmer of light inside.

Rawlings followed his glance. 'The Reverend Calvin will be at 'ome in his vicarage on the 'igh Street by now. 'E's in 'is dotage and goes to bed early on a night. You might just catch 'im before 'e retires if you 'urry.'

'Thank you,' Lavender said. 'To be honest, apart from talking to the vicar, I don't think there's much more we can accomplish tonight. You've been very helpful, Mr Rawlings. Don't let us detain you if you want to return to Mrs MacAdam. We'll see you tomorrow afternoon in Bow Street.'

For a moment, the tall man hesitated. He glanced back at the church and sighed sadly. 'It's a shame, it is.'

'What is?' Woods asked sharply.

But Rawlings shook his shaggy head, said 'Goodnight to you both' then walked back through the graveyard towards the gate.

'Do you want to eat first before we call on the vicar?' Lavender asked Woods.

'There's somethin' amiss here,' Woods replied, frowning.

'That's a bit of an understatement, considering the circumstances.'

'No, I meant with Rawlings and Mrs MacAdam. Wait here for a moment.' Woods strode towards the church porch and disappeared inside the dark building. When he emerged, there was a wide grin stretched across his broad face.

'I knew it!' he said. 'I knew there were more to his friendship with Mrs MacAdam. They're betrothed and are due to be married in two weeks' time.'

'What? Rawlings and Mrs MacAdam?'

'Yes, their names are on the list of marriage banns posted on the wall inside the porch. I thought there were somethin' between them when I saw how comfortable he were by her hearth. Did you notice he kept his coat in the bedchamber?'

'That's well thought through, Ned,' Lavender said. 'I confess I was too distracted by the prospect of the exhumation to notice much. I hope she finds more happiness than in her marriage to MacAdam. Rawlings seems a decent man.'

Woods gave him a funny look. His next statement surprised Lavender. 'No, sir, you've misjudged him. Rawlings is a sly man, despite his slow speech and easy-goin' ways.'

'Sly?'

Woods nodded eagerly. 'Yes, he knows the two of them are suspects for the murder of MacAdam.'

'They are?' The mysterious Collins was currently Lavender's first choice of suspect in this murder inquiry. That man had a lot of questions to answer.

Woods stared back at him in disbelief. 'Of course they're suspects! Gawd's teeth, sir – it's not often I'm one stride ahead of you in a case.'

'How are they suspects? They thought MacAdam was already dead.'

'Yes, but suppose they were both lyin'? Imagine they knew MacAdam were still alive and had feigned his own death. You heard the woman say how she'd kill him herself if she'd known about it.'

Lavender hesitated, then nodded. 'To be honest, I found Mrs MacAdam's shocked reaction quite genuine. Most people would react like that to such a horrendous prank. It's a natural outburst of anger considering the extent of her husband's deception.'

'But if MacAdam were still alive – and they found out about it – it'd ruin their nuptials and their plans for a life together. You must confess, sir, they've got a strong motive to kill MacAdam. And Rawlings were in London yesterday, on the day of his murder. How do we know she weren't with him?'

'Yes, you're right. We need to question them again. We must keep an open mind and explore every possibility. This is good thinking, Ned.'

Woods' cheeks flushed at Lavender's praise. 'Right, let's visit this vicar and see what he has to say for himself.' He turned and strode enthusiastically towards the road.

Chapter Nine

The streets of Chelmsford were quieter now as darkness fell. The shops had closed and the townsfolk hurried home for their suppers. They stopped a helpful pedestrian who directed them towards the vicarage.

The Reverend Calvin received them in his drawing room, sitting in front of the fire wrapped in a plaid blanket. He was white-haired and frail and his rheumy eyes squinted painfully behind his spectacles. The plain middle-aged woman who'd admitted them into the house was his daughter and it quickly became obvious she was also his nursemaid. 'Please try not to tire him,' she begged. 'He struggles to follow conversation at this time of night.'

The woman wasn't jesting. Lavender had trouble explaining the purpose of his call. Miss Calvin turned pale with shock when Lavender told them about MacAdam's cruel trick on his family but she soon rallied and asked a series of quick questions to clarify the situation. The vicar, however, struggled to grasp what had happened.

'What's he saying, Annie?' he whined plaintively. 'Is David MacAdam still alive? Did we bury a man alive in the churchyard? Was the corpse still breathing?'

She leaned forward and took his mottled hand in her own. Calvin's skin was paper thin and looked like it might tear at any moment. 'No,

Father, no. It's nothing like that. Please don't upset yourself. Detective, may I speak to you outside?'

Lavender nodded. He and Woods walked back out into the hallway and waited while she settled the old man and joined them.

She closed the door to the study behind her and turned her ashen face to Lavender. 'I'm so sorry, Detective, but I feel the shock of this may kill him. He's in terrible health and should have retired years ago. I feel this distressing turn of events may be the end of his career.'

'It may well be,' Lavender said sternly. 'I'm not sure what protective measures the church has in place to make sure it doesn't bury the wrong man but protocols clearly weren't followed in this case. If there were any documents brought from London with the coffin, then I need to see them.'

Her face crumpled in distress. 'My father can't see to read any more. I deal with the administration and sometimes I'm not sure what I'm doing. I can't remember receiving any documents before the funeral.'

'I understand your father knew MacAdam personally, that he'd helped him with his elocution.'

'Yes, that was some years ago. Mr MacAdam was such a charming man. We were sad to hear he'd died so young. I organised the sexton to dig the grave, took father to the burial and wrote him a eulogy to deliver for Mr MacAdam – but he forgot to read it out. Oh dear, what a terrible situation – and it's probably my fault!'

Lavender watched tears well up in her eyes. Despite his frustration, he felt a pang of sympathy for the woman. His maternal grandfather had been Dean of St Saviour and St Mary Overie's church in Southwark. He knew from his grandfather that many English parish churches were run by elderly and incompetent vicars, who refused, usually for financial reasons, to relinquish their homes and their livings and retire. Their wives and families usually bore the brunt of the parish workload.

'How long has your father been the rector in Chelmsford?'

She hurriedly wiped a tear from her cheek. 'For nearly fifty years.'

'Well, we won't detain you any longer, Miss Calvin, but you do realise, don't you, I'll have to write to the bishop to obtain a faculty for exhumation? We need to find out who – or what – is in that coffin.'

She swallowed hard and nodded. They said farewell and left.

'Right, we need a tankard of ale and some supper to help us think this through.' Lavender set off back towards The Great Black Boy coaching inn and Woods fell into step beside him. 'David MacAdam is – was – the most twisted liar I've ever come across in my thirteen years as a police officer and my head is reeling at the extent of his duplicity.'

Lavender's hopes for a quiet spot by the fireside in the tavern were dashed the moment they ducked beneath the low lintel and entered the inn. It heaved with townsfolk engaged in rowdy games of dice, noisy hard-faced farmers and inebriated soldiers from the local barracks in their brilliant red uniforms. Half a dozen tired and hungry sheepdogs were also sprawled across the taproom floor, like a matted black and white carpet. Occasionally, a drunk soldier would stand on a stray paw and the whole pack would leap to its feet, yelping and growling. This led to a lively exchange of cursing and recrimination between the militia and the agrarians. The tavern stank of tobacco smoke mingled with wet dog.

They found a small round table in the far corner and sank wearily into their wooden chairs. A blowsy barmaid with missing teeth was soon by their side with two tankards and a pitcher of ale. Lavender asked her for food and was told that the whiting, caught locally, was one of the most popular dishes served at the inn. Lavender ordered himself a plate of the fish. 'What about you, Ned?'

'Nothin' for me, sir – I'll just drink my ale tonight.'

Lavender frowned, unsure how to proceed. Woods never turned down food. In fact, he usually ate enough for the both of them. 'Are you sure?'

'Yes, sir.' The barmaid shuffled impatiently from one foot to the other and Lavender dismissed her.

'What's this about?' he asked, once they were alone. 'Why won't you have supper?'

'I'm not hungry, that's all.'

'Not hungry – rubbish! I can hear your belly rumbling from here.' Lavender's eyes narrowed as a new thought flashed through his mind. 'This is something to do with Sir Richard's comment about how you need to wear stays, isn't it?'

Woods glanced away and waved his big hand dismissively in the air. 'Can't a fellah just say "no thank you" without an interrogation? Now, what about this case, sir? What are your thoughts about this sharper, MacAdam?'

Woods was trying to distract him. Lavender remembered Magdalena's comment about how sensitive Woods was at the moment about his weight and decided to change the subject. It wouldn't hurt his constable to miss a meal or two.

Lavender sat back, sipped his ale and thought quietly for a moment. 'Well, MacAdam is less of an enigma than he was when we left London this morning. We now know he wasn't the charming, genial character described by his London friends but an unscrupulous liar and a cheating husband intent on bigamy. He lied about his background to the Howards and connived with his friend, Collins, to fake his own death. He wanted to release himself from his family in order to marry an heiress.'

'It's like he led two lives.'

'Maybe three, if there's a red-headed woman involved in his life as well,' Lavender pointed out.

'He's gulled everyone.'

'Yes. It might help if we worked out how long this went on for. When did Drachmann say MacAdam left his employment?'

'It were May, I think.'

'May? Of course!' Lavender slammed down his ale on the table. Froth slopped over the side. 'The same month he met Miss Howard. A young woman like that would expect a lot of time and attention.'

'What? You think he left his job to court her?'

'Possibly – he was pretending to be a baronet's son, remember? A wealthy gentleman of leisure has plenty of time to escort his beloved around town.' Lavender frowned. 'But that doesn't explain how he supported himself through this summer. Mrs Palmer claims he always paid his rent on time and I found a receipt from his bank for £50. MacAdam got money from somewhere.'

Woods shrugged and sipped his drink. 'Maybe he went to a money-lender. They've been known to turn nasty if you welch on your debt – and have murdered debtors in the past.'

'Perhaps.'

'Maybe his young woman gave him money?' Woods suggested. 'MacAdam wouldn't be the first man to become a petticoat pensioner and from what you've told me Miss Howard were so besotted and innocent he'd have found it easy to gull her.'

'Yes, although I'm sure if that happened, her grandfather didn't know about it. I need to question both of them about this tomorrow – and I need to go to his bank.'

'But what about this faked death, sir?'

The barmaid suddenly returned with a generous plate of sizzling whiting and thick-cut slices of warm bread and fresh butter. She paused to fill up their tankards. Woods gazed at Lavender's food with the desperation of a starving street orphan.

'Are you sure you don't want something to eat?'

Woods averted his eyes and gave another dismissive wave. 'No, no.'

Lavender paid the woman and asked for a room to be prepared for them for the night. She gave him a toothless smile, bobbed a curtsey and left them alone again.

'Meeting Miss Howard changed the course of MacAdam's life,' Lavender said between mouthfuls. 'A month later, he'd left his employment and persuaded his unscrupulous friend, Collins, to help him stage his own death. On MacAdam's instructions, Collins brought a sealed coffin back to Chelmsford with the story that the commercial traveller had died from a hideously disfiguring and infectious disease, thereby ensuring no one would want to open the coffin and examine the body too closely.'

'He'd spent time with the vicar and knew he were frail and useless at his job,' Woods added.

'Exactly. It was a huge risk – but the two men carried off the deception. No one would come to London looking for MacAdam now. He was free to carry on the pretence that he was the impoverished second son of a baronet and claim the hand of Miss Howard.'

'But what does that Collins fellah get out of this? Why help MacAdam to fake his own death?' Woods spoke directly to Lavender's plate of food.

'Money. MacAdam must have promised Collins a large amount of money in order to secure his help with the deception, probably to be paid after his marriage to Miss Howard. Collins, whoever he is, must be as twisted and evil as MacAdam. Finding him is our first task when we get back to London.'

Woods stared at Lavender's food with moist lips. He swallowed the spittle back hastily. 'That wheedlin' sawbones said Collins were in Yorkshire.'

Lavender frowned and nodded. His fork hesitated over his fish. The pathetic look of hunger on Woods' face was putting him off his food. 'We'll find Collins,' he said firmly. 'Collins is complicit in this despicable fraud and it's possible he's also responsible for MacAdam's death.

If MacAdam refused to pay Collins for his part in the deception, they may have had an altercation that led to the stabbing.'

They paused for a moment while Lavender took another self-conscious mouthful of his meal and washed it down with a swig of ale.

'So, if David MacAdam weren't the corpse in the coffin . . .' Woods said quietly to Lavender's fish, 'who the devil was it?'

Irritated, Lavender pushed his plate away. 'I think I've lost my appetite.'

Woods looked scandalised at the waste of food and sat back in his chair, nursing his ale.

'I've no idea, at the moment, who – or what – is buried in that grave, Ned. It'll take days to arrange the exhumation. But I've a horrible feeling that when they open that coffin, we'll have another murder to solve.'

Chapter Ten

T hey took the first coach back to London and arrived in the capital just before nine o'clock. Woods had missed breakfast. The journey was uneventful apart from the constant loud growling from his stomach. The noise brought him plenty of funny looks and comments from the other passengers and Woods spent most of the journey apologising. Embarrassed, Lavender buried himself in his book of heraldry and drafted a letter to the bishop in his notebook, requesting an exhumation.

'We'll go to Bow Street first and then call on Mrs Palmer,' Lavender said. 'I need to tell Magistrate Read about the developments in this case.' He desperately wanted to go home to see Magdalena but duty came first. 'I'd also like to have a word with Mr Bentley today. He might know something about the devious plan of his fellow lodgers. We'll wait until Mrs MacAdam has identified her husband before we visit the Howards this afternoon.'

The stable yard at the back of Bow Street Magistrates' Court and Police Office was a hive of noisy activity, bustling with officers, stamping horses and jangling harnesses. Several of the big, hard-faced men glanced up and hailed Woods in a friendly manner. Lavender wondered if Woods missed the companionship of the horse patrol. His role with Lavender was essential but more sedentary. Had the lack of exercise over the last few months contributed to Woods' expanding waistline?

'Da! Da!' Woods' son Eddie pushed his way through the crowd of men. Beaming smiles lit up the round moon faces of both father and son when they greeted each other. Eddie had grown another two inches this summer and was now as tall as his father, though not quite as broad. He'd changed in other ways, too, according to his mother, Betsy. She'd quietly confided in Lavender a few weeks ago that the constant company of the powerfully built, gruff – but often humorous – officers of Bow Street had curtailed his childish temper and made him quieter. Her firstborn was growing into a thoughtful young man.

But Woods didn't seem to care that his son was now a man in a man's world. He threw his arm round the lad's shoulders, hugged him tight and ruffled his curly brown hair like he'd done since he was a child.

'Gerroff, Da!' Eddie struggled to free himself and smooth down his curls.

Lavender laughed and felt a pang of jealousy.

It was nearly three years since he'd first met Sebastián, Magdalena's child from her first marriage. He got along well with his stepson when Sebastián was home from boarding school but he knew their relationship lacked the spontaneity that Woods enjoyed with his own sons. Sebastián had always called him 'Sir', for a start. Was it too late to change and become less formal? Maybe their new child would change things. He'd heard that a new baby in the house could change everything.

'Detective Lavender?' The Chief Clerk, Oswald Grey, picked his way through the mud and horse dung littering the cobbled yard towards them. 'Magistrate Read wants to see you both – urgently.' Grey was a dour man at the best of times but there was something in his frown and his tone that sounded sinister. Lavender and Woods exchanged puzzled glances.

'You have a few minutes with Eddie,' Lavender said. 'I'll go up to the office and see what Magistrate Read wants.'

Lavender found James Read behind his cluttered desk, enveloped in his voluminous black court robes and wearing his wig of office. He glanced up and scowled deeper when Lavender knocked and entered. He didn't suggest that Lavender sit down in the battered chair opposite his desk. 'Ah, Lavender – you've caused me trouble this morning.'

'I have?'

'Yes, I've had a visit from Sir Richard Allison. The man is furious. He wants me to give this Park Lane murder case to another officer. He requested John Townsend.'

'Ah.' Lavender took off his gloves and sat down anyway. 'Why is he so incensed?'

'Oh, do make yourself comfortable, why don't you, Lavender?' Read said sarcastically. 'Apparently, Sir Richard asked you to conduct your inquiries discreetly but you sent Woods around the neighbourhood alerting most of Mayfair to the murder at number ninety-three.'

'Sir Richard should have known better,' Lavender said firmly. 'We don't conduct murder investigations discreetly. Alerting the public is the best way to get witnesses to come forward. And as for his suggestion that you replace us, I doubt old Townsend would be able to handle this case. He works better in London ferreting out criminals amongst his close network of criminal "acquaintances". Woods and I have already found another victim in Essex, a suspected murder – and it's linked to the death on Park Lane. The complexity of this case would baffle Townsend.'

Read frowned, removed his itchy wig and scratched his close-cropped greying head. 'Suspected murder? Was the second victim murdered, or not?'

'We'll have to dig him up first to be sure.'

'Dig him up!'

'Yes.' Lavender explained what they'd learned about David MacAdam and his treachery to the horrified magistrate. 'We need to ask the Bishop of London for an exhumation of the grave.' He pulled out the letter he'd drafted to the bishop and passed it to Read.

The lines in Read's furrowed brow deepened. He sighed heavily and shook his head. 'This is a nasty case. You're right – you're the only one of my officers with the intelligence to untangle this web of deceit. Townsend would be out of his depth. You'll just have to use your charm and placate Sir Richard – and you'll need to do that, Lavender, because you'll need his help with those remains in Chelmsford when you exhume them. I know he can be a difficult man at times but his experience is invaluable – he's the best in London when it comes to explaining how our murder victims met their grisly fates.'

Lavender nodded. 'To be honest, I hadn't thought so far ahead but yes, I'll need Sir Richard's help.'

'Then don't antagonise him further.' Read scanned the notes Lavender had handed him. 'I'll contact the bishop today and ask him for haste in issuing the faculty for exhumation. Meanwhile, we'll open the inquest into MacAdam's death tomorrow morning at nine o'clock. Make sure you and Woods are present.'

'Thank you. To be honest, sir, I'm concerned about how involved Sir Richard is in this case. He seems to be overly familiar with Mrs Palmer and her household and I don't know why. He seems to have lost his professional detachment as far as MacAdam's murder is concerned.'

Read's eyebrows gathered together into one long line across his piercing eyes. 'Is this why your wife was questioning *my wife* about Sir Richard's background yesterday?'

'Ah, I take it Magdalena wasn't as discreet as she promised to be?'

'Your wife was discreet after a fashion – Charity had no notion she was being probed for information about the Allisons but *I* recognise an interrogation when I hear about one. What's happening, Lavender?'

It was Lavender's turn to sigh. 'I needed information to placate Ned Woods. I can't see it myself but he's convinced Mrs Palmer is Sir Richard's mistress.'

Read laughed sharply then frowned again. 'In May, Sir Richard pulled a pistol ball out of Woods' shoulder and saved his arm from amputation. Has none of this softened his dislike of the surgeon?'

'No. It seems to have intensified it, if anything. Ned doesn't like being beholden to anyone for anything.'

Read shook his head, turned back to his paperwork and gestured Lavender towards the door. 'Pride, sheer pride,' he muttered darkly.

Lavender rose and turned to go.

'If you want to know more about Sir Richard's relationship with Mrs Palmer, Stephen,' Read called after him, 'ask him yourself.'

Lavender and Woods made a short detour to Lavender's home on their way to Park Lane. He left Woods in the street with their horses and bounded up the steps two at a time.

Magdalena was delighted to see him when he walked into the house and fell into his arms. He buried his face in her sweet-smelling ebony hair and pulled her warm, plump body closer.

'I haven't got much time,' he whispered. 'How are you both?'

Smiling, she disentangled herself from his arms and sat down, reassuring him that she and the baby had spent a comfortable night. He sat on the chair opposite, still holding her hand. He'd heard that women 'bloomed' in the middle stages of pregnancy and he saw this in Magdalena. Her flawless olive complexion glowed with health and her glossy black hair was thicker than ever.

'We're on our way to see Mrs Palmer again and Sir Richard may be there. I want to know what you found out from Charity Read yesterday.'

Sadness clouded her bright eyes. 'It's a terribly sad story. Sir Richard had a tragic childhood.'

'He did?'

'Yes, his mother died when he was born and his elderly father died when he was only ten years old. The family wasn't wealthy at all.'

Lavender frowned. 'So what happened to him? Who brought him up?'

'He was passed around from the care of one relative to another. He had no real home.'

'So how did he progress from being a penniless, friendless orphan to become such an eminent London surgeon?'

'Fortunately, he was an exceptionally bright student, and ambitious. His family scraped together enough money to train him as a doctor at Oxford, but without money or contacts, his career was never destined to amount to much. It was his marriage to Katherine Willis that launched him.'

Lavender searched his memory. 'Willis? I know that name . . .'

'Lady Allison was the only daughter of the Reverend Doctor Francis Willis.'

'Of course! The King's famous physician who cured him of his first bout of madness.'

'Well, after their marriage, Sir Richard's career advanced quickly at Guy's Hospital and it wasn't long before he was knighted for his services to medicine.'

'Was it a marriage of convenience, do you think?'

Magdalena shrugged her pretty shoulders. 'Who knows? Charity Read told me they're an amicable couple and seem happy together – although they've never had children. Katherine Willis never expected to find a husband and was delighted her marriage elevated her to the peerage.'

'Why didn't she expect to marry?'

Magdalena leaned forward with a twinkle in her eye. 'Because she had settled into spinsterhood. She's quite a plain woman and was over forty when they married. She's fifteen years older than Sir Richard.'

Lavender sat back, surprised. 'Good grief.'

'Will you tell Ned?' Magdalena asked, smiling.

'What? About the age difference between the Allisons? Definitely not. He's already convinced Sir Richard has a penchant for older women and that Mrs Palmer is his mistress. It'll only fuel his prejudice against the man.'

Chapter Eleven

Lavender's heart sank when he saw both Mrs Palmer and Sir Richard standing at the open doorway of the house on Park Lane. They were with a short man in a hat and a light-coloured coat over a vivid red and orange checked waistcoat. Following Read's warning, he expected a tense confrontation with Sir Richard and knew it would take some persuasion before the surgeon accepted them back on to the investigation. He'd hoped any confrontation would take place in the parlour but now it looked like they would have to plead their case for readmission out here on the street.

But raised voices reached their ears when they drew nearer. Sir Richard and Mrs Palmer were in dispute with the man on the doorstep. The surgeon was red with anger and shouting. Mrs Palmer looked pale and clutched her shawl tightly round her shoulders.

The features of the fellow with the gaudy waistcoat were hidden beneath the brim of his hat but Woods grinned when he heard his angry tones and thick accent. 'I know that voice.' He leapt out of his saddle, threw his reins for Lavender to catch and strode towards the argument. 'Well, well, if it ain't young Billy Summersgill causin' trouble.'

The man glanced up in horror at the sight of the burly Bow Street officer bearing down upon him, and Lavender caught a quick glimpse of a pale, pock-marked face and small, beady eyes. The fellow turned and was off down the road in a flash, racing away like a young hare.

Woods laughed and yelled after him: 'There ain't nowhere to run, Billy. I know where to find you.' He turned back to Lavender. 'Shall I get him, sir?'

'Who is he?'

'He's a debt collector for his da's firm of moneylenders in the Seven Dials. They're an unscrupulous bunch of rogues, the Summersgills.'

'Why did he run?'

Woods shook his head. 'I don't know – guilt over somethin', most likely. Shall I give chase, sir?'

'Wait a minute.' Lavender turned to the red-faced surgeon. 'What did he want, Sir Richard? Is this relevant to the murder inquiry?'

'He wanted payment for the interest on a debt of a hundred guineas run up by MacAdam,' Sir Richard snapped angrily.

'When my maid told him MacAdam was dead, he wanted entry to the house,' Mrs Palmer added. She shuddered and pulled her shawl even more tightly round her thin shoulders. 'I'm so glad you're here, gentlemen. He'd become most unpleasant.'

Lavender was relieved to hear her welcome. 'Why did he want entry into the house?'

'The damned man wanted to come inside and search MacAdam's room for some ring or other,' Sir Richard said. 'And if he didn't find it, he said he was within his rights to take Mrs Palmer's furniture instead of the interest owed on the debt.'

'So Summersgill is playin' the bum-bailiff now, is he?' Woods said, smiling. 'Do you want me to get him, sir?'

'Yes, drag him into the cells at Bow Street and question him about MacAdam and this ring. I'll meet you back there.'

Woods swung himself into the saddle and cantered off down the street in pursuit of Billy Summersgill.

'The shame of it!' Mrs Palmer wailed miserably. 'First a murder in my house – and now there's debt collectors and bailiffs at my door.'

'Let's go inside, ma'am,' Lavender said gently. 'Woods will deal with Summersgill – he won't bother you again. I need to talk to you both about David MacAdam and what we've discovered in Essex. May I come in?'

Mrs Palmer nodded but Sir Richard hesitated and narrowed his eyes.

Lavender knew he was weighing up his request. 'I know you've asked for another officer to take over this case, Sir Richard, but Magistrate Read has refused to remove us. You'll understand why if you let me explain what we now know about David MacAdam. John Townsend would be out of his depth with a case of this complexity.'

There was an awkward pause, then Sir Richard nodded. Lavender tied his horse to the park railings and followed them inside to the parlour. Sir Richard took the fireside seat opposite Mrs Palmer and glared coldly at Lavender, who remained standing by the door.

'What is this ring Summersgill spoke about? One hundred guineas is a lot of money for one item of jewellery. Did either of you see MacAdam with an expensive ring – or notice one in his room, yesterday morning?'

Mrs Palmer shook her head. 'I assume it's something he bought for his sweetheart.'

'So you knew MacAdam was courting a young woman?'

Mrs Palmer lowered her eyes and nodded. She looked embarrassed and twisted her shawl in agitation. 'I once overheard him bragging to my other lodgers that he'd caught himself a wealthy heiress.'

Lavender took a sharp intake of breath. 'That's not a pleasant way to talk about a young woman.' He paused for a moment and eyed her bowed head thoughtfully. 'But you also knew – or suspected – that MacAdam was already married, didn't you? I saw some hesitation yesterday when I questioned you about his family.'

'I say, Lavender!' Sir Richard flushed angrily. 'I won't have you accusing Mrs Palmer of evasion. You're back on this case on sufferance – don't forget that!'

Mrs Palmer leaned forward and placed a calming hand on the surgeon's knee. 'No, please, Richard – he's right. Yes, Detective, Mr MacAdam accidentally let slip some months ago that he had a wife and family back in Chelmsford but he seemed to regret the slip and covered it up quickly.'

'Good God, Sylvia!' Sir Richard looked scandalised. 'Are you saying you knew the fellow was married but was still chasing other women?'

'No, no, Richard, I didn't know anything for sure.' She seemed genuinely distressed by the surgeon's censure. 'And if he was married, I hoped it was just a harmless flirtation that would fizzle out. My gentleman lodgers all get lonely sometimes . . . and they all have dalliances.'

'You condone this?' Sir Richard looked worried.

'Nothing improper happens under my roof,' she retorted.

'I'm afraid it was worse than a dalliance, Mrs Palmer,' Lavender said. 'MacAdam was about to commit bigamy. He'd proposed to the young woman.'

Her elegant hand fluttered to her mouth in shock and Sir Richard cursed. 'What else did you overhear when MacAdam boasted about catching his heiress?'

Mrs Palmer swallowed hard. 'They were in their cups that night and he never mentioned the name of his heiress.'

Sir Richard interrupted her with the questions in Lavender's mind. 'Drunk? But you claimed yesterday that they hardly drank at all. What else are you concealing, Sylvia?'

'Nothing! I promise you, Richard, that I'd never heard Miss Howard's name mentioned until Detective Lavender asked about her yesterday. Then I remembered that Mr MacAdam once asked me to post a letter bearing her name and address on Bruton Street. It was then I made the connection and realised she must be Mr MacAdam's young woman.'

'Where are your other lodgers at the moment, ma'am?' Lavender asked. 'I need to speak to them both urgently.'

Mrs Palmer continued to stare sadly at Sir Richard. It was the surgeon who turned and answered his question. 'Bentley is at work at the Grosvenor Estate office and, like I told you yesterday, Mr Collins is away on business – he works for a tea importer. Why do you need to speak to him?'

'Because I'm afraid MacAdam's intention to commit bigamy wasn't the worst of his sins and I suspect both of your other gentlemen lodgers were involved in his scheming.'

'What scheming?'

He told them how MacAdam, with the help of Collins, had faked his own death.

Sir Richard looked furious and Mrs Palmer was in tears by the time he had finished. 'I can't believe it!' she wailed. 'What a terrible thing to do to his poor wife. He . . . he seemed such a nice man as well!'

'He also told Mr Howard he lived with his aunt in a mansion on Park Lane,' Lavender said. 'Are you and MacAdam related, by any chance?'

'They're not!' Sir Richard yelled. 'That man has gulled us all shamefully! I understand now why someone wanted to murder him!' He rose to his feet and stomped over to the bell pull to summon the maid. She appeared quickly and Sir Richard angrily demanded that she fetch Mrs Palmer some tea and the brandy decanter for himself.

Lavender pulled up a chair and sat down, waiting patiently for their anger and distress to subside. The maid returned with the brandy. Sir Richard gulped down a generous measure of the spirit while Mrs Palmer dried her eyes.

'Tell me about your other lodgers,' Lavender said.

'Mr Collins works for Raitt's Tea Company on St Martin's Lane,' Mrs Palmer said, 'but he's been away on business in Yorkshire since June.'

'June?' Lavender asked sharply. 'That's a long time to be out of town on business.'

Sir Richard leaned forward towards the woman. 'What about his rent? Is his rent up to date, Sylvia?'

She shook her head. 'He wrote to me in the middle of August and sent me more money for the room – but I've had nothing since then.'

'Oh, Sylvia!' Sir Richard moaned. 'So MacAdam owed you two weeks and Collins owed you at least a month's rent. You're too soft-hearted with these lodgers of yours.'

Mrs Palmer looked wretched at his criticism. 'Mr Collins has been my lodger for years. I'm very fond of him and he's never disappointed me before.'

'Do you still have the letter?' Lavender's hopes rose. 'Did it give his address in Yorkshire?'

'No. It was more of a note than a letter. There was no address.'

Lavender shook off his disappointment. 'I need a description of this Collins – and his full name.'

'Frank, Francis Collins,' Sir Richard said. 'He's a big fellah, very loud and in his late twenties. He's got longish, dark hair with a reddish tinge – and a prominent wart on his chin . . .' Sir Richard's voice fizzled out and he shook his head in disbelief.

'He's a very strong character,' Mrs Palmer added. 'It was always my impression the others looked up to him and followed his lead – especially Mr Bentley.'

Lavender nodded. It would take a strong, dissolute and brazen character to carry out the fraud Collins had perpetrated in Chelmsford. Maybe the fake burial had been his suggestion rather than MacAdam's?

'Have you any idea how Mr MacAdam supported himself after he left Drake's in May?'

She shook her head. 'I had no notion he'd left his employment. He must have found another job. He always came down to breakfast at the same time and dressed smartly as if he was going to work.'

'I need to search MacAdam's room for this ring, in case we missed it yesterday,' Lavender said, 'although I suspect it's already on the finger of Miss Howard. There may also be a receipt for this ring amongst his papers that I overlooked yesterday. I also need to search Collins' room for clues about his whereabouts. Do you have a spare key?'

Mrs Palmer nodded. 'I'll take you there.'

'Then I'll go to the Grosvenor Estate office to interview Mr Bentley and Raitt's Tea Company to find out what I can about the whereabouts of Collins.'

He paused. Sir Richard nodded but neither of them said anything.

'But before I go, there are a few other questions I need answering.' Lavender pulled out the rough sketch he'd drawn of the crest Jackson claimed adorned the side of MacAdam's bone-rattling carriage and leaned towards Mrs Palmer. 'According to Mr Howard's secretary, MacAdam kept a carriage and horse and this was the emblem on the side of the vehicle. Do you recognise it?'

She shook her head, bewildered. 'He didn't keep horses or a carriage to my knowledge. No, I've never seen that coat of arms before.'

Disappointed, Lavender pocketed the drawing and showed her the other coat of arms, the one he'd sketched after seeing Bentley climb into a carriage yesterday morning. 'And what about this one?'

Mrs Palmer hesitated and for a brief second Lavender thought he saw shock in her face. 'I can't be sure but I think this is the family crest of my friend Louisa Fitzgerald, who lives in Berkeley Square.' She was holding something back.

Sir Richard frowned. 'Why? How is Lady Louisa involved in this crime, Lavender?'

'She's not – at the moment. Unless she's a redhead. Does she have red hair?'

Mrs Palmer shook her head in confusion. 'No, she's older than me and grey-haired.'

Lavender rose to his feet and his glance swung significantly between Sir Richard and Mrs Palmer. 'I've one final question. I want to know how you two know each other. You're far more intimate than a doctor and his patient.'

'Ha! Nothing escapes you, does it, Detective?' Sir Richard snapped bitterly.

'What is the connection between you?' Lavender persisted.

Sir Richard bristled. 'I don't see how that will have any bearing on the case . . .'

'Oh, Richard, stop it.' Mrs Palmer turned to Lavender, her lined face creased with worry and concern.

Lavender steeled himself for the imminent revelation.

'Sir Richard is my younger brother,' she said.

'Your brother?' He glanced between them – then cursed himself for not seeing the resemblance before. Sir Richard's face was fleshy and Mrs Palmer's thin and lined but they shared the same bulbous nose and pale eyes.

'Yes, we had the same father but different mothers. I was Sylvia Allison before my marriage.'

Sir Richard looked awkward. His voice dipped. 'I didn't tell you before, Lavender, because I thought it might complicate things.'

'How so?'

'I didn't want anyone to doubt my impartiality in this case. It's important to me that I'm part of this investigation and that the murderer is swiftly brought to justice, for Sylvia's sake. But I didn't know whether – because of my family connection – you would doubt my evidence about the deceased and his injuries. Or, indeed, if the courts would do so later, when we finally track down MacAdam's killer.'

Lavender exhaled with relief and allowed himself a small laugh. 'I'd never doubt your evidence, Sir Richard,' he said firmly. 'And I'd make sure no jury did either. In fact, I sincerely hope when the exhumation of MacAdam's coffin takes place, you'll come up to Essex with me to examine the remains.'

'You can rely on my help,' Sir Richard said. 'I'm as determined as you to get to the bottom of this devilish murder, Lavender.'

Chapter Twelve

B illy Summersgill had already reached Piccadilly by the time Woods caught sight of him again. The moneylender darted across the busy thoroughfare between the rear end of a hansom cab and an oncoming brewer's dray and narrowly missed a trampling. The driver cursed loudly but Summersgill wasn't listening. He swerved to avoid a man with a handcart and stumbled on to the pavement. He bent double to relieve a stitch. His shoulders heaved with his laboured breaths.

Woods grinned and calmly trotted across the road behind him, confident that the clip-clop of his horse's hooves would be drowned out by the rumble of traffic. He swung out of the saddle, scattering a crowd of startled pedestrians, and had a metal handcuff round one of Billy's wrists before the fugitive had time to straighten up.

"'Ere! Gerroff me!' Summersgill yelled. 'I've done nuffin'!' His uncuffed fist swung at Woods' head but the man had no energy left and Woods avoided the blow easily. 'You're under arrest.' Woods grabbed his other shoulder and swung the moneylender round like a child, knocking his hat to the floor. The second cuff snapped into place.

'I've done nuffin'! What you arrestin' me for?'

Woods paused for a moment with the writhing man in his arms and wondered himself. He was about to say 'because Detective Lavender says so' but a crowd had gathered around them and he thought better of teasing the fellah in public. Besides which, he had the reputation of Bow Street Police Office to consider. He decided to give the good folks of London a show. 'Billy Summersgill, by the power invested in me by His Royal Highness, the Prince Regent, in the name and on behalf of His Majesty King George III, I arrest you on suspicion of the murder of David MacAdam.'

The crowd gasped in horror.

''E's a killer!' someone shrieked.

'I didn't kill 'im!' Summersgill squeaked. 'Show me your warrant.'

Woods yanked on the cuffs to silence him.

'You're so brave, officer!' a woman exclaimed. Woods nodded solemnly.

'I'll fetch your horse, Constable,' said one of the gentlemen in the crowd.

'That'd be most kind of you, sir.'

Woods' well-trained patrol horse had stopped calmly by the side of the road when he'd leapt from its back and it was easily led towards the two men. Woods attached a chain between Summersgill's cuffs and his saddle amid the cheers and excited chatter of their audience. He remounted and rode back towards Bow Street with the wild-haired, hatless and complaining moneylender stumbling beside him.

He pondered how best to conduct the interrogation while he rode beneath the arched entrance of the Bow Street stable yard at the rear of the building. *In for a penny, in for a pound,* he decided. *Might as well scare the livin' daylights out of him.*

Eddie rushed forward across the cobbled yard to take his horse after he'd dismounted.

'Thanks, son. Where's David MacAdam's body?'

'In the morgue, like Detective Lavender told us,' Eddie replied, 'but there's another corpse in there, Da. They've just hauled it out o' the Thames and it stinks to high heaven.'

'Good.' Woods thanked Eddie, grabbed the chains and hauled the squealing Summersgill towards the stinking morgue.

Eddie was right about the foul stench. It hit Woods' nostrils before he'd even forced open the creaking door. Four stone slabs stood in the centre of the room. An open wooden coffin stood on one of them, while a pile of decomposing flesh and sodden rags lay on the one in the far corner. Woods pushed the moneylender towards MacAdam's coffin and pressed him to peer over the edge. The undertakers had dressed MacAdam before they brought him to Bow Street; he looked quite smart and angelic in death.

'Take a good look at your handiwork, Billy!' he yelled.

'I didn't do it, guvnor!' Summersgill snivelled. 'That bleedin' dustman's nuffin' to do wi' me!'

'And why should I believe you? He welched on his debt – and within hours you're at his home, threatenin' violence to an old lady. You're a murderous cove, Billy.'

'I didn't offer no violence!'

'You threatened to steal her furniture!' Woods roared. His indignant fury made the sentence sound like a hanging offence.

'I'm sorry! I'm sorry!' Large tears rolled down Summersgill's pockmarked cheeks. Woods didn't know whether it was fear, self-pity or the stench from the drowned corpse that made his eyes water.

He grabbed the moneylender by the collar and, ignoring the man's rank breath, hauled his face up to his own. 'How do we know you didn't kill him for defaultin' on his loan?' he hissed.

'I swear on me old ma's life, I never touched that swell.'

'You ran from the law!'

Summersgill hesitated and in that instant Woods knew there was more than just a business transaction behind his association with MacAdam. 'It weren't that, it were somethin' else. I don't want no trouble.'

'You'd better tell me everythin'.'

'I will, I swear on me old ma's . . .'

'Don't bother.' Woods stopped him abruptly. 'Your ma was a Covent Garden nun who died of the pox two years ago.' He pushed Summersgill out of the door and into a small interview room in the adjacent cell block. Summersgill slumped on to a hard-backed chair and Woods sat opposite him. His empty stomach contracted in a vicious cramp and rumbled loudly. He contorted his features to make it look like he was glowering rather than grimacing with pain.

'Now tell me what happened with MacAdam.'

Summersgill sniffed and wiped his streaming nose on the back of his coat sleeve. His chains rattled when he moved. "E came to me about a month back, askin' for a loan of a 'undred guineas. Said 'e'd seen a lovely ruby sparkler 'e wanted to buy his gal from Robbie's on the Strand.'

'So, you loaned him the money?'

The moneylender bristled with indignation. 'I didn't. I'm a sharp businessman, I am, Constable. 'E 'ad no security for the loan – or job as far as I could see. I don't just furnish every bushed nob who walks into my shop with an 'undred yellow boys.'

Woods' eyes narrowed. 'So how did he persuade you to give him the chinks?'

Summersgill shuffled uncomfortably in his seat. "E said 'e'd got a rich 'eiress danglin' from 'is arm and 'e needed the ring to ensnare 'er. I weren't rightly comfortable wi' that.'

Woods snorted. 'Don't tell me you're growin' a conscience, Billy?'

His prisoner drew himself up and bristled again. 'I'll 'ave you know I'm a respectable man, I am, Constable – and I respect the gals.'

Despite the griping pain in his stomach, the side of Woods' mouth twitched. 'That's fine talk for a whoreson.'

"E said 'e'd drive past my shop at one the next day to prove it.'

'And did he?'

The moneylender's eyes widened at the memory. 'Aye, 'e did – in a spankin' black phaeton. They looked an 'andsome couple, despite her brown skin. I thought about it and decided to take a chance on the fellah.'

'So when he came back, you gave him the chinks – probably at a sky-high rate of interest – and today he was supposed to make the first payment on the loan?'

'Yesterday. 'E were supposed to pay yesterday. That's why you know I didn't kill 'im – I don't have no reason to kill 'im. I want me money back.' Summersgill's face turned ugly. 'The ring's mine now 'e's dead.'

'Oh no, it's not,' Woods said sharply. 'If he's given it to his sweetheart it's hers now. And you'll stay well away from her and from Mrs Palmer's house, do you hear me? When MacAdam's estate is settled – that's if he's got one – you can join the line of other debtors at the lawyer's door.'

'That ain't fair!' Summersgill yelled. 'That ring is mine. I loaned 'im the yellow boys to buy it. And I lost me 'at when you clapped me in irons.'

Woods leapt to his feet and the chair fell over with a crash. He grabbed the moneylender by the throat again and slammed him up against the cell wall. 'Sod your hat! And you'd better forget about the ring, Billy – and leave those people alone.'

The terrified moneylender whimpered.

Woods flung open the door and pushed the snivelling wretch into the arms of the gaoler. 'Lock him up,' he said. 'Detective Lavender may want a word with him when he gets back. I'm goin' out again.'

'Where are you goin', Woods?' the gaoler asked.

Woods took a deep breath, pulled back his shoulders and smiled. He felt curiously light-headed and happy. The misery and irritation that had haunted him since he stopped eating yesterday had lifted and he wasn't even bothered by the pain in his guts any more. 'I'm goin' to Robertson's jewellers on the Strand to follow up a lead. If Detective Lavender gets back before me, let him know, will you?'

The man nodded.

Woods strode out of the prison block into the sunny yard – and promptly blacked out and fell in a heap on the cobbles.

After a fruitless search for the missing ring in MacAdam's room, Mrs Palmer fetched her keys and let Lavender into Mr Collins' stuffy bedchamber. It reeked of stale tobacco smoke and there were several clay pipes on the mantelpiece spewing out a trail of fine tobacco on to the surface. He pushed up the sash window to let in some air. 'When did someone last come in here?' he asked.

'I haven't been in here since he left,' Mrs Palmer replied from the doorway. 'My maid cleaned in here the week after Mr Collins left for Yorkshire but it's been locked up since then. Do you need me for anything else, Detective? Because if you don't, I'll leave you in peace.'

'No, thank you. You can go.'

She turned and disappeared down the stairs.

Collins was an untidy beggar. He'd left a pair of muddy boots on the floor and a dirty cravat and a spare coat flung across a chair. Lavender wondered which bits of the room the maid had actually cleaned because every surface was covered with books, pamphlets, crumpled bits of paper and personal items.

There was even a pile of unswept ash on the hearth, although strangely enough it looked like someone had tried to clean the thin, grubby carpet around the edge of the hearth. One patch was paler than the rest and less marked.

Lavender examined the books first; every one of them had an equestrian theme. Collins obviously liked his horses and followed racing. The crumpled pamphlets were from horse fairs and races held earlier in the year; the small, screwed-up pieces of paper were gambling slips. The man had even used some old gaming tickets as bookmarks between the well-thumbed pages of his books.

Lavender paused thoughtfully and remembered MacAdam's earlier career with horses. Collins and MacAdam had obviously shared a passion for the animals but following racing was an expensive pastime for a layman, especially if he was a reckless gambler. Had Collins run up gambling debts? Lavender searched through the scattered papers looking for letters from creditors or anything else to give him an idea about the state of his suspect's financial affairs. He found nothing.

Biting back his frustration, he examined the coat on the chair and found some dog-eared trade cards in the pocket. They showed an elegant green tea canister encased in a swirling wreath of foliage, flowers and small Grecian urns. It read: 'Raitt's Tea Warehouse, May's Buildings, St Martin's Lane. Fine Teas, Coffee and Chocolate. Wholesale and Retail.' He pocketed one of the cards with the address and noticed the breadth of the shoulders of the coat. Sir Richard was right – Collins was another big man, about the same size as MacAdam and Woods.

He opened the closet door and was surprised at the number of garments hanging inside. The elusive tea merchant must either have an extensive wardrobe, or he had taken hardly anything with him to Yorkshire. Several flame-coloured hairs were caught on the hem of the pantaloons and breeches. Lavender pulled them off and rubbed their silky texture between his fingers, frowning. For the first time, he considered the possibility that these were dog hairs. They were almost identical in colour and texture to the hair he'd found on MacAdam's clothes, which he'd initially thought belonged to a woman.

Collins had also left behind his razor, shaving brushes and soap, but Lavender didn't read much into that. He himself had two sets of shaving equipment, one of which stayed permanently in his travelling bag in case an investigation ever called him out of town in a hurry. He found more gambling slips in the pockets of the coats and a short, sweet letter to *'Uncle Frank'* scribbled in a childish scrawl, from Collins' niece.

He gave the room one last glance and noted a broken tile in the corner of the hearth before he descended the stairs to the parlour and returned the key to Mrs Palmer. 'You don't keep a dog, do you, Mrs Palmer?'

She shook her head.

'Did any of your lodgers have friends who own dogs with a red coat? Perhaps an Irish setter?'

She looked startled but shook her head again. 'Is this relevant to the case, Detective?'

He shrugged. 'Maybe.' He excused himself and let himself out of the house into the sunlight.

Young Will, the road sweeper, was standing by the park railings with his horse, beneath the shade of a towering oak.

'Where's yer fat friend today?' the boy asked when he held out his hand for Lavender's penny.

Lavender smiled. 'Be off with you, you cheeky imp.' He turned back to his mare and stroked her silky neck, enjoying the freshness of the light breeze and the whispering of the leaves above. Weak sunlight filtered through the canopy of the leaves, creating a soft, dappled effect on the horse's glossy neck and flank.

The ruby ring had added a new dimension to MacAdam's murder. A missing jewel of such value brought robbery back into the investigation as a motive. MacAdam's murderer may have been happy to leave the pocket watch and small change in his pockets once he'd uncovered such a dazzling article.

But it was only twenty-four hours since the investigation began, so there was plenty of time to get to the bottom of this case. It seemed longer, though.

He glanced up at the position of the sun and realised it was nearly noon. Mrs MacAdam would arrive at Bow Street to view her husband's body in the morgue at two o'clock. He only had enough time left to visit the workplace of one of Mrs Palmer's lodgers.

He swung himself up in the saddle and turned his horse in the direction of Collins' employer in St Martin's.

Chapter Thirteen

Woods woke to find a pale-faced crow flapping above his throbbing head. When his eyes finally focused, he realised it was Magistrate Read in his voluminous court robes scowling down at him. A small crowd of smirking ostlers had also gathered around him. His frightened son was amongst them.

'What happened, Woods?' Magistrate Read demanded.

Embarrassed, Woods sat up and tenderly explored the sore, bloodied patch on the back of his head where it had hit the cobbles. 'Nothin' happened, I tripped and fell over, that's all. Fetch me a drink of water, son.'

While Eddie raced over to the pump, Woods pulled himself to his feet. One of the officers made a crack about 'being foxed on duty' and another suggested he watered down his ale, but Woods barely heard them. Both the light-headed sensation and the terrible gnawing in his stomach returned when he stood up. Despite his desire to brush off the incident, he staggered and grimaced with pain.

'Are you sure you're all right?' Read asked. 'You've got a nasty lump on your head.'

Eddie returned with a cup of water, which Woods gulped down gratefully. The water temporarily filled the emptiness of his belly and settled the hunger pangs.

'Your head looks bad, Da,' the lad said.

'It's nothin' a bit of vinegar and brown paper won't put right,' Woods replied with a wink. 'Remember that old rhyme, son? *Jack and Jill?*'

Eddie smiled ruefully.

'Well, if you're sure you'll be all right, Woods . . .' Read said.

'Yes, sir, I'm fine.'

'Then back to work, everyone.'

The crowd dispersed and Magistrate Read continued his journey to the courthouse.

Only Eddie remained, his young face etched with concern. 'Da . . . ?'

Woods managed a smile. 'I'll be fine, son. Now stop fussin' and get me my horse.' While Eddie went into the stables, Woods brushed the muck off his uniform and staggered to the water pump. He soaked his face and the back of his head to remove the blood. By the time Eddie returned with the saddled horse, Woods was wet but more alert and he'd stopped quivering.

But it took all of his energy to haul himself up. Conscious of his son's sharp eyes, he fixed a smile across his face. It vanished the second he cantered out of the stable yard and the stomach pains returned.

Just for a week, he promised himself. *Just for a week . . .*

Lavender enjoyed the strong aroma of the coffee when he rode past the famous New Slaughter's Coffee House on St Martin's Lane. He had the time to call in for a bowl. He and Magdalena were coffee drinkers and both of them liked it strong.

Once a leafy lane leading to the heart of the capital, bordered by the gardens and large homes of the nobility and officials of the royal court, St Martin's Lane was now a bustling and thriving commercial thoroughfare. A row of four-storey stuccoed family houses with flat roofs towered above him, casting the street into shadow and jostling for space with the older, wood-gabled shops and taverns. The Chippendales lived here on St Martin's Lane and had converted two of the houses into a workshop for their celebrated furniture business.

May's Buildings, a relatively new commercial building, was constructed around a paved central courtyard with a broad archway leading out on to the main street. Several bow-fronted shops looked out on to the courtyard. A sign displaying the elegant green tea canister and elaborate Grecian foliage of Raitt's Tea Warehouse swung out of the wall above a doorway.

At the rear of the courtyard, the large wooden doors of the tea-packing warehouse had been slid open. Men were taking measured quantities of the pale green leaf out of large tea chests and packing them into smaller boxes. The aromatic scent of the plant drifted on the breeze towards Lavender.

He entered the building through the door beneath the swinging wooden sign.

A middle-aged bald man with wire spectacles glanced up from behind several sets of the brass scales on the counter and greeted him. The grassy vegetable aroma of tea was stronger in here. Open boxes of tea were everywhere, labelled with exotic names like 'Bing', 'Hyson' and 'Imperial', but there were also bowls of delicate, reddish-brown leaves called 'Bohea'. The shelves behind the counter glittered with expensive silver tea sets. There was everything the discerning house-wife would need, from a teapot on a stand to the teaspoons and sugar tongs.

Lavender introduced himself to the proprietor, Mr Alistair Raitt, and explained he was looking for a worker at the company called Francis Collins.

'Ha!' the little man exclaimed, 'and so are the rest of us.'

Lavender frowned and adjusted his ears to the Scotsman's strong accent. 'What do you mean, sir? I understand Collins works for

Raitt's Tea Company but may be away on business at the moment in Yorkshire.'

'So that's the story the rascal tells, is it?'

'Where is Mr Collins?'

The black shoulders of Raitt's jacket shrugged. 'I dinno, I've niver seen him for months. Yes, he was supposed tae be in Leeds on ma company's business but he niver arrived there – or returned back here. I've replaced him now.'

'When did you last see him?'

'It was in June. He set off with a wee shipment of tea for my business partners in Leeds and Harrogate. He was instructed tae get us more trade and were supposed tae be back here in three weeks.'

'May I have their address?'

'Aye, but I've wrote tae them since and he niver arrived.'

'I'll take a copy of that address anyway, sir. What was Collins' position in your company, Mr Raitt?'

The shopkeeper reached for a pencil and a piece of paper. 'He did a bit of everythin' but mostly sellin' here in the shop or promotin' the business in the tea shops of London and with provincial buyers and warehouses. He's a silver tongue, has Collins, and he's good at his job.' He handed Lavender the address.

'Didn't you make any other enquiries about his absence? Contact his family – or his landlady, for instance? He may have met with an accident while on your company business.'

Raitt scowled at Lavender's suggestion. 'I'm a busy man, Detective. I canna be chasin' around England lookin' for workers who've deserted. Collins was niver mah responsibility.'

'Did the shipment of tea disappear with him? Did you contact the constables about the theft?'

Raitt shook his head. 'It was only a wee shipment. The bigger loss was the trade he didna get for me.'

'On what date in June did Collins set off for Yorkshire?'

'I canna remember.'

Sighing with frustration, Lavender thanked him and left.

Eddie Woods frowned, bent down to the horse's fetlock with his stiff-bristled dandy brush and began to remove the mud from the animal's lower legs. The stallion snorted and shuffled uncomfortably. It was loosely tied to a ring on the outside of the stable wall.

'Shh, Beresford,' he soothed. It had become a tradition amongst the stable hands to name the Bow Street horses after the British generals, especially those who fought alongside the newly elevated Marquess of Wellington. Even the mares were named after military men. The experienced mare his Uncle Stephen rode was called Abercromby.

Beresford calmed down and remained still while Eddie resumed his firm brushing of the animal's hocks. Mud fell away on to the cobbles.

The rhythmic work gave him a few moments to think about his da. Finding his father unconscious on the ground had alarmed and unsettled Eddie. His da was never ill and had never taken a day away from work that Eddie could remember – apart from when he was shot in the shoulder, last spring. Was this swooning a sign of something bad? He didn't know whether or not he should tell his ma. His da probably wouldn't like it but his ma wanted to know everything. If he didn't tell Ma, she might give him a slap.

He was dimly aware that his mother's attitude had changed towards him this summer. She was more loving these days and he'd seen a softness shine in her brown eyes when she looked at him. She listened closely to what he said and she'd also stopped slapping him. She gave him bigger portions than his brother because she said he needed a man's strength to do a man's job and she often sneaked him small treats when the others weren't looking. He didn't want that to stop – or for her to slap him again. To tell Ma? Or not to tell Ma? It was a conundrum. As his da often said, it was addling his noddle.

He sighed, stood up and regarded Beresford's clean fetlocks with satisfaction. He'd fetch a pail of water and swill away the mud from the cobbles. He might as well comb Beresford's blond mane and swish his pale-coloured tail in the water while he was at it. Both looked a bit grubby.

'Excuse me, sir.'

Eddie spun round. Two black-gowned, heavily veiled women stood behind him. He'd been so lost in thought he hadn't heard them approach.

'Yes, ma'am?'

'We understand the late Mr MacAdam has been brought here to rest.' He couldn't see much through the veil but the woman who spoke had dark eyes and she sounded young. 'We'd like to pay our last respects to him.'

For a moment, Eddie didn't know who or what she meant. Then he remembered the dustman the undertakers had brought to the morgue yesterday. 'Yes, ma'am.' He pointed towards the building with his dandy brush. 'It's over there. Are you Mr MacAdam's family?' He knew Mrs MacAdam was expected shortly.

'No.' The young woman followed the line of his arm and stared at the door a few yards away. She seemed to hesitate.

'Do you want me to come with you?'

'No, sir. Thank you.'

'I'm afraid there's another body in there too. It's a bit ripe.'

The young girl braced herself before she led her companion towards the morgue. They opened the door and hesitated. He thought it might be the smell that stopped them but they'd only paused so the other woman could take off her gloves and button up her coat against the chill of the room. They disappeared inside.

When they reappeared, the older woman was sobbing. The younger woman took her arm and led her through the arch out of the stable yard.

Eddie sighed and led Beresford back inside the stable. His Uncle Stephen was right; solving mysterious murders was the most exciting thing in the world – but dealing with the sadness of the friends and relatives of the victims was hard.

Chapter Fourteen

Robertson's Jewellers, known locally as 'Robbie's', was one of the most famous high-class establishments in the mile-long parade of shops on the Strand. Despite the fact that the seedier nature of Covent Garden had swept down the street like a tidal wave over the last few years, by day the Strand remained a popular shopping area for Londoners of quality. The interior dazzled customers with its glass cases full of glistening diamonds, sapphire-encrusted necklaces and sparkling emerald rings and bracelets.

The shop was also carpeted, which always embarrassed Woods because he was never sure about what he may have picked up on the bottom of his muddy boots from the stable yard; but the proprietors were always friendly and helpful towards the Bow Street officers. Over the years, they'd helped them retrieve several items of stolen jewellery.

Woods entered and asked for the proprietor. While he waited, he studied a stylish gold pocket watch and a diamond-encrusted cravat pin, under the watchful eye of several male shop assistants. When the shop owner arrived, Woods explained he wanted information about a recent transaction involving an expensive ruby ring purchased by a big fellah called MacAdam.

The elderly man immediately called for the sales ledgers and examined them studiously. 'Here,' he said, jabbing his finger into the book.

'It was three days ago. Mr MacAdam bought one of our ruby rings for one hundred guineas. It was an exotic piece, brought over from the Indian subcontinent.'

'Indian, eh?' Woods said. No doubt Miss Howard would have appreciated that. 'Can you describe it, sir?'

'It was previously owned by a Mughal empress and contained a floret of rubies around one central large stone. The leaves were carved from turquoises. The turquoise leaf design continued part way around the gold band.'

'Sounds like a pretty little sparkler,' Woods said. 'Who served the gentleman?'

The proprietor glanced down at the ledger and then called over a young man called Perkins. Woods asked him to describe the customer. Perkins' description matched MacAdam.

'Were Mr MacAdam alone when he came into the shop?'

'Yes, sir, but he was in a hurry. I believe there was a lady waitin' outside for him in his carriage.'

'A lady? Did you see her?'

'No, officer. It was just somethin' he said when he left about how he "mustn't keep the old gal waitin'".'

'*Old gal?*' Was this just a crude slang way of talking or a clue? 'Can you describe the carriage?'

'Describe it, officer?' Confusion flashed across Perkins' pale, freckled face.

'Yes, the vehicle. Were it a flashy black phaeton, for example?'

'No, it were just an ordinary carriage with smart chestnut horses.'

'Were there a crest on the side, a coat of arms?'

Perkins shook his head. 'There were market traders with stalls outside on the pavement. I only caught a glimpse of it over their heads when it pulled away.'

Woods glanced up at the jewelled face of the elegant French long clock that stood at the end of the counter. It was a quarter off two o'clock. He had to get back to Bow Street. 'You've been very helpful, gentlemen, thank you.'

◆ ◆ ◆

Lavender was standing talking with Eddie in the stable yard when Woods trotted beneath the arched entrance. He pulled up beside them and dismounted. 'I've a lot to tell you, sir,' he said, 'and I've got a description of the ring MacAdam bought.'

Lavender nodded. 'That's good news, Ned. Your son has also been doing some detecting on our behalf while we were out.'

Woods saw the gleam of excitement in his boy's brown eyes. 'Oh, yes? What's been happenin' here?'

'According to Eddie, the late Mr MacAdam has had visitors,' Lavender continued. 'Female visitors.'

Woods raised his eyebrows in amusement. 'I hope MacAdam were courteous, made them tea and offered them both a comfy chair.'

'Don't be daft, Da,' Eddie said, annoyed. 'He's dead.'

'Well, I'll wager they didn't stay long in that stinking morgue.'

'No, they didn't,' Eddie gabbled. He was bursting to tell his story. 'They said they wanted to pay their last respects to Mr MacAdam – at least, the young one did. The older one never spoke.'

'You said they were both heavily veiled, Eddie,' Lavender said gently. 'How could you tell the difference in their ages?'

'It were her hands, sir. The older one took her gloves off for a moment to button up her coat. Her hands were wrinkled and had those brown old people's spots that Ma has.'

Lavender bit back his smile and Woods chuckled.

'You'd best not mention to your ma she has "old people's spots",' Woods said.

'But it's good observation, Eddie,' Lavender pointed out.

Eddie beamed at the praise.

'Did you ask for their names, son?'

The youngster's face fell. 'No, it didn't seem right to question them. They was only inside the morgue for a moment and left quickly. The older woman seemed upset.'

'Did they arrive in a carriage?' Woods asked.

Eddie shook his head. 'I don't know, they went out of the archway into the street.'

'Did the younger woman have a thick foreign accent? How did she sound?' Lavender asked.

'No, she sounded just like me – but I thought she were dark.'

'Thought it, or saw it, Eddie?' Lavender asked quietly.

Eddie hesitated. 'Thought it – I'm not sure. Did I do wrong? Should I have questioned them harder?'

Lavender patted him on the back. 'No, Eddie – you've been very helpful, as always. Keep your eyes peeled, though, in case they come back.'

They left him glowing with praise and walked inside the police office to wait for Mrs MacAdam and Ike Rawlings.

'Did you think one of those visitors may have been Miss Howard? Did she come to say goodbye to her fiancé?' Woods asked.

'Yes, I wondered if it might have been her – especially when he said he thought she was dark-skinned. I've not met Miss Howard yet but I doubt she speaks just like Eddie.'

The gloomy hallway entrance of the police office heaved with the dregs of London society. A sorry collection of petty criminals waited morosely in handcuffs and chains by the desk for the clerks to record the details of the charges against them. Once the administration was complete, they would be taken by the constables to the cramped and overcrowded cells at the back of the building.

Woods glanced at the sour-faced Chief Clerk, Oswald Grey, and his beleaguered staff behind the desk. 'That reminds me, sir, I've kept Billy Summersgill below the hatches in case you wanted a word with him.'

He told Lavender the information he'd gleaned from the moneylender and explained how it had led him on to Robertson's, the jewellers where he got the description of the ruby ring.

'You've done well, Ned, but ask Grey to release Summersgill. With any luck, this stint in the cells will have frightened him and he'll leave Mrs Palmer alone. The ring isn't in her house.'

Woods nodded. He sidestepped a drunk who'd slid down the greasy wall on to the floor and went to the desk to organise Summersgill's release. A new thought struck him when he returned to Lavender's side. 'The jeweller said an "old gal" were waitin' in a carriage for MacAdam while he purchased the ring. Maybe it were the same old trot who's just been to view MacAdam's body?'

'This case gets more intriguing by the hour,' Lavender said thoughtfully. 'We need to find out more about MacAdam's London friends and associates and track down this mysterious carriage he claimed to own. Now Collins has vanished into thin air and that lead has gone cold, we'll make tracing MacAdam's last journey home from the Howards' our main priority. Somewhere between climbing aboard that coach and the steps of his home on Park Lane he received a fatal injury.'

'Collins has vanished?'

'Yes.' Lavender told him about his visit to Raitt's.

Woods was stunned. 'That's a real mystery, that. Why would he disappear – especially if MacAdam had promised to make him a rich man? It don't make sense.'

Lavender shrugged. 'I've no explanation for his disappearance. Perhaps he didn't help MacAdam for the money. I may be wrong about that.'

'Maybe Collins got drunk in a dockside tavern and were press-ganged into the navy,' Woods suggested.

Lavender shook his head. 'No, he's gone to ground somewhere in the country. He sent Mrs Palmer a brief note with some rent money in August. To be honest, I think it might be worth raising a hue and cry for him.'

Woods was thoughtful for a moment. 'I wondered if Mrs Palmer may have been the "old gal" waitin' in the carriage for MacAdam?'

Lavender shook his head. 'She claims no knowledge of any carriage – but then again she had a suspicion MacAdam was married and never mentioned it. To be honest, Ned, I think Mrs Palmer knows far more about David MacAdam than she's told us. She's keeping something back.'

Mrs MacAdam and Ike Rawlings walked through the entrance into the hallway. They looked pale and glanced around awkwardly. She wore a fraying dark coat over her gown and a battered bonnet. Her clothes and Rawlings' old coat were dusty from their journey.

'Oh, and there's something else she and Sir Richard held back from us yesterday,' Lavender said before they went to greet the visitors.

Woods growled at the mention of Sir Richard's name. 'What's that then?'

'They're brother and sister.'

Woods looked like Lavender had just slapped him round the face with a wet kipper. 'You're jestin' with me, surely?'

'No.'

'How can that sweet little old woman be related to Sir Slyboots?'

Woods' shocked reaction made Lavender smile. 'Well, they are. Same father, different mothers. Now forget about Sir Richard and come with me. I need you to concentrate on the reaction of Mrs MacAdam and Ike Rawlings when we go into the morgue.'

It only took Mrs MacAdam a few seconds to identify the body of her husband, so mercifully the time they spent in the stinking morgue was short.

Outside in the fresh air and sunshine of the stable yard, the woman exploded. 'I can't believe the lyin', cheatin' scoundrel did that to us! What were 'e thinkin' of?' Her cheeks flushed and her plain face became ugly with anger. She shook off Rawlings' hand when he reached out to soothe her. 'Why did 'e pretend to be dead?'

'We think he'd met another woman and wanted to marry her,' Woods said gently.

'Well, she were welcome to 'im!' she shouted. 'The lyin' wrinkler!'

'We're sorry for your loss,' Lavender said.

'No, no – don't be sorry. It were good riddance when 'e died in June – and it's good riddance 'e's died again. The scum!'

'We'll open the inquest into his death here, tomorrow morning at nine o'clock. You'd be welcome to attend.'

'I don't think so!'

Lavender turned to Rawlings in the hope he might be less emotional but was surprised to see the carrier wipe a hasty tear from the corner of his eye. 'Are you feeling all right, sir?'

Rawlings nodded his shaggy head and cleared his throat. 'It were just a bit upsettin', that's all. I've known Davy for years. 'E were a rogue, yes, but it's awful to think of 'im murdered like that.' He fumbled in his pocket for his pipe and tobacco.

'You're a soft-hearted fool then, Ike Rawlings,' the little woman snapped. 'I'll not shed no more tears over 'im after the way 'e's carried on.'

'We've requested the exhumation,' Lavender said. 'When the bishop sends the permission, we'll bring Mr MacAdam back up to Chelmsford so you can bury him again.'

'And no doubt that'll cost me!' Her eyes rolled up to the sky and she threw her hands up in frustration. 'Lord knows what I've done to offend God so much I'm cursed wi' 'avin' to bury the same 'usband twice.'

Lavender had no answer to that. He turned back to Rawlings. 'I need to know something, sir. You've told us you travel to London regularly to bring stone to a building merchant in the city.'

'Yes, I come to Eggerton's stonemasons in Spitalfields. Why?'

'During your time in the city, have you ever met David MacAdam – or seen him in passing? Did you know where he lived?'

Rawlings stopped filling his pipe and glanced up. 'No, our paths never crossed. I knew 'e lodged somewhere in the city but I didn't know where.' A red flush crept up his neck above his dirty blue neckerchief. His soft brown eyes blinked rapidly then dropped beneath Lavender's steady gaze.

'What's this all about?' Mrs MacAdam asked angrily. 'Why do yer want to know about Ike?'

'Mr Rawlings has already told us he was in London the day your husband was murdered,' Woods said.

'What?' She glanced quickly between the strained faces of the three men. 'What?' She gave a short, brittle laugh. 'Don't tell me you think Ike may have killed Davy?'

'We have to examine every possibility,' Lavender said.

'And Mr Rawlings had a motive,' Woods added. 'We know you planned to wed each other soon.'

'What's that got to do wi' anythin'? Yer jestin' wi' us, surely? You can't think Ike had anythin' to do wi' Davy's murder?' Rawlings remained silent and rooted to the spot. A few shreds of tobacco floated unheeded from his pouch down to the cobbles.

'At the moment, we don't know what happened,' Lavender confessed, 'but we will soon. And you, madam, have you ever been to London before?'

'I 'ave not! And I tell you somethin' else, Detective – I won't be comin' again!' She grabbed Rawlings' arm and half-dragged the tall man and his unlit pipe through the arch and out of the stable yard.

Chapter Fifteen

A re you lettin' them go?' Woods asked, as Rawlings and the indignant Mrs MacAdam disappeared from sight and out into the street.

'For now,' Lavender replied. 'We know where they are if we need to question them again and we'll be back in Chelmsford soon for the exhumation.'

Rawlings and the indignant Mrs MacAdam disappeared from sight out into the street.

'He looked shocked.'

Lavender nodded thoughtfully. 'Yes, there's something not right there. He was surprisingly upset to see MacAdam's body.'

'Were it guilt, do you think?'

'I don't know, but my instincts tell me Ike Rawlings knows something about MacAdam's death. We'll let him brood on it for a few days and question him again in Chelmsford. In the meantime, Ned, I want you to go over to Eggerton's stonemasons in Spitalfields and find out what you can about Rawlings. We need to know if he went straight home after he made his delivery two days ago, if he stayed in London – and if he was alone when he arrived.'

'What about you, sir?'

'I intend to question Mrs Palmer's third lodger, Alfred Bentley. After that, I'll go to Bruton Street to see the Howards and I'll call in at MacAdam's bank on the way. I'll meet you back here later.'

Before they separated, they approached Oswald Grey at the custody desk. Bow Street's Chief Clerk was aptly named. A tall, pallid, greying man of sixty with pale humourless eyes and a preference for drab clothing, Grey rarely smiled. His was a responsible position, which he carried with diligence, intelligence and occasionally a sardonic quip or two about both the felons and the officers.

Woods signed for the release of Billy Summersgill, then departed. Lavender asked Grey to contact the newspapers and ask them to raise the hue and cry and write a 'Wanted' notice for Francis Collins, tea salesman, formerly of Park Lane, London.

'He's in his late twenties and is well built and about five foot ten inches tall. He's got longish dark hair with a reddish tinge – and a prominent wart on his chin.'

'Any known aliases?' Grey asked.

'Not at the moment. He was called "Frank", though.'

'Aren't they all.' Grey made a note of the nickname. 'And he's wanted on what charge?' He paused with his quill poised above the paper.

Lavender hesitated for a moment while he thought carefully. 'Perjury and deception.'

Grey raised a quizzical eyebrow behind his wire spectacles. 'That's not very exciting for a hue and cry notice, Lavender. It needs to be more dramatic or no one will bother to read it.'

'I've not come across a case like this before,' Lavender confessed.

'Do you need me to help you, Detective? I've got thirty years of experience of drawing up charge sheets.'

Lavender felt amused by Grey's patronising tone. 'Frank Collins took an unidentified body in a coffin to a vicar to bury and gave him false evidence. That's definitely perjury.'

'An unknown corpse?' Was there a tinge of excitement in the clerk's voice? 'Did he murder the dead man?'

'We don't know yet.'

'Well, if he wasn't a murderer, was he a body-snatcher? Did he dig up the victim in the coffin?'

'No – well, not as far as I know.'

'You don't seem to know much,' Grey said. His tone was full of disdain but his face expressionless. 'What about a shroud? Did he steal a shroud with the body? That's a hanging offence on its own and any mention of a death shroud always excites the ghoulish public.'

Lavender smiled. 'I honestly don't know.'

'Did he obstruct a lawful burial? That's another hanging offence.'

Lavender thought for a moment. 'Possibly – we need to find the damned man and hold the exhumation before we can uncover the true extent of his crimes.'

Grey's long, thin nose sniffed. 'There's no need to curse, Detective. I suppose we'll just have to settle for perjury, deception and fraud then.' He sighed heavily while he wrote down the three words.

'I'm sure when I finally apprehend this felon, there'll be a long list of charges against him,' Lavender said.

'Yes, and no doubt I'll get cramp in my hand when I write them down – and a dry throat in court when I read them out. I'll look forward to that. Personally, I'm just surprised the felon used his real name. If half of what you've told me is true, he'll swing for this, for sure.'

Lavender thanked him, pulled his hat back on his head and strode out of the building into the sunshine.

But he'd barely descended the steps when he stopped short, frowning. Grey had raised a good point. What if it hadn't been Frank Collins who'd taken the coffin back to Chelmsford? He remembered the description Rawlings had given him of a dark-haired young man. He'd never mentioned a prominent wart on his chin. Perhaps Collins had innocently continued his journey up to Yorkshire and some mishap had befallen him up there in the provinces?

But if Frank Collins hadn't accompanied the coffin to Essex, then who the devil had impersonated him?

The manager at the bank of Messrs Down, Thornton and Gill was busy with other customers when Lavender called in to the bank. Frustrated, he made an appointment for first thing the following morning to discuss David MacAdam's finances and left the bank clerk in no doubt that this was a matter of urgency. Next, he made his way to the Grosvenor Estate office.

He was introduced to the manager, who scowled at his request to interview Bentley. He was taken into a large room where Bentley sat in silence behind a high bench with a row of other junior clerks. His dark head was bowed over his work when they entered. He glanced up and his good-looking young face flashed with alarm when he saw Lavender. The lad had probably just turned twenty.

The manager led them to a small unused office for the interview. It was dirty, dark and full of broken furniture, which smelled of mould. 'You'd better not be in any trouble with the law, Bentley,' he said when he turned to leave, 'or we'll have to reconsider your position here.'

'I'm not in any trouble, am I, Detective?' Bentley stammered.

'Not that I know of – yet.' Lavender pointed to a rickety wooden chair and waited while Bentley sat down. Despite his youth, the clerk was smartly and fashionably dressed, with a pristine, creaseless cravat below his strong jawline and a well-cut dark blue coat over his athletic frame. Lavender cleared his throat. 'As you know, we're investigating the murder of David MacAdam and we need to know your movements on the night of his death.'

Relief flooded across Bentley's face. 'Oh, that's . . . easy. Yes, poor Davy. It's quite a shock.'

'Where were you the night he died?'

'I was out earlier in the evening but came home around seven o'clock. I read for a bit in my room before I went to sleep.'

'Did you hear MacAdam come home just after nine o'clock?'

'No, I was already asleep by then. I heard nothing.'

'Not even when Mrs Palmer wished MacAdam goodnight?'

'No.'

'MacAdam's bedchamber is on the floor above yours. He would have passed by your door on his way up there.'

Bentley shook his head. 'I heard nothing,' he insisted.

'How close were you to your fellow lodgers?' Lavender asked. 'How much time did you spend with them?'

'I knew them a bit. I've only lodged with Mrs Palmer for a few months, since I started working here.'

'Did you ever go out drinking with Collins and MacAdam? Did you visit taverns with them?'

'Yes, sometimes.' Bentley fingered the buttons on his waistcoat nervously. 'They were good company and we enjoyed a glass or two of brandy together.'

'Where is Frank Collins?'

'He's away in Yorkshire on business.'

'No, he's not. He's disappeared. I ask you again: where is Frank Collins?'

Bentley looked confused. 'I don't know, Detective. I haven't seen or heard from him in months.'

'Did you know MacAdam was courting a young woman called Amelia Howard?'

'Was he? No, I didn't know about that.'

'That surprises me,' Lavender said, 'because Mrs Palmer claims she once overhead MacAdam boasting to you and Frank Collins that he'd caught himself a young heiress.'

Bentley flushed. 'Well . . . yes . . . he might have mentioned something once. I, I don't remember. MacAdam was full of plans and schemes to get rich. I didn't pay much attention to him, to be honest.'

'Did you know MacAdam was already married?'

'Was he? No, I didn't know that.' He was sweating. Lavender could smell it.

'And did you know he planned to fake his own death in order to get out of his marriage and wed his heiress?'

Confusion flashed across Bentley's face and his mouth flapped open and shut like a dying fish on a slab in the Billingsgate market. 'He did what? Good grief! That's scandalous! I knew nothing about this. I can't . . . I can't believe he did something so evil.'

'I didn't say MacAdam did the deed. I simply said he planned to do it.'

'You're confusing me,' Bentley wailed plaintively. 'Even to think such a thing is foul – never mind actually carrying out such an evil plan.'

Lavender regarded him coldly. Everything about the young man's demeanour, his evasive eyes and nervous swallowing, told Lavender he was lying. 'Why don't I believe you, Mr Bentley? Don't lie. You knew about his plan to fake his own death and commit bigamy – and you knew Frank Collins helped him.'

Bentley's voice became shrill. 'I didn't. I swear I didn't!'

Lavender paused and wondered idly whether to haul the young fool down to Bow Street and let him languish and sweat in the cells for a few hours. A spell under the hatches often loosened tongues. Failing that, he could try fishing for information.

'Someone took a coffin back to Essex. Perhaps it wasn't Collins. Perhaps it was you?'

'No! I swear I had nothing to do with this.'

'It would be easy enough to check with your employer whether or not you were here in London at work on that day.'

'Please – no!' Bentley lowered his voice and looked beseechingly at Lavender through his big blue eyes. 'Please don't ask him any questions – I'm already in trouble. He says I'm absent too often from my desk. I'll lose my position.'

'Why weren't you at work yesterday? We saw you at Mrs Palmer's.'

'I'd taken the day off again,' Bentley said. 'I was upset by Davy's death – and I had some family business to attend to.'

'Family business? With Lady Louisa Fitzgerald in Berkeley Square?'

Again, Bentley's mouth flapped like a fish. 'Lady Louisa Fitzgerald?'

'Yes, I saw you climb into her coach outside Mrs Palmer's house.'

Bentley glanced nervously at the closed door. His forehead glistened with a thin sheen of sweat. 'Please don't mention it to my employer, or I'll lose my position here.'

'Why?'

'I'd told them I needed time off work to attend my grandfather's funeral.'

'Where did you really go?'

Bentley swallowed hard again and said, 'I went out to a racecourse in Surrey with my friend, Matthew Fitzgerald. He's Lady Louisa's son.'

Lavender doubted that but Bentley's story was easy enough to verify. The young man looked wretched and bowed his head, hiding his eyes. His long, dark eyelashes fanned out over his cheeks. Most women would pay a fortune for eyelashes like those, Lavender thought.

'This is a murder investigation,' Lavender said, 'and I have more important things to deal with than protecting a young man who lies to his employer – and lies to police officers. We need to find this murderer and bring him to justice on the gallows.' He paused for a moment before adding slowly: 'Because we *will* find MacAdam's murderer – and he *will* hang.'

Bentley gave what sounded like a gulping sob.

Lavender nodded towards the door. 'You can return to work but don't leave town, Mr Bentley. I'm sure I'll want to talk to you again.'

Chapter Sixteen

M r Howard's turbaned footman showed Lavender into the large drawing room of the house on Bruton Street. The stucco carvings on the heavily decorated white plaster ceiling were so elaborate that Lavender felt the weight of them bearing down on him. Sumptuous purple silk wall hangings lined the walls. Bordered with emerald green and blue birds of paradise and brilliant orange chrysanthemums, they were embroidered in silver and depicted scenes of scarlet-robed maharajas in battle, maharajas holding court beneath glittering awnings and maharajas riding on bejewelled elephants. Exquisite ornaments of jade and ivory stood on the mantelpiece and side tables.

Howard himself sat in front of the fire, on a traditional wing-backed chair. He'd discarded his flowing banyan today and wore a plain black coat with matching pantaloons. He looked worried and older. Opposite him, a raven-haired young woman in a red gown with a high empire waist was draped elegantly over the sofa. She had the same caramel-toned skin as the young woman Lavender saw the previous day in the phaeton, but she had bulging brown eyes beneath heavy black brows and a sour expression on her face.

'Ah, Detective Lavender,' Howard said. 'May I introduce my younger granddaughter, Miss Matilda Howard?'

A small hand jerked out imperiously towards him. 'Detective Lavender.'

He shook her hand and bowed politely. He estimated her age at sixteen or seventeen but she was small in stature and could have been younger. She'd drawn her tongue back in her mouth when pronouncing the two 't's in 'Detective' and they'd erupted with a curious popping sound, giving her strong accent a sing-song quality. He remembered Mr Jackson's comment about the poor education received by the Howard girls and he wondered how much time they'd spent with English speakers during their youth and how much of it they had been banished to the company of Indian servants and ayahs.

'This is a bad business, Lavender, a bad business,' Howard continued. 'Poor Amelia has been devastated to hear about the death of her fiancé. The girl is inconsolable and refuses to leave her room.'

Lavender nodded sympathetically. 'So she hasn't left the house today?' He still half-wondered if Miss Howard had been one of the two mysterious women who'd visited the Bow Street morgue.

Howard shook his head.

Miss Matilda smoothed down the silk of her skirts and her lips curled into a smug smile. 'My sister has stayed at home and I've used the phaeton and been to the Row. Her catastrophe is my blessing.'

'I'm sorry to hear Miss Howard is so distressed,' Lavender said sharply.

'The silly mare has swollen red eyes with crying,' the young woman continued. 'Her looks are very, very spoilt now; she will not leave the house or find another beau like this.' Her thick accent didn't mask the irritation and coldness in her tone. There was clearly no love lost between the two girls.

'That's hardly surprising, Matilda, my dear,' her grandfather admonished patiently. 'To find out MacAdam is dead is shock enough but to then learn he was murdered is another dreadful blow on top of the first one.'

The girl shrugged her thin shoulders. 'Let her wallow in the self-pity. At least I can drive the phaeton now her beau is dead.'

Lavender bit back his disgust at her callousness. 'I'd hoped to speak to Miss Howard today about MacAdam – and some other issues that have come to light.'

'Oh, what other issues?' Miss Matilda turned her head like a curious cat and gave him a half-smile.

Lavender cleared his throat, unsure how much of MacAdam's sordid behaviour he should reveal in front of the young woman. 'I'm sorry to have to inform you, sir, but David MacAdam wasn't the man he claimed to be.'

'How so?' Howard asked.

'He wasn't the second son of Baron MacAdam from Colchester. He was a commercial traveller with Drake's tailoring company from Chelmsford.'

'What!' Howard's jaw dropped open.

'Or, to be more accurate, he was a commercial traveller until May,' Lavender continued, 'when he appears to have given up his paid employment altogether. Isn't that the month he met Miss Howard?' The question was rhetorical; he already knew the answer but he left it hanging there. Howard was an intelligent man. He'd work out the significance.

'What is this commercial traveller?' Matilda Howard asked. 'It's a common pedlar, yes?' Lavender nodded and she burst out laughing. 'Poor Amelia – she has been duped by a dirty pedlar! Yes?'

Lavender and Howard ignored her obvious glee.

'I don't understand.' Howard's tone was incredulous. 'The man kept a carriage and horses and gave Amelia a beautiful ruby ring as a token of his love only a few days ago. It must be a question of mistaken identity, surely?'

'I'm afraid there is no mistake,' Lavender said. He hoped Howard wouldn't ask him how he was so sure MacAdam was a Chelmsford salesman. He needed Miss Matilda out of the room so he could talk privately with Howard. 'This commercial traveller from Chelmsford and David MacAdam are the same man.'

Matilda waved her hand dismissively in the air and laughed again. 'That ring was nothing – a mere trinket.'

'No, Matilda,' her grandfather said sternly, 'I examined the ring myself and it's an exquisite piece with real rubies and turquoise.'

'I haven't solved the mystery of the carriage and horses yet,' Lavender said, 'but we know MacAdam borrowed heavily to pay for the ring.'

'He did what?'

'He borrowed a hundred guineas from a moneylender in the Seven Dials to pay for it.'

'The Seven Dials?' Howard looked horrified.

His granddaughter let out a peal of spiteful laughter. 'I knew he was only after her money! But she thought it was true love – that he wanted her for her true self!'

He remembered the line in Amelia Howard's letter to MacAdam about her sister's jealousy. At the time, he'd dismissed this phrase as normal sibling rivalry but there was nothing natural about the perverse delight Matilda was taking in her sister's misfortune.

'I need to speak to Miss Howard,' he said urgently. 'Can we ask her to join us? And I would appreciate a moment or two in private with you, sir.'

'Matilda.' Howard's voice caught in his throat. 'Please go to your sister's chamber and fetch her downstairs.'

Petulant anger flashed across the young woman's face at the dismissal. Then she shrugged, rose to her feet and walked to the door. 'I shall take the pleasure to give her the news about her lying, cheating beau,' she said.

'You'll do no such thing!' Howard called after her, alarmed. 'Simply ask her to join us. I'll inform Amelia of Detective Lavender's latest discoveries.'

The girl didn't respond and slammed the door shut behind her.

'I apologise for Matilda's behaviour, Lavender,' Howard sighed wearily. 'Matilda has been difficult since Amelia met MacAdam. I think she's jealous. She's the cleverer of the two girls and a competent horsewoman but she has never been blessed with Amelia's good looks or pleasant nature.'

'I'm afraid there is worse news to come about MacAdam,' Lavender said quickly. 'He was already married. He had a wife and family in Chelmsford. His wife has been down to Bow Street this afternoon to identify his corpse. That's why I'm so sure of my facts.'

Howard said nothing but the twitching muscles in his neck and his reddening facial colour suggested a volcano of fury was building at the other side of the room.

'On top of this,' Lavender continued, 'in June, MacAdam faked his own death. He arranged for a friend to take a coffin back to his wife in Chelmsford and claim it contained his dead body. The fraud only came to light yesterday when I visited Mrs MacAdam.'

'Damn the fellow to hell!' Howard clenched his arthritic fists, rose to his feet, marched to the marble fireplace and leaned on the mantelpiece, breathing heavily. After a moment, he glanced up at Lavender's reflection in the mirror. 'Tell me everything,' he growled.

Howard listened silently while Lavender talked but shock and anger flashed across his features in his reflection in the mirror. 'We've asked the bishop for an exhumation of the coffin in MacAdam's grave,' Lavender concluded. 'We're fearful it will lead to a second murder inquiry; there's probably another body in the coffin – placed there by MacAdam. I fear we've barely scratched the surface about the true extent of MacAdam's treachery.'

Howard stared back at him blankly. His tone was bitter when he eventually spoke. 'Was all this just to get his hands on my granddaughter's fortune?'

Lavender nodded. 'I believe so. You must prepare yourself for more grisly revelations. He may have been a murderer as well as a lying, cheating lothario.'

'So who murdered MacAdam? Was it his much-maligned wife?'

'I'm afraid I don't know yet,' Lavender confessed. 'Mrs MacAdam's reaction suggested she was innocent of the vile deception practised upon her.'

'It's a good job he's dead,' Howard snarled. 'Or I would have murdered the lying bastard myself!' His clenched fist crashed down on the mantelpiece, nearly knocking off an exquisitely carved ivory elephant. 'I can't believe how easily he fooled us. What an idiot I was not to make more enquiries about the man.'

Lavender was about to reply when he heard a faint scratching at the door, which he thought was followed by a stifled laugh. Frowning, he moved quickly towards it and swung it open. Miss Matilda virtually fell into the room. She pulled herself upright, smiled and smoothed down her gown. Shameless about her eavesdropping, she announced loudly: 'Amelia is crying again. She says she's very, very upset and can't come downstairs.' She promptly turned on her heel and flounced away with rustle of red silk.

Howard's face crumpled at the news of his elder granddaughter's distress. He reached for the bell pull at the side of the fireplace. 'I'm sorry, Detective, but I must go to Amelia. No doubt Matilda has disobeyed my instructions, told Amelia the truth about MacAdam's lies and turned the knife in her heart. I'm afraid I must ask you to leave.'

Lavender frowned. 'I really need to speak to Miss Howard. There are many questions only she can answer about MacAdam.'

'I'm sorry but you'll have to return tomorrow.'

'There is one other thing,' Lavender said hastily. 'The moneylender who loaned MacAdam the money for the ring he gave Miss Howard is causing trouble. He's already tried to force his way into MacAdam's lodgings to retrieve the item, or items commensurate with the value.

My constable has warned him off and sent him away with a flea in his ear, but please alert your servants in case the fool tries to approach Miss Howard in the street. He's called Billy Summersgill.'

Howard moaned. 'Dear God, is there no end to this nightmare?'

The door opened and the footman arrived to show Lavender out. He bit back his frustration, bowed and left.

Chapter Seventeen

Eggerton's stonemasons in Spitalfields was a large, dusty yard, appropriately sited on Brick Lane. Woods' ride through the bustling street market to the yard was both slow and painful. Slow because of the heaving crowds of shoppers and painful because of the delicious aroma of freshly baked pies and roasting chestnuts wafting from the stalls and carts of the street vendors. His treacherous stomach cramped in protest at its emptiness.

Originally home to London's Huguenot silk weavers and merchants, the area had declined with its industries over the last few decades. The old merchant dwellings had degenerated into slums where several generations of the same family huddled into a single room and the low, dilapidated houses of the surrounding streets cowered together in narrow, dark lanes and alleys, haunted by pickpockets and cut-throats.

Eggerton's stood between the brewery and the premises of the Spitalfields Soup Society. A long line of thin, rag-clad paupers and beggars snaked out on to the cobbled street from the door of the charity. Fortunately, the smell of the brewery hops overrode any waft of watery beef gruel that may have floated Woods' way. He promised himself a glass of ale after this business at Eggerton's had concluded. The alcohol should take the edge off his gnawing hunger. Two wagons piled high with great blocks of pale stone stood in the centre of Eggerton's yard beneath a crane. Sweating men strained on the end of ropes to unload the cargo. Beneath the wooden awnings lining two sides of the open space, more men in brown hessian aprons used massive two-man diamond-tipped saws to cut these rough blocks into squares. Others stood behind trestle tables, using chisels to work the stones into the required shape or cleaving slate into thin wafers for roof tiles. The constant ring of their hammers on the chisels and the rhythmic grind of the saws echoed round the yard. Mountains of finished stone blocks were piled at the far end of the yard, ready to feed the insatiable demands of builders in the burgeoning city. Everything was covered with a fine film of greyish-white dust, including the faces of the workers as they concentrated over their work. It gave them a ghoulish appearance.

Woods led his horse towards the low office, tied its reins to a post and asked a passing workman to take him to the foreman. The man grunted and led him to a corner of the yard.

A small, wizened, bald man stood there, surrounded by a group of bright-eyed apprentices. He held a chisel and a hammer in his scarred, calloused hands. The chisel had paused above a block of stone on the bench in front of him. One glance at its intricately carved wreath of foliage told Woods this was where stone craft crossed over into an art form. The master mason glanced up at Woods' uniform and his blue eyes twinkled.

'A runner, eh?' He turned his head to speak to the young men gathered around him. 'It looks like the law 'as finally caught up wi' me, boys.' The apprentices giggled.

'I'm Constable Woods from Bow Street Police Office.'

The elderly man put down his chisel and brushed the grime from his hands before extending one of them to Woods. 'Sam Eggerton, master stonemason.'

'I'm here to ask about a fellah called Ike Rawlings,' Woods said as he shook Eggerton's hand.

'Ike?' The old mason nodded. 'Yes, 'e's a carrier, 'e brings us several loads a week down from the quarry at Chelmsford. Nice fellah.'

'Were he here two days ago?'

Eggerton rubbed his stubbly chin thoughtfully. 'Aye, I think 'e were.'

'What time were that?'

''E usually arrives about midday, 'elps us unload and then goes 'ome. What's this about, officer?'

'Does he always go straight back to Chelmsford?'

The mason shrugged. 'I can't say as I know. Sometimes the carriers 'ave other errands to do while they're in town.'

'Did he ever mention a man he knew here in town? A man called MacAdam?'

Eggerton shook his head and Woods felt his heart slump with disappointment. He knew Lavender was right to want him to explore every aspect of this case, but tracing a man's movements in a city the size of London was like trying to follow a rat through the old sewers.

'I'm interested in his trip here two days ago.' Woods glanced at the wide entrance to the yard and the busy street beyond with its constant stream of traffic. 'Which way would he turn to get the road back to Essex?'

The mason thought for a moment, then said: 'Left. That'd take 'im to Mile End Road and out o' town.'

'But 'e didn't go that way two days ago,' said an excited high-pitched voice. A carrot-topped little fellow with a face full of freckles elbowed his way forward. The boy was so small he almost tripped over the filthy man-sized apron strapped round his thin frame. 'I saw 'im – 'e turned to the right and nearly caused that carriage to overturn. Don't you remember, Master Eggerton?'

'Oh, yes,' said the old man. 'I remember now. It were quite a commotion. Well done, young Nibbs.'

'What happened?' Woods asked.

'Ike weren't lookin' out properly. 'E turned straight into the traffic in front of an 'ackney cab and their 'orses collided. It were a devil of a job to sort it out because the traces got tangled. The cab driver were furious and cussin' like Old Nick himself.'

Woods frowned. 'Is Rawlings normally such a poor driver?'

'No, 'e's one of the best. You won't find a safer pair of 'ands wi' that 'eavy wagon in the whole of Christendom. But come to think on it, 'e were a bit diverted two days ago.'

'Diverted?'

'Aye, dreamy like. Ponderin'. I know 'e's to wed soon and I thought 'e may 'ave been ponderin' about his nuptials – or thinkin' about his little woman.' The apprentices giggled again. 'I always tell the boys to steer clear of women, don't I, lads?'

'Yes, guvnor.' Young Nibbs puffed out his chest with pride as he repeated the mantra. 'Women are the tools of the devil. They're sent by Beelzebub to distract a good mason from the straight line 'e's carvin'.'

'The only good woman is the one carved in marble,' another boy added for Woods' edification.

Woods smiled.

'Now, what's this about, Constable? Rawlings didn't leave 'ere and cause another accident wi' 'is wagon, did 'e?'

Woods shook his head. 'It's just a routine enquiry, sir. Thank you for your help – and you too, young Nibbs.'

The young lad bristled with pride.

Woods took his leave and walked back to his horse, barely able to contain his excitement. So, Ike Rawlings had been distracted on the day of the murder, had he? And he hadn't left the stonemasons to return to Essex but had turned his wagon towards the west of the city instead. It was only a small piece of information, but enough to justify questioning the man further when they returned to Chelmsford. Inch by slow inch, they were gathering the evidence to make a case against Rawlings.

Suddenly he was flushed with joy and that giddy light-headed feeling returned. He stumbled slightly as he led his horse towards The Black Eagle tavern attached to the towering brewery that overshadowed the stonemason's yard. He salivated at the thought of a tankard of ale. His stomach screamed out for sustenance. He'd earned a drink.

Lavender decided to visit the mews on King's Street at the back of Park Lane. His investigation had come to a grinding halt. He couldn't speak to MacAdam's bank manager or to Miss Howard until tomorrow and the only clue left for him to explore this warm afternoon was the mystery of the coach used by MacAdam. When he rode back towards Hyde Park, he saw the sunlight glittering on the Serpentine in the distance and it lifted his spirits a little.

King's Street Mews was a narrow, muddy back street, littered with piles of horse dung and clumps of rotting straw. Built in a uniform style for the utilitarian purpose of providing accommodation for the horses, coaches, ostlers and groomsmen of the nearby wealthy homeowners, the mews had little to endear itself to a stray pedestrian and reeked of horses and manure. Mindful of his boots, Lavender stepped carefully over the slow rivers of dirty urine draining away from the stables down to the block drain in the middle of the street. One of the upstairs windows had a window box of red geraniums beneath it, but the human residents of King's Street Mews had made no other attempt to bring a touch of cheerfulness to break up the plain, smoke-blackened brick buildings.

Lavender paused to allow a groom to lead a horse out of one of the stables. Then he tied his own horse to an iron ring on a wall and pulled a notebook out of his pocket. Several of the coach house doors had been slid open on their rusty iron runners. Ignoring the curious stares of the ostlers and grooms, Lavender peered inside their dark interiors, searching for a vehicle whose coat of arms bore some resemblance to the red shield, coronet and two rampant black stallions in his sketch. He saw a wide variety of gleaming barouches, a fashionable landau and other assorted carriages, but none of them matched Howard's description of MacAdam's old boneshaker with its distinctive coat of arms.

'Can I 'elp you, guvnor?' An elderly, whiskered groom sat on an upturned barrel. He was using wadding and a bottle of polish to bring back the shine to the brasses on a leather harness.

Lavender approached him. 'I'm looking for a carriage that was kept here and used by a man called David MacAdam.'

The groom shook his shaggy head. 'I've never 'eard of 'im – and I know the owners of all these stables and coaching 'ouses.'

'He may have borrowed it from someone else.' Lavender held out his sketch towards the man. 'It had a distinctive coat of arms on the side, possibly with a coronet and two black rampant stallions.'

The groom glanced at his drawing and shook his head again. 'Never seen it.'

Lavender thanked him, retrieved his horse and led it back to Park Lane. He stood for a moment in the dappled shade of the trees opposite number ninety-three, looking at the plain front of Mrs Palmer's house. Sighing, he realised he might as well pack up for the day and go home to Magdalena. His investigation was going nowhere.

Think, think, he told himself. Even without confirmation from the bank, Lavender knew MacAdam couldn't afford to keep horses and a carriage. Yet he'd visited the Howards in an old brown coach with a coat of arms. He'd also travelled to the jewellers on the Strand in a coach – possibly the same one – to purchase the ring for Miss Howard. And on this occasion, he'd travelled with a woman – maybe an older woman. He must have borrowed a coach and horses from someone. MacAdam had been a charmer, especially with the fairer sex. Women of all ages, from Mrs Palmer and her friends to Miss Calvin, the vicar's daughter in Chelmsford, all seemed to have adored or trusted him. It had to be a woman who'd loaned him the coach.

He felt rather than saw Will the road sweeper sidle up next to him. 'If you've come to see Mrs Palmer from number ninety-three, yer too late.' The boy's high-pitched voice shattered Lavender's thoughts. 'She left wi' that nasty old trot from number eighty-five.'

Lavender struggled to keep his face straight. 'It's impertinent to talk about Lady Tyndall in such a manner, son.'

''Ave you found the killer of the fat guy yet, guvnor?'

'Not yet.' Obviously, nothing, not even MacAdam's use of a corset, had escaped the urchin's sharp eyes.

'D'you need 'elp? I 'eard about the murder this mornin' from Daisy the 'ousemaid at number ninety-seven. She often stops and passes the time of day wi' me on 'er way to work.'

'I'll take any help I can get with this case at the moment. What do you know?'

'Is there a reward if I 'elp you catch the killer?'

Lavender glanced down at Will thoughtfully. He was clutching the handle of his broom with both grubby little hands and had rested his peaked chin on top of them. He looked up at Lavender with intelligent brown eyes beneath his long, matted fringe.

There wasn't a reward offered in this case. No one in MacAdam's acquaintance – except Mr Howard – could afford to put up a reward for information. But after the revelations this afternoon, Howard would probably be more disposed to buy the killer a glass of brandy than assist with his capture.

For a second, Lavender wished Woods were there; he'd do a much better job of questioning the urchin and, with or without a monetary reward, he'd wheedle and charm information out of the boy. But Ned wasn't there. He'd just have to be as gentle as he could.

'There may be a bigger reward out soon for capturing the villain,' he said cautiously, 'but at the moment, I can only offer threepence a time to witnesses who tell me anything about MacAdam.'

Will looked thoughtful. 'But I can tell you lots about 'im, guvnor. I sweep all of Park Lane. I do the full road – and round the corner to the toll gate. I often saw that geezer comin' and goin' out the 'ouse. I tell you what, give me thru'pence now and I'll tell you 'alf. Then you can come back later wi' another coin for the rest.'

Lavender didn't know whether to laugh or clip the cheeky urchin around the ear. *React like Ned,* he thought – and use the boy's name to put him at ease. He smiled. 'Just tell me what you know, Will. If it's good enough I'll give you the full sixpence today. Now tell me what you know about MacAdam.'

A wide grin lit up the boy's thin face. ''E used to leave early for work but not so much lately.'

'Was he alone when you saw him?'

Will nodded. 'Mostly, but sometimes 'e'd go down to Rotten Row wi' the other geezers from the 'ouse and watch the nobs drive past in their carriages.'

Here was another witness to the friendship between MacAdam and Mrs Palmer's other lodgers. Bentley had lied to him and downplayed his acquaintance with MacAdam. 'Did you ever see him climb into a carriage?'

'What, 'ere or down on the Row?'

'Both.'

Will pulled himself up to his full height proudly. 'I've done more than that – I've seen 'im drivin' a fancy black carriage wi' a young gal down on the Row.'

This wasn't new information, Lavender thought. He pulled out his notebook and pointed to his sketch of the mysterious coat of arms with the rampant black stallions. 'Did you ever see MacAdam board an old carriage with an emblem like this?'

Will studied it carefully but shook his head. 'No, guvnor.' Then he grinned and prodded the other coat of arms, the Fitzgerald emblem, with his grubby forefinger. 'I've seen 'im use that carriage, though.'

'What? The coach belonging to the Fitzgerald family?'

'Aye, the old lady often gave 'im a ride – and the rest o' them fellahs.'

'The old lady?'

'Lady Louisa, they call 'er. She's a pal of 'er at number ninety-three – a pal of all of 'em who lives there, from what I can see. Can I 'ave my tanner now?'

'One last question, Will. Did you ever see MacAdam meet anyone else out here in the street?'

'No.'

'Did it ever look like anyone was following him?'

'That's two questions. No.'

'So, you've seen nothing suspicious – or unusual?'

Will frowned, and Lavender realised the child was worried he might not get his reward. 'I don't know what you mean about suspicious – but there were the geezer with the wagon.'

'What geezer?'

'You know – I told you yesterday. The wagon wi' the dirty stone that spills out the dust and gravel on to my road.'

Lavender froze, barely able to believe his ears. 'Did it come here often? Was it here on the afternoon of the murder?'

Will thought for a moment, then nodded. 'Yeah, it were. The driver's an old fellah like yer fat friend. 'E sits and smokes 'is pipe watchin' number ninety-three.'

'And you're sure he was here two days ago, on the afternoon of the murder?'

'Yes, 'e were. Can I 'ave me tanner now?'

Lavender fished in his pocket for the sixpence. 'One last question, Will—'

'What? Another 'un?'

'Would you recognise this man if you saw him again?'

''Course I would. E's an 'airy fellah wi' a beard.'

A flood of satisfaction swept through Lavender when he handed the boy the coin.

Finally, this case was getting somewhere.

Chapter Eighteen

Lavender rode to Berkeley Square to find the Fitzgerald family home. The ornate cream facades of the town houses lining the square gleamed in the sunlight. The contrast between the MacAdams' cramped back-street cottage back in Chelmsford and these imposing, elegant homes struck him anew. David MacAdam's journey through life had taken him from one end of the social scale to the other. These were the homes of the nobility, politicians and wealthy businessmen. The Prince Regent's stylish friend Beau Brummell lived here, as did one of the Prince's female favourites, the indomitable Lady Jersey. Half the fashionable world sought entrée to her receptions held at number thirty-eight.

A group of uniformed nursemaids stood beneath the shade of the plane trees watching their young charges playing on the lawn in the centre of the square. Lavender dismounted and led his horse towards them.

Lady Louisa Fitzgerald was well known to the nursemaids. Apparently, she kept a pack of large, ferocious dogs, which were sometimes exercised here in the grassy centre of the square. Delighted to have the attention of a police officer, the young women told Lavender they had feared the drooling animals would eat the young children in their care. Lavender nodded and hid his amusement. He thanked them and promised to mention their concerns to Lady Louisa.

The Fitzgerald house was a dilapidated building compared to its neighbours and in urgent need of some exterior maintenance. Lavender tied his horse to the rusty railings, leapt up the stone steps to the peeling door and rang the bell. It unleashed a tirade of barks behind the door. When one canine voice drew breath, another took over, so loud and so close that Lavender's fingers instinctively went to the loaded pistol he always carried in his coat pocket. Not for the first time today, he wished Ned was by his side. Woods had a natural ability with every kind of animal, from his beloved horses to escaped cows from Smithfield meat market. He was especially good with large, angry dogs.

He heard a man shouting and cursing the animals inside the building. Then an interior door slammed shut and the barking ceased.

When the door finally swung open, a flushed footman in a moth-eaten wig and faded livery glared at him down his pinched nose. His waistcoat swung open over his stained shirt, which had a button missing.

'Detective Stephen Lavender from Bow Street, to see Lady Louisa Fitzgerald.'

The footman's sharp eyes took in every detail of the smart tailoring of Lavender's black coat and hat. Then his lip curled and Lavender smelt the alcohol on his breath. 'The tradesmen's entrance is round the back.' He tried to shut the door in Lavender's face.

Anger flashed through Lavender. If a former horse dealer like MacAdam could ride in a carriage with the Fitzgeralds, he certainly wasn't creeping round the back like a tradesman on the say-so of a slovenly footman. He stepped forward, raised his tipstaff and set it firmly against the edge of the door. 'If I were a tradesman, I'd use it – but I'm not. I'm a Principal Officer with the police office at Bow Street and I'm conducting a murder inquiry. It's essential I see Lady Louisa as soon as possible – and I warn you against obstructing me while I'm undertaking my duty. Think carefully, my man.'

The footman grudgingly let him enter the dark, musty hallway of the great house.

'I'd also like to see her son, Master Matthew Fitzgerald,' Lavender continued. 'Is he at home?'

The man's lip curled in disdain. 'Son? There ain't no son of the 'ouse as far as I know. She's a spinster. Mind you, I wouldn't put it past 'er to 'ave 'ad a by-blow in her youth.'

The news that Bentley had lied to him – again – made Lavender pause. The footman turned on the heel of his filthy buttoned shoes and strode towards a large pair of double doors at the back of the hallway before Lavender could rebuke him for his insolence. He disappeared inside the room, presumably to announce Lavender's arrival.

Lavender smoothed down his coat, wrinkled his nose at the strong smell of dog that permeated the whole house, and frowned. He felt like he had stepped back in time two centuries. The hallway was full of heavy old Jacobean furniture: ancient dressers and chairs carved from age-darkened wood. The marble floor was filthy and covered in muddy paw prints. Dog bowls and half-chewed bones lay abandoned on the floor beneath a scuffed settle in a dirty pool of spilled water. Piles of books and other items were piled on the bottom steps of the grand, unswept staircase as if some maid had left them there to take upstairs and then forgotten their existence. Even the large oil paintings added to the gloomy atmosphere of the house. These weren't ancestral portraits but smoke-blackened paintings of long-dead racehorses, their owners and their owners' dogs. And all the dogs were the same breed: red Irish setters.

Biting back his mounting anger, Lavender strode towards a discarded grooming brush that lay on one of the hall tables and picked it up. The matted flame-coloured dog hair in the brush was the same he'd found on the clothes of MacAdam and Collins. Mrs Palmer had lied to him when she'd disclaimed any knowledge of an acquaintance who owned dogs.

But he didn't have time to dwell on her duplicity for long. On the same table was a crumpled pamphlet from a Surrey race meeting held the previous day. Beside it was a discarded pair of women's gloves. Young Will had claimed that all the lodgers at Mrs Palmer's house travelled in the Fitzgeralds' coach. Maybe there was some truth in Bentley's claim he'd visited a Surrey racecourse the previous day – but his companion clearly hadn't been the son of the house.

Bored with waiting, and desperate to meet Lady Louisa Fitzgerald, preferably without her blasted dogs, Lavender walked over to one of the doors that stood ajar. He pushed it gently and peered inside the gloom. It was another reception room, but was obviously unused; the drapes were closed and the furniture shrouded with dust cloths.

To his relief, the surly footman stomped back down the hallway and informed him Lady Louisa was ready to receive him.

Her ladyship's drawing room was as oppressive and antiquated as her hallway and even more claustrophobic. The tall, black-wood furniture seemed to lean in towards Lavender and compress him. He was instantly surrounded by three great, hairy red hounds, who growled threateningly. He held out a placatory hand, only to snatch it back when one dog dropped a rancid bone to snap at the fully fleshed one on offer.

'Rufus! Donal! Eoin! Enough!' The dogs turned their heads to acknowledge their mistress's order but continued to eye their visitor.

Ignoring them, Lavender braced himself and spoke firmly. 'I apologise for arriving without an appointment, Lady Louisa, but I need to ask you some questions about your association with Mrs Palmer of Park Lane – and her lodgers.'

'Of course,' replied the woman by the fireplace. 'Mr MacAdam's death is very disturbing. Mrs Palmer sent me a note yesterday – and called earlier – to tell me about it. Very tragic.' Her voice was confident, deep and gravelly – almost masculine. She didn't sound disturbed. She seemed more interested in her dogs' behaviour.

The dogs sniffed Lavender's calves then retreated and threw themselves down on the carpet.

Meanwhile, their smirking mistress, a big-boned, flat-chested and white-haired woman, held out a china plate of half-eaten cake towards a small whippet at her feet. The little dog whimpered with excitement as she fed it morsels. The setters' eyes tracked the route taken by the cake to the whippet's mouth but they stayed down, drooling on the carpet.

'Mrs Palmer visited you today?'

'Yes, she's just left. She told me all about poor Davy's murder and warned me you were asking questions about my carriage and my dogs.'

'Warned you? Do you have anything to hide, Lady Louisa?' The room stank of coal smoke and dogs and was dark. The windows were filthy and the heavy drapes hadn't been properly pulled back. The equestrian theme was continued in here with bronze statues of hunters and thoroughbreds on the mantelpiece and more ugly paintings of racehorses lining the walls.

She glanced up from the whippet, smiling with amusement at his comment, and waved her large, bony hand towards the chair opposite in an invitation to sit down. 'No, I don't have anything to hide, Detective, and as I've just tried to explain to Sylvia, we shouldn't play games and withhold evidence from an officer of your standing – although she pleaded with me to do so.'

He stepped over the sprawling hounds cautiously and went to join her by the fire.

'We've all read about your success in the news-sheets,' she said slyly, as he sank down into the lumpy, horsehair-stuffed chair she'd offered. 'You're quite the darling of *The Times*, aren't you, Lavender?'

She was a plain woman with a large, square face, a prominent nose and strong jawline. Her bony facial features matched her angular body. This woman had never been a beauty in her youth but her eyes glimmered with intelligence. 'I'm glad to hear you propose to be honest with me, Lady Louisa, because I'm heartily sick of the lying and evasion I've experienced in this case so far – especially from Mrs Palmer.'

'Oh, I wouldn't call Sylvia a liar,' she said reproachfully. 'She just tends to be a bit vague with the truth. You'll learn all you need to know from her when you need to know it.'

Lavender bit back the angry retort that sprang to his lips. The woman was toying with him now and had enjoyed his discomfort from the moment he'd stepped into her dog-infested drawing room. But it wouldn't help the case to antagonise her. 'How are you acquainted with Mrs Palmer?' he asked.

She pointed to a large portrait in one of the alcoves beside the fireplace. 'My dear father, Lord Fitzgerald,' she explained. 'He was one of Colonel Palmer's oldest and dearest friends. My father was also god-father to Clarissa's husband.'

'Clarissa?'

'Clarissa is Lady Tyndall. She, Sylvia Palmer and I have been good friends for many years – especially since they were widowed. We've a close and supportive relationship – along with some other single and widowed women of our acquaintance.'

'Who are they?'

'Mrs Mary Willis and Miss Deborah Anderson – although Deborah has abandoned us recently and married a parson in Dulwich.'

'Is Mrs Willis the widow of Doctor Willis, the former physician to the King?' he asked.

'Yes, that's right. Does this answer your questions about our acquaintance, Detective? Do our long-standing friendships break some ancient law?' Despite the humour in her question, he heard a slight reproach in her voice.

'Again, I apologise for the intrusion, Lady Louisa. I'm also inter-ested in your acquaintance with Mrs Palmer's lodgers.'

'Ah,' she said slowly. 'So, you do want to know about that – Sylvia said you might.' She put down the plate in front of the whippet, to the quivering indignation of the setters. But they didn't move. They just glared their hatred of the smaller dog. The remains of the cake were wolfed down in a second.

He smiled reassuringly. 'Yes, I saw Bentley climb into your coach yesterday and both MacAdam and Frank Collins had red dog hairs on their clothing, presumably from your dogs. You must all be well acquainted.'

'You've a nice smile, Detective,' Lady Louisa observed. 'It makes you quite handsome when you smile.'

He dropped his smile and cleared his throat. 'Mr Bentley claims he travelled to the horse races in your carriage with your son, Matthew, yesterday. But I've since learned from your footman that no such young man exists.'

'Ah,' she said again, slowly. 'I'm afraid Mr Bentley has told you a falsehood, Detective. Alfred was with me. He accompanied me and my maid to Surrey.'

'Why?'

'Because I enjoy his company,' she confessed. 'Sometimes I tire of female company and the ceaseless chatter of my maid. Like all of Sylvia's lodgers, Alfred is a good-looking young man and quite charming, although Frank has always been my favourite. He's a very funny man.'

Her frankness confounded him into silence for a moment.

A smile twitched at the corners of her wrinkled old mouth. 'Does this shock you, Detective?'

'No, ma'am.'

'Alfred is pleasing to the eye,' she said firmly. 'They all are. Frank has that silly wart on his face, of course, but it doesn't disfigure him. And just because a woman reaches sixty, it doesn't mean she's immune to flattery – can't appreciate the attentions of a handsome man – or that she loses her sense of fun.'

'Quite so,' Lavender said hastily. 'Were all of Mrs Palmer's lodgers so accommodating when you required company?'

She nodded. 'We all shared a mutual interest in horses and racing. Apart from being handsome and charming, they are – were – all so . . . so *obliging*.'

I'll wager they are, Lavender thought grimly. *How much had she paid them for their companionship?*

'Are you married, Detective?'

Her sudden change of subject threw him for a moment. 'Yes, ma'am – Mrs Lavender and I are expecting our first child this winter.'

Her eyes twinkled and again her mouth curled with amusement at his discomfort. She muttered something under her breath, which he thought sounded like the words: 'That's a shame.'

He cleared his throat. 'Who proposed yesterday's outing to the races?'

'Well, I did, of course.' She laughed. 'It would hardly have been appropriate for a penniless clerk to ask out the daughter of an earl, would it?'

He hesitated, and for the first time she seemed to sense the censure in his mind.

'Oh, it's nothing untoward, Detective.' She waved her large hand dismissively in the air. 'There's nothing improper in our behaviour and Sylvia is being a silly goose if she thinks any society gossip would be interested in the company kept by a woman of my age. Personally, I think she's more bothered about the reaction of her prudish younger brother to our amicable arrangement than anything else.'

'Arrangement?' Lavender almost dreaded her reply. He had the uneasy sense he was about to discover something immoral, if not illegal.

'Yes, Sylvia knows how much I enjoy the company of handsome young men and has always been accommodating. She never hesitated to introduce me to her lodgers.'

'And Sir Richard . . . ?'

'Sir Richard knows nothing about this – and she doesn't want him to. I trust you'll respect her privacy? Sir Richard and Lady Allison want

Sylvia to sell up her home and move in with them, but she values her independence.'

Lavender gave a silent sigh of relief. He was glad his colleague was unaware of the secret trysts his sister had been facilitating between her friend and her lodgers. *But how best to approach the issue of money?*

'I understand Mr Bentley lied to his employer about his where-abouts yesterday and he probably lost a day's pay for his absence.'

Lady Louisa smiled again. 'I paid Alfred generously to reimburse him for his lost wages. I always do when he takes a day away from his dreadful little job.'

'Did you have the same arrangement with Frank Collins and David MacAdam?'

'Yes. They've all benefited from their willingness to accommodate the whims of an old lady. I haven't seen Frank for a while, of course – he's been away on business – and when Davy became involved with Miss Howard, he had less time to spend with me.'

'You knew about MacAdam's courtship of Miss Howard?'

'Of course! I encouraged it! I wanted to see Davy happily married and I looked forward to the wedding – it's been years since I was last invited to a wedding. A few days ago, I went to the jewellers with Davy to purchase the ring he bought for Miss Howard. This was the last time I saw him alive.'

Her mention of the ring reminded Lavender of the moneylender Summersgill. 'Did MacAdam ever ask to borrow money from you?'

She snorted. 'Yes, once – for the ring – but I refused. I'm not a complete fool, Detective. I gave him a small gift of money occasionally to thank him for his kind attention to an old lady, but I didn't loan him any money.'

Lavender almost rolled his eyes. Did the woman not realise the scandal that would ensue if her aristocratic acquaintances got wind of the fact she paid impoverished younger men to escort her around town?

But if she did, did she care? 'Two women visited Bow Street morgue this morning to pay their respects to MacAdam. Was that you?'

She gave a short, barking laugh and shook her head. 'Certainly not. I consider that a ghoulish practice. I prefer to remember Davy as the vibrant young man I knew.'

'Did you think it entirely appropriate for a commercial traveller to pay court to a wealthy young woman like Miss Howard?'

She shrugged. 'I didn't see any fault with it – after all, her grandfather was in trade, wasn't he?'

'MacAdam spun the Howard family a string of lies about his ancestry. He claimed to be the second son of a baronet.'

She shrugged again and laughed. 'Well, they were fools to believe him! And let's be honest, Lavender, the little chee-chee was hardly likely to attract a husband from the aristocracy, was she?'

Stung by her prejudice, Lavender replied sharply. 'Unfortunately, "husband" is the opportune word here, Lady Louisa. Did you know MacAdam was already married?'

For the first time in their conversation, Lady Louisa's confidence faltered and a shadow passed over her features. 'No, I didn't. Sylvia told me about this today.' Her gaze shifted to the whippet at her feet. The animal was licking parts that shouldn't be mentioned in polite society, never mind displayed in such a manner, but its mistress seemed amused rather than offended.

Lavender seized the advantage. 'Did MacAdam have any enemies? Do you know of anyone who would want to kill him?'

'Oh, for heaven's sake, Detective! We flirted and talked about horses and racing. Why on earth would he share information like that with *me*? Are we finished now?' She picked up a bell and rang for the footman, who reappeared quickly. Lavender wondered if he'd been listening at the door.

'I've just a couple more questions, Lady Louisa.' He pulled his notebook out of his pocket and showed her his sketch of the unidentified coat of arms. 'Have you ever seen this emblem before?'

'No.'

Disappointed, he returned the notebook to his pocket. He stood up to take his leave. 'Did you ever lend your own carriage to David MacAdam?'

She continued to watch the antics of the whippet. 'No, I didn't – but I can't vouch for the others.'

'The others?'

'Yes, I told you.' She glanced up at him, frowning as if he were an imbecilic child. 'Mary Willis, Deborah Anderson and Clarissa Tyndall.'

He paused, his mind reeling with this latest revelation. 'Are you telling me that Mrs Palmer's lodgers escorted *all* of your friends around town?'

She laughed. 'Stop it, you bad boy!'

For a moment, Lavender thought she was addressing him, then he realised the whippet's activities had become too much to tolerate, even for her ladyship.

She nudged the dog with her slippered foot then turned back to Lavender. 'Of course they did. My friends and I have no secrets from each other and once they saw how much I enjoyed the company of these young men, they soon joined in the fun.'

Lavender's jaw dropped. 'What? All of them?'

'Yes, although Deborah has now settled for her vicar in Dulwich. Mind you, we had no idea Davy would turn out to be such a rogue.'

Conscious that his mouth was now flapping like that of a fish out of water, Lavender gave a small bow, thanked her ladyship, veered round the prostrate hounds and left with the footman.

Once he was out of the door, an almighty dog fight broke out in the drawing room, punctuated by high-pitched squealing from the whippet and yells from Lady Louisa. He could only assume that the setters had made up for their lack of cake by punishing the whippet for its vile manners. He brushed a hair from his sleeve and sniffed. He'd ask Magdalena to get his breeches and coat cleaned as soon as he was home.

Chapter Nineteen

G awd's teeth! Let me get this straight in my old noddle.' Woods' eyes were wide with surprise.

They'd met up back at Bow Street. Lavender had an urgent need for a strong drink and suggested a visit to The Nag's Head. While they strode across the street towards the welcoming glow in the small windows of the tavern, he'd told Ned what he'd learned from Lady Louisa Fitzgerald.

The ceiling of the ancient inn was low and smoke-blackened. Behind the bar, tiers of mirrored shelving displayed a wide range of brandies and other spirits in a wonderful array of glass bottles, which glittered in the light from the chandeliers of dripping tallow candles. The place was popular with the Bow Street officers and the landlord nodded to them in recognition. They crossed the uneven floorboards to the back of the inn, where they found a couple of vacant settles next to the stone fireplace.

A barmaid with a stained gown and a mob cap on top of her thick mop of unruly hair appeared by their side. She poured them both a glass of ale and gave Lavender a beaming smile when he tossed her a coin and told her to leave the jug.

Woods was struggling with these latest revelations. 'So, all them fellas at Mrs Palmer's are petticoat pensioners,' he said at last, 'and she's been pimpin' them out to the wealthy old trots in her circle of friends.'

Lavender choked on his ale. 'It's not clear if any petticoats have been lifted, Ned – although I doubt it, considering the age of the women involved.'

Woods raised his bushy grey eyebrow to show his cynicism. 'We have laws in this country against pimpin',' he muttered darkly. 'Men or women – it don't matter.'

'I've no notion what Mrs Palmer may or may not have gained from this arrangement, apart from the gratitude of her friends,' Lavender said. 'There's no suggestion money changed hands.'

'You didn't ask?' Woods continued to stare at him, his ale poised halfway to his mouth. 'Sir Richard told us yesterday she were short of the chinks and had been forced to take in lodgers. Maybe she charged her lodgers out by the hour.'

'It didn't seem appropriate or necessary to delve any deeper . . .'

'You're the best detective in all of England – but you didn't have the gumption to get to the bottom of this case?'

Lavender choked again. 'That's not an appropriate turn of phrase, Ned. Besides which, it's not necessary to know how far these relationships have gone. I've found out how Davy MacAdam supported himself after he left his employment with Drake's and that's all I need to know.'

Woods shook his head knowingly. 'You were too embarrassed to ask because they're toffs and a bit long in the tooth and you're a saphead around women. It's a good job Magistrate Read made me your assistant so I can go back and ask the right questions. It's a shame I weren't there today.'

'Heavens, no! If you'd been there, Lady Louisa would have soon uncovered your passion for horses and dogs and roped you into her stable of escorts. The woman is shameless, Ned. She even asked me if I had a wife.'

'I might have enjoyed it,' Woods grinned.

'Not if Betsy found out, you wouldn't.'

'Well, at least we now know why that wheedlin' sawbones wanted us to be discreet. The scandal sheets will have a field day if this story comes to light.'

'Lady Louisa was adamant that Sir Richard is ignorant of this cosy little arrangement between his sister, her lodgers and her friends.'

Woods' raised eyebrow again signalled his disbelief. 'What about MacAdam's murder? Could one of the old trots have done it?'

Lavender took a long swig of his drink. 'I have absolutely no idea if any of them had either the opportunity or a motive to kill him. That needs more thought and investigation. However, my main suspect for his murder at the moment is Ike Rawlings.'

'I've found a witness at Eggerton's who saw him turn towards the west of the city when he'd delivered his load on the day of the murder,' Woods said. 'He definitely didn't go straight home to Essex.'

'Good – that's excellent news. Young Will, the road sweeper, also saw a man matching Rawlings' description sitting on a stone wagon watching number ninety-three Park Lane on the same afternoon,' Lavender said.

'He were there?' Woods' voice rose with excitement.

'Someone matching his description was there,' Lavender said cautiously, 'according to a child witness.'

'It's got to be him! The wily old fox! He knew all along MacAdam were still alive – and he killed him so he could wed his wife! I told you he were our chief suspect, didn't I, sir?'

Lavender smiled at Woods' enthusiasm. He took a long drink from his glass, sat back and undid the buttons of his greatcoat. The alcohol relaxed him and the tension eased from his tired body and mind. It was always good to talk through the latest developments in a case with Ned. 'It's all circumstantial evidence,' he warned, 'and a jury might not believe the child's account – but with your witness as well, we've got enough to justify questioning Rawlings further. We'll arrest him when we return to Chelmsford for the exhumation. It seems he's another one who's lied to us. You were right to suspect him, Ned.'

Woods smiled at the praise. He drained his tankard and poured himself another drink from the jug. 'But what about all these women MacAdam were escortin' around town? Jealousy can be a powerful motive for murder and MacAdam were a right lothario.'

'That's what I was wondering,' Lavender said. 'As we've agreed many times, I'm not an expert on the fairer sex—'

'No, you're not.'

'But it was obvious, even to me, that this *friendship* with MacAdam was an arrangement of convenience for Lady Louisa. It wasn't an affair of the heart. She didn't seem particularly upset by his death.'

'What about the others?'

'I don't know. I need to interview them – one of them must have loaned MacAdam the carriage he used to visit the Howards. I need to find that damned carriage – and the coachman who drove it.'

'It sounds to me like you need some help investigatin' this wicked coven of elderly aristocrats.'

'Yes,' Lavender agreed thoughtfully. 'And I think I know of someone who can help me.'

'You mean that aristocratic doxy, Lady Caroline?'

Lavender nodded. He put down his tankard, stood up and buttoned up his coat. 'Excuse me, Ned, but I have to go. Can you finish the rest of the ale?'

Woods winked up at him and reached for the earthenware jug again. 'Can a fish swim?'

Chapter Twenty

My Dearest Magdalena,
Duddles is married.
I am wretched and in great need of consolation.
Please call on me at your earliest convenience.
Yours affectionately,
Caroline Clare

'Oh dear.' Magdalena put down Lady Caroline's note, fetched her cloak and asked Mrs Hobart to find her a hackney carriage. She'd been dreading this day.

Her good friend Lady Caroline was twice widowed and for years had enjoyed the companionship of a sweet-natured young man called Henry Duddles. Unfortunately, Duddles was the heir to his uncle's shipping fortune and Baron Lannister had recently placed the young man under considerable pressure to marry and produce an heir – something the childless and older Lady Caroline couldn't provide. The baron had threatened to cut Duddles off without a penny if he didn't settle down and do his duty and had even found a suitable young woman for him to marry from a wealthy neighbouring family.

Lady Caroline claimed she was sanguine about the situation and had repeatedly wished Duddles happiness in his new life. But

Magdalena suspected her friend still harboured a secret hope that this loveless match wouldn't take place and Duddles would return to her arms.

Magdalena asked Mrs Hobart to delay their evening meal then hurriedly descended the steps towards the waiting carriage. To her delight and surprise, she saw Stephen walking down the street towards her. She hurried to greet him. In a breathless babble of English, peppered with a few Spanish expletives about the cruelty of Baron Lannister, she told him of her urgent mission to Lady Caroline's.

Stephen glanced down the street and frowned. 'But where's Teresa? Surely you didn't intend to travel out alone? I've asked you to take Teresa with you when you leave the house.'

'Oh, I forgot. She has the afternoon off and is with her beau, Alfie Tummins.'

The young coachman had been courting Teresa for several years and Magdalena dreaded the day Teresa would leave her to become Mrs Tummins. Alfie was besotted with her Spanish maid, although Teresa seemed more excited about the prospect of Magdalena's new baby than walking up the aisle just at the moment. But Magdalena knew everything would change once she held the infant in her arms and Teresa thought about having a child herself.

'Never mind,' Stephen said. 'I'll come with you instead. I need to speak to Lady Caroline myself regarding a police matter.'

'Please don't tell me she's been misbehaving again,' Magdalena said as he helped her climb into the carriage.

He smiled. 'No, I just need to ask her about a group of elderly aristocratic women whom she may know.'

'Lady Caroline knows more men than women.'

Stephen's attractive dark eyes twinkled and he raised one eyebrow sardonically. 'I think most of London is aware of that.'

Magdalena smiled and silently agreed. The younger daughter of the impoverished Earl of Kirkleven, Lady Caroline had first scandalised the high society of London when she'd eloped with Victor Meyer Rothschild, a member of the wealthy Jewish banking family. After Victor's death, she'd married again, this time to a minor baronet, and lived quietly in the country until he too died. Her second husband had left her penniless and forced to earn an income from her painting. This, plus her unconventional lifestyle and penchant for younger men, added to the notoriety surrounding Caroline Clare. But she'd always been a good friend to Magdalena and Stephen.

While the carriage wound its way through the traffic towards Lincoln's Inn Fields, Magdalena asked Stephen about his murder case and he told her about MacAdam's relationship with Mrs Palmer's friends.

Magdalena burst out laughing. 'Why, those naughty old women!'

'I'm glad you think it amusing, my dear. There were times during Lady Louisa's candid explanation of the situation when I wanted the ground to open up and swallow me whole. I dreaded to hear what she would confess to next.'

'Well, thank goodness for her frankness – at least this has moved your case forward and explained several mysteries that eluded you. And we shouldn't be too harsh on them. All these women have done is pay younger men to escort them around town. Lady Caroline has been walking out on the arm of a younger man for years.'

Stephen frowned. 'Yes, but these women are twenty years older than Lady Caroline. They should be wrapped up in shawls and nodding beside the fire with a cup of chocolate, not gallivanting around town with young bucks. Their friends and families will be scandalised.'

Magdalena laughed again. 'Perhaps they don't have any family to care? Maybe they live for the excitement of the company of these young men.'

'MacAdam is not just a young man. He's a murder victim who may have been a murderer himself. He was married yet intent on becoming a bigamist. Their association with him will scandalise high society if it becomes common knowledge. I dread the moment I'll have to tell Sir Richard about his sister's behaviour.'

'He knows nothing about this?'

Stephen shook his head. 'Mrs Palmer also lied to me on several occasions and was evasive in order to throw me off the scent. I don't know how much she knew about MacAdam's antics but she made protecting the reputation of her friends her priority.'

Magdalena patted his leg affectionately and smiled. 'Then she's a fool. She should have known better than to try to mislead Bow Street's finest police officer.'

They found Lady Caroline in the glass-vaulted orangery at the rear of her apartment, which she used as her painting studio. A paint-splattered easel dominated the space, along with a mismatched daybed and a chaise longue. A large table scattered with paintbrushes, paints, rags and a clean glass of water was pushed up against the wall.

Lady Caroline lay wearily on the chaise longue, wearing a dark-print day dress with an embroidered fichu draped around her neck and tucked into her bodice. She was wringing a wet handkerchief in her long, artistic hands. A crumpled copy of *The Times* lay abandoned beside her. The skin around her green eyes was puffy and her mouth drooped, emphasising the lines around her lips. Today she looked every one of her forty-five years.

She managed a small smile when they entered and sat up. 'Magdalena! My dear, you're so kind – and you too, Lavender. I apologise – you find me wretched, I'm afraid.' She asked the maid who'd shown them into the orangery to fetch coffee. Magdalena sat beside her, put her arms around Lady Caroline and hugged her. Stephen sank down on to the daybed opposite.

'I'm so sorry, Lady Caroline,' Magdalena said. 'I know how fond you were of Duddles.'

'Yes, I'm sorry for your loss,' Stephen said awkwardly.

Magdalena flashed her husband a slightly reproachful glance. 'I know you were prepared for this eventuality, but the news of Duddles' marriage must have been a terrible shock even so.'

'I always liked Duddles,' Stephen said. 'He was a funny chap at times but he was genuine.'

'He's not dead, Stephen,' Magdalena hissed. 'Don't talk about him in the past.' Her husband jerked at her reproach and sat up straighter.

Lady Caroline sniffed and dabbed her nose with her handkerchief. 'Yes, he's a lovely man, but alas, no longer mine – and he's not as genuine as we thought. I think it's his treachery that has upset me the most,' she added sadly.

'Treachery?' Stephen frowned.

Magdalena wondered if she'd done the right thing bringing Stephen with her. Lady Caroline had always been a bit prone to exaggeration and the dramatic but this wasn't the time to question her feelings. She hurried to intervene with soft words. 'It must be dreadfully upsetting to think of him with another woman.'

'I know – and such a woman!'

'What other woman?' Stephen asked. 'He's married the young girl picked out for him by his uncle, hasn't he?'

'Good grief, no! Haven't you read the papers today?' She picked up the crumpled copy of *The Times* that lay beside her on the couch and waved it towards him.

'Who has Duddles married?' Magdalena asked, startled.

'Lady Danvers is Duddles' new wife.' Lady Caroline's voice rose with distress. 'He's married the widow of his worst enemy!'

'What?' Magdalena and Stephen uttered the exclamation in unison.

The previous May, Duddles had accidentally offended the brutish Baron Danvers, who'd responded by challenging the young man to an illegal duel. Persuaded by Stephen and Lady Caroline, Duddles stayed at home and didn't participate in the duel. Unfortunately, a gang of villains had lain in wait for Baron Danvers at the appointed place and killed him. In the confusion that followed, Duddles narrowly avoided being charged with Danvers' murder. The villains responsible for this atrocity were still at large; it was one of the few unsolved cases of Stephen's distinguished career.

'Eliza Danvers, that mousy little woman, is now the new Mrs Henry Duddles,' Lady Caroline continued. 'It's all here in today's paper. They married by special licence yesterday.'

'But I don't understand,' Magdalena said. 'Duddles hardly knew the woman – and she's older than him – and already has two children. His uncle can't approve of the match, surely?'

'Well, he clearly does. Lannister posted the announcement himself. She's older than Duddles, of course – but obviously fertile.' Lady Caroline's tone was bitter. 'Maybe that's all that matters to Baron Lannister. And yes, you're right. The evening of my soirée, when Danvers challenged Duddles to the duel, was the first time he'd met Lady Danvers.'

Magdalena and Stephen were quiet for a moment while they remembered the young man's awkward, and very public, attempt to flirt with the cowed and abused wife of the monstrous Danvers.

'Duddles felt sorry for the poor woman,' Stephen said at last. 'And, if I remember rightly, she was grateful for his attention. Danvers was a brute. I remember the way she waved at Duddles when her husband hauled her out of the party.'

'Yes, and he waved back – like a love-struck puppy!' Lady Caroline's voice trembled. 'I knew he felt sorry for the woman after her husband was murdered and he called on her to offer his condolences but I had no idea he'd continued the acquaintance.'

For a moment, Magdalena thought her friend was about to break down again, but fortunately, the maid arrived with the coffee. Lady Caroline rallied and she became an attentive hostess.

They sipped the hot beverage quietly, then Stephen put down his cup and cleared his throat. 'Why is this match so offensive to you, Lady Caroline?' he asked gently. 'You knew Duddles had to marry – his uncle had threatened to cut off his allowance if he didn't. It's the duty of men of his class to provide an heir. Does it make any difference to you whom he's married?'

Lady Caroline's face crumpled and fresh tears rolled down her cheeks. 'I'm upset because . . . because I suspect Duddles may have genuine affection for Eliza Danvers.'

Magdalena put her arm around the quivering shoulders of her friend and gave Stephen a warning glance, which he ignored.

'No, no. I don't accept that. Ned Woods is always telling me I don't understand women, but after years of acquaintance I presume to understand you a little, Lady Caroline.' He leaned forward and took hold of her hand.

'You're not a vicious woman. Yes, maybe a loveless match between Duddles and some unknown, faceless young woman from the country may have been easier for you to bear at the moment. But in time, I think this would sadden you. You would be sad to think of Duddles trapped in an empty, loveless marriage.'

Lady Caroline sniffed and nodded, encouraging him to continue.

'If it's true that genuine affection has grown up between Duddles and Eliza Danvers, then I think, with time, you'll be happy for him – for them both. God knows, the poor woman deserves some happiness after the misery Danvers put her through – and Duddles too. He deserves to be happy in his marriage – like you were with your first husband, Victor Rothschild.'

Lady Caroline sniffed again and dabbed her eyes. 'Yes, you're right, Lavender. You know me so well. It's wrong of me to be jealous of Duddles' happiness. And Ned Woods is wrong – you do understand the fairer sex. Magdalena is a lucky woman to have you for her husband. You see the world so clearly.'

Stephen sat back, satisfied. Magdalena breathed a sigh of relief and decided to change the subject. 'What happened to that young artistic apprentice of Joshua Reynolds?' she asked. 'You told me the boy was quite smitten with you last week.'

Lady Caroline smiled and a little colour flooded back into her sallow cheeks. 'Unfortunately, his master heard of his infatuation and hauled him back into his own studio. It was such a shame – I've never known a man so keen to clean my brushes and mix my paints for me before.'

They laughed and had a short conversation about other mutual friends and acquaintances while they sipped their coffee. When Magdalena thought her friend was strong enough to leave alone, she indicated to Stephen it was time for them to return home.

'Before we go, Lady Caroline,' Stephen said, 'can I talk to you about a few of the elderly female inhabitants of Mayfair? I would value your opinion and knowledge about these women.'

'What's this?' Lady Caroline joked. 'More police work for me? I'm sure if Magistrate Read knew how often my expertise was sought to solve the cases overwhelming Bow Street Police Office, the man would pay me a retainer.'

Stephen smiled. 'And you would deserve it. I need to ask you about five women: Mrs Sylvia Palmer, Miss Deborah Anderson, Lady Tyndall, Mrs Mary Willis and Lady Louisa Fitzgerald.'

'Good grief! Why do you want to know about that coven of old witches? Have you found them practising necromancy on Hampstead Heath?'

Stephen smiled again. 'I take it you know the women I mentioned?'

'No, not all of them. I've never heard of the first two but yes, I do know of Lady Tyndall and Lady Louisa and their social-climbing friend, Mrs Willis.'

'Was this Mrs Willis married to the doctor who cured the King's madness?' Magdalena asked.

'Yes, she was his second wife. Willis was well rewarded for his successful treatment of the poor king but his wife thought he should be more recognised by high society. She's a shrill woman and she forced her way into many of the card parties and soirées I attended. But the good doctor died several years ago and she's had to live quietly since then.'

Stephen frowned thoughtfully. 'Is this the same woman who is the mother of Lady Allison, wife to Sir Richard?'

'No, she's her stepmother.' Magdalena felt Stephen sigh with relief; it would make his job easier now he knew there was no blood connection between this Mrs Willis and Sir Richard's wife. 'To be honest, I haven't seen or heard much about the wretched woman for a while,' Lady Caroline continued. 'I understood she'd retired to Lincolnshire to nurse her dying brother and has been there some months.'

'But what about Lady Louisa Fitzgerald and Lady Tyndall?'

Lady Caroline sighed and shook her head. 'Louisa Fitzgerald is a domineering old spinster. She's the only surviving child of the late Earl Fitzgerald. A distant cousin inherited the title and the family seat in Ireland after her father's death. She inherited a small annual income and that huge mausoleum of a house in Berkeley Square. It's too big for her and she uses it as a dog kennel, I understand.'

'Is she an honest woman, do you think?' Stephen asked. 'I met her this afternoon and was quite startled by her candour.'

Lady Caroline nodded. 'Yes, Louisa Fitzgerald is a brutally honest woman. She's extremely confident and never holds back her opinion on any subject. You do realise, don't you, Lavender, that you'll have to share with me the reason for your interest in this circle of old harridans.' Light had returned to her green eyes and she was smiling now.

'I'll do that happily in a moment,' Stephen said, 'but first tell me about Lady Tyndall. Ned Woods met the woman but as yet, I've not had the pleasure.'

Lady Caroline frowned. 'Poor Woods! Clarissa Tyndall is the worst of them. I try to avoid her if she attends the same social function, which thankfully is rare. She's very bossy and quite bad-tempered. It's rumoured she drove her first husband to his death with her nagging. The poor man hanged himself from the bannisters of the family home on Park Lane.'

'Heavens!' Magdalena exclaimed. 'What did she harass him about?'

Lady Caroline leaned forward towards them and lowered her voice dramatically. 'It was said she'd found out about his mistress. But rather than turn a blind eye to the affair, as most sensible women would, she was driven by jealousy and harassed the poor man relentlessly. Harassed him to his death, in fact.'

Magdalena struggled to keep back her smile. Her friend's lax morality still had the power to surprise her sometimes. 'She truly sounds a dreadful woman.' She shuffled uncomfortably in her seat. The baby was restless this evening and she suddenly felt tired.

Lady Caroline turned back to Stephen. 'So why are these women of interest to Bow Street Police Office, Lavender?'

Stephen explained about MacAdam's death and his relationship with the elderly widows and spinsters of Mayfair.

Lady Caroline burst into laughter and had to dab her eyes to stop tears of merriment coursing down her cheeks. 'I haven't heard such a wicked story for weeks. Imagine! All of them sharing the same young men in their beds!'

'There is no evidence to suggest . . .' Stephen began hurriedly.

Lady Caroline held up her hand to stop him. 'Oh, I'm sure there isn't any evidence – but that's what everyone will think when this comes out, isn't it? Don't spoil the picture that has formed in my mind. This is the most amusing tale.'

'Yes, it seemed to amuse Magdalena too. Well, if you'll excuse us, Lady Caroline, I can see Magdalena is tired. We must leave you now.'

'Oh, of course, yes. But before you go, at what number on Park Lane does this enterprising Mrs Palmer reside?'

'Why?'

Lady Caroline's eyes twinkled with amusement. 'Well, now Duddles has abandoned me I may need to call on her services to find another young man to escort me around town.'

Chapter Twenty-One

Lavender helped Magdalena up into the hackney carriage, climbed in after her and shut the door. The vehicle jolted and pulled away. He shook his head and gave a half-smile as they settled back into the seat. 'You and Caroline Clare are incorrigible. I'm forced to delicately tiptoe around a group of amorous and titled sexagenarians trying to uncover the truth about their relationship with a dead man – and all you women can do is laugh.'

'*Sexagenarians?*' Magdalena giggled.

He gave a glance of mock disapproval. 'Your Latin is as good as mine, Magdalena. You know what the prefix means.'

'Yes, I know the word – and I also know you English have a totally different meaning for the word *sexual . . .*'

'Don't!' He held up his hand to interrupt her. 'I've already had Ned Woods musing about *petticoat pensioners.*'

She laughed again and settled back in her seat for the journey. Then she frowned as a worrying thought crossed her mind. 'Are these women really suspects in David MacAdam's murder?'

Lavender sighed. 'I honestly don't know what to think. MacAdam was an unscrupulous lothario who used his good looks and charm to win over every woman he met. Did this cause jealousy? I don't know.

Was his behaviour enough to drive one of the women he toyed with to murder him? I don't know. What do you think?'

'We never stop loving,' she said slowly. 'Our joints swell with arthritis and the skin sags and wrinkles but the heart still pounds and hot blood pulses through our veins. We never lose that sparkle in our eyes and the passionate beat of our heart.' Lavender turned his head to listen.

'Tonight, we distracted Lady Caroline from her misery,' she continued. 'But by now, her pain over Duddles will have returned. She'll have a sad and restless night. It doesn't matter how many times we love and lose, or how old we are, the pain from heartbreak is still as sharp as ever. We're all excited, infatuated fifteen-year-olds trapped in ageing bodies.'

'What are you suggesting, my love?'

'I don't think you can dismiss these amorous old ladies as foolish clowns, Stephen. Passion never dims – and, as you've taught me, jealousy is often the greatest motive for murder. You need to take these women seriously as suspects in the murder of David MacAdam.'

He squeezed her hand affectionately. 'I don't know what I would do without your love and support, Magdalena.'

'Good.' She pulled away her hand and wagged a warning finger at him. 'Because should you ever be tempted to take a mistress, when I'm fat and worn out with childbearing, I won't look the other way and ignore it – as Lady Caroline suggests. I'll hound you like Lady Tyndall instead.'

He smiled. 'That's a terrifying thought. I promise to behave.'

Mrs Hobart was waiting on the steps of their home for them as Lavender helped Magdalena down from the carriage. She looked worried and twirled a folded note in her hands, which she handed straight to Lavender. 'This came from Bow Street, sir – and young Eddie Woods is waiting to see you both in the kitchen.'

'Eddie?' Magdalena said. 'I hope there's nothing wrong. I'll go down to him now.'

'Excuse me, ma'am, but he wants to see both of you – Detective Lavender too.'

Magdalena paused on the steps. 'Very well, we'll go together. What's the message, Stephen? Please tell me you don't have to go back to work?'

Lavender shook his head as he read the note. 'No, I don't have to return to work tonight.' He followed the women into the house. 'The Bishop of London has replied to Magistrate Read's request for an exhumation of the grave in Chelmsford. Woods and I are to take MacAdam's body there tomorrow afternoon and stay overnight. The exhumation will take place the following morning at dawn and we're to bury MacAdam in the grave before it's sealed up.'

'Ugh. You call this good news?' Magdalena removed her cloak and handed it to Mrs Hobart. 'Come with me now to see Eddie.' Mrs Hobart followed them downstairs to the kitchen.

Lavender knew the moment he saw Eddie's face that something was wrong. The lad was pale and stood awkwardly by their kitchen table, still wearing his coat.

'Good evening, Eddie . . .' Magdalena said pleasantly.

'Evenin', Aunty Magdalena.'

'Is something wrong at home, son?' Lavender asked.

'My da were foxed when he came home tonight, Uncle Stephen.'

'Ah, yes, I left him in the tavern with a jug of ale.' Lavender frowned. *Foxed?* Woods handled his drink better than any man he knew; he couldn't remember the last time he'd seen his constable inebriated.

'He hasn't had anythin' to eat since yesterday mornin',' Eddie continued, 'the ale went straight to his noddle.'

'What?' Lavender and Magdalena exclaimed in unison. This didn't make sense. Woods had a legendary appetite and love of food. Even Mrs Hobart looked startled.

'Where is he?' Lavender asked.

166

'He's sleepin' off the ale in the kitchen. Ma's right worried about him. I came straight here.' His words came out in a torrent.

'Is he unwell?' Magdalena asked, concerned. She sat down on one of the kitchen chairs.

Eddie shook his head. 'No, he's just refusin' his food. He turned up his nose at his supper tonight and when Ma pressed him for a reason, the truth came out. Thankfully, he were in his cups – otherwise I don't think we'd have got to the root of the problem.'

'What's this truth?' Lavender asked.

'He says he's starvin' himself for a week.'

'He's *what*?' Magdalena was incredulous.

'He didn't eat supper last night in Chelmsford,' Lavender said thoughtfully. 'Or breakfast this morning.'

Eddie's brown eyes narrowed as he frowned. 'Did you know he swooned like a gal at Bow Street this afternoon?' Eddie's voice rose with the distress he was trying so hard to contain. 'He's starvin' himself and makin' himself ill.'

'Why is he doing this?' Lavender asked.

'Ma thinks somethin's upset him. He says he's too fat and this is his way to lose weight.'

Lavender groaned. 'It'll be that comment Sir Richard Allison made yesterday about how he needs a man's corset.'

Eddie's cheeks flushed with wrath. 'That popinjay of a surgeon said that about *my* da?' Lavender heard the fury in his voice. Eddie had the height and build of his father but everyone who knew the family was aware he'd inherited his mother's fiery temper rather than his father's genial nature. His battles with his mother were legendary.

'How can we help, Eddie?' Lavender said hastily. 'Do you want me to stop taking your father into taverns after work?'

'No, Uncle Stephen, I want you to make him eat again.'

'I don't see how . . .'

'You're his Principal Officer. *Order* him to eat a pie. That's why I've come here tonight. To get you to make him eat.'

There was a short silence in the room. Magdalena and Mrs Hobart looked at Lavender expectantly, as if the young man's request was the simplest, most logical thing in the world.

'Right, yes, of course. Leave this with me, Eddie. I'll make sure he eats something tomorrow.' He said the words confidently but he hadn't the faintest idea how he would accomplish the task. He wasn't sure that force-feeding his burly constable steak and ale pie was physically possible but he had to do something. Eddie expected it – and he didn't want to let the boy down.

Relief washed over Eddie's face and his anger abated. He turned to Magdalena and asked when Sebastián was next expected home from boarding school. Magdalena's son and the Woods boys had become good friends over the last two years.

Lavender made his excuses and went to wash and change for dinner. Weariness swamped him when he dragged himself up the stairs. It had been a long and exhausting day.

Chapter Twenty-Two

Wednesday 23rd September, 1812

Lavender and Magdalena were awakened just before five o'clock by an incessant hammering on the front door.

Lavender lit a lamp and pulled his breeches over his nightshirt.

'What is it?' Magdalena asked sleepily from her pillows.

'I don't know. Stay in bed. I'll deal with it.' He padded downstairs in his bare feet and pulled back the bolts on the door.

A muddied and pale-faced night patrol officer from Bow Street stood on the chilly doorstep. Behind him in the gloom, two saddled horses were tied to the railings.

'Mornin', sir,' the officer said. 'You're called out to work urgently. They've sent me to fetch you.'

Lavender ran his fingers through his tousled hair. 'What's happened?'

'There's been a burglary at Mr Howard's home in Bruton Street. 'E's asked for you to attend the scene personally.'

Lavender nodded. *Burglary?* Was this connected with the murder of David MacAdam? This case became more complicated by the hour. 'Give me five minutes to dress. Do you want to step inside?'

The officer shook his head. 'No, I'll stay out 'ere with the 'orses.'

Lavender dressed quickly and splashed cold water on his face while Magdalena watched him from the pillows. He ran his hand over the stubble on his chin but there was no time to shave. He kissed his sleepy wife on the forehead, grabbed his coat and descended the stairs.

The night patrol officer returned to his duties, leaving Lavender to wend his way through the dimly lit streets towards Mayfair. London never slept. Broughams and curricles sped by, taking home the late-night revellers and spraying up filth from the gutter. Staggering drunks were still weaving their way home after a noisy night in the taverns and gin shops and shadowy figures lurked down the narrow alleyways. Meanwhile, the steady stream of wagons from the country were already heading for the capital's markets, heavily laden with produce to feed the gargantuan appetite of the biggest city in the world.

Lavender took his horse to the stables at the rear of Howard's home in Bruton Street and left it with a sleepy groom. The building blazed with light; the entire household must be roused. He strode across the stable yard to gain entrance through the servants' quarters and braced himself for whatever shock lay inside.

A grim-faced and hastily dressed Indian footman led him through the chilly marble hallway to the drawing room, where the family waited. The man hadn't had time to pull on his turban and his long black hair wound down his back like a sleek ebony snake. In the weak light from candles and lamps, Howard's impressive arsenal of Mughal daggers and sabres took on a more sinister appearance. Their evil glimmer mocked him for his failure to find the knife that had killed MacAdam.

'Lavender! Thank goodness you're here at last!' Howard said. 'This is a damned shocking business!' He wore his flowing green silk banyan over his nightshirt. It flapped and rustled as he paced angrily in front of the hearth. Every candelabra and lamp in the opulent drawing room had been lit. The warm glow bounced off the shimmering silk wall hangings, the ivory statues and the gold leaf and jewel-encrusted ornaments.

'What's happened?' Lavender spoke to Howard but his eyes were drawn to the two young women sitting demurely on the sofa in plain high-necked dressing gowns. Both wore lacy nightcaps over their unbound hair.

It was the first time he'd been in the same room with the elusive Miss Amelia Howard. She sat with her head bowed, wringing her hands in her nightgown. Her silky black hair fell forward, obscuring part of her pretty face, but he saw enough to confirm his suspicion that she was the beauty of the family. Both girls were small and slender but there the similarity ended. Miss Howard's facial features were softer than those of the sourpuss beside her.

'We've been robbed.' Howard was red with fury. 'Matilda saw a man sneaking along the landing and raised the alarm. You warned me about the fellow – I should have been more alert.'

What fellow? Did he mean that the intruder was Billy Summersgill?

Lavender turned to the younger girl. 'When was this, Miss Matilda? And exactly what happened?'

Matilda shrugged. 'I sleep on the floor above my sister's room. I looked over the bannister and saw a stranger lurking outside her bed-chamber. I knew it wasn't one of the servants because he wore a hat pulled low over his ugly, pale English face.'

'You saw his face?'

'Yes – but only enough to see his pasty skin. When I screamed, he ran down the stairs. Grandfather came running – and Amelia. It was an hour ago.'

Lavender hesitated. This sounded more like Miss Howard had been entertaining a nocturnal male visitor than a burglar. Stranger things had happened in wealthy Mayfair homes. But Howard's next statement left him in no doubt they were dealing with a robbery.

'We've found where the damned scoundrel broke into the house. It's the laundry door to the rear yard. He broke the glass and pulled out the key from the inside to let himself in.'

'Did the servants . . . ?'

'No, no one heard anything.'

'It may have been the breaking glass that woke me,' Matilda said. 'I sleep at the back above the laundry.'

'What's been stolen?' Lavender asked.

'Ha!' Howard exclaimed. 'That's how we know it was your man. Amelia's jewellery box has been rifled. The ruby ring MacAdam gave her has gone. You need to arrest that moneylender you told me about – he's behind this.'

Lavender glanced around in disbelief at the priceless jewelled ornaments and artefacts adorning every surface of the well-lit drawing room. 'Are you sure that's all that was stolen?'

'The servants have done a thorough search while we waited for you to arrive. Nothing else is missing.'

Lavender frowned. It seemed unbelievable that a burglar had ignored the rest of the wealth in the house and made his way straight to a young girl's jewellery box. 'I need to examine the scene of the crime. Please take me to Miss Howard's room.'

They all accompanied him up the curved marble staircase to the floor above. There were many doors on this landing and a small night lamp flickered on an onyx table next to the door to Miss Howard's room.

'Was this lamp lit at the time of the burglary?' It would have made it easier for Matilda to glimpse the face of the thief.

Matilda answered, 'Yes, my sister is scared of the dark – the silly mare.' Lavender heard the derision in her tone. Miss Howard didn't respond to her sister's taunt and remained standing beside her grandfather with her head bowed.

Lavender glanced upwards. The staircase continued to sweep up in a spiral for at least another two floors.

'Where do you sleep, Miss Matilda?'

She pointed her long, thin hand to the open door of a room on the upper balcony opposite. Lavender nodded. She would have had an excellent view of the prowling thief.

After the vivid colour and brashness of the rest of the Howard home, Miss Howard's bedchamber was tastefully decorated and furnished in pastels, with peach and cream striped upholstery. The material was also used in the heavy satin drapes, which were still closed against the waning night outside. The silk sheets and satin coverlet on the elegant four-poster bed were crumpled and looked like they'd been thrown back in haste. The contents of Miss Howard's jewellery box lay scattered on the surface of a carved light-oak dressing table by the window. Lavender walked across and examined the scattered jewellery carefully, fingering the silver filigree earrings and painted glass bangles. The Howards watched his every move in silence.

'It does seem that the burglar intended to steal Miss Howard's ring,' Lavender said thoughtfully. 'I wonder if there's more to the history and value of that item than we know.' He'd heard stories of the drastic lengths some Asian and African communities had gone to in order to retrieve precious artefacts and jewels, taken or stolen by British traders. Often these pieces were imbibed with religious or spiritual significance. He turned back to Miss Howard. 'Did Mr MacAdam tell you anything of its history when he presented it to you?'

She sat down on her bed and shook her head. 'No, nothing. I can't get over the horror of what has happened.' She had a quiet, melodious little voice. 'It's awful to think of that man in here while I slept, going through my possessions.'

'Yes, you could have been murdered in your bed,' her sister said cheerfully.

'But you saw and heard nothing until Miss Matilda screamed?' Lavender asked.

She shook her head again. 'I'm a heavy sleeper.'

'What I don't understand,' Howard interrupted, 'is how the deuce he knew which one was Amelia's bedchamber?'

'He may have had an accomplice inside your house, who told him where she slept,' Lavender said. 'The only other explanation is that the thief visited several rooms before he found her.'

The Howards all shuddered at the thought.

Billy Summersgill knew what Miss Howard looked like. MacAdam drove past Billy's moneylending shop with her in the phaeton. But Lavender was still unwilling to leap to the same conclusion as Howard. Rogues from the Seven Dials, like Summersgill, didn't walk through a home bursting with valuable artefacts to simply steal a ring from a young girl.

'It doesn't matter about the stupid ring,' Miss Howard exclaimed. She sounded close to tears. 'My grandfather told me about the true extent of Davy's betrayal. I never want to see that ring again!'

'Nonsense!' Howard said. 'That's not the point, Amelia. Some villain has broken into our home and robbed us. We must investigate the theft and bring the culprit to justice. Matilda, comfort your sister. Lavender, come with me – I'll show you the broken door where the scoundrel entered.'

Lavender set off to follow Howard down the stairs, then paused and turned back. 'I know this is a bad time, Miss Howard, but before I leave, may I have a moment or two of your time to ask you some questions about MacAdam?'

'Ha!' said the sad young woman. 'It's never a good time, Detective – not for the last two days – but yes, very well. We're all wide awake now. We may as well talk.'

Relieved he'd finally secured an interview with the young woman, Lavender followed Howard and the footman down several flights of stairs and through a maze of narrow passages. Frightened servants lurked in the shadows. Some bobbed a curtsey to Howard as they passed. The musty laundry was a long, narrow room, white-tiled and stone-flagged and crammed with mangles and large washing tubs. Lavender felt the cold draught from the broken window. The others stood back when he approached the half-open wooden door with its shattered glazing.

He noticed the omission immediately. He should have felt and heard the broken glass crunching beneath his boots but there was no glass in the laundry. He grabbed the handle and pulled the door further open. The iron key had been wrenched out from the inside of the door and was now inserted into the lock on the outside. But the broken glass from the smashed window was glimmering in the moonlight on the step *outside* the door.

'We've a problem, Mr Howard,' Lavender said.

'What's that?'

'This glass has been shattered from the *inside* of the building, by someone standing here in the laundry.'

'What?'

'This is an amateurish attempt to make it look like someone broke into the house, when no such thing happened.'

'By Christ, Lavender! What are you suggesting?'

'Miss Howard was either robbed by someone who lives here – or alternatively, someone let the thief into the building then smashed the window to try to throw us off the scent.'

Chapter Twenty-Three

For a moment, Howard stood in silence, staring down at the broken glass. Then he swore and clenched his arthritic fists. 'Betrayed by one of my own staff? I'll flay the hide off the bastard when I find him!'

'We need to interview your servants as well as Billy Summersgill, the moneylender,' Lavender continued. 'Everyone who has slept in the house tonight is now a suspect in this burglary.'

Howard nodded, his jaw rigid with anger. 'I can't believe I didn't notice this before – it's so obvious now you've pointed it out.'

'You were shocked by the burglary. It's understandable,' Lavender said. 'I'll go back to Bow Street and organise officers to arrest Summersgill and search his premises for the stolen ring. Unfortunately, I can't do it myself. I have an appointment at MacAdam's bank at eight, then the inquest opens at nine into his murder.'

'Yes, yes, I know solving MacAdam's murder is your priority. I've sent for my secretary, Jackson. We'll interview the servants together – and find the damned villain who did this.' A vein throbbed in the sagging folds of his neck above the open collar of his nightshirt. 'I don't take betrayal lightly from anyone in my household, especially when it endangers my granddaughters while they're asleep in their beds.'

Relieved to leave this particular task to Howard, Lavender nodded. 'I leave for Chelmsford this afternoon but I'll send you a message when we've got Billy Summersgill in custody – and you can contact me through Bow Street. The bishop has agreed to the exhumation of MacAdam's grave at dawn tomorrow, which is why I need to return to Essex.'

'Do you like digging up dead people, Lavender?' Matilda Howard asked. The girl had slid up behind them and was leaning nonchalantly against a mangle. A sly smile played around her lips.

'I told you to stay with your sister,' Howard snapped. The girl shrugged at his irritation.

Lavender ignored her and turned back to Howard. 'I'll make sure Billy Summersgill is thoroughly interrogated by the Bow Street police and his premises searched,' Lavender said. 'You're right to suspect he's involved in this crime. From what we saw of him yesterday, he's obsessed with reclaiming that ring – and sometimes obsession can lead men into foolish criminal acts. Now if you don't mind, just before I leave, may I speak with Miss Howard?'

'Yes.' Howard frowned. 'I suppose there will be newspaper reporters at the inquest?'

Lavender nodded. 'There usually are.'

'I'd appreciate it if you can keep Amelia's name out of this dreadful affair. Her relationship with MacAdam had no bearing on his murder.'

'I'll do what I can,' Lavender said, 'but once they find out MacAdam faked his own death, they'll ask questions about why he went to such extreme lengths.'

Howard shook his head sadly. 'What a damned mess this is.'

Lavender made his way back upstairs to Miss Howard's room. She waited patiently for him in an armchair by the cold fireplace. Her pretty face was clouded with sadness but he was pleased to see she was dry-eyed. Her Indian ayah hovered around in the background, folding clothes.

Lavender sat down in the companion chair on the other side of the hearth. 'May I first give you my condolences, Miss Howard. I appreciate you must be very distressed by David MacAdam's death – and everything else you've learned about him since.'

'I've cried until I've no tears left, Detective,' she said. 'Now all I feel is a deep sadness. I'm sad he's dead – and I feel very sorry for myself. My foolish dreams are shattered.'

'I'll not take much of your time,' Lavender promised, 'and I'll try not to distress you further. I only have a few questions. First, can you please tell me what happened the night he died? I know he was here with you and your grandfather until about nine o'clock.'

'We had a very pleasant evening – full of laughter. Davy was a funny man. But I was tired and went to bed early. Davy drank brandy with my grandfather and then he went home.'

'In his carriage? The old one with the coat of arms with the two rampant black stallions?'

'Yes.' A small smile flitted at the corner of her young mouth as she remembered something. 'It was a dreadful vehicle compared to our phaeton, very uncomfortable. It rattled and creaked. But Davy was fond of it. He said it had been his grandmother's coach and she'd bequeathed it to him when she died.'

Lavender didn't correct her. 'So sometimes you travelled with him in the coach?'

She nodded. 'Not often. We were always more comfortable in Grandfather's phaeton. Davy's carriage was an ancient landau with saggy leather straps and a stale odour. But it didn't have rampant black stallions in the emblem, Detective. They were unicorns and they were red.'

Lavender breathed an inward sigh of relief, mingled with frustration. No wonder no one had recognised the crest he'd shown them. Mr Jackson, Howard's secretary, had given him an inaccurate description. 'Do you know anyone who might want to harm Mr MacAdam? Did he ever mention any enemies?'

The glossy curls peeping beneath her nightcap wobbled when she shook her head. 'No, Davy was a popular man. I can't . . . can't imagine how anyone would want to hurt him . . .' Her voice broke and Lavender realised that despite her courage, she was on the verge of tears again.

'Did he ever talk about his friends Francis – Frank – Collins and Alfred Bentley?'

'Yes, sometimes. They shared a passion for horse racing.'

'Did you ever meet them?'

'No, he promised me they would be at our wedding and I'd meet them there.' Her luminous eyes filled with tears again at the thought of her ruined nuptials.

'Just two last questions, Miss Howard,' he said. 'Did you ever give David MacAdam any money?'

She shook her head again and her glistening eyes fixed dreamily on the wall. 'No, Davy was a gentleman. I knew his family wasn't as wealthy as mine but he would never ask to borrow money from a woman.'

How little you knew him, Lavender thought, remembering his conversation that afternoon with Lady Louisa Fitzgerald.

'Finally, I'd just like to know if you visited MacAdam yesterday morning to pay your respects. Two women came to Bow Street and spent time with his corpse.'

She looked startled. 'No, that wasn't me. I was too distressed to leave my room.'

Lavender thanked her and rose to leave. She couldn't help him further. MacAdam had kept this young woman ignorant about his real life and his evil intentions.

He reached into his coat pocket and pulled out the wooden box of billet-doux she had written MacAdam. 'These are yours, I believe, Miss Howard. I thought you'd appreciate it if I returned them.'

She took the box in trembling hands. Large tears rolled down her cheeks as he bowed again and left.

Dawn was breaking over the smoking chimneys and spires of London when Lavender rode away from the house on Bruton Street. Faint pink streaks reached out across the lightening sky above. It promised to be another clear day, but for the first time that month Lavender felt the chill of autumn in the dawn air.

The city was stirring. Shopkeepers in long aprons pulled back shutters, swept refuse away from the front of their stores and chased away the beggars who had slept in their doorways overnight. They carried out displays of their wares and stacked them on the pavements. Workers scurrying to their jobs veered round them. The smell of fried breakfast ham mingled with the drifting coal smoke reminded Lavender that he hadn't eaten. He wondered if the indomitable little Betsy Woods had managed to beat some sense into her stubborn husband and force him to break his ridiculous fast.

When he approached Bow Street, he saw a light already glimmering in James Read's office and once again he felt a surge of respect for the court's Chief Magistrate. Read worked long hours like his police officers and took his responsibilities seriously.

Oswald Grey had also arrived and was at his post at the desk in the hallway. Grey had responsibility for organising the workload of the police constables so Lavender went to him to arrange the re-arrest of Billy Summersgill.

'We'll have to wait until the day shift arrives,' Grey said, 'and this will take a group of several men. I can't send a solitary officer into the Seven Dials – he'd never come out alive.'

Lavender nodded. One of the most notorious parts of London, the Seven Dials was a maze of gin shops, hovels and secret alleyways divided by open sewers. Cut-throats lurked around every dark corner and Bow Street officers were often attacked, especially if they ventured there alone after dark.

Lavender thanked Grey, then went up the scuffed stairs to report to his employer.

Read sat behind his cluttered desk with a quill in his hand and a pile of papers in front of him. He glanced up when Lavender entered and gave him a welcoming smile. 'You're early, Stephen.'

'I had a rude awakening.' Lavender sat down on a hard-backed chair opposite the magistrate. 'There was a burglary at the Howards' home in the early hours.'

Read put down his quill and frowned. 'Is it connected to the murder of David MacAdam?'

'I don't know,' Lavender confessed, and proceeded to update Read about all the developments in the case. Read listened in grim silence. Only the occasional raised grey eyebrow or tightening of his square jaw indicated his surprise.

'I suspect MacAdam left his job to spend all his time courting Miss Howard and seducing her into marriage. I'm sure the bank will later confirm my suspicion that he received regular payments from his group of admiring old ladies.'

'Have you had any luck tracing that carriage or the murder weapon?'

Lavender shook his head. 'Not yet, but thanks to Miss Howard, I've got a new lead about the carriage – and a strong suspicion where I'll find it. I'll deal with that before we go to Chelmsford for the exhumation.'

Read sighed. 'At which point, you'll probably get another murder to solve.'

Lavender nodded. 'At the moment, Ike Rawlings is my main suspect for the murder of MacAdam but the evidence is circumstantial. I'll keep an open mind. In the meantime, I've raised a hue and cry for Frank Collins and asked Grey to send out officers to arrest Billy Summersgill to question him further about this missing ring – we need to find them both.'

Read sat back in his chair and rolled his eyes to the ceiling. 'What a tangled mess this case is!'

'Yes,' Lavender said grimly. 'And to be honest, I think there'll be a few more nasty surprises ahead. Heaven knows what the exhumation will reveal.'

'Did you say that Sir Richard's sister facilitated this extraordinary arrangement between her lodgers and her friends? And his mother-in-law is one of these wicked old women with a penchant for younger men?'

'Yes, although I heard last night that Mrs Willis has been out of town for a few weeks, nursing her sick brother in the country. If this is correct, I won't need to question her.'

'Sir Richard should be able to confirm this,' Read said. 'I'll ask him at the inquest.'

'He'll be shocked,' Lavender warned. 'I don't think he knows the full extent of what his female relatives have been up to.'

Read shrugged. 'Well, he'll have to be told. But I don't feel we need to mention these shenanigans in court at the inquest. Just stick to the main facts about your investigation at this stage, Lavender.'

'Mr Howard requested that we try to keep his granddaughter's name out of the investigation.'

Read grimaced. 'That may be harder, but you can try.'

Lavender picked up his hat, pushed back his chair and stood up. 'I'll leave you now, sir. I want to catch Ned Woods before I visit the bank.'

'Ah yes, Woods. Is he ill, do you think, Lavender? He fainted clean away in the stable yard yesterday. We can't do with an officer with the fainting sickness.'

Lavender smiled. 'He's fine, sir. He was just hungry, that's all – he'd missed a meal.'

Read's eyebrows shot up in shock. 'Woods missed a meal? Have the four horsemen of the apocalypse ridden into town? Is the end of the world nigh?'

Lavender laughed. 'I'll make sure it doesn't happen again, sir.'

Chapter Twenty-Four

L avender found Woods in the stable yard talking with a couple of the bleary-eyed night patrol officers. Hard-faced and powerfully built men, their boots and uniforms were splattered with the mud of the outlying roads of the capital where they had spent the night on patrol. The group laughed at something Woods said and Lavender wondered how his starving constable managed to remain so cheerful despite the gnawing ache in his belly. But when he drew nearer, he saw the glimmer of pain and something akin to disorientation in Woods' brown eyes. His fleshy cheeks had shrunk into his round moon of a face.

'Mornin', sir,' Woods said brightly. 'Oswald Grey tells me he's organisin' officers to arrest Billy Summersgill. Do you want me to join them?'

'No, Ned, I want you to come with me.'

Without another word, Lavender led his constable out of the stable yard and across Bow Street into bustling Covent Garden market.

Despite the early hour, Inigo Jones' grand Italian piazza was already a noisy, heaving mass of humanity and commerce. Stallholders shouted until they were hoarse to attract the shoppers to the mountains of potatoes, turnips, swedes, dried herbs and stringy beans piled high on their tables. Their customers argued about the prices and complained about the poor choice. The smell of fresh bread and stale ale wafted from the brick-built shops that lined the square, where bakers and retailers of genever and other spirituous liquors rubbed shoulders with haberdashers, ironmongers and cook shops. Housewives and servants jostled down the narrow aisles with their baskets. Drunks staggered out of the gin shops.

'Where are we goin'?' Woods asked.

Lavender ignored him and scanned the crowds for Simple Simon the pieman. This wasn't the man's real name, of course. He'd been given the nickname by the Bow Street officers who'd merged the two characters in the popular children's nursery rhyme. Simple Simon wore a battered hat with a mangy feather over his long, greasy hair. The victim of a minor seizure, the right corner of his mouth and his right eye drooped but, despite his unusual appearance, there was nothing simple about this Simon. He charged a good price for the famous pies he sold from a wooden tray slung around his neck.

Lavender spotted Simon's hat and feather bobbing about in the sea of heads on the western edge of the square, amongst the better-class fruiterers and florists. 'This way, Ned.' He led his constable past a couple of aristocratic ladies and their liveried servants who were examining a colourful display of exotic hothouse blooms. When they reached Simon, with his well-stacked tray of gleaming, golden-crusted pies, Woods hesitated and held back. The aroma of steak, gravy and warm pastry was tantalising.

The pieman's eyes flitted over Woods' distinctive uniform and his lopsided mouth lifted into an awkward grin over his toothless mouth. 'Good mornin' to you, officers. 'Ow can I serve you today?'

'Help yourself, Ned,' Lavender said firmly. 'I'm treating you to breakfast today. I presume you haven't had any?' He handed a couple of coins over to Simon, reached out for a pie and took a bite. The flaky pastry melted in his mouth and his tongue swirled through the meaty gravy. 'Mmm, this is delicious.'

Woods continued to hold back but Lavender could see the desperation in his eyes. His broad nose twitched furiously at the smell emanating from the tray. 'It's all right, sir, I'm not hungry.' His voice caught as his rebellious throat – under instructions from his starving stomach – tried to strangle the lie.

'Eddie came to see us yesterday evening,' Lavender said between mouthfuls. 'He told us about this ridiculous notion you have about starving yourself to lose weight.'

Woods said nothing, his eyes still riveted on the tantalising golden mound of food on the tray.

'Come along, guvnor,' Simon said, 'which one do you want?' He thrust his tray towards Woods, who flinched.

'I understand you were sprawled out unconscious on the stable yard cobbles yesterday too,' Lavender continued. 'You do realise, don't you, that you're killing yourself with this silly abstention?'

Alarm flashed across the drooping face of the pieman. 'Killin' 'imself? Not wi' my pies, 'e ain't! I don't know what this abstention thing be – but there's nothin' wrong wi' my pies!'

'It's just for another day or two, sir,' Woods said. 'I already feel lighter.'

'Lighter in the head, maybe,' Lavender snapped. 'You're making yourself ill, Ned. This isn't the way to do it. And a constable who faints on duty is no use to me. If you want to lose weight, try eating one pie instead of three – and use a normal bowl instead of Betsy's mixing bowl for your porridge. Now eat a pie.'

'Yes, eat!' shouted the indignant pieman. 'There ain't nothin' wrong wi' my pies.' His raised voice attracted the attention of a small crowd.

'What's amiss, fellah?' someone asked.

''E's refusin' to eat my pies,' Simon said.

'Oooh, that's bad, that. They're right tasty, them pies of yourn.'

Still Woods refused to move. Oblivious to the indignant crowd and angry pieman, Woods was caught in a trance, his eyes fixed on the tray of food.

'Do you want one of my ruddy pies or not?' Simon yelled.

'Does 'e think they're bad?' asked a woman with a wicker basket full of posies for sale. The pieman looked like he was about to explode.

Lavender shoved the last of the pie into his mouth, grabbed Woods' arm and dragged him away. It was no use – and definitely time to leave. Smaller incidents than this had triggered riots in Covent Garden. 'Keep the change,' he yelled over his shoulder to Simon. The pieman responded with a string of curses, which rang in their ears as they pushed their way back through the heaving throng.

'You're a stubborn saphead, Ned Woods,' Lavender said angrily.

'Yes, sir,' Woods grinned cheerfully. A smile spread across his broad face. 'But I'll be a slimmer saphead soon.'

Lavender shook his head and sighed as his anger faded. Ned would come to his senses soon but in the meantime, he would have to keep him close. Ideally, he should have sent Ned out to the Seven Dials with the other officers to arrest Summersgill but he couldn't risk it. Woods was now on the third day of his self-imposed fast. If he kept up this daft notion much longer he would become weak and disorientated. Lavender had failed in his promise to Eddie to make Woods eat something; the least he could do now was keep an eye on his father for him. He owed them both this much.

Mr Underhill, the manager of the bank of Messrs Down, Thornton and Gill, was both obese and bald. His domed pate gleamed with a fine sheen of sweat and his chin sunk deep into the elaborate folds of his cravat. His small, sharp eyes were deep-set in his plain, fleshy face.

However, he greeted them cordially and he'd taken the trouble to prepare for Lavender's appointment. A full written summary of MacAdam's account was spread out on the large mahogany desk that dominated his office.

Underhill picked up a sheet of paper with his podgy hand and handed it to Lavender. His gold ring flashed in the sunlight pouring through the high window. 'Mr David MacAdam has left ninety-six pounds, ten shillings and six pence in his account.'

'That'll please his widow,' Woods said. 'At least she'll be able to afford his second burial now.'

Underhill looked surprised by the comment but he didn't ask for an explanation.

Lavender grimaced. Woods wasn't normally so indiscreet; he was trying too hard to appear normal. 'Does this amount include the deposit he made recently of fifty pounds?' He pulled out the crumpled receipt he'd found in MacAdam's bedchamber and showed it to the manager.

Underhill nodded. 'Yes, I think Mr MacAdam was struggling with money. He'd recently approached us for a loan of one hundred guineas but he had no surety and we declined his request.'

'That'll have been to pay for that blessed ruby ring for Miss Howard,' Woods said. 'Once the bank turned him down, he'd no choice but to approach a moneylender.'

Mr Underhill raised a greying eyebrow and pressed his lips tightly together.

Lavender remembered Magistrate Read's request for discretion at the inquest and made a mental note to keep Woods out of the witness box.

'I believe this recent deposit was made by banker's draft,' Lavender said hastily. 'Who paid him the money?'

'The fifty pounds was drawn on the bank of Lady Tyndall.'

'Well, the lyin' old trot!' Woods exclaimed. 'She told me she hardly knew MacAdam.'

Lavender was less surprised than Woods by her ladyship's lies, but excitement still surged through him at this latest revelation. 'Have there been similar deposits from Lady Tyndall in the past?'

Underhill peered at the sheets in front of him through his piggy eyes. 'Yes, he presented us with a draft to be drawn on her bank nearly every month since May. I understood she was his aunt?'

'His aunt?' Woods burst out laughing.

Lavender kicked him in the ankle to shut him up. 'Were they always for the same amount: fifty pounds?' he asked.

'No. They were mostly for twenty pounds.'

Lavender nodded. With this and the occasional cash handout from Lady Louisa Fitzgerald and the other women, MacAdam would have had enough to tide himself over while he spent his time courting his little heiress.

'There was one other deposit from Lady Tyndall back in January,' Underhill continued, 'but the payments didn't become regular from her until May.'

'That were when he left his job,' Woods said.

'Has he had any other source of income besides these payments from Lady Tyndall?'

'Not that I can see,' the manager said. 'If he had received money from other quarters it never made its way into his bank account.'

Lavender pushed back his chair to rise. 'Thank you, Mr Underhill, you've been most helpful. I shall pass on the bank's address to Mrs MacAdam so she can claim the remaining money in her husband's account.'

They blinked when they walked out on to the crowded street. Bright sunlight had chased away the early morning tinge of autumn and it promised to be another fine day. Excellent weather, Lavender thought sardonically, for taking a coffin in a cart to Chelmsford.

'We need to pay a visit to that old harridan,' Woods said.

'We'll go to her carriage house first.'

'She's fed me a pack of lies – just like Mrs Palmer lied to you. These old women have done nothin' but obstruct this investigation from the start.'

'Well, I'm just glad someone managed to feed you something over the last two days.'

'There's no need to get testy,' Woods said.

'I'm not testy – but you need to concentrate on what you're saying. You've become light-headed with lack of food and your mouth's running away with you.'

Woods looked hurt and began to protest, but Lavender had already turned in the direction of Bow Street. 'Come on, we need to return for the inquest. Hopefully, we'll have time to deal with Lady Tyndall before we leave for Essex.'

Chapter Twenty-Five

T he coroner, Sir Edmund Sylvester, opened the inquest into David MacAdam's death at nine o'clock prompt. Ten jurors were present in the stark wooden courtroom, along with Magistrate Read, Sir Richard Allison and his sister, Mrs Palmer.

Tunnels of sunlight streamed in through the high windows down on to the gnarled wooden benches, but they did little to lighten the sombre mood. Cobwebs hung down from the rafters above the heads of the spectators and officials.

Lavender glanced up to the public gallery and recognised the lanky frame and pock-marked face of Vincent Dowling, a reporter with *The Day*, amongst the other journalists and curious bystanders. This wasn't good news; Lavender knew him for a perceptive man. Dowling had previously worked for the Home Department as a spy and their paths had crossed several times.

The purpose of the inquest today was primarily to establish the identity of the deceased person, to explain how the death occurred and the cause of death and, if possible, to establish when and where the death occurred.

Mrs Palmer was the first to be called to the imposing stand to give evidence. Dressed demurely in black, she bowed her head to hide her pale face in the shadow of her bonnet as she quietly confirmed that the dead man had been her lodger at number ninety-three Park Lane. She explained how she had seen MacAdam on the landing the night before and then found him dead in his room the next morning.

Next, Sir Richard Allison took the stand. 'Mrs Palmer is a patient of mine,' he lied confidently, 'and her lodger, David MacAdam, was also known to me. On Monday morning, I received an urgent request from Mrs Palmer to examine the dead man at her premises.'

He explained to the courtroom how MacAdam had been stabbed with a thin, four-inch curved knife, which had penetrated his liver. 'Initially, due to the fact he died in a locked room, I assumed the death was self-inflicted. However, it is now my belief the victim was deliberately stabbed by a person or persons unknown on his way home that evening.'

'He died in a room that was locked from the inside?' The startled coroner asked for clarification.

Sir Richard pulled himself up to his full height and with all the confidence of a compère at a vaudeville performance, he explained to his fascinated audience how the dead man's corset had restricted the blood flow and contained his injury until he'd undressed later in his room. A murmur of amazement rippled round the court. Lavender glanced up and saw the quills of the journalists in the public gallery working feverishly over their notebooks.

'The cheeky whiddler made it sound like this was his deduction!' Woods whispered furiously in Lavender's ear. 'He hadn't a clue about how MacAdam died until you explained it to him.'

'It doesn't matter,' Lavender replied. He was called to the stand next and made a short statement about how the Bow Street inquiry had progressed so far.

'Constable Woods and I discovered Mr MacAdam was a commercial traveller from Chelmsford. We located his wife, who came to London yesterday and also identified the deceased. We now know Mr MacAdam visited the Howard family on Bruton Street the evening before his death. He enjoyed a brandy nightcap with Mr Howard and then left for home in a carriage, which I believe to have been borrowed from a friend. Somewhere between Bruton Street and Park Lane he received that fatal stab wound, administered by a person or persons as yet unknown. So far, we've been unable to establish where and when the attack took place. The inquiry is still ongoing but we're treating this incident as murder.'

Then the coroner asked the question that Lavender had hoped to avoid. 'If both Mrs Palmer and Sir Richard had already identified the victim, why did you feel it was necessary to bring his widow over from Essex?'

Lavender cleared his throat. 'Because she already believed her husband to be dead. It has transpired that Mr MacAdam successfully faked his own death in June by sending a coffin home with one his acquaintances. The coffin was buried in St Mary's church and is marked with a gravestone. Francis Collins, MacAdam's accomplice in the deed, has since vanished. We've raised a hue and cry for his arrest.'

The sombre courtroom suddenly burst into life. Gasps of shock and cries of indignation rippled round the public gallery. Journalists shouted down questions and the coroner had to bang his gavel to regain order. 'Who – or what – lies in that coffin in Chelmsford, Detective?' he asked.

'We don't know yet, sir. We've been granted a faculty for exhumation by the Bishop of London and the exhumation is to take place tomorrow at dawn.'

Lavender heard the scratching of quills on parchment above and wondered how many of the reporters would turn up in Chelmsford for the exhumation. Such events were rare but they always caused a sensation amongst the public.

'Is this killer on the rampage in London, Lavender?' one of the jurors asked in alarm. 'Do you think the same person who murdered MacAdam also murdered the victim in the coffin? Will he strike again?'

Fortunately, Sir Edmund was a stickler for protocol during his inquests and he intervened quickly. 'We must stick to the facts in this inquest, sir – and avoid speculation.' He turned to Lavender. 'Do you and your constable have any more pertinent facts you can share with us at the moment, Detective?'

'No, sir. The investigation is still ongoing. Constable Woods has shadowed me throughout this investigation so he'll have nothing further to add to my testimony.'

The coroner nodded and turned to the jury for a brief discussion. To Lavender's relief, they decided to adjourn the inquest pending further information. 'We feel we've established without reasonable doubt the identity and cause of death of David MacAdam,' Sir Edmund said. 'His death is suspicious; he was feloniously murdered by a person or persons unknown. Detective Lavender and Constable Woods need to pursue further inquiries. Let's all hope this investigation is quickly concluded and these villains are apprehended and brought to justice. I declare this inquest adjourned until further evidence is available.'

Relieved, Lavender climbed down from the witness stand. Across the room, Magistrate Read pulled Sir Richard to one side. Lavender couldn't hear what was said but he guessed the nature of their conversation from the shocked expression on Sir Richard's face. A faint, discernible line of colour touched Sir Richard's jawline and he glanced furtively across the room at Lavender.

'Well, that went well,' Woods said.

Lavender rolled his eyes; Woods' forced cheerfulness was grating on him. 'Yes, all the more so because I kept you out of the dock,' he snapped. 'You do realise how indiscreet you were at the bank, don't you?'

Woods looked hurt but didn't have chance to reply. Suddenly Vincent Dowling was by their side, with his pencil and notebook clutched in his inky fingers. 'So why did he fake his own death,

Lavender? Was this an insurance fraud – or was he dallying with another woman?'

'I can't tell you anything more at the moment.'

Dowling's long, greasy hair swayed when he laughed. 'I have other ways to find out, Lavender.'

'I'm sure you do – if you must.'

'Oh, I must. I think I can help you too, Lavender. I saw the pathetic hue and cry notice you placed in the news-sheets this morning; I doubt you'll get much response from that. What the public needs is a good scandal to attract their interest and my readers will love the scandal of a man faking his own death. You'll soon catch your man with their help.'

'We're not prepared to say any more at the moment,' Lavender said firmly. He gave Woods a knowing stare. Woods replied with an almost imperceptible nod.

But Dowling wouldn't let it drop. 'It sounds like the dead man went to elaborate lengths to deceive his poor wife – and there must be a reason. Is she a suspect in his murder, by the way?'

Magistrate Read beckoned Lavender across the room.

'Excuse me, Dowling.' He walked over, leaving Woods alone with the journalist, silently praying Woods wouldn't succumb to pressure from the man to reveal any more about the case.

'Sir Richard would like a quiet word with you, Lavender.' Read walked across to speak to the coroner, leaving them alone.

Sir Richard coughed to clear his throat. 'Well, this is a devilish situation, Lavender. I had no notion of what my sister and her friends were up to with her damned lodgers.'

'I believe you.'

The surgeon paused in surprise and scanned Lavender's face. 'Well, as I'm sure you appreciate – this must never come out. We need to be discreet. Nothing to the newspapers, eh? I dread to think what Lady Allison will say when she finds out about Sylvia's part in this. We've tried to persuade Sylvia to sell her house and move in with us – but I don't know if Katherine will be so keen now.'

Lavender half-smiled and glanced across to Mrs Palmer, who sat on a bench, waiting patiently for her brother. Sir Richard seemed more concerned about his wife's reaction to this revelation than the public scandal it would cause. He wondered idly about the strength of character of Lady Allison. Was Sir Richard like the rest of the married men he knew, including himself – master of his own house in name only?

'Is it true your mother-in-law, Mrs Willis, has been out of London for some time?'

'Mrs Willis is the second wife of Lady Allison's father. Strictly speaking, she's my *step* mother-in-law, Lavender. No relation.'

'The news-sheets won't be so discerning – they won't care. Any scandal involving Mrs Willis would still reflect badly on you and Lady Allison.'

'Yes, I know, I know. But to answer your question, Mrs Willis has been in Hampshire with her dying brother for some weeks now. The fellow is taking an infernally long time about his dying. She's nothing to do with this damned case.'

'Good, this reduces the number of these women I need to question.'

'But what about it, eh, Lavender? The discretion I mentioned? I watched you in the witness stand there – you did a good job sticking to the pertinent facts and avoiding lurid speculation.' There was a fine sheen of sweat on Sir Richard's high forehead and the gleam of desperation in his pale, lashless eyes. The man was pleading with him. 'Can we get through this without mention of my sister and Mrs Willis?'

Lavender glanced across at Woods, who was now alone at the other side of the courtroom. Believing himself unobserved, his constable was leaning heavily on a wooden bar. Pain flitted across his face from some abdominal spasm. This had got to stop.

'Perhaps we can have an arrangement, Sir Richard.'

'An arrangement?'

'Yes – if I do my best to keep the women in your family out of the scandal sheets, you can undo some of the damage you inflicted two days ago on Constable Woods.'

'Woods? What the devil does he have to do with this?'

'Your comment about how he needs to wear a man's corset upset him badly and there have been repercussions.'

Sir Richard laughed. 'Surely you don't expect me to apologise for speaking the truth, Lavender? The man is quite overweight.'

'No, I don't expect an apology,' Lavender replied grimly. 'I just need you to be the doctor and medical professional you are. Woods has thrown himself into a ridiculous fast – he hasn't eaten anything for three days now in the belief that this will help him lose weight.'

'That's ridiculous!' Sir Richard exclaimed.

'Yes, I know. But he's a stubborn man. I'm concerned he's injuring himself with this starvation. Give him your medical opinion, some advice, some help.'

'Of course he's hurting himself – I've never heard such nonsense!' Sir Richard laughed again. He obviously found the whole situation amusing.

Lavender fought back his irritation and steeled himself not to react. 'He's a stubborn fool,' he agreed, 'but he needs guidance, not mocking. His wife and I have both tried to talk sense into him and failed.'

Sir Richard stopped laughing and held out his hand to seal the pact. 'Very well, Lavender, if that's what you want from me in return for your cooperation and discretion, I'll do it. I'll help persuade your idiotic constable to eat again. Shouldn't be hard. I must take Sylvia back home now but I'll see you both at The Great Black Boy coaching inn in Chelmsford this evening.'

A niggling doubt crossed Lavender's mind when he shook the surgeon's proffered hand. A wicked glint had replaced the distress in Sir Richard's eyes. Had he just made a pact with the devil? Woods would certainly think so. But a desperate situation required a desperate solution.

There was no time to worry about it. He had less than two hours before they were due to leave for Chelmsford with the body of David MacAdam – and he needed to find that damned carriage and its driver.

Chapter Twenty-Six

L avender and Woods paused at the top of King's Street Mews and surveyed the activity in the narrow, muddy back street. Grooms were leading out horses. A liveried coachman wrung out a leather cloth over a bucket of water then disappeared back through the open doors of the coach house and continued to wipe down the gleaming barouche inside. There was a forge halfway down the mews and the metallic clang of the blacksmith's rhythmic hammering filled the air. Old axles and a pile of rusty iron wheels leaned against the wall of the smithy. Weeds sprouted at their base.

They tied the reins of their horses to an iron ring on the outside of one of the stables and Lavender found the same ostler he'd spoken to the day before, mashing up bran for the horses in a tub. He asked where they would find the coach house owned by Lady Tyndall and they were directed to the building next to the blacksmith's forge. The huge doors were closed but unlocked. They slid open easily on their iron runners.

''Ere, what you doin'?' The leather-aproned blacksmith, a big man with black bushy hair and whiskers, had left his anvil and was standing glowering beside them. His hammer dangled menacingly in his hand.

Lavender pulled out his brass-topped tipstaff and held it up. 'I'm Detective Lavender from Bow Street. I need to see Lady Tyndall's carriage and speak to her coachman.'

The hairy forge master hesitated, then nodded. 'Runners, eh? I recognise yer uniform now. You investigatin' that murder on Park Lane?'

Lavender nodded.

'Well, I'm sorry I disturbed you, sir, but I can't be too careful – what wi' all the thievin' coves who come down this street.'

'Do you know Lady Tyndall's coachman and where I can find him?'

'That'll be Tolly Barton you want. It's 'is afternoon off. 'Er ladyship is always *at 'ome* on a Wednesday. She don't require the carriage so Tolly gets some time off.'

Lavender glanced up at the accommodation above the coach house. The small window was one of those with a window box of red geraniums. Their colour was a vivid splash of brightness against the smoke-blackened brick. 'Does he live here?'

'Yes – but he ain't 'ere. 'E always goes to visit 'is old mother in Cheapside on a Wednesday.'

Lavender bit back his frustration. He'd have to wait to speak to the coachman until after his return from Essex, but at least Lady Tyndall was *at home* – and receiving callers, by the sound of it. She wouldn't be pleased when a pair of Bow Street officers arrived in her drawing room if she was surrounded by her friends and acquaintances, but pleasing Lady Tyndall wasn't one of his priorities today.

Woods slid both coach house doors fully open to let in more light and they stepped inside.

Miss Howard was right. The coach MacAdam had borrowed was a low-slung, ancient landau with a rounded roof and sagging leather harnesses. Lavender brushed his hand over the two rampant red unicorns on the faded coat of arms on the door and felt a surge of satisfaction that this part of the mystery of MacAdam's fateful last journey had finally been solved. 'We need to examine the entire area. We know there won't be much blood – if any – but let's see if we can find any other clues.'

Woods grabbed the handle and wrenched open the stiff door of the coach, releasing the musty stale odour from inside. The vehicle rocked as he clambered up the wooden steps to examine the interior.

Lavender carefully picked his way around the floor of the coach house. Kicking aside the clumps of rotting straw, he peered beneath the undercarriage but saw nothing. He found a dark stain near the door that could be dried blood, but whether it was human or animal he couldn't tell. This could be nothing more than the site of a successful feline strike on a rat.

A high shelf ran along the back wall, crammed with dusty bottles and pots of silver polish, glycerine, rat poison and grease, interspersed with boxes of spare nails and studs and old brushes. Below the shelf, harnesses, ropes and chains hung from rusty hooks, along with a selection of broken reins waiting to be re-stitched. He rattled the chains and moved the pots and jars to see behind them. Nothing.

Woods emerged from the interior of the coach with a small piece of white lace in his hand. 'I found a woman's handkerchief lost behind the seats but nothin' else.'

Lavender sighed. 'It was too much to hope we'd find evidence of the attack on MacAdam here.'

'Maybe he weren't stabbed here. Did you go through there?' Woods jabbed a finger towards a door at the rear of the coach house. It was partially hidden from sight by a line of horse blankets hanging from hooks on the wall.

'It leads into the forge, I think,' Lavender said.

They tried the handle and the door swung open easily. They were at the back of the forge close to the hot furnace, where a startled young apprentice worked the groaning bellows amidst an angry shower of sparks. The blacksmith was hammering out a horseshoe on the anvil with his back to them. The apprentice called out to get his attention.

Lavender and Woods walked up to the smith, away from the blistering heat and noise of the furnace. 'I apologise for disturbing you again, but is this door always left unlocked?'

The blacksmith immersed the glowing red horseshoe in a pail of water. There was a loud hiss and a billowing cloud of steam. Once it subsided, he placed the shoe to one side, wiped his hands on his apron and shook his head. 'No, the darned thing is supposed to be locked at all times. I didn't realise it were open again.'

'How long has it been unlocked, do you think?'

The blacksmith frowned. 'I asked Tolly Barton to make sure it were locked on 'is side about a month ago, when me other 'ammer were taken. Looks like 'e didn't do it.'

'Have you had items stolen recently?' Lavender asked sharply.

The big man sniffed and nodded. 'Aye, I've just lost a knife. I can't turn me back for a minute. I blame the youngsters – they're always roamin' up and down this street on the lookout for somethin' to lift.'

'What did this knife look like?' Lavender asked.

The man gave a short laugh. 'Why? You runners goin' to find it for me and 'ang the little villain who took it?'

'No, but we're looking for a murder weapon – a knife.'

The big man stepped back, alarmed, and held up a hand. 'Whoa! This murder ain't nothin' to do wi' me and me farrier's knife!'

Woods turned sharply to Lavender. 'A farrier's knife could have killed MacAdam. It's the right length and curved. They use it to trim the sole and frog in the feet of horses. When did you notice this knife missin', fellah?'

The blacksmith frowned while he tried to remember. 'A few days ago, maybe . . . no, it were on Monday when we came to work after the Sabbath.'

Lavender and Woods glanced around the cluttered forge. There were hoof nippers and gauges, nail clinchers and rasps. Metal gleamed everywhere. 'Are you absolutely sure it's not here?'

'Ha! I've turned this place upside down lookin' for it!'

Lavender nodded, thanked him and he and Woods left. They walked out of earshot of the blacksmith and the grooms and coachmen who milled about the cobbled street. Both men were thoughtful.

'It looks like we've found the murder weapon,' Woods said.

'Not yet, we haven't,' Lavender said. 'It's still missing. But at least we know what we're looking for now. It's a good job you spotted the door to the forge, Ned. I was so busy staring at the floor looking for clues I missed it. In fact—' He stopped suddenly. 'How did the murderer know he could get such easy access into a room full of lethal weapons?'

'Do you think he knew about that doorway and lay in wait for MacAdam to return home in the carriage?'

'Possibly. The killer may have been snooping about and chanced on that grim array of metalwork in the blacksmith's forge by accident.'

Woods frowned as a new thought struck him. 'You don't think that MacAdam disturbed a burglary in the forge, do you? And that he was stabbed in the gut to stop him from raisin' the alarm?'

Lavender hesitated for a moment, then shook his head. 'No. I doubt it. That would have led to a tussle and the blacksmith didn't mention that anything had been disturbed. But what we need to do is search this street and the alleyway leading to the back of Mrs Palmer's house. The killer may have dropped the weapon when he fled.'

Silently, they retraced their steps up the mews, peering into the central drain that ran down the street and turning over clumps of rotting straw and other debris with the toe of their boots. They retrieved their horses and slowly walked the animals down the back of the row of houses, scanning every inch of the route. Nothing.

Lavender sighed. 'It's no use. It's not here. Come on, we need to speak to Lady Tyndall. I've a lot of questions I want to ask that woman about her relationship with MacAdam.'

Chapter Twenty-Seven

They left their horses tied to the back fence and sought entrance to the house through the rear servants' entrance, which Woods had used two days before. The elderly butler took them into the tiled servants' hall and left them there while he went to speak to his mistress. Lavender fidgeted irritably with the delay.

A mousy young housemaid in a blue-striped uniform and a white apron was sewing at the large table in the centre of the room. Her sharp, jerky actions with the needle and the frown across her pretty young face suggested needlework wasn't her strongest skill.

'Mornin', treacle,' Woods said cheerfully.

The girl just glared at him and continued to stab at the hem of the elaborate dark-green silk gown on her lap.

Another maid in the same uniform popped her freckled face round the door. 'Will you be long, Sarah? Only we've got them upstairs chambers to clean yet.'

'I'll be as quick as I can,' the needlewoman said wearily. She pointed to an overflowing basket of freshly ironed laundry at her feet. 'She wants them put away and I need to lay out 'er gown for tonight.'

The other maid nodded, sighed and withdrew.

'Shouldn't her ladyship's maid be doin' that?' Woods asked the girl sympathetically.

'Yes, but she ain't here, is she?'

The butler returned and informed them Lady Tyndall couldn't see them. She was too busy entertaining her visitors to spare them the time.

Lavender's temper snapped. This was the final straw. Over the last two days of this investigation he'd been lied to by most of the witnesses he'd interviewed and been left dangling with unanswered questions by a distressed young woman, a bank manager and now a coachman on his day off.

'Please return to Lady Tyndall,' he said, 'and tell her I need to speak to her urgently about the murder of David MacAdam. If she doesn't cooperate I'll come back here with a warrant for her arrest. I've already got plenty of evidence she's perverted the course of justice and hindered my investigation into this murder. I'll use it to get an arrest warrant if I need it.'

The young maid gasped and the butler's jaw dropped. Horrified, he hurried away with Lavender's reply.

'She's a right harridan,' Woods warned, grinning.

'And I'm a Principal Officer with the Bow Street Police Office,' Lavender replied.

The chair scraped noisily across the stone floor as the needlewoman rose to her feet and gathered up the gown in her arms. She looked flushed but the faint glimmer of a smile flitted around the edge of her lips. 'I'd like to be a fly on the wall in the room when 'e tells 'er what you've just said,' she said. 'I'll wager she bites 'is 'ead off.' She turned to pick up the overflowing basket of laundry but Woods was beside her in an instant.

'Let me help you with that, treacle,' he said. 'I can see you've had a busy mornin'.'

'Bless you, sir, but no, I can manage.' Smiling, the girl left the room.

The elderly butler looked pale and ill when he returned. 'Follow me,' he said.

He led Lavender and Woods into the light and spacious hallway of the house and steered them towards a small antechamber. A low murmur of female chatter and laughter and the clink of teacups and saucers emanated from the partially open drawing-room door.

Lady Tyndall waited for them on a high-backed chair. Stiff-backed and rigid, she glared at them coldly through her tortoiseshell lorgnette. The butler remained in attendance by the door.

'Well, if it isn't Detective Stephen Lavender and his grubby little constable.'

Lavender clenched his jaw together and made a small formal bow. He felt Woods stiffen beside him.

'And look at the state of you, Lavender!' she snarled. 'Unshaven! You're nearly as bad as he!'

Lavender resisted the urge to run his hand over his stubble and met her ice-cold glare with one of his own. 'Yes, I didn't have time to shave. Unfortunately, I was dragged out of my bed at an ungodly hour this morning to deal with another development in this case. A case, I may add, that I would have solved a lot quicker if you'd been honest with Constable Woods about your intimate relationship with David MacAdam.'

She didn't flinch but Woods gave him a quick sideways glance of surprise. 'I'd heard such wonderful reports about the smart Bow Street officers,' the woman continued. 'The pair of you are a disappointment.'

'You like smart, well-dressed men like MacAdam, don't you, Lady Tyndall?' Woods asked, taking his cue from Lavender's more strident attitude. 'And you liked MacAdam – even though you told me you barely knew the man.'

She shrugged. 'My friendship with the late Mr MacAdam was none of your business and bore no relevance to his murder or your case.'

'I'll decide what's relevant and what's not,' Lavender said firmly. The butler shuffled uncomfortably behind him.

'I've not perverted the course of justice or hindered your investigation, as you so rudely claim.'

'You knew MacAdam had been out in your carriage on the evening of his death but you failed to mention it to Constable Woods. That, madam, is obstructing justice.'

She shrugged her shoulders and gave a small laugh. 'It slipped my mind.'

'So, what was the nature of your relationship with the dead man?' Lavender asked sharply. 'I'm sure most of London, especially the newspapers, would love to know.'

A small smile curled at the edge of her wrinkled mouth. 'Don't try to browbeat me, Detective; I can assure you it won't work. You already know about my little arrangement with Mr MacAdam. I believe Louisa Fitzgerald opened her big blabbermouth and explained everything to you yesterday.'

'What arrangement is that?'

'It's very simple. I like to take tea at the better hotels in the city and sometimes I would ask Mr MacAdam to join me, that's all. There's nothing outrageous in this. Absolutely nothing to interest the tattling gossips.'

Lavender laughed. 'You paid MacAdam a regular monthly income and loaned him your carriage, like he was your paramour. Excuse my scepticism, Lady Tyndall, but I think there was more to your relationship than you claim.'

Her grey ringlets quivered as she gave a short, cold laugh. 'Then you're wrong. It was friendship, companionship – that's all.'

'Why did you pay MacAdam money?' Woods asked.

'He'd left his employment and struggled for money. I'm a generous woman, Constable, I like to help my friends.'

'To the tune of twenty pounds a month?' Lavender intervened. 'That's excessively generous of you, madam.'

'I'm excessively rich.'

She was matching them phrase for phrase, batting their questions back like they were involved in a tennis rally. Lavender decided to change tack.

'Did you visit MacAdam's corpse with your maid at Bow Street yesterday morning?'

'I did not.' Nothing. No response. He switched subject again.

'How did you feel about MacAdam's relationship with Miss Howard?'

This time she gave a small, almost imperceptible flinch at the sound of the young girl's name. 'I didn't care about her.'

'Didn't you?'

'Of course not. That's why I was quite happy to loan him my carriage when he went to visit her. Have we finished now, Detective? I have guests waiting.'

'Just one last question, madam. Where were you on the night of MacAdam's murder?'

'Ha!' she laughed. 'So, I'm to be accused of his murder now, am I? Dear me, I thought better of you, Lavender.' She leaned forward, snarling. Spittle flew out of her mouth. 'I'm sure your grubby little constable here has already told you. I was tucked up in my bed by nine o'clock – like the rest of my household.'

She rose angrily to her feet and smoothed down her dark gown. 'This interview is over, Detective. I shall contact Magistrate Read when my guests have left and inform him of your insolence and bullying.'

'I'm sure you will.'

'Your attitude is intolerable.'

'And so, madam, is yours.' Lavender gave a curt bow, turned and strode out of the door, which the shocked butler only just managed to open in time.

◆ ◆ ◆

'I take back what I said about you yesterday!' Woods burst out laughing as they went to retrieve their horses. 'You're more forceful than that reporter, Dowling, when you want to be.'

Lavender just shook his head. The encounter with her ladyship had left him drained. He needed to think. They left the dark back alleyway and walked the animals out into the sunshine on Park Lane.

'Do you really think that old harridan murdered MacAdam?'

'I don't know. We don't have any evidence linking her to the crime but Magdalena warned me not to dismiss these old women lightly. Lady Tyndall had the opportunity to kill him. She was one of the few people, maybe the only person, who knew where MacAdam was that evening – and where and when he would return.'

'Ike Rawlings had been stalkin' MacAdam, too, don't forget. He knew where MacAdam was that night.'

Lavender's mind was still on his recent encounter with Lady Tyndall. 'Personally, I don't believe that nonsense about her generosity. She strikes me as the kind of woman who might try to *buy* herself a man and use the promise of money to bind him to her.'

'Oooh, that's scary,' Woods said. 'Do you think she might have been jealous of his courtship with Miss Howard?'

'Yes. And I think she's capable of great anger and passion.'

'But why loan him her carriage to visit her rival? It don't make sense.'

'Perhaps she didn't know where he went. Maybe he lied to her.' Lavender lifted his foot to the stirrup and swung up into the saddle. 'We'll talk to her coachman tomorrow when we return from Essex – and it won't hurt to seek out her maid and ask her a few questions, too. But right now, we have to take David MacAdam home to Chelmsford.'

It always helped talking things through with Ned, but Lavender knew he'd wandered off into the realm of speculation about Lady Tyndall. The woman was probably one of the most unpleasant creatures he'd ever met, but that didn't make her a murderer. They still didn't know where MacAdam had been stabbed and they didn't have a murder weapon. Without that – and some witnesses to the crime – he would struggle to bring this case to a conclusion.

It was a pity. He'd hoped to be further along with solving this mystery by now. He preferred to work on one case at a time but now the exhumation loomed and he had an ominous feeling that by dawn tomorrow he would have another murder to solve.

Heaven knew what gruesome horrors the exhumation would reveal.

Chapter Twenty-Eight

L avender sent Woods ahead to Bow Street while he called home to have a shave and collect his bag for his stay in Chelmsford. When he arrived back in the stable yard, Woods, Eddie and the ostlers had already loaded MacAdam's coffin on to the back of a wagon and hitched two chestnut horses between the shafts.

Oswald Grey stood with Woods beside the impatient animals. 'Ah, Lavender, I'm glad you're back. I've a message for you from Mr Howard on Bruton Street.'

Lavender swung out of the saddle and handed the reins of his mare to Eddie, who led her inside the stable. 'Has he had any success tracing the member of his household who assisted the burglar?'

'It appears not. He's interviewed all of his servants and made no progress. He requests your assistance when you return from Chelmsford.'

Lavender frowned. 'Damn it. I knew I should have interviewed them myself. Have we arrested Billy Summersgill?'

Grey's long nose sniffed with disapproval. 'I've told you before there's no need to curse, Detective. No, our officers came back without the villain Summersgill. He'd left home early to meet with a customer apparently. We'll try again tonight.'

'Let's hope Billy's meetin' isn't with his fence,' Woods growled, 'or the Howards may never see that ring again.'

'I've some good news though, Lavender,' Grey said. 'I've received a message from a Lady Louisa Fitzgerald. She's prepared to put up a fifty-pound reward for the capture of the murderer of David MacAdam.'

'Thank you, that is good news,' Lavender said. 'The offer of a reward may loosen some tongues.'

'In fact,' Grey continued, 'I've had a busy morning at the desk dealing with your cases. I've already been visited by four journalists who want to know more about the MacAdam case and the exhumation. I'm quite exhausted with fending them off and have come out here for a moment's reprieve, away from their incessant questions.'

Lavender smiled. 'I'm grateful for all your hard work, Mr Grey. Thank you.'

'And I've also had an unusual complaint from a Mr Thaddeus Thornton to deal with.'

'I don't know him.'

'He's the pieman in Covent Garden. A very angry pieman. Allegedly, this morning two of our officers insulted his pastry. You don't know anything about this, do you?'

'I'll fetch a tarpaulin to cover this coffin.' Woods turned on his heel and went into the stable.

'No,' Lavender stuttered. 'How – how bizarre!'

Grey's eyes followed Woods' broad back as it disappeared. 'Yes, that's what I thought. Very bizarre. I can do without nonsense like this, Lavender. Bow Street is a place of serious business – not high jinks and japes. We've a respectable reputation to maintain. Anyway, I won't detain you any longer. I can see you and Constable Woods are keen to go and dig up your dead body. I'll leave you to it.'

It took them a while to negotiate the traffic of London and leave the bustling city. They joined a long line of hackney carriages and wagons and found themselves behind a coal merchant when they crawled up

Cornhill. The incline caused the dusty coal to shift and slither on the wagon and lumps fell on to the road. A pair of barefoot children darted out into the street to retrieve it, coming perilously close to their horses' hooves. Woods cursed as he jerked back on the reins.

They picked up speed once they left the city. Woods urged the horses into a trot, which ate away the miles. They flew through the small hamlets that lined the road, scattering squawking hens as they went.

Woods glanced over his shoulder at the coffin beneath the tarpaulin. 'He's the quietest passenger we've ever had,' he joked.

Lavender smiled and felt himself relax. The market gardens that fed the city had given way to gently rolling countryside and a broad common of vivid green pasture dotted with a herd of peacefully grazing cows. A bird of prey soared in leisurely circles above their heads. 'I don't think we'll have any complaints from him about your driving.' The breeze rushed by his face and he pulled his hat down over a flapping strand of dark hair.

Woods raised an eyebrow. 'Well, he'll be the only one who isn't complainin' about us today, by the sound of it. Did you get chance to warn Magistrate Read we've upset Lady Tyndall?'

'No.'

Woods held the chestnuts to a steady pace as they wound up a gradual incline. The twisting road was suddenly thrown into shade by a row of poplars. Lavender yawned. It had been an early start and the last few days had been exhausting.

'That were good news about the reward from Lady Louisa,' Woods said. 'It looks like she wants this murderin' cove found as much as we do. I guess we can take her off the list of suspects.'

Lavender shrugged. 'Not necessarily. Do you remember the Travis case?'

'Ah, yes – I'd forgotten about him. Nasty piece of work, he were.'

Three years previously, Lavender had travelled to Birmingham at the request and expense of a wealthy landowner who wanted an officer from Bow Street to help the local constables solve the murder of his brother. Like Lady Louisa Fitzgerald, Travis had also offered a generous reward for the capture of the villain. It didn't take Lavender long to realise that Travis had, in fact, killed his own brother. A braggart and an overconfident liar, the landowner also had a low opinion of police constables and a high opinion of his own guile and cunning. He thought he could deceive everyone. Travis was still professing his innocence when he mounted the steps of the gallows after his conviction for murder.

'He tried to throw you off the scent by offerin' that reward,' Woods said, 'but he underestimated you.' He paused for a moment, then asked: 'Do you think Lady Louisa murdered MacAdam, then?'

Lavender shook his head. 'I have to keep an open mind but, no. Stabbing's not in her nature. If Lady Louisa Fitzgerald wanted someone dead, she'd just let her ruddy hounds eat them alive.'

Woods laughed and the two men lapsed into companionable silence. The steady, rhythmic clip-clop of the hoof beats on the well-maintained road, the soft churning of the wheels and the warmth of the sun made Lavender sleepy. He lowered his chin to his chest and closed his eyes for a moment. Beside him, he felt Woods' shoulders relax and sink down into his blue greatcoat.

It was the shrill cry of a crow overhead that jerked Lavender back awake. He glanced at Woods and realised with shock that his white-faced constable had lost consciousness again. He was nodding forward with the reins slack in his hand.

The wagon jolted as the left-hand horse led its fellow into a field to graze. The vehicle tilted sharply as it left the road. Its wooden joints strained and gave an unearthly groan as it lunged towards a ditch. Behind them, the coffin slid and crashed into the side of the cart with a thud and a curious metallic clang.

Lavender yelled. He grabbed Woods with one hand to stop him toppling to the ground. With the other, he seized the reins and hauled on the horses. It wasn't enough – he needed the strength of both hands. He let go of Woods and pulled back the animals with all his might. Woods jerked awake, regained his balance and reached out to help. Together they hauled the horses and the vehicle safely back on the road.

'You ruddy saphead!' Lavender yelled. 'We're supposed to bury MacAdam in St Mary's – not drop him in a roadside ditch!'

'Sorry, sir! Sorry!'

'You swooned again, you saphead!'

Woods grimaced as Lavender uttered a string of insults. 'Right, that's it. This stupid fasting has gone on long enough. We'll stop at the next tavern and you'll eat something before you kill us both with this fainting.'

Woods ignored him and leapt down on to the dusty road. He went to calm the wide-eyed and snorting horses.

Still cursing his constable, Lavender also clambered down. He went to the back of the wagon, bent down and peered beneath at the metal axle. Something metal had definitely broken, he'd heard it. But the axle seemed intact. He walked round the other side and checked again. Nothing. He reached inside the vehicle and fingered the heavy metal chains used to raise and lower the tailgate. *Had it been their rattle he'd heard?*

His heart rate was calming now. His ears strained against the other noises in that quiet lane: the stamping of the horses, the gentle lowing of a cow and the wind swishing gently through the sweet-scented grass. *What was it he'd heard?*

Woods joined him. 'What's the matter?'

'Nothing. I thought I heard something unusual, that's all. But everything seems fine – although I can give you no thanks for that!'

They climbed back on to the vehicle and Lavender snatched the reins out of Woods' hands. 'I'll drive.'

Woods grinned. 'I'll be fine, sir. And there's no need to stop at a tavern for food.'

Lavender shook the reins angrily and the horses jerked forward. 'I'm serious, Ned. This nonsense about starving yourself has to stop before you do yourself, or someone else, an injury.'

Woods' grin broadened. 'I'll be fine,' he reiterated.

'You might be,' Lavender snapped, 'but what about the rest of us who have to live with you?'

Night had wrapped its dark cloak around Chelmsford when they finally crossed the arched stone bridge over the River Can. Dusty and weary, they drew up in front of the white brick arches of the new Shire Hall in Chelmsford. There was a small morgue in the corner of the building and they'd arranged to leave the coffin there overnight; Magistrate Read had deemed it inappropriate to send it back to Mrs MacAdam and had asked his colleague, Chelmsford's town magistrate, Thomas Nulty, to oversee the exhumation.

The morgue attendant and Magistrate Nulty came out to greet them as they dismounted stiffly from the vehicle. Nulty, a thin man with straggly grey hair in a dark coat, looked nervous when he shook Lavender's hand. 'Welcome, Detective – and Constable Woods. Magistrate Read has apprised me of all the details of this dreadful case. My, this is a sobering business. Very irregular, very irregular indeed.'

The lamp-lighter was busy at his work on the far side of the square but the town was nearly deserted. A few people scurried past on their way home. One or two glanced curiously at Lavender, Woods and the burly morgue attendant when they pulled back the tarpaulin and lifted MacAdam's coffin down from the cart. Awkwardly, they manoeuvred it through the doors towards the morgue.

Woods stumbled and lost his grip as they approached the large stone slab in the centre of the poorly lit and chilly room. Lavender and the attendant struggled to hold the coffin, which crashed down on to the surface of the slab.

'Oops! Sorry!' Woods said.

Lavender stood back to stare at the cheap wooden box. He'd heard it again. The faint but unmistakable clang and roll of something metal.

'Have you got a crowbar?' he asked the attendant. 'Or something to prise off the lid?'

'I don't think we'll have damaged him,' Woods joked.

Nulty frowned. 'What's amiss, Lavender?'

The attendant went to a pile of tools in the corner of the room and came back with a metal spike. 'Will this do, sir?'

'Yes, help me to get off the lid. I think there's something in there.'

The smile vanished from Woods' face and Magistrate Nulty shuffled nervously from one foot to the other. 'This is most irregular, Detective, most irregular.'

Lavender ignored him and, with help from the attendant, prised open the coffin lid. It screeched and groaned in protest as the nails were ripped out.

The sickly smell of MacAdam's decomposing flesh filled the room. The men fumbled in their pockets for their handkerchiefs and covered their faces. Trying not to look at the dead man's pale, waxy face and lifeless body, he peered over the edge.

In the corner of the coffin by MacAdam's boot lay a small hand-held tool. A thin, curved knife with a wooden handle. The surface of the four-inch blade was stained dark with blood.

He picked it up and held it up to the light. 'Well, what have we here?' he said slowly.

'Heaven and hell! That's the missin' farrier's knife,' Woods said.

'These look like bloodstains on the blade. Are they human or equine, I wonder?'

'They're not from the horses. Any blacksmith who draws blood on a horse while slicin' away the frog and the sole has done a poor job.'

'What is this all about, Lavender?' The magistrate was desperately trying not to retch into his own handkerchief. 'Why is that knife in the coffin?'

'I think we've just found the weapon that killed David MacAdam,' Lavender said slowly, 'but how the devil it came to be in his coffin alongside his corpse, I've no idea.'

Chapter Twenty-Nine

For a moment, the four men stood silently in the dim light of the stinking morgue and stared at the knife.

Then Lavender made a grim decision. 'Ned, go to The Great Black Boy coaching inn and find out if Sir Richard Allison has arrived yet. Tell him I think I've found the murder weapon and ask him to come straight here as a matter of urgency. I need his help; there's something only he can confirm.'

Woods nodded and left.

With the attendant's help, Lavender slid the lid back over the coffin to try to contain some of the smell. 'Let's step outside and wait for Sir Richard in the fresh air,' he suggested.

Magistrate Nulty hastily agreed and led the way.

Outside, the stench of market animals and their excrement still hung in the air but this was better and more wholesome than the smell of David MacAdam. Lavender breathed heavily and leaned back against the wall of the Shire Hall. The three men stood in grim silence while they waited. Wisps of straw rustled across the cobbles in the light breeze.

How the devil had that knife ended up in the coffin?

It was inconceivable that the undertakers had found it in MacAdam's chamber and just popped it in with the corpse. Someone else must have put it there later and had probably hidden it beneath the body, confident it wouldn't be found. After all, who went rummaging around in an open coffin? But who had done this? The coffin lid hadn't been nailed down until after Mrs MacAdam and Ike Rawlings had visited Bow Street.

Was it them? Had he missed something during those brief moments when Mrs MacAdam had identified her dead husband?

The only other people who'd had access to the open coffin were Mrs Palmer and the two mysterious women who'd visited MacAdam to pay their last respects. But Mrs Palmer had no motive to kill her lodger. What had he missed?

He turned to Magistrate Nulty. 'Can you draw up an arrest warrant for Isaac Rawlings, the stone carrier who lives down by the riverside?'

'What, Ike Rawlings?' Nulty was genuinely surprised. 'He's a respected member of our community – a regular churchgoer at St Mary's and a member of the Temperance Committee.'

'He's also the main suspect in my murder inquiry – and he had an opportunity yesterday to place this knife in the coffin. We suspect he knew MacAdam was still alive and he's about to marry MacAdam's widow – so he has a motive to kill him. I want Rawlings in a cell where I can question him further about his movements on the day of the murder.'

'Very well, Detective. I'll do it now.' Magistrate Nulty hurried back inside and went upstairs to his office.

Four figures strode out of the shadows towards them: Woods, Sir Richard and two of the surgeon's interns. Lavender wasn't surprised Sir Richard had brought some of his students with him. An exhumation was a rare occurrence. It appeared that it wasn't only the newspapers who were interested in those grisly remains in the coffin in St Mary's churchyard. It would be crowded at the graveside in the morning.

Sir Richard was in an excellent mood. 'Lavender! I understand you've found something of interest. You remember young Kingsley and Hodge, my students?'

Lavender nodded, shook the men's hands and led everyone back into the morgue. The attendant removed the coffin lid. The three doctors seemed immune to the smell emanating from MacAdam's corpse.

Lavender held out the farrier's knife. 'I need you to confirm that this is the knife that killed David MacAdam.'

Sir Richard's sharp eyes took in the situation at once. He asked the morgue attendant for more light. Then he crossed his arms and turned to his students. 'So, Kingsley, how will you confirm Detective Lavender's suspicions?'

The young man's long fringe fell over his face when he stared down at the corpse. Lavender felt Woods shuffling uncomfortably beside him. Sir Richard was notorious for bullying his students.

Kingsley pushed back his fringe and cleared his throat nervously. 'Should we see if it fits?'

'Fits what?' Sir Richard asked sharply.

'The wound?'

'Excellent idea, Kingsley. Get on with it then. Help him, Hodge.'

The young doctors stepped forward and began to remove the dead man's clothing. They unbuttoned his coat and pulled up his shirt but when Kingsley unbuttoned the flap on MacAdam's breeches, Sir Richard exploded.

'Oh, for heaven's sake, man! Why are you taking off his breeches? This corpse was stabbed in the liver. Do you expect to find it down there?'

'What on earth is happening?' asked a muffled voice behind Lavender. Magistrate Nulty had returned with the warrant for Ike Rawlings' arrest. In his other hand, he held his handkerchief over his nose and mouth. His eyes were watering again.

Lavender took the warrant from him and pocketed it. 'This is Sir Richard Allison and his students. They're confirming this is the knife used to kill MacAdam.'

The morgue attendant arrived with another lamp and held it above the coffin, illuminating the decaying flesh on the corpse and the wound in the abdomen. Kingsley gently inserted the knife into the gash in MacAdam's stomach. 'This is most irregular! Most irregular!' Nulty wailed.

'But most necessary.' Sir Richard beamed with satisfaction. 'Well, Kingsley?'

'It slid in easily and fits, there's no resistance. I can confirm, sir, that this was the murder weapon.'

'Excellent.' Sir Richard turned to Lavender. 'There you go, Detective. Your murder weapon is confirmed by three of London's finest doctors. All you need to do now is find the hand that wielded the knife.'

'Thank you, Sir Richard.'

The surgeon pointed to the morgue attendant. 'You, man – you can re-dress the corpse. We'll return to our supper at The Great Black Boy tavern now. I can heartily recommend their mutton stew, Constable,' he added with a knowing glance at Woods.

'I'm grateful for your help, sir,' Lavender said. How the surgeon could even think about food while such a noxious stench swamped his nostrils was beyond him.

Suddenly, Woods emitted a loud and unearthly groan. His knees gave way and he slithered to the floor in an ungainly heap.

'Ned!'

'Good grief!' exclaimed Magistrate Nulty. 'Is your constable unwell?'

A broad grin lit up Sir Richard's face as he observed Woods' prostrate form. 'Is he still refusing to eat?'

'Yes.' Lavender moved towards Woods but Sir Richard held out his arm to stop him.

'Then it's time for me to fulfil my part of our bargain.' The surgeon's eyes glimmered with amusement in his smiling face. 'Leave this with me.'

'What are you going to do?' Lavender asked in alarm.

Sir Richard ignored him. 'Kingsley? Hodge? Take an arm each and hold the constable down firmly.' The two young men dropped to their haunches and grabbed Woods by the arms, pinning him to the floor.

Grinning wider, Sir Richard turned to his medical bag and extracted a large, curved knife that glinted evilly in the lamplight. 'This is my biggest,' he said with satisfaction.

Lavender watched with horror as Sir Richard, knife in hand, sat down on Woods' legs and straddled him. The flickering lamplight cast a grotesque shadow on the tiled wall of the morgue.

'What on earth do you plan to do with that?' Every instinct in Lavender's brain screamed at him to go to Ned's assistance but he was rooted to the spot.

Sir Richard spoke over his shoulder. 'Sometimes we doctors have to treat our patients' minds – rather than their bodies. And playing to their greatest fears can be part of this.'

Sir Richard slapped Woods' face sharply to bring him round. Woods blinked groggily, then his eyes opened wide with horror. He screamed. A loud primeval scream of terror that tore at Lavender's heart. Woods struggled and tried to throw off the three men, but failed. Three days without food had taken its toll on Woods' legendary strength.

Sir Richard laughed and leered over him further, brandishing his vicious knife. 'Damn it! You've come round, Constable,' he drawled slowly. 'We thought you were dead, didn't we, Kingsley? Lavender tells me you've been starving yourself. What a pity you've recovered. I wanted to extract your shrivelled organs to pickle in jars.'

'Blast your eyes! You scraggin' body-snatcher!' Woods struggled in vain against his captors.

Sir Richard laughed again. 'Do you know what happens to the bodily organs when they're starved of food, Woods? They wither, bleed – and die. The kidneys, the liver, the heart – everything shrivels away to nothing.'

To Lavender's horror, Sir Richard tapped the hilt of his knife on Woods' crotch. Woods winced and every man in the room held his breath. 'Even the testicles shrivel away, bleed and die when starved of food.' Sir Richard paused for dramatic effect. 'Shrivelled testicles make fascinating specimens for surgeons.'

'Gerroff me, you evil bastard!'

'Very well – I'll wait a few more hours until you faint again.' Sir Richard winked at Woods. 'Then I'll be back.' He climbed to his feet, still holding the knife. 'Release him.'

The two young doctors moved back and Lavender held his breath.

Woods leapt to his feet, his face purple with fury. For one awful moment, Lavender thought his stricken constable might hit Sir Richard. Then Woods turned and pelted out of the door, swearing.

'This is most . . . most irregular,' murmured the shocked magistrate from behind his handkerchief. 'You gentlemen from London have most irregular methods.'

Sir Richard laughed, replaced his gruesome knife in his bag and brushed down his coat. 'That's my debt discharged to you, Lavender, I think?'

Lavender nodded, swallowed and finally found his voice. 'I thought you intended to *talk* to him – not butcher him!'

Sir Richard shrugged. 'Did it work when you and his wife *talked* to him?'

Lavender shook his head.

'Then the threat of butchering was needed.'

Lavender glanced desperately at the door. 'I need to go after him – and quickly. God knows where he'll be.'

'He'll be on his third bowl of mutton stew in The Great Black Boy by now, I should think,' Sir Richard said, smirking.

Sir Richard was right. Lavender found Woods glowering in the bar in the tap room of the coaching inn, with a tankard of ale in his large, shaking hand.

'Don't you speak to me!' he yelled when Lavender approached. 'You stood by while that blasted sawbones tried to cut off my nutmegs. You're no friend of mine!' Ale slopped down from the tankard on to his coat as he spoke. Other customers glanced up from their card games in alarm at his tone.

Lavender nodded and retreated to a far corner of the warm, smoke-filled tavern. He sat at a vacant table, took a tankard of ale from a barmaid in a mob cap and waited and watched.

Woods ordered another ale, which he downed more slowly, pausing occasionally to belch and wipe his mouth on the back of his coat sleeve.

Then a barmaid appeared by Woods' side, carrying a huge bowl of steaming stew and a platter containing half a loaf of freshly baked bread and a gleaming pat of yellow butter. Woods glanced around for a vacant seat but there weren't any, apart from at Lavender's table.

Lavender raised his hand and waved him across. Woods hesitated, glowering, then reluctantly walked towards him. The barmaid followed him with his food.

Woods slumped down into the seat opposite Lavender, gave him a withering look and picked up his spoon.

The meaty aroma of the mutton wafted across the table and made Lavender's own stomach rumble. He asked the young girl to bring him a bowl, then sat back and watched with satisfaction while his constable shovelled spoon after spoon of the delicious-smelling stew into his mouth. 'I wouldn't have let him hurt you,' he said gently.

Woods just glared across the table. He tore off a huge chunk of the loaf and rammed it into his mouth.

Lavender sipped his ale, repressed his smile and waited. His own food arrived quickly. He paid the barmaid for both meals and she disappeared.

Woods jabbed his spoon angrily in Lavender's direction. 'You should have arrested him! That's assault, that is. I were assaulted.' A shower of breadcrumbs flew from his mouth when he spoke.

'He didn't harm you.'

'Didn't harm me?' Woods yelled. 'I'm scarred for life now, I am. I'll never be able to look at my poor nutmegs again without seein' them floatin' in vinegar in a jar on his desk!'

His outburst brought sympathetic gasps from the group of farmers at the next table.

Woods threw down his spoon with a clatter on to the table and resumed his assault on the loaf of bread. He smeared it generously with a knife full of soft butter.

Lavender lowered his face over his bowl to hide his smile. 'He didn't harm you,' he repeated quietly.

'Ha! You're the finest detective in England – but you choose to turn a blind eye to a blatant injustice handed out to your closest friend? Where's the reason – where's the loyalty – in that?' A trickle of butter slid down his grey-stubbled chin.

'And where's the reason in an intelligent man starving himself to death until he faints and stumbles all over the place?' Lavender asked quietly, conscious of the curious glances of their neighbours. 'Come on, Ned. Sir Richard's methods may be brutal and, er, a bit unorthodox – but they usually get a result. He's probably just saved your life – again.'

Now the knife was jabbed menacingly in Lavender's direction – not a finger. 'Don't you even mention the incident last May! The damned fellow only took the pistol shot out of my shoulder so he could hover around my house in case I snuffed it. He was after my poor nutmegs back then.'

Lavender repressed another smile and ate his food in silence. Sir Richard had been right about something else too: the stew was delicious.

A satisfied belch from the other side of the table announced Woods had finished his meal. 'That were good, that,' he said grudgingly. Some natural colour had returned to his cheeks and there was a twinkle in his eyes again. 'Besides which, if I hadn't stumbled with that damned coffin – or driven the wagon off the road – you wouldn't have heard the knife rattlin' around inside it. I may be stubborn and stupid sometimes – but I reckon it's a useful kind of stupid.'

Relieved the conversation had finally turned away from Sir Richard's extraordinary behaviour, Lavender smiled and nodded. 'Yes, that was a stroke of luck.'

'You've got sharp ears next to that sharp mind of yours.'

Lavender brushed away the compliment and sipped his ale thoughtfully. 'It's still a mystery though, Ned, isn't it – the murder weapon in the coffin.'

'Who do you reckon put it there?'

'The murderer,' Lavender replied shortly.

'Then it were a brilliant ruse to hide the weapon beneath the dead man. Who'd have thought to search in the coffin? It's most . . . most irregular.'

Lavender smiled. Woods was regaining his good humour. His imitation of Magistrate Nulty was unmistakable. 'Irregular, yes,' Lavender said, 'but maybe it's not that clever. Not if the knife is found. It narrows down our field of suspects to those who had access to the coffin before it was sealed.'

'The morgue at Bow Street's often unlocked,' Woods pointed out.

'Yes, but there's always stable hands and officers in the yard and everyone's more alert now since Nidar's gang dumped the body of Baron Danvers on our doorstep last spring. Not many people had access to David MacAdam's body after he was found dead.'

'True,' Woods said. 'Our Eddie's always on the lookout for strangers lurkin' in the stable yard.'

'Did you see anything unusual when Mrs MacAdam and Ike Rawlings were in the morgue at Bow Street?'

'What? You think one of them may have slid the knife in the coffin while we were stood next to them?' Woods thought for a moment, then shook his head. 'It's always dark in that room but I didn't see any sleight of hand.'

Lavender downed the last of his ale and pushed back his wooden chair. It scraped across the flagstones. 'Are you ready?'

Woods glanced longingly at his empty bowl. 'What for? I'd thought to have another one of these.'

'That, Ned, is how you got into this mess in the first place. From now on, it's one bowl of stew at a time for you – like a normal man.'

Woods sighed, pushed his chair away from the table and stood up. 'Where are we goin'?'

'I think it's time we had another word with Ike Rawlings. And I want to see how Mrs MacAdam reacts to the news that Rawlings knew her husband was still alive.'

'Do you think he killed MacAdam?'

'I don't know,' Lavender replied honestly, 'but I think a night in the town gaol may make him more talkative – and I have a warrant for his arrest in my pocket.'

Chapter Thirty

Mrs MacAdam bristled with annoyance when she found Lavender and Woods on her doorstep. Reluctantly, she let them into the cottage. 'I don't want to 'ear any more nonsense about Ike killin' Davy,' she said.

Rawlings was sitting by her fireside, smoking his pipe. The lanky man stood up when they entered. There was no sign of the two young boys. 'Good evenin', officers,' he said. 'Do you 'ave some news for us?'

'Not yet,' Lavender said, 'but we need to ask you some more questions. Firstly, do either of you remember if Mr Collins, the man who brought you the coffin in June, had a prominent wart on his chin?'

Rawlings and Mrs MacAdam glanced at each other, bewildered, then shook their heads.

'I can't remember much about 'im at all, except 'e were young and dark,' Mrs MacAdam said. Rawlings sucked on his pipe and nodded agreement.

'Would you recognise him if you saw him again?' Lavender asked.

Mrs MacAdam shrugged her shoulders and raised her hands in confusion. 'I don't know. I were mightily upset to 'ave my 'usband brought 'ome in a coffin.'

'I might know 'im again,' Rawlings said.

Lavender cleared his throat. 'I also need to ask if either of you recognise this.' He pulled the bloodstained farrier's knife out of his pocket and held it out.

Neither Rawlings nor Mrs MacAdam flinched. They just stared quietly at the weapon in his hand.

'Is that what killed Davy?' Rawlings asked.

Mrs MacAdam frowned. 'Why should *we* recognise it?'

'Because you've been lying to me,' Lavender replied firmly. 'Or at least you – Rawlings – have done so.'

Rawlings shuffled uncomfortably and his eyes dropped beneath Lavender's stare.

Mrs MacAdam pulled herself up to her full height and put her hands on her hips. ''Ow so? What you accusin' 'im of now?'

Lavender ignored her. 'You didn't go straight home after you delivered your cargo to Eggerton's on the day of the murder, did you, Rawlings?'

'No, I . . . I 'ad an errand to run.'

'In the west end of the city?' Woods asked.

'I can't recall.'

'So how is it we've got a witness who saw you in your wagon outside MacAdam's lodgings on the day of the murder?' Lavender asked.

Silence. Rawlings nodded and hung his shaggy head in shame.

Mrs MacAdam slumped down into a chair in shock. 'Did you . . . Ike, did you know Davy were still alive?'

Pink spots appeared on Rawlings' high cheekbones beneath his beard. 'Winnie . . . I . . .'

Mrs MacAdam's voice rose in distress. 'You knew 'e were still alive? But you still asked me to wed you! Oh, Ike – 'ow could you?'

'I didn't know what to do, Winnie,' Rawlings said in desperation. 'I were so shocked to see 'im drive past in that fancy black carriage wi' that young girl by 'is side.'

'Young girl!'

Rawlings dropped his voice to a mumble. 'Aye, 'e were with a chit of a girl.'

'Why the devil didn't you tell me?' She slammed her fist down on the arm of her chair. 'Is every man I ever meet set to betray me?'

They heard movement from the attic above. 'Are you all right, Ma?' asked a nervous young voice from the top of the wooden ladder.

Lavender glanced up and saw the pale faces of Mrs MacAdam's young sons staring down at them. 'I think we'll take this conversation to the town gaol.'

He pulled out the warrant from his pocket and showed it to the shocked couple. 'Isaac Rawlings, by the power vested in me by His Royal Highness, the Prince Regent, in the name of and on behalf of His Majesty King George III, I arrest you on suspicion of the murder of David MacAdam.'

Woods pulled out his handcuffs and clamped them round the wrists of the stunned stone carrier. Mrs MacAdam's sobs and screams rang in their ears when they dragged Rawlings, stumbling, out of the house into the moonlight.

The dilapidated County Gaol of Essex was a crumbling fortress about three-quarters of a mile out of Chelmsford. Surrounded by a high brick wall, it had a platform over the entrance gateway where the condemned were publicly executed. The interior of the cramped compound was as bleak as the exterior and it was noisy. The low, ugly murmur of male voices, the yells of the insane and the screams of a woman prisoner suggested that the shared cells were overflowing ahead of the quarter sessions. Lavender and Woods pulled out their handkerchiefs to protect their noses from the overpowering stench of urine, faeces and unwashed bodies as they nudged Rawlings ahead of them.

Lavender showed his arrest warrant and his Bow Street tipstaff to one of the gaolers on duty. The man nodded and led them through a series of draughty and stone-flagged corridors to a small interview room. The iron keys on the ring dangling from his belt jangled when he walked.

The peeling walls and the rotten beams in the ceiling dripped with damp. The weak lantern on the table and the silver moonlight pouring through the high window failed to light or warm the cold, shadowy corners of the bleak cell.

Rawlings slumped down into a battered chair with his head bowed forward. He hadn't uttered a word since they dragged him out of the house. The gaoler stood behind him, waiting for further instruction from Lavender.

Lavender took Woods outside for a moment. 'What did you think of Mrs MacAdam's reaction?'

'It seemed real enough to me. I don't think the poor woman knew anythin' about Rawlings' deception. Neither of them seemed to recognise the knife, either. If they did hide it in the coffin, I think they'd be more alarmed.'

Lavender gave a short nod. Woods had confirmed his own thoughts. Mrs MacAdam was no longer a suspect for the murder of her husband and the case against Ike Rawlings for the murder of MacAdam wasn't as strong as he'd like. There should have been more reaction when he produced the murder weapon. 'Let's see what he has to say for himself.'

They returned and sat down at the table opposite Rawlings. The silent gaoler shifted his weight from one foot to the other and his keys jangled again.

'You haven't been honest with us, Rawlings,' Lavender said. 'You knew all along David MacAdam was still alive and had faked his own death.'

Rawlings' shaggy head nodded sadly. He raised his eyes to Lavender's. He looked wretched. 'Yes. Winnie will never forgive me for that.'

'It's not Mrs MacAdam you need to be worried about right now, fellah,' Woods said. 'You're facin' a charge of murder. If you're found guilty, you'll be hanged.'

'Tell us how you found out MacAdam was still alive,' Lavender said.

'It were like I said at the 'ouse.' Rawlings' voice dropped with despair. 'I were in my wagon and I saw 'im drivin' past in a fancy black carriage wi' a young girl. I saw it clear as day.'

'What did you do?'

'I pulled out into the traffic and followed 'im. I didn't believe it at first. I 'ad to make sure.'

Woods was sceptical. 'Are you tellin' us your creakin' old wagon managed to keep up with that flash phaeton?'

'The traffic were slow. No one were movin'. I followed them to 'er 'ouse near Berkeley Square. 'E 'elped 'er and the maid down from the carriage. 'E raised 'er 'and and kissed it then the women went inside. I knew by the look on 'er face the gal were sweet on 'im. 'E seemed right fond of 'er too. One of their fancy servants took the coach and 'orses and Davy walked 'ome.'

'Did you follow him back to Park Lane?'

'Aye, and I watched 'im go inside.'

'Didn't he see you?'

'I took care to stay back. 'E only 'ad eyes for the gal anyway.'

'When was this? Woods asked.

'About a month ago.'

Woods sat back in his chair and gave a short, unfriendly laugh. 'So you've known for a month MacAdam was still alive – but you never thought to tell his grievin' widow?'

Rawlings' handcuffs clanked as he twisted his large hands together in his lap. 'I didn't know what to do. I swear, Officer, I didn't know what to do. I wrestled wi' me conscience for weeks. I knew 'im and Winnie 'ad never been 'appy together. She wouldn't want 'im back.'

'And in the meantime, you'd decided you wanted Mrs MacAdam for yourself.'

Rawlings ignored Lavender's jibe and continued: 'I were mightily torn about what to do, Detective. It were like a paralysis 'ad set in my mind. I couldn't believe it were 'im. I kept goin' back to the 'ouse on Park Lane, wantin' to catch another glimpse of 'im to make sure I'd got it right.'

'Yes, we know,' Lavender said coldly. 'Our witness saw you there several times. You do realise, don't you, Rawlings, that faking a death is a criminal offence? If you'd reported MacAdam to the police he'd have been arrested and probably transported for his crime.'

'Yes – I know that. But 'ow would that 'ave 'elped poor Winnie?' Rawlings' tone became stronger as he defended the woman he loved. 'She'd 'ave still been bound to 'im by marriage while 'e were on the other side of the world. Without an 'usband to take care of 'er and the boys back in Chelmsford, they'd 'ave ended up in the workhouse – or worse.'

There was a short silence while Lavender and Woods digested Rawlings' words. The carrier was right. A few wives and families went out to New South Wales with their transported husbands, but most didn't. This cruel system of punishment devastated families even more so than the death penalty. At least after a villain was hanged, the widow was free to find another man to support her and her children. By faking his own death, MacAdam had done his wife a huge favour as well as himself; he'd released her from an unhappy union to marry again.

'So, you decided to become her new husband,' Woods said flatly.

Rawlings nodded. 'I've always been fond of Winnie – and she grew fond of me. But I thought I'd make it right wi' Davy.'

Lavender frowned. 'How so?'

'I decided to approach 'im.'

'You intended to confront him?'

'I were goin' to tell 'im I knew what 'e'd done – but that it were all right because I wanted to wed Winnie. I were goin' to tell 'im to stay away from Chelmsford then it would be all right. 'E could 'ave 'is life in London – and we'd 'ave ours in Essex.'

It was Lavender's turn to sit back in his chair, startled. 'That's complicity to fraud. You do realise, don't you, that makes you an accomplice to MacAdam's fraud?'

Rawlings nodded sadly. 'Well, maybe it would 'ave done if I'd done it – but I didn't. I never got chance to speak to 'im. I followed 'im for a couple of days but couldn't find the pluck to call out to 'im.'

'You lost your mettle, did you, fellah?'

Lavender heard the sympathy in Woods' voice. 'Were you following him on the day of his murder?' he asked.

'Aye. I intended to talk to 'im that day. A carriage turned up at Park Lane to take 'im to 'is sweetheart's in the evenin'. I followed it and waited. It were dark when 'e finally left and I could see by the way 'e stumbled down the steps 'e'd had a glass or two of strong drink. I followed the carriage back to the mews. I left my wagon on the main road, climbed down and waited in the shadows of the mews at the top of the road for 'im to walk back to 'is lodgin's. I were determined to speak to 'im that night.'

Lavender tensed and Woods held his breath beside him. 'What happened next?'

Rawlings shrugged. 'I didn't see 'im. The coachman backed the carriage into the coach 'ouse and took the 'orses into the stables.'

'Where was MacAdam?'

'I don't know. I must have missed 'im in the dark. Maybe 'e went 'ome a different way. When the coachman went up to 'is rooms above the coach 'ouse, I gave up and come back to Chelmsford, sorely disappointed. I went to London the next day but didn't try to see 'im again; I were too tired. The next thing I knew you were at the door of Winnie's cottage tellin' us 'e'd been murdered in his lodgin's.'

Lavender cleared his throat. 'But we didn't tell you MacAdam was murdered in his lodgings.' He paused to make sure his next words had maximum effect. 'He was stabbed on his way back from the mews to the house. He managed to stagger home and died later in his bedchamber.'

The colour drained away from Rawlings' face. 'You mean, the murderer were out there in the street wi' me and 'im?'

'Yes, Mr Rawlings, the murderer was out there on the street. The attack took place somewhere between the mews and his lodgings – in the exact same place you've just told us you waited for him in the shadows.'

The silence hung heavy in the room. Rawlings' Adam's apple moved painfully in his dry throat as he tried unsuccessfully to swallow. 'So that's why you think I killed 'im?'

'Do you blame us?' Lavender asked. 'You had a motive to kill him, the opportunity to do it – and now the knife that stabbed him has turned up in a coffin you stood next to yesterday morning. Someone tried to hide it in there.'

'I didn't do it.'

'It's not lookin' good for you, fellah,' Woods said. 'This is your last chance to tell us what happened. Think hard. Were there anyone else there? Did you see, or hear, anyone else?'

Rawlings shivered and the metal cuffs rattled. His tone became desperate. 'Apart from the coachman, I never saw anyone else. The mews were deserted apart from a couple of cats. There were a few lamps glimmerin' in the rooms above the stables and I 'eard a dog barkin' and a couple quarrellin' . . .'

'A couple quarrelling? You mean a man and a woman?'

'Aye, they were havin' a right spat – she sounded well vexed.'

Lavender hesitated. Many families lived in the accommodation above those stables and coach houses on the mews. It was a warm night. Windows may have been open and an argument would carry on the still air . . . 'Can you remember anything else?'

Rawlings put his head in his hands and shook it. 'Nothin'.'

Lavender pushed back his chair and picked up his gloves and hat. 'We'll leave it there for tonight, Rawlings. I need to speak to the coachman. I'll arrange with the gaolers to have you transported to Bow Street for further questioning before I charge you. The journey will give you time to reflect on your predicament.'

Suddenly Rawlings became agitated and tried to rise to his feet. The gaoler shoved him roughly back down on the chair. 'I didn't do it! I'm no murderer! I just wanted to talk to Davy – not kill 'im!'

'If I were you, fellah,' Woods said gently when they turned to leave, 'I'd forget hirin' a parson to wed you to Mrs MacAdam and think about hirin' a solicitor for your defence instead.'

Chapter Thirty-One

L avender and Woods strode in grim silence through the sleeping town towards St Mary's. The medieval tower of the church was barely visible against the black sky. They'd consumed a hasty bowl of porridge before they left the tavern but the food did little to alleviate the churning of Lavender's stomach. He shivered and pulled his hat firmly down over his head against the chill. It had rained overnight and their boots splashed through invisible puddles on the dark streets.

A small group of men with lanterns waited for them by MacAdam's grave, surrounded by the dark shape of crumbling tombstones leaning drunkenly amongst the nettles. The flickering light cast grotesque shadows on to the flint-stone walls of the silent church – the demonic outline of those about to disturb the dead.

Lavender winced when the screeching of the rusty gate shattered the eerie silence of the night. Magistrate Nulty, Sir Richard and his students greeted them in hushed tones. They fell silent beneath the dripping yew trees when the sombre, rhythmic thump of the spades on the earth began to echo round the graveyard.

Lavender shuffled from one cold foot to the other as his boots sank into the sodden ground. He distracted himself by watching the slow glow of light spread from the east. Rooftops, smoking chimneys and the church tower gradually took form. Bats flitted silently overhead, returning to their roost in the belfry.

The weak daylight brought some comfort and normality to the dismal scene. Crows called to each other from nests in the treetops then rose, circling and wheeling in pairs and groups of three before they headed to their favourite feeding grounds.

The gravediggers were about four feet down now. They slowed when the soil became wetter and stickier. They wiped muddied hands across their brows and breathed heavily with the exertion.

'Looks like they've buried him deep,' Woods whispered beside him.

Lavender said nothing. A small crowd had gathered at a respectful distance on the road. Vincent Dowling, the reporter, was amongst them and so was the Reverend Calvin and his ashen-faced daughter. The frail old man leaned heavily on his stick and Miss Calvin.

Sir Richard moved alongside him and Woods. 'What do you expect to find here, Lavender?' Even the normally loud and confident surgeon had lowered his voice.

'With luck, the coffin will be filled with rubble,' Lavender replied.

'And if it's not? If it contains a cadaver?'

Lavender's chest tightened. 'Then we need to identify the body and discover the cause of death – if possible.'

'You do realise, don't you, that after three months the corpse will have decomposed badly? There'll be little left of the tissue, with only the skull and the bones remaining.'

Lavender swallowed hard and nodded.

The pounding of the spades ceased and the sextons called for a lantern to be passed down into the grave. One of them had found a coffin nail and held it up for examination.

'Well, at least we know somethin's down there,' Woods said.

The minutes dragged on as the gravediggers resumed their work. They were shoulder-deep in the hole now. Their hats bobbed up and down as they bent over their work and rose to deposit another spadeful of sloppy earth on to the edge of the gaping hole.

'Well, it can't be as bad as that poor fellah they hauled out of the Thames this week,' Woods said cheerfully.

'It'll be worse,' Lavender replied grimly.

A dull thud and a scrape announced to the tense spectators that a spade had hit wood. Lavender held his breath and the birds in the trees stopped their merry chirping as if on cue.

Everyone inched forward to the edge of the extended hole. The rotting wooden lid of the coffin was now visible. The sextons were squashed on a ledge beside it. They scraped away the top layer of mud and their smeared faces glanced up for further instructions.

Sir Richard took control. 'Remove the lid. Let's see what we're dealing with.' He turned to his students. 'Hodge, Kingsley – help them remove the lid.'

Hodge reached for pliers and pulled a crowbar out of the wheelbarrow of tools standing beside the grave. Kingsley dropped down to his haunches and slid down the muddy hole, oblivious to the damage to his tailored coat and breeches. His young face was paler than any of them. Hodge passed down the tools.

Beneath the force of the crowbar the lid cracked and came away easily, releasing the foul smell of the dead into the fresh morning air.

Everyone spluttered and groaned. Kingsley and Magistrate Nulty retched.

'Gawd's teeth!' Woods muttered, wrinkling his broad nose in disgust. He pulled out his handkerchief and covered his lower face.

Lavender's eyes watered and obscured his vision. He brushed away the tears, braced himself and stared down at the skeletal corpse in the pit. The morning sunlight strengthened, illuminating the grave in all its viscous, gory detail.

Sir Richard had been right. The putrefying cadaver had decomposed almost down to the skeleton. The mouldering clothing of a man lay flat over his bones in the sticky pool of noxious black liquid staining the base of the coffin. Gnarled, blackened claws protruded from the cuffs of the coat.

Lavender forced himself to look at the skull. Only a few peeling shreds of purple flesh and wisps of dry, dark hair remained. The lips had gone entirely, exposing a full set of strong white teeth tightly clenched in the grimace of death. The sunken cheeks were green hollows and the empty eye sockets leered up at Lavender in defiance, challenging him to name these grisly remains. He groaned with disappointment. It would be impossible to recognise the man who'd once inhabited that body.

'I have something!' Kingsley shouted from behind his own handkerchief. Coughing and retching, he crouched down and rummaged in the stinking coffin amongst the mangled remains. When he stood up, he held a rotting black leather bag in his gloved hand. He tossed it up on the side of the grave.

Lavender picked up the mouldering bag and walked away out of the shadow of the trees into the soft sunlight. Woods and Sir Richard followed him.

He reached inside the bag and pulled out a small, waterlogged box. It immediately disintegrated in his hand. A shower of black clumps spilled out on to the ground and Lavender caught the faint aroma of tea. He cleared the dirt from the sodden cardboard and pointed to the faded green markings. 'I think I know who he is.'

The ink had run in the damp and the emblem was faint, but an elegant green tea canister and the elaborate Grecian foliage of Raitt's Tea Warehouse were just about decipherable.

'It's Frank Collins.'

'That's not possible!' Sir Richard exclaimed.

He examined their find more closely. The bag contained a dozen soggy boxes of tea. 'Collins' employer, Raitt, said samples of tea had had gone missing along with the man.'

'But how is this possible?' Woods asked. 'He were the one who brought the coffin here – how the devil did he end up inside it?'

'It wasn't Collins who brought the coffin here,' Lavender said. His brain whirled as he pieced together the final pieces of the mystery. 'It was someone else – someone masquerading as Collins. We should have realised no one would have used his own name to carry out an audacious crime like this.'

'But how can he have been dead since June?' Sir Richard's small, pale eyes were upset and confused beneath his frowning brow. He ran his muddy hand across his forehead, oblivious to the streak of dirt he left behind in his carefully styled hair. 'He sent my sister some rent money in August.'

'Again – that wasn't him,' Lavender said. 'The killer – or killers – sent the rent money to Mrs Palmer to maintain the illusion Collins was still alive and in Yorkshire on business.'

'Well, who in hell's name has done this?' Sir Richard demanded. 'Sylvia will be devastated – that's two of her lodgers confirmed dead in the space of a week!'

'I'm afraid your sister's woes aren't over yet,' Lavender said slowly. 'The only other person who was privy to the affairs of both MacAdam and Collins was her third lodger, Alfred Bentley – and he answers the description we have of the young man who brought the coffin to Chelmsford.'

Sir Richard gave a short humourless laugh of disbelief. 'You can't be serious, Lavender, surely? Collins was a big fellow and Bentley is barely shaving. He's just a boy – a weak, impressionable boy. It seems improbable that he murdered Collins and came up with this heinous plan to fake MacAdam's death.'

'Stranger things have happened,' Lavender said grimly.

'Perhaps MacAdam killed Collins?' Woods suggested. 'If the Bentley fellah is as weak-minded as you think, maybe MacAdam persuaded – or forced – the younger chap to help him cover up the murder and bring the coffin here.'

'That makes more sense,' Lavender said thoughtfully. 'Ike Rawlings is under arrest and on his way to London with his gaoler. He said last night he might be able to identify the young man who brought this body to Chelmsford.' Another thought struck him. 'Sir Richard, did you tell your sister that we would be exhuming the grave today?'

'Yes, why?'

'If she told Bentley – then he might run.'

'We need to get back to London – and fast!' Woods said.

Lavender shoved the crumbling boxes of tea back into the bag and closed it. 'We'll arrest Bentley and take him to Bow Street, where Rawlings may be able to identify him.'

'My poor sister!' Sir Richard groaned. He looked wretched. 'She'll be devastated.'

'I'm sorry, but we must go,' Lavender said.

The surgeon nodded glumly.

Lavender glanced back at the gaping hole in the ground. 'Please continue with the autopsy, Sir Richard. I know it won't be easy for you but if you can find any clue about how Frank Collins met his death, it would be very helpful.'

Sir Richard nodded irritably. 'Just catch the bastard responsible for this, Lavender.' He turned and walked back to his gruesome task across the sodden ground.

Chapter Thirty-Two

L avender and Woods caught the first coach back to London and strode into Bow Street at about half past nine.

'I'll get a warrant for Bentley's arrest while you saddle up the horses,' Lavender said. He leapt up the scuffed wooden stairs to Read's office two at a time.

Read was halfway across the room, resplendent in his court robes and wig, when Lavender entered. 'You just caught me, Stephen. I'm due in court in five minutes.'

'I need an arrest warrant for a man named Alfred Bentley.' Quickly, he explained what they'd discovered at the exhumation. 'If Bentley found out from Mrs Palmer that we did the exhumation this morning then he'll know the game is up. He might try to run.'

'Good grief!' Read retraced his steps across the room and grabbed a blank warrant and his quill from the inkstand. 'What charge?'

'We'll start with the murder of Francis Collins. Oswald Grey and I will need to sit down with a legal dictionary to work out the rest of the crimes the cove has committed. The charge sheet will be extensive.'

As if on cue, there was a sharp tap on the open door and Grey stepped into the room. 'Detective Lavender, you need to come downstairs to the desk immediately.'

'Why?'

'There's a Mr Jackson here, an employee of Mr Howard's on Bruton Street. He's very distressed and says they urgently need your help. Apparently, Miss Howard has eloped to Scotland and her grandfather has sent for you to help give chase.'

'What?' Lavender spun round. This didn't make sense. 'Her fiancé has just died – she can't have eloped.'

'Apparently, she's gone north with some penniless wastrel called Bentley.'

Lavender gasped and snatched the warrant from Read's hand. 'I'm on my way.' He flew across the room and down the stairs.

'The ink's still wet!' Read yelled after him.

Howard's secretary stood wringing his hands in the grimy hallway. The broken veins on his pale cheeks were flushed red with anxiety. 'Lavender! Thank goodness, you're here! This is a terrible business.'

'What's happened?'

'She went out for an early ride in the phaeton this morning. About half an hour later, her ayah confessed to Mr Howard that the wicked girl planned to meet up with this chap Bentley and elope to Gretna Green. She had forced the servant woman to help her pack and load her belongings into the carriage and sworn her to secrecy. But the ayah was wracked with guilt.'

Forced? Lavender couldn't imagine the gentle Miss Howard forcing anyone to do anything.

'Mr Howard is furious,' Jackson continued. 'He called for his landau, and gave chase immediately. He insists you join him in the hunt.'

'This doesn't make sense,' Lavender said. 'Miss Howard seemed genuinely in love with David MacAdam. Why has she run off with Bentley?'

'Oh, I'm sorry – I'm so flustered – I haven't been clear. It's not Miss Howard who's eloped with Bentley,' Mr Jackson said hastily. 'It's Miss *Matilda* Howard, her sixteen-year-old younger sister.'

'Good grief!' Lavender's brain spun. Events were fast moving out of his control. He didn't know what the devil was going on but he knew they needed to catch Bentley. 'Do you know which route they took north?'

'The ayah said they intended to take the Great North Road.'

'How long has the girl known him?'

Jackson looked embarrassed. 'The ayah said Miss Matilda has secretly met Bentley since June. Mr MacAdam introduced them privately. Miss Howard knew nothing about this either – she's devastated.'

June. The same month when Collins was murdered and MacAdam faked his own death. Is that why Bentley helped MacAdam? To gain an introduction to the second Howard heiress? These men were despicable.

Lavender turned to Oswald Grey, who'd followed him downstairs. 'I need more men.'

'Most of the officers are either on patrol or still searching for Billy Summersgill,' Oswald told him.

Summersgill. Lavender had forgotten about him and the burglary. An idea flashed in Lavender's brain and another piece of the mystery fell into place.

'Constable Barnaby is out in the yard,' Grey added. 'Take him.'

Lavender nodded and strode towards the door, with Jackson trailing behind him. Barnaby was quick, intelligent and a fast rider. 'I'll take Eddie Woods too,' he called over his shoulder to Grey.

'We don't know how they intend to pay for this flight,' Jackson said breathlessly as he struggled to match Lavender's stride. 'It'll take them at least four days – and nights – to reach Gretna Green. They'll need fresh horses and accommodation. Mr Howard is terrified the cad will get cold feet and abandon Miss Matilda at the side of the road. She doesn't have much money of her own.'

'Oh yes, she does,' Lavender corrected him.

Woods, Eddie and Barnaby stood talking by the stables. Eddie held the reins of two saddled horses.

'You're all coming with me – now!' Lavender yelled. 'Get two more horses saddled. Quick!' Woods, Barnaby and Eddie dived into the stables.

'I don't understand,' Mr Jackson continued, his eyebrows drawn together in confusion. 'Mr Howard only gives Miss Matilda a small allowance. What makes you think she has any money?'

Lavender hauled himself up into the saddle, gathered up the reins, then leaned down to the secretary.

'Did you ever find the burglar's accomplice amongst your servants?'

'No.'

'Think about what's occurred this morning, Jackson. Then ask yourself: who do you *now* think stole that valuable ring?'

Five minutes later, Lavender and his men trotted out of Bow Street and joined the heavy traffic heading towards Clerkenwell. Their faces were grim with determination. They wouldn't be able to pick up much speed while they were in the confines of the city but Bentley and Miss Howard wouldn't have moved quickly through London either.

Lavender tried to work out how much distance lay between them and the fugitives. The average coach travelled at six miles an hour but that phaeton wasn't an average vehicle and, according to her grandfather, the young girl was an exceptional horsewoman. She'd fled with Bentley about two hours ago. They didn't know they were being pursued by her grandfather and the Bow Street officers but they wouldn't dawdle. They may have reached Stevenage by now. It would be a long, hard ride.

He glanced ahead at Woods' broad blue-coated shoulders rising and falling in rhythm with his trotting horse and felt a sudden pang of guilt. He'd forgotten about Ned's shoulder injury. A furious dash north on horseback wouldn't help his constable's recovery. But it was too late to turn him back. Besides which, the stubborn fool would probably refuse to go back anyway.

Gradually, the city fell away. The sun strengthened above them and they whipped their horses into a gallop. The rush of wind in their ears and the drumming hoof beats drowned out all other sensation. Lavender leaned over his horse's flying mane and peered through the dust cloud kicked up by the thundering hooves to concentrate on the road ahead.

At some points, the rutted historic highway was hundreds of yards in width. Over the years, feet, hooves and vehicles had sought firmer ground on the broad, grassy common away from the ruts and widened the road. The four horsemen weaved effortlessly in and out of the other vehicles, passing everything that threatened to slow them down.

Woods set the pace and Lavender was happy to let him. Every now and then, the experienced patrol officer would pull on the reins to slow his panting horse, especially if the road narrowed or they wound up a gradual incline. Then Woods would set his spurs to his animal's flanks once more and they'd thunder ahead. They clattered through small hamlets, splashed through shallow fords and stopped only for tollgates. But most of the keepers opened the gates wide to let them pass unhindered once they saw the distinctive uniform of the Bow Street patrol officers bearing down upon them.

Lavender watched Eddie veer away from a couple of small, ragged children playing with a mangy dog in the dust of a village street. Flushed with the excitement of the chase, Eddie was as good a horseman as his father and exceptional for his age. Lavender had done his best to teach Sebastián but he knew his stepson would never sit as comfortably in the saddle of a horse as Woods' son. It was like Eddie had been born to it.

Woods slowed when they approached the coaching inn at Hatfield and indicated they were to change their horses. They pulled up in the cobbled yard and dismounted stiffly from their tired, sweating animals.

Woods strode into the stables bellowing for the best horses, with Barnaby and Eddie trailing in his wake.

Lavender questioned the other stable hands in the yard about any sightings of Miss Matilda or her grandfather. No one remembered the old man but everyone remembered the dark, exotic girl and her expensive black phaeton when it called there to change horses.

'She'd been thrashin' those poor horses,' one of the grooms said. 'She nearly mowed down a young woman wi' a child when she swung out o' the yard.'

'When was this?' Lavender asked.

The groom glanced at the clock on the village church tower, just visible over the roof of the inn. 'Just over an hour ago.'

Woods and the others reappeared leading fresh horses. 'These are the best I can find,' he grumbled. 'They've got a right stable of queer prancers here.'

'We're making up ground on the fugitives,' Lavender told them when they swung back up into the saddles. 'They're an hour ahead of us.'

The news reinvigorated his weary crew. They urged the fresh horses forward and cantered out of the stable yard. The countryside flew past in a haze of dust. The road became an endless brown ribbon undulating through fields of stubble, small woodlands and over the gently rolling hills. Lavender's calf muscles screamed in agony from the endless pressure of standing in his stirrups. His rigid back ached and his shirt stuck to it with sweat. Only the wind whipping past his face kept him cool.

To take his mind off the pain, he tried to make sense of the complicated case of the Park Lane petticoat pensioners and the two Howard girls.

MacAdam's deceptive courtship of Miss Howard started in May. A month later, MacAdam introduced Bentley to the younger Howard sister, and the two of them began a clandestine liaison of their own. Their secrecy suggested that the young girl knew from the start Bentley wasn't a suitable sweetheart or future husband – but she obviously didn't care. Perhaps it had always been their intention to elope?

MacAdam had a beguiling and dangerous charm; he lied about his background and prospects and acted his part as a baronet's son with ease. Bentley didn't have those skills, but he was a good-looking young man who had honed his seduction techniques on a group of amorous old ladies. Matilda Howard was plain and childish; Bentley would have swept a young girl like her off her feet.

Had he confided in her his involvement with MacAdam's scheme to fake his own death? Did she know about the murder of Collins? And if she did, did she care? A girl who robbed her own sister had no conscience.

He'd no doubt Matilda had staged the burglary and stolen the ring to finance their elopement. It would have been easy for her to sneak into her sister's room and remove the ring from the jewellery box. Next, she probably crept downstairs to smash the window in the laundry and make it look like they'd had an intruder. Then all she had to do was raise the alarm and the household descended into turmoil.

To Lavender's relief, Woods slowed his wide-eyed and sweat-flecked animal when they approached The Sun coaching inn at Biggleswade. Scared that his stiff legs would buckle beneath his weight once he dismounted and tried to stand, Lavender pulled up at the mounting block to make his descent easier.

The sun was high in the sky now and unseasonably hot. Lavender's hair was plastered to his flushed head beneath his hat. It was the same with the others; young Eddie glowed like a ripened tomato.

While Woods sought out some decent fresh horses, Lavender sent Barnaby into the inn to fetch them all a drink. There was no news of the fugitives or Mr Howard here in Biggleswade, but Lavender knew they weren't far ahead.

The thirsty men and Eddie downed their ale in a few gulps and then hauled themselves on to the backs of their new horses.

They came across Mr Howard about twenty minutes later. His landau had pulled over by the side of the road. Lavender would have ridden straight past him if it hadn't been for the distinctive jewelled turbans and flowing red-silk livery of the two coachmen. The servants were changing a rear wheel of the carriage.

Howard stood holding the horses still. His burnt, leathered face was lined with worry but it flooded with relief when Lavender reined in beside him. 'Lavender! Thank God you came! We nearly had them, by God! We saw them in the distance, where the road crests that hill.'

Lavender followed Howard's pointing finger to the hilltop about half a mile away. 'How long ago was this?'

'About fifteen minutes. Then the damned wheel started to wobble.'

'We'll go ahead and catch them,' Lavender said. 'Is Miss Matilda still driving the phaeton?'

Howard nodded angrily, and pointed to one of his silk-swathed coachmen. 'The little minx tricked my coachman. She persuaded him to climb down from the carriage, scrambled into the box and drove off without him. We picked him up at Potters Bar tollgate. It's good of you to come, Lavender. If we can catch them before nightfall we might be able to salvage something out of this madness.'

'I'm sorry to tell you this, but we're not here to save Miss Matilda's reputation,' Lavender replied. 'We're after Bentley. He's wanted on a murder charge.'

Lavender had no time to explain further. He set his spurs to the horse's flanks and surged forward, leaving the horrified East India man at the edge of the road.

They soon crested the hill where the phaeton had last been sighted and dipped down into a small wooded valley before rising again. Lavender wanted to charge on ahead but Woods held them at a steady trot as they twisted up the gradual incline.

'It's all downhill from the top of this hill to St Neots,' Woods yelled over his shoulder. 'Let's give the horses chance to get their breath before we gallop again.'

Woods was right. The road fell away rapidly before them after this second hill. They thundered down it towards a sharp bend.

When they turned the corner, they saw a slow-moving line of wagons and coaches about three-quarters of a mile ahead, winding its way along the narrow road. The vehicles were hemmed in by another woody copse and the phaeton was the third vehicle in the line.

'Stop!' Lavender yelled, desperately hoping the others heard him above the rush of the wind and the drumming of the hoof beats. His officers sat back in their saddles, pulled up their horses and turned their flushed faces towards him.

For a second there was silence, apart from the whispering breeze in the tall grass and the gentle lowing of a cow.

'They're down there,' Lavender said breathlessly, 'caught in that line of traffic. I want to trap them at the St Neots' tollgate just outside of the town. If we pace ourselves it should be easy. If Miss Matilda sees us, I wouldn't put it past her to bolt off the road with the phaeton and turn it over. That's why we need to hem them in at the tollgate.'

They moved forward at a steady trot with one eye on their prey. Slowly the gap decreased between themselves and the line of vehicles. Every time the phaeton disappeared around a bend in the road, they moved forward a little faster.

They timed it to perfection. By the time they rounded the last bend, the carriage was only a few hundred yards ahead, stationary and trapped in the queue for the tollgate.

Yelling with satisfaction, Lavender whipped his horse forward. The others thundered at his heels.

Bentley glanced over his shoulder in alarm. His face turned pale with shock at the sight of the officers bearing down on them. He leapt nimbly down from the carriage and ran.

Barnaby was on him in an instant. In a swift, graceful move, the young officer swung down from the saddle of his still-moving horse and landed on the fleeing clerk, knocking him to the ground.

Miss Matilda screamed, then picked up the reins. But Woods had already reached the lead horse of the carriage and had his hand firmly on its harness.

Lavender drew up sharply beside her. 'Get down from the carriage, Miss Matilda!' he yelled. 'Get down – now!'

'Or else, what?' Her face contorted with fury beneath the dark-green pleated satin rim of her bonnet. She pointed with her whip towards Barnaby. 'You will knock me to the ground like he did to poor Bentley?'

'No, madam.' Lavender drew out his pistol from his pocket and aimed it. 'If you refuse to cooperate, I will shoot you in the leg instead. You're under arrest for the theft of your sister's ring and your grandfather's phaeton. Clap her in irons, Eddie.'

Chapter Thirty-Three

L et me help you down, miss.' Eddie dismounted from his own horse and reached up his hand to help Matilda Howard.

Her grip tightened on her whip. Lavender held his breath, half expecting her to lash out at Eddie, but she leaned forward instead and sank her teeth into his proffered hand.

Eddie yelped, grabbed the girl roughly by the legs and hauled her down from the carriage. She landed in a crumpled heap of silk taffeta on the ground. He threw her over, yanked her arms behind her back and slapped the iron cuffs on her thin wrists. She screamed and yelled out in a foreign language. Lavender didn't need to know Bengali or Hindi to know she cursed them.

Woods burst out laughing as he steadied the stamping horses. 'Steady on, son. That's not your brother you're tacklin'!'

'She bit me, Da!' Eddie straightened up and held up his bleeding hand as evidence.

Woods shook his head and tried to keep a straight face. 'I've warned you before, son. Women are the same as horses. When they're in a mood – always keep away from the sharp end.'

Barnaby reappeared round the side of the vehicle, pushing a cuffed and dishevelled Bentley before him. The clerk's hat had gone and his coat and breeches were covered in mud. His long dark hair flopped over a puffy left eye where the skin was discoloured and swelling. He'd soon have a nasty shiner to spoil his good looks.

'How are we goin' to get them back?' Woods asked. Lavender noticed he was rubbing his injured shoulder.

Lavender pocketed his pistol and slid gratefully out of his saddle. 'Get them inside the carriage and put the hood up. We'll tie our horses behind the coach and you can drive the vehicle back to London, Ned. I'll travel inside with them.'

The men nodded and quickly did his bidding. He gestured to the fugitives to climb back inside the carriage.

'You don't tell me what to do, Lavender!' the girl screamed in his face. 'You're nothing more than a servant! Grandfather shall hear about this!'

'Sooner than you think, madam.' Lavender spoke between gritted teeth as he pushed her roughly up the steps.

A few moments later, the hood of the phaeton was raised and fixed in place. Woods mounted the box on the carriage, confidently called to the horses and shook the reins. The phaeton jolted forward then swung round smoothly.

Lavender sank back in the plush comfort of the red leather seats and sighed with satisfaction. He'd caught Bentley and although he could have wished for better company, the carriage was well sprung and comfortable. He didn't expect any trouble from his captives. Even they weren't stupid enough to throw themselves out of a moving vehicle while handcuffed.

He sat back and coldly observed the couple sitting opposite him. With their hands cuffed behind them, both were precariously balanced on the edge of the seat. Bentley looked dejected and stared down at the floor but Matilda Howard glared back at Lavender defiantly. Her gown was ripped and muddied and her hair pins had fallen out. Her bonnet was askew and strands of wiry black hair fell in a tangled mess over her shoulders. She glanced to Bentley for reassurance but he avoided her eyes, and continued to stare mournfully at the floor. His ridiculously long, dark eyelashes rested on his cheekbones.

Lavender turned to Bentley. 'Do you understand why we've arrested you?'

The young man shrugged and mumbled: 'Because I've eloped with Matty and she's not twenty-one.'

'Yes, there is that,' Lavender said slowly. 'We'll have to add abducting a minor to your list of crimes when we reach Bow Street.'

'It's a false arrest,' Matilda Howard said confidently. 'My grandfather will not press charges against him once he sees how much we are in love. You waste your time, Lavender.'

Lavender repressed the urge to smile. 'Do you love her, Bentley?'

'Of course he does!' Matilda insisted, nudging Bentley with her elbow. But he stayed silent.

'Go on then, Bentley,' Lavender goaded. 'Tell her how much you love her.'

Bentley turned his head and stared out of the window. 'I should have run yesterday when I had the chance,' he muttered bitterly.

'Alfie! Alfie, speak of your love for me!'

Lavender laughed. 'He can't, Miss Matilda – because he loves your fortune more than he loves you.'

'You're wrong!'

'I don't think so.'

She sank back into the corner of the coach glowering, but doubt flickered in her protruding eyes.

Lavender turned back to the silent youth. 'So what was your plan today? Did you hope that if you whisked Miss Matilda to Gretna Green and married her, her money – and her grandfather – would protect you from the law?'

Still Bentley said nothing.

'Alfie has done nothing wrong,' Matilda said.

'I don't think you understand British law, Miss Matilda,' Lavender said firmly. 'He murdered Frank Collins and hid his body in a coffin.

255

Then he took it to Chelmsford to bury and falsely claimed it was the body of MacAdam. That's at least three capital offences in British law.'

'He did not!' Matilda exclaimed.

Bentley finally glanced up and fixed his blue eyes on Lavender. 'I didn't kill Collins – you can't lay that one at my feet!'

'But you don't deny your part in faking MacAdam's death?'

Bentley's mouth flapped in confusion. 'No! Yes! Yes, I do deny it. I had nothing to do with MacAdam.'

The coach jolted over a rut and Bentley nearly fell off the seat. Lavender grabbed him by the lapels and shoved him back, leaning in close to the young man's terrified face. 'We've identified the body in the coffin,' he hissed. 'I've got witnesses who will confirm you accompanied it to Essex. You're going to hang for Collins' murder, Bentley – and your other despicable crimes.'

'I swear I never touched Collins!' Bentley squealed.

Lavender gave him one last shove and sat back in his own seat. 'Talk then. Tell me what happened.'

'Say nothing to him, Alfie!' Matilda yelled. 'I will beg my grandfather to get you a lawyer—'

Lavender's patience with the girl finally ran out. 'Be quiet, madam! Your grandfather is about ten minutes away in his landau. From what I've seen of his mood, he's more likely to take a horsewhip to you both and flay Bentley alive than get him a lawyer.'

She sank back in her seat in shock and sniffled.

Lavender turned back to Bentley. 'Now, tell me what happened to Frank Collins.'

Bentley swallowed hard. Lavender could smell him sweating.

'They'd been drinking.'

'Who?'

'Collins and MacAdam. Mrs Palmer was away visiting her friend in Dulwich – the one who married the vicar. They got drunk every night she was gone.' Bentley poured out the rest. 'They had a fight. MacAdam hit Collins hard and he went down. MacAdam killed him.'

'Where and when was this?'

'Back in June – in Collins' bedchamber. He cracked his head on the hearth and died instantly.'

Lavender paused and remembered the cracked tiles he'd found on the corner of the hearth in Collins' room. 'What did they argue about?'

Bentley stared at the floor. A muscle in his neck twitched above his muddy cravat. 'MacAdam said he intended to marry Amelia Howard – and damn his wife and children. Collins said this was wrong. He argued that a light flirtation was fine but he shouldn't trick Amelia into marriage when he was already married.'

'Well, I'm pleased to hear at least one of you three had some moral scruples,' Lavender said drily. 'What happened next?'

'We were shocked he was dead and didn't know what to do at first. MacAdam said a police investigation would scupper his chances with Amelia and pleaded with me not to tell anyone until he'd worked out how to get rid of the body. The next morning, he came up with the plan to send the body back to Chelmsford and fake his own death. He forced me to help him.'

'Really? Are you sure he didn't promise you something else instead?' Lavender glanced at the girl in the corner of the carriage. 'Like an introduction to a silly young heiress, for example?'

'No! He forced me! He knew some bad people, did MacAdam. He threatened me. He bought a cheap coffin from someone in St Giles and organised a man to arrive the next day with a wagon. A man whom he'd paid well for his silence. I was to accompany the coffin back to Chelmsford and tell his wife he'd died of the pox.'

Lavender didn't believe him for one minute. 'And then, to thank you, he kindly introduced you to Miss Matilda.' He turned to the girl. 'Did you know about any of this?'

She turned her head haughtily and looked out of the window.

Lavender laughed, a cruel dry laugh. 'It's a shame you're going to hang, Bentley, because the two of you deserve each other. It's a long time since I've met a young couple so perfectly matched in deviousness. What was your plan after that? How did you intend to convince Mr Howard to accept you as a suitor for Miss Matilda?'

Bentley swallowed again. 'We intended to elope the day after MacAdam and Amelia's wedding. MacAdam promised to do his best to help convince the old man to accept the match. We didn't want Howard to cut her off without a penny.'

'No, of course you didn't.'

'Howard liked MacAdam. He would listen to him.'

'But MacAdam's sudden and unexpected death spoilt your plans, didn't it? And you decided to elope anyway. Miss Matilda stole Miss Howard's expensive ring to finance your trip to Scotland. To whom did you sell it, by the way?'

Matilda and Bentley exchanged a furtive glance. 'Matty heard you mention some fellow called Summersgill when you were talking with her grandfather.'

'Yes, I thought she was listening at the keyhole,' Lavender said drily. 'It's not an attractive trait in a young lady.' Matilda scowled at him.

'I tracked Summersgill down yesterday morning after Matty passed the ring on to me. The damned fellow would only give me ten pounds for it.'

Lavender gave a short laugh. Billy Summersgill knew the true value of that ring. He'd make nearly all of his money back when he sold it on.

'Look, I'm helping you out here, sir, Lavender – is there any chance you can soften the charges against me?'

Lavender ignored Bentley's request. 'You also knew we were about to exhume Collins' body. You knew that because Miss Matilda also listened in to my conversation with her grandfather on the night of the fake robbery.'

Bentley's face suddenly flushed with anger. 'I should never have let her persuade me into this madness. I should have taken the money and made a run for it yesterday while I had a chance.'

'Alfie!' Matilda wailed.

'What kept you from running?' Lavender asked, smiling. 'Was it love?'

Bentley scowled. 'She said you'd never be able to identify the body after such a long time.'

Lavender laughed. 'And you believed a sixteen-year-old girl? More fool you, Bentley.'

There was a short pause. 'She said she'd seen something . . . something horrible . . . in India.'

'I'm sure she has,' Lavender interrupted sharply. 'But do you know what gave the game away, Bentley? What led us to identify Collins?'

Bentley shook his head and his metal handcuffs rattled behind him.

'It was the bag of Raitt's tea we found in the coffin. The one you'd hidden in there when you cleaned up the room after the fight.'

'I didn't put any tea in the coffin!'

Lavender laughed again. 'Then I guess it was MacAdam who placed it there while you were distracted. MacAdam wanted everyone to believe Collins had left for Yorkshire with his samples, didn't he? He couldn't leave them lying around.'

'The bloody fool,' Bentley muttered beneath his breath.

'Yes, your dead friend, your partner in crime, sealed your fate for you. He helped us identify Collins. He's ensured that you'll soon be joining him in hell.'

Chapter Thirty-Four

B entley turned pale at Lavender's comment but he didn't get chance to respond. He jerked forward and almost fell off the edge of the seat again as the coach suddenly slowed and came to an abrupt stop. Mr Howard and his servants had finally met up with them.

Lavender opened the door and climbed down. A refreshing breeze brought the sweet scent of the long grass in the fields. He relished the fresh air after the stuffiness and tension inside the carriage.

A red-faced Mr Howard climbed out of his own vehicle and strode towards him. 'Where is she? Is she hurt?'

'She's fine – but she's under arrest . . .'

Howard pushed past him, climbed into the coach and hauled his squealing granddaughter down the steps.

'Grandfather! Grandfather – you must save Alfie – I love him!'

Howard ignored her. 'I'll take over from here,' he said to Lavender. 'She travels back with me.'

Lavender grabbed his arm. 'She stole your phaeton and her sister's ring.'

For a split second, Howard hesitated. Then his blind love for the writhing girl in his grasp won over. 'I won't press charges against her. She's my granddaughter, for Christ's sake. Remove the handcuffs, please.'

Lavender bit back his disappointment and pulled out his key. There was nothing he could do if the troublesome girl had her grandfather's support.

The cuffs snapped open and she glared at Lavender in triumph. 'Now rescue Alfie, Grandfather! Please!'

Howard frowned and glanced at the phaeton. 'What about him? Is he a killer?'

'Please, Grandfather – I love him!'

'He claims MacAdam murdered Frank Collins – the body in the coffin in Chelmsford,' Lavender said. 'But he helped MacAdam fake his own death and hide Collins' body.'

'Do you believe him – about the murder?'

'I'm not sure yet. We need your vehicle to transport him to Bow Street for further questioning.'

'Do you have enough to hang him?'

'Oh, yes.'

'Good.'

'Grandfather!' For the first time, the young girl's arrogant belief in her infallibility crumpled. She burst into tears and hung on to Howard's arm, desperately pleading with him to help Bentley. It was a pitiful sight. Howard beckoned over one of his servants. The Indian peeled the distraught girl off Howard's arm, dragged her over to the landau and bundled her inside.

Howard sighed with relief when the landau door shut on his wailing granddaughter. 'She's young. She'll get over him. If you've enough evidence to arrest and charge Bentley for his other crimes, then you don't need to charge him with abducting Matilda. We can keep her name out of this and preserve her reputation.'

'Not necessarily,' Lavender warned. 'MacAdam used your rich granddaughter as bait to persuade Bentley to help him with the fraud. This might come out in court. It was his motive.'

For a moment, Howard looked like he might argue; then his face softened. 'Do you have a daughter, Detective?'

'No – at least, not yet.' Lavender's mind leapt to Magdalena and his unborn child.

'Well, when you do have one – you'll understand. Girls are precious. They can be misguided sometimes but they are always . . . precious. Just do what you can, Lavender, please. Keep her name out of this sordid affair.'

Howard turned and gestured to the other silk-liveried coachman to join them. 'I'll leave you one of my coachmen. He can return the phaeton to Bruton Street after you've finished with it.'

Howard returned to his landau, climbed inside and yelled through the open window for the coachman to drive on. The carriage turned back to London, then drew away briskly, leaving Lavender and the phaeton standing in a cloud of swirling dust.

Lavender was thoughtful as he watched the rumbling vehicle disappear round a bend. Peace descended on to the road, disturbed only by birdsong and the whisper of the breeze. He had a premonition this was the last time he would see Howard.

If a grandparent could love such a foul young woman so strongly, so blindly, what chance did parents have against the wiles and manipulation of such an immoral youngster? He thought of his own mysterious, half-formed child and his stomach knotted with his sense of his own inadequacy. How would he ever cope if the child turned out like Matilda Howard?

Woods handed over the reins of the horses to Howard's coachman and climbed down from the box to join him. 'Well! He could have thanked us for gettin' her back!'

Lavender managed a small smile. 'I think he's too embarrassed to remember his manners. Did you hear everything?'

'Yes, and it's disappointin'. He were foolish to take her away – a night in a Bow Street police cell would have done that little madam the world of good.'

Despite his black mood, Lavender gave a short laugh. 'That's an interesting approach to parenthood, Ned. Somehow I can't see you willing to let Rachel or Tabitha spend a night with the prostitutes and drunks in one of our cells.'

'Ah, that'll never happen. My little gals are both takin' the veil when they're old enough – before they get into trouble with the fellahs.'

Lavender's smile broadened. 'You're not a Catholic.'

'It don't matter. There's too many cads out there wantin' to whisk away our daughters and dangle with them. I'll find a nunnery to take Rachel and little Tabby, you see if I don't.'

Their return trip to Bow Street was far less frenetic than their mad dash up the Great North Road and the journey was far more comfortable for Lavender inside the carriage and Woods up on the box next to Howard's coachman.

The first time they stopped to change horses, Lavender took his officers inside the low-beamed, smoky tavern and treated them to a hearty meal. They left Bentley securely attached with a second set of handcuffs to the interior of the carriage.

Lavender raised his tankard and toasted and praised his men, young Eddie included.

'Yes,' Woods said to Barnaby. 'That were a spectacular dismount from a gallopin' horse. I ain't seen anythin' like that since the gypsies put on a horse show at the Vauxhall Gardens. Are you sure you don't have Romany blood?'

Barnaby grinned at the praise and ignored the teasing. 'I knew I'd have a soft landin'.'

Lavender laughed. 'I'm surprised you didn't knock Bentley's teeth out.'

'That'd have spoilt his goods looks,' Woods said drily.

Lavender turned to Eddie. 'And you rode well, too, Eddie. Once you're old enough I won't have any reservations about recommending you for the horse patrol.' Two pink spots of joy appeared on the young lad's round cheeks. Beside him, Woods' chest swelled with pride and he raised his tankard of ale. 'To another Woods in the family business!' The men all tapped their drinking vessels together.

Young Eddie got carried away and continued to drain his tankard long after the others had finished the toast. He belched loudly and wiped the froth from his face with his sleeve as he banged his empty vessel down on the table.

Woods laughed. 'Steady on, son, you don't want to be foxed on the ride back – you'll fall off your horse and we'll have to pull you out of a ditch.'

Their lamb cutlets arrived and for a while they were silent while they devoured the food.

Woods finished first. He gave a satisfied belch, put down his cutlery and turned to Lavender. 'So Bentley claims he didn't kill Collins and MacAdam were responsible for his death. Do you believe him?'

Lavender nodded. 'Yes. And it'll be hard to prove anything else now MacAdam is dead.'

'That's convenient for Bentley. What about MacAdam's murder? We said at the start that Bentley had the opportunity to kill him. MacAdam walked right past his bedchamber on his way to his own room.'

Lavender swallowed his last mouthful and chewed it thoughtfully. 'He had the opportunity but he doesn't have a motive. From what he's told me, he needed MacAdam alive to smooth his way with Howard after his elopement with the girl. Besides which, he didn't have the opportunity to put the farrier's knife into MacAdam's coffin. He was out with Lady Louisa Fitzgerald at the races when the undertakers brought the coffin to Park Lane. As far as we know, he didn't go near the Bow Street morgue.'

'Then we're back to Ike Rawlings as MacAdam's killer?'

'Yes. Or the two mysterious women who turned up at Bow Street the morning after his murder.'

Woods sat back in his chair. 'We need to find out who they were.' The fingers of his right hand tapped his tankard and his greying eyebrows gathered close together as he pondered the mystery. It was good to have him back to his normal self. 'Have you ruled out both the Howard sisters? That young filly we chased today is a wild one. I wouldn't put anything past her.'

'Neither of them had a motive to murder MacAdam.' Lavender shook his head and sighed. 'And Matilda needed him alive.'

'Mrs Palmer? Lady Louisa Fitzgerald?'

'I just can't see either of them murdering MacAdam with a farrier's knife. Neither of them appears to have a motive and Lady Louisa Fitzgerald strongly denied visiting MacAdam's corpse.'

'They're all denyin' it,' Woods reminded him. 'Lady Tyndall denied it too.'

The two men sat quietly thinking for a moment. The two young men watched them in respectful silence.

'Wait a minute,' Woods finally said. 'Eddie, did you say that you thought the younger woman of the two were dark?'

His son nodded his head vigorously. 'It were difficult to tell with the veil and the shadows, Da – but she had very dark eyes and I thought she were dark-skinned as well.'

'Is that significant, Ned?' Lavender asked.

'Well, it could be nothin' but Lady Tyndall's maid is a little darkie. I think her grandaddy were probably an African.'

Lavender frowned. 'But the girl we saw in the house yesterday . . .'

'Was called Sarah. That weren't her personal maid – she's called Harriet. I'll go back to Lady Tyndall's first thing in the mornin' if you want me to?'

'Yes, please, Ned. And don't take any nonsense from that household. Clap the whole lot of them in irons and drag them to Bow Street if they won't cooperate. Speak to the girl and find out if she accompanied her mistress to Bow Street.'

Woods grinned. 'Yes, sir.'

'Meanwhile, I need to go back to Park Lane and have another look at Collins' bedchamber. Bentley claims that's where the fight took place. I'll see if they left any clues to verify his story. Come on, let's go home.'

The men rose from the table and returned to their fresh horses and the carriage containing their prisoner.

It was dark when the weary police officers finally drew up outside Bow Street. Their faces and uniforms were streaked with dust from the road and they dismounted stiffly. Despite the relative comfort of the coach, every bone in Lavender's body ached; it had been a long and bruising day.

Lavender said goodnight and Woods, Eddie and Barnaby took the horses round to the stables. Lavender hauled Bentley out from the carriage and pushed him up the steps into the grimy hallway. Behind him, Howard's coachman urged the horses forward and the phaeton disappeared down the street.

Oswald Grey stood behind the desk and one of the gaolers sat nonchalantly on a nearby chair. Grey was bent over a document on the desk, straining to read it by the weak light of a lantern and the smoking tallow candles in the wall sconces. A cold and unwelcoming place in daylight, at night it was downright dismal.

Lavender felt Bentley stiffen with fear when he pushed him forward. The young man had been silent since Howard dragged his granddaughter away. This had suited Lavender. Bentley sickened him.

'You're working late, Mr Grey.'

The Chief Clerk looked scathingly at Lavender over the top of his spectacles. 'Yes, Lavender. I'm still doing the records for your cases.'

'Oh? How so?'

'Well, the prisoner Rawlings arrived about an hour ago from Essex. I've had to organise his incarceration in one of the cells. Are we charging him with the murder of MacAdam?'

'I'm not sure yet.'

Grey's frown deepened. 'You're never too sure these days, are you, Detective?'

Lavender shrugged and gave a weak smile.

'Then your fellow Summersgill was finally dragged in, protesting his innocence.'

'Really?'

'Yes. It was nonsense, of course. We found the stolen ring in his possession – but bizarrely he claims he bought it yesterday morning from the owner, Miss Howard. Anyway, I've charged him with receiving stolen goods.'

'Ah, he probably did.'

'What? Receive stolen goods?'

'No. He did buy the ring from a Miss Howard. Miss *Matilda* Howard – she's the sister of the owner and the one who stole it. Knowing Summersgill, he probably didn't know the difference between two Indian girls with the same name.'

'Are we charging the girl with theft?' Grey asked hopefully.

'No, her grandfather won't bring charges against her, which means we can't charge Summersgill either. We might as well let him go.'

Grey paused dramatically with his quill in midair. 'What, again?'

'Yes.'

'Earlier this week you arrested Summersgill – then released him. Two days ago, you asked us to catch him again – but now you want to let him go – again.'

'Yes.'

Grey drew a long line across the paper. The quill scratched so loudly that Lavender winced.

'Well, that was a waste of our time, wasn't it, Detective? I've had officers looking all over London for him for the last two days.'

'Sorry,' Lavender said.

'Who's this?' Grey jabbed his quill in Bentley's direction. The young man's shoulders were slumped and his head bowed.

'This is Alfred Bentley.'

'Ah, the child kidnapper. At last you've brought me a villain I can charge, imprison and take into court.' Hope gleamed in Grey's eyes behind his spectacles. He pulled out a fresh sheet of paper and raised his quill.

'The girl's grandfather doesn't want him charging with the abduction.'

Grey sighed heavily. 'Detective, I feel obliged to remind you this is a police office. Here, we bring in arrested men, charge them and imprison them until their trial. We don't just haul in random men off the streets, keep them for a bit and then let them go.'

A smile twitched at the corner of Lavender's mouth. 'You can charge Alfred Bentley with helping MacAdam to fake his own death.'

Grey's eyebrows shot up and he suddenly looked interested. 'Ah, so *he's* the body-snatcher as well as a child abductor.'

'I didn't rob any graves!' Bentley exclaimed.

Grey ignored him. 'I thought you were after a man called Frank Collins for that crime?' he said.

'We were, but it turns out Collins was the dead body in the coffin. This fellow was involved in his death.'

'Is he a murderer?'

'Possibly.'

'Possibly?'

'I need more evidence before we can charge him with murder. But he's definitely impeded a lawful burial.'

Satisfaction spread across Grey's face. His quill flew across the page. 'Fraud, deception and impeding a lawful burial. Are there any more charges I can add, while we're at it? Stealing a shroud, perhaps? I've always liked that one.'

'I've never touched a damned shroud!' Bentley yelled.

Lavender smiled. 'No, I can't think of any more but I'll let you know in the morning if I do. I'll leave him with you.' He beckoned across to the gaoler to take Bentley to the cells.

'Don't you want to see that Rawlings fellow, Lavender?'

'Not now,' Lavender said, fighting back his exhaustion. 'Right now, I'm going home to my wife.'

'Oh, by the way, before you leave, Sir Richard Allison is back in London and he sent you a message.' Grey passed across a folded note.

Sir Richard's message was brief. He'd completed the autopsy in Chelmsford and discovered that Frank Collins' skull had an irregular shaped hole. He believed the man had died following a massive blow to the back of his head.

Lavender sighed. This evidence supported Bentley's claim that Collins had fallen against the corner of the hearth. Sir Richard's writing swam before his eyes. His head ached. He desperately needed sleep.

'Is there a problem, Detective?' Grey asked ominously, his quill poised over the charge sheet. 'Do I need a fresh piece of paper?'

'No. Goodnight, Mr Grey.' Lavender thrust the note in his coat pocket and made a hasty escape.

Chapter Thirty-Five

Lavender slept heavily that night but was up before dawn fretting about Ike Rawlings' involvement in the MacAdam murder. Oswald Grey's comments about his indecision had been made in dry jest but they irked him all the same.

He knew he should charge Rawlings and be done with it. The man had both the motive and the opportunity to kill MacAdam. He also had the opportunity to place the farrier's knife in the coffin, although this was the weakest point in the case against the stone carrier. A good barrister would argue Rawlings had plenty of opportunity to simply throw the knife away somewhere on the road between London and Chelmsford; he didn't need to keep it and hide it in the coffin. Was it possible Rawlings had just been in the wrong place at the wrong time on the night of the murder?

Lavender decided to leave his decision about Rawlings until after he'd spoken with Lady Tyndall's coachman. He arrived at the mews adjacent to Park Lane just as first light illuminated the narrow, cobbled street. He was pleased to see the blacksmith was already at work and firing up his forge.

He dismounted, led his horse across to the smithy and pulled the farrier's knife out of his pocket.

A huge grin spread across the big man's hairy face when he saw the knife in Lavender's gloved hand. 'Well, I don't believe it! You found me ruddy knife after all.'

'Is it definitely the same one that vanished from your forge?' Lavender asked.

'Yes, though it weren't stained like that. Where'd you find it?' The blacksmith wiped his hand on his leather apron and reached out for the knife.

Lavender shook his head and put it back in his pocket. 'I'm afraid I can't let you have it back just yet. It was used to kill David MacAdam on Sunday night. I need to keep it as evidence.'

The blacksmith's face flashed with a mixture of shock and disappointment but he nodded and said he understood.

Lavender tied his horse to one of the iron rings in the wall next to the forge and climbed the short flight of stone steps up to the dwelling above Lady Tyndall's coach house. He rapped on the door and admired the window box of red geraniums alongside while he waited.

Tolly Barton still had sleep crusted in the corner of his eyes when he answered the door. He'd thrown on a grubby shirt over his breeches. His braces dangled down behind him and his feet were bare. He was a grey-haired, gruff fellow, probably in his late fifties. He was also a little deaf. Lavender had to explain the purpose of his visit twice. Eventually the man invited him inside.

The small, smoky kitchen was crammed with furniture, cooking utensils and other items. A startled woman glanced up from the hearth, where she was frying ham over the coal fire. Like Barton, she'd also dressed hastily and her grey hair was still down round her shoulders. Above her head, a drying rack, laden with damp laundry, swung on the end of two ropes.

'Please excuse my visit at such an early hour, Mrs Barton,' Lavender said, 'but I need to ask your husband some urgent questions about a murder we're investigating.'

'Ah, the poor chap who were killed at Mrs Palmer's? We 'eard about that, didn't we Tolly?' She spoke very loudly to compensate for her husband's deafness. The coachman nodded but didn't respond. 'Such a shame,' the woman continued. 'Such a nice man. Lady Tyndall loaned 'im 'er coach sometimes, didn't she, Tolly?'

Again, Barton simply nodded. His wife was obviously the more talkative of the pair. Lavender wondered how much of what she said her husband actually heard.

He turned to Barton and raised his voice to the same level as the man's wife. 'I believe you took MacAdam to Bruton Street on the night of the murder and brought him home again, Mr Barton. I need you to tell me about your return journey. I need to know every detail.'

Barton shrugged. 'It were just another trip. I brought 'im 'ome, settled the 'orses down and came up 'ere for me supper.'

'We 'ad a bit o' tripe,' his wife added helpfully, obviously taking Lavender's request for information to the extreme.

'Was MacAdam in good health? Where did he climb out of the carriage?'

''E came back to the mews with me,' Barton replied gruffly. ''E seemed fine.'

'It's shockin' to think 'e were murdered a few hours later,' his wife murmured.

'He was murdered sooner than that,' Lavender said loudly. 'We believe the attack took place just after you arrived back here in the mews – possibly outside the coach house or in the vicinity.'

Mrs Barton gasped. 'What? You mean the killer were in our street?'

'Mr Barton, did you see – or hear – anything at all?'

Barton hesitated.

'For the love of God, Tolly, if you know somethin', tell the Detective!' Mrs Barton shouted. 'That killer needs catchin' and hangin' – it may be one of us next! It gives me the shivers to think of 'im still roamin' the area.'

'I'm thinkin', woman, don't nag me.' Barton screwed up his face while he tried to remember. The gentle sizzle of the ham in the pan was the only sound. Finally, he shook his head. 'I saw nothin'. There were no one else around in the mews – but I were distracted wi' the 'orses and the carriage.'

'Well, 'e might not 'ave 'eard somethin', on account of 'is affliction, but I 'eard somethin',' Mrs Barton said. 'I were up 'ere waitin' for Tolly and I 'eard a couple quarrellin'.'

'That's not what 'e means,' her husband protested.

Lavender frowned and held up his hand. 'Let her speak.'

'It were a man and a woman. She were a quarrelsome 'arridan and were shoutin' at him.'

'One of your neighbours, perhaps?' Lavender suggested.

She shrugged. 'They're a peaceful lot round 'ere, by and large. I didn't know the voices.'

'Have we done?' Barton asked abruptly. 'I need to get to work.'

'One final question, Mr Barton. Did Lady Tyndall know about MacAdam's trips in her carriage to Bruton Street to see his young woman?'

Barton shifted uneasily on his bare feet and glanced away. 'She didn't. Well, not until Sunday, at least. MacAdam asked me to tell 'er that 'e used the carriage to meet up with 'is friends at The Porcupine in Covent Garden – but I knew what were goin' on. The girl 'ad taken a few trips wi' MacAdam in the coach. I'd seen 'em together – and I'd seen the ring on 'er finger. My ears might be bad but there ain't nothin' wrong wi' me eyes.'

'Did you lie for MacAdam?'

'I didn't lie – I just didn't say nothin'. I do as I'm bid and drive where I'm told. Lady Tyndall don't ask my thoughts and rarely speaks to me. I keep me mouth shut.'

'You said "she didn't" know about Miss Howard but she found out on Sunday. What happened then?'

Barton shuffled uncomfortably again. 'I may 'ave let somethin' slip about MacAdam's young woman when I brought 'er ladyship back from church.'

'How so? What happened?'

'She said I were to drive MacAdam to The Porcupine again that evenin'. I were distracted with one of the 'orses – she had a loose shoe – and without thinkin' I just said: "To see 'is wench on Bruton Street, you mean?"'

'That's more than lettin' somethin' "slip",' his wife said, frowning.

'Well, I were fed up of 'im actin' like 'e were a bloody lord,' Barton replied angrily. ''E'd told that gal it were 'is carriage.'

'How did Lady Tyndall react?' Lavender asked.

'She were annoyed and demanded I tell 'er the truth about 'is visits to the gal.'

Lavender waited for Barton to elaborate further but he said nothing else.

He didn't need to. Lavender had the information he needed. He thanked them both, left the smoky kitchen and walked out gratefully into the fresh morning air.

Lavender felt dazed as he collected his horse, walked it round to Park Lane and tied it to the railings. He intended to visit Mrs Palmer's to tie up some loose ends about the Collins murder but he needed to think about what he'd just learned before he moved on to the other case. He stood thoughtfully beside his horse, stroking her neck, and watched a couple of groomsmen gallop over the grass of Hyde Park, exercising their horses.

Mrs Barton had just confirmed Ike Rawlings' story that there was an arguing couple somewhere in the mews on the night of the murder. Was it MacAdam and a woman? Did some furious woman kill MacAdam?

In all of Lavender's career, he'd only ever arrested three women for murder. Two of them had his sympathy; they'd both been battered and abused by their husbands. One had slowly poisoned her husband to death with arsenic. The other had grabbed a bread knife in the heat of an argument and slit her drunken spouse's throat. The third woman, a particularly nasty creature he'd met in Northumberland a few years ago, had finished off her frail stepmother by sprinkling digitalis from the foxglove plant in her food.

Poison was always a woman's preferred method when it came to murder but as his murderess with the bread knife showed, women were as lethal as men in the heat of an argument. It wasn't beyond the realm of possibility that during an ugly argument with MacAdam in the back of the smithy, some woman grabbed the farrier's knife and plunged it into him.

Carefully, he considered the women in MacAdam's life. Mrs Palmer and Lady Louisa Fitzgerald had no motive to kill the man. Amelia Howard adored MacAdam and was ignorant of his lies and deceit. Her vixen of a little sister was probably quite capable of murdering a man in cold blood but Lavender struggled to see what Matilda Howard would gain from killing the lothario. Matilda and Bentley needed MacAdam alive. Besides which, as far as he was aware, both the Howard girls had remained in Bruton Street after MacAdam climbed in the coach to travel home.

That left Lady Tyndall. A woman with a reputation for jealousy who'd financed MacAdam and loaned him her coach. She'd tried to give him the impression that she was unconcerned by MacAdam's relationship with Miss Howard but according to Mr Barton she was ignorant of his trips to see his fiancée in Bruton Street – until Sunday. The day he died. She knew where MacAdam was that night – and she probably knew about the open door into the smithy at the back of her carriage house. Did she creep out of her home and confront him about his deception? Did they end up in the smithy arguing? Did she stab him?

Everything now depended on what Woods discovered from Lady Tyndall's maid, Harriet. In the meantime, he needed to tie up loose ends in the Collins murder.

Lavender shook his head to clear his mind and walked to Mrs Palmer's.

The tousled and sleepy maid who answered the door told him Mrs Palmer was 'still a-bed'.

'Never mind,' Lavender said. 'Don't disturb her. I just need to visit the bedchamber of Frank Collins to look at something, if that's all right with you?'

The girl nodded and led him upstairs to the murdered man's untidy room. She used her key to open the door and hovered nervously in the doorway. 'Sir Richard came to see Mrs Palmer last night. 'E told 'er Mr Collins were dead and you were after Bentley for the murder. Did you catch 'im?'

'Yes.' Lavender walked across to the hearth, bent down on one knee and examined the broken terracotta tile at the corner. 'I imagine Mrs Palmer was upset?'

'Oh, yes. She were right upset. We both were. She said she's ruined. She sent me round to 'er friends askin' them to call on her this mornin' and comfort her.'

'So Lady Tyndall and Lady Louisa Fitzgerald will be here later today?'

'Yes, at eleven.'

Lavender nodded and turned his attention back to the shattered tile. It had been hit with some force and was cracked into tiny pieces. 'How long has this been damaged?'

The maid inched her way across and peered over his shoulder. 'I don't know.'

Lavender took off his glove and ran his hand over the recently cleaned area of thin carpet next to the hearth. It had the stiff, matted feel of material that had been heavily soaped and left to dry out. 'Did you clean this bit of carpet?'

'No. The gentleman lodgers 'ad accidents sometimes with their pipes and tankards of ale. They'd borrow a bucket of water and a cloth from the kitchen and clean it up.'

Lavender took out the penknife he always carried in his coat pocket and prised up the stiff carpet from the edge of the hearth. It ripped away from the tacks that held it with a series of sharp pops.

'What you doin'?' the girl asked in alarm. 'Mrs Palmer won't like that.'

'Looking for evidence of the biggest "accident" your gentlemen lodgers ever had.'

'What do you mean?'

A dark stain pooled across the floorboards beneath the carpet.

'What is it?' the maid asked in alarm.

'The blood of Frank Collins,' Lavender said. 'This is where he fell to his death and cracked his head open on the hearth after MacAdam hit him.'

Chapter Thirty-Six

I t was mousy young Sarah, the housemaid, who answered the door to the servants' entrance of Lady Tyndall's house. She grinned when she saw Woods on the doorstep. 'Ooh, you're a brave one comin' back 'ere after last time.'

'Good morning, treacle,' Woods said, smiling. 'It's all right – I've not come to rouse the dragon. I were just hopin' to have a quick word with Lady Tyndall's maid, Harriet.'

Sarah shook her head and smoothed down the apron over the skirts of her blue-striped uniform. 'Well, you can't. She's gone back to her mother's. She were dismissed from her post two days ago.'

'Dismissed? Why, what happened?' Despite the obvious tension between mistress and maid on Monday, Woods was surprised. Had Lady Tyndall dismissed the girl to cover her tracks? Did young Harriet know too much?

Sarah rolled her eyes and jerked a thumb in the direction of the upper storeys of the building. 'She's what happened. She's forever dismissin' 'er personal maids. They don't last long 'ere.'

Woods nodded, kept his opinion to himself, and asked for the address of Harriet's mother.

◆ ◆ ◆

The narrow house on busy Long Acre was crammed between a butcher's and a cobbler's. It was a dilapidated and mean neighbourhood. Harriet answered the door and looked at him with confusion.

'Good mornin', Harriet,' Woods said. 'Do you remember me? I'm Constable Woods.'

The girl's dark eyes took in the bright blue coat and scarlet waistcoat of his distinctive uniform and she nodded. 'You're the constable who were askin' Lady Tyndall questions about Mr MacAdam.'

'That's right. Can I have a word with you?'

She hesitated for a moment then opened the door wider and led him through a narrow passage into a small and chilly parlour. She stood awkwardly, clutching at the apron over her threadbare brown gown. 'My ma's gone out with the little ones.'

'It's you I wanted to see, Harriet. I understand you've left Lady Tyndall's employment now, is that right?'

She nodded and lowered her head. 'I weren't good enough for her.'

'I find that hard to believe,' Woods said gently. 'I can tell from lookin' at you that you're a hard worker – and you've such pretty hair, too.'

She flushed and raised her hand to push back some of the wiry black curls escaping from her cap.

'Did she give you a reference?'

Harriet shook her head and brushed a tear from the corner of her left eye.

'That's a shame. I could see you were doin' your best when I came round on Monday. How long did you work for her?'

'Nine months. I lasted longer than any of her other maids.'

'It's a shame you've lost your job.'

'My ma needs all the help she can get with the rent. I've let her down.' Her face fell and her voice trembled.

'Well, I might be able to help you, treacle.'

She looked up hopefully. 'Do you know someone who needs a maid? I'm trained as a lady's maid but I'll do anythin' – and I'm nineteen next week.'

'No, I'm afraid I don't know anyone who needs a maid – but I do know there's a handsome reward out for anyone with information that will lead to the capture of the man – or woman – who killed David MacAdam.'

Harriet's dark face crumpled. 'But I don't know anythin' about that.'

'Let's see, shall we? Shall we sit down and be more comfy?'

The girl nodded and the two of them perched on the edge of a pair of battered and faded chairs.

'First off,' Woods said, 'what can you remember about Sunday?'

'Sunday?' She thought for a moment. 'I went with Lady Tyndall to church as usual, then we came home. She received no visitors that day, ate alone, then went to bed early.'

'Did you sleep in the next room?'

'No, I shared an attic room with one of the housemaids, Sarah.'

'Would you know if she got up again later that night and went out?'

'But she never goes out without her maid!' Harriet looked quite scandalised at the suggestion.

'As far as you can remember, did anythin' unusual happen on Sunday? Either with Lady Tyndall or with any other member of the household?'

The girl wrung her hands in her apron again. 'She were in a bad mood when we came back from church – and snapped at me . . .' Her voice trailed away hopelessly.

'But what you're sayin', treacle,' Woods' tone softened, 'is there were nothin' unusual in that?'

She nodded.

'What about the next day? The day the murder was discovered. What was Lady Tyndall's mood like then?'

'She were upset after you'd told her about MacAdam's death. Very upset.'

'Did she know him well?'

Harriet nodded again. 'He'd often come with us on outin's in the carriage. Sometimes he'd take tea with us in town.'

'She must have liked him very much.'

'She did. It were the only time I heard her laugh, when she were with him. He were a funny man – but I didn't like him much.'

'You didn't?' Woods was impressed. Harriet must be the only female who knew MacAdam who didn't warm to him.

'No, there were somethin' false about him. He flirted with her – and it, it didn't seem natural. I think he were after her money.'

'Do you think she were overly fond of MacAdam?'

Suddenly the girl looked wary. 'Constable, why are you askin' about Lady Tyndall?'

'She's been a bit difficult, treacle. You know how she can be?' Harriet nodded. 'Anyhow, we think she knows somethin' about MacAdam that she's not tellin' us. I'm hopin' that you can help me get a better idea of their relationship. After all,' he added, 'she's let you go without a reference. You don't owe her anythin' any more, do you? I'm sure a share of the reward will come in handy.'

'I'll get a reward if I help you?'

'There's a fifty-pound reward to be shared out amongst those who help solve the case of MacAdam's murder.'

'Fifty pounds!'

Woods could see she was torn between the prospect of the money and loyalty to her former mistress. He didn't have to be a police officer to work out that this household, with its shabby and damaged furnishings, needed money. There wasn't even any coal in the scuttle.

He paused for a moment, to let her think, then asked again: 'Do you think Lady Tyndall were overly fond of David MacAdam – for a woman of her age and station, that is.'

'She were besotted with him,' Harriet said sharply. Her voice hardened with disgust. 'It weren't right for a woman of her age. She hung on his every word and often pleaded with him to come around and see her. Imagine it! A lady of her status – *pleadin'* with a man like him.' Months of frustration poured out of the girl in a torrent. 'And she kept touchin' 'im.'

Woods' eyebrows shot up his forehead. 'How so?'

'She were always pattin' his leg or touchin' his face – brushin' back his hair and strokin' his cheek. It weren't . . . it weren't *seemly.*'

'Did she give him presents?'

'Often. An expensive pocket watch, a tie pin – and then that thing after he'd died.'

Woods sat up straighter. 'What thing, treacle?'

'She made me go with her to see MacAdam at the morgue in Bow Street.'

'That must have been difficult for you,' he said gently. He held back, knowing she'd tell him in her own time.

Harriet wrinkled her nose in disgust at the memory. 'It were foul. The place stank of death but she didn't seem to notice – or care. She wanted to give him a "goodbye" present, she said.'

'What was it?'

'I don't know.' The girl's voice caught in her throat and her face screwed up in horror. 'She leaned over the coffin and kissed his corpse! Can you imagine it? It were . . . horrible! Disgustin'! I looked away.'

'So you didn't see the present she gave him?'

'No, I looked away. But she had somethin' long and thin in her hand. She put it in the coffin with the body.'

Magistrate Read had his wigless head bowed over his paperwork when Lavender and Woods knocked and entered his office. 'Morning, gentlemen,' he said, without looking up. 'I gather from Oswald Grey that our cells are full of your suspects.'

Lavender and Woods sat down in the chairs opposite Read's desk.

'Yes,' Lavender said. 'And I'm about to add to their number. I want an arrest warrant for Lady Tyndall.'

Read's hand jerked and the quill scratched over the paper, spoiling his letter. 'Lady Tyndall?'

'Yes, we have irrefutable evidence that she stabbed David MacAdam during a heated argument.'

Shock flashed across Read's face. He pushed aside his ruined letter and laid down his quill. 'This had better be irrefutable evidence, Lavender. She's a wealthy aristocrat – the widow of a baronet. It'll be devilish hard to convict her.'

'She's also a possessive, bad-tempered and unstable old woman who allegedly nagged her husband to death after finding out about his liaison with another woman.'

'Nagging is not a capital offence,' Read said, 'and rumours are not evidence. You'll have to do better than that.'

Carefully, Lavender and Woods explained everything they had uncovered regarding the woman's involvement with MacAdam. Read winced when Woods mentioned that Lady Tyndall had kissed MacAdam's corpse.

'I believe she'd fallen in love with the rogue,' Lavender said. 'That's the only explanation for the generous gifts, the money she gave him and the liberties she allowed him with her carriage. She was ignorant of his plan to court and wed the Howard heiress until the morning of the murder. I suspect she brooded on it all day and went out to the stables to confront MacAdam when he returned from Bruton Street. She was one of the few people who knew where he was on Sunday night and his mode of transport. I think they went into the forge next to the carriage house to talk. This turned into an argument, then she grabbed the farrier's knife and stabbed him. We've got two witnesses who heard a man and a woman arguing: Ike Rawlings and Mrs Barton, the coachman's wife.'

'Is Mrs Barton a reliable witness to the argument?' Read asked. 'Because once Lady Tyndall's lawyers find out Ike Rawlings intended to marry MacAdam's widow, they'll tear his evidence to pieces in court if you put him in the witness stand. Like you, they'll suspect he murdered MacAdam himself.'

'We've also got her maid's statement that she left a "goodbye" present in MacAdam's coffin,' Woods said.

'Which can only be the farrier's knife we found in the coffin in Chelmsford,' Lavender added.

Read still didn't look convinced. 'Juries tend to be dismissive of the testimony of servants who've been sacked from their employment. They recognise that the young girl may want revenge.'

'She told me the story without promptin',' Woods said. 'I believe her.'

'Whether the case holds up in court or not – I'm convinced Lady Tyndall murdered MacAdam,' Lavender said firmly. 'MacAdam was a rogue and a lothario but even he deserves justice. I want an arrest warrant.'

'Good grief, Stephen,' Read said unhappily as he reached for his quill. 'You'll cause a sensation with this case.'

Chapter Thirty-Seven

A black barouche with four handsome chestnuts waited outside Mrs Palmer's house on Park Lane when Lavender and Woods arrived with the prison wagon they'd borrowed from Newgate gaol.

'Looks like she's got company, all right,' Woods said as he pulled on the reins. He stopped the distinctive vehicle a few yards down from the house. Lavender didn't want anyone in number ninety-three to look out of the window and see it.

'That'll be Lady Louisa Fitzgerald's carriage,' Lavender said. 'Let's hope we're not too early and that Lady Tyndall is here.'

'Are you sure you want to arrest her here? You'll have an audience.'

Lavender nodded. 'It's for the best. I have a hunch that she'll say something in her defence when surrounded by her shocked friends. She'll feel pressurised to explain herself here. When we take her back to Bow Street, she'll clam up like an oyster until her lawyer arrives.'

'So you're hopin' for a confession?'

'Yes – with witnesses.'

They climbed down from the box. Young Will raced across the road towards them, grinning. Woods tossed him a penny to look after the horses.

The maid who answered the door looked unsure when Lavender asked to be shown into the parlour. 'Mrs Palmer has guests,' she said, 'their ladyships are here and so is Sir Richard.'

'I know – I want to see them too.'

The narrow room was crowded. The three women were all dressed sombrely in black and sitting on chairs near to the fireplace. Mrs Palmer was red-eyed with crying and fiddled with a damp handkerchief in her lap. Sir Richard sat on a hard-backed chair by the table in the window. His crimson silk waistcoat brought the only splash of brightness to the dark room.

Lady Tyndall slammed down her cup, slopping tea into the saucer, and glowered angrily at Lavender. 'What are you doing here? I don't know how you've the bare-faced cheek to show your face after the way you talked to me the other day.'

'I've news for you all,' Lavender said simply.

Sir Richard held up his hand to silence the angry woman. 'Steady on, Clarissa. Lavender knows that I haven't been happy at times with how he's conducted this investigation but he usually gets his man and we need to hear him out. Did you catch Bentley, Lavender? They told me at Bow Street yesterday that you were pursuing him.'

Lavender nodded. 'We arrested Bentley on the Great North Road. He's now in the cells at Bow Street.'

'Oh dear.' Mrs Palmer's thin shoulders drooped and she blinked back more tears.

'So, have you solved the case, Detective?' Lady Louisa asked. 'Do you know who murdered Davy?' She had her whippet on her knee and was letting it lap at cold tea out of her saucer, oblivious to the mess the splashes made on her gown.

'Yes, I have.'

Lady Louisa turned to Lady Tyndall in triumph. 'That's ten guineas you owe me, Clarissa. I said Lavender would solve the mystery within a week.'

Lavender bit back his urge to smile. 'Thank you for your faith in us, ma'am.'

'Well, I don't want to hear about it.' Lady Tyndall gathered up her reticule. 'There's no need to bother your maid, Sylvia. I shall see myself out.'

'Oh, do sit down, Clarissa!' Lady Louisa said firmly. 'You know you're as intrigued as the rest of us. You're dying to find out what happened to poor Davy.'

'Huh!' Lady Tyndall exclaimed, but she remained seated, glaring coldly at Lavender.

'Come on then, man,' Sir Richard said. 'Don't keep us in suspense. What's happened to my sister's lodgers?'

Lavender cleared his throat. 'Firstly, it would appear that Frank Collins was accidentally killed in a drunken brawl in his room in June.'

'Your lodgers were more partial to their drink than you suggested when we first met,' Woods said to Mrs Palmer.

The elderly woman grimaced. 'Frank died here? In my house?'

'Yes,' Lavender said. 'Did you go to Dulwich for a while in June to visit your friend?'

Mrs Palmer nodded.

'During your absence, MacAdam and Collins had an argument about Miss Howard and MacAdam's plan to marry her. Collins thought the plan was appalling. It seems Frank Collins was the only person in Mayfair with any moral scruples.'

'That's a bit below the belt, Lavender,' Sir Richard warned.

Lavender ignored him and continued. 'MacAdam hit Collins. He fell and smashed his head on the corner of the hearth in his room.'

There was a short silence, then Lady Louisa groaned softly. 'Poor Frank.'

Mrs Palmer's elegant hand fluttered to dab her eyes with her handkerchief. Only Lady Tyndall seemed unmoved.

'Such an injury is consistent with the wound I found on Collins' skull,' Sir Richard said.

'When I came here early this morning I discovered bloodstains on the floorboards around the hearth and there are cracked tiles in the corner.'

'So, it looks like Bentley's story is true – MacAdam killed Collins,' Sir Richard said thoughtfully.

'Unless Bentley hit him,' Woods suggested.

Sir Richard shook his head. 'Even in his cups, I can't imagine Bentley knocking down a man as big as Collins – but MacAdam was his equal in strength and size.'

'So if Davy killed Frank, why don't you release young Alfred?' Lady Louisa asked. 'Did he kill Davy?'

'No, he didn't kill MacAdam – but he did aid and abet MacAdam in his devious plan to hide Collins' body in a grave in Chelmsford. MacAdam rewarded Bentley with an introduction to Miss Matilda Howard, whom Bentley wooed for the same reason MacAdam was after the older sister – the girls' future inheritance from their grandfather.'

'Oh dear, what a tangled web we weave,' Mrs Palmer sighed. She looked wretched. 'I suppose Alfred will spend a long time in gaol for his part in the fraud?'

'He'll be lucky to escape the death penalty, ma'am,' Lavender replied.

Mrs Palmer shuddered.

Lady Louisa shook her head sadly. 'What a waste of his life,' she said. 'I always enjoyed Alfred's company. Why can't people just be satisfied with what they have and stop scheming after more?'

Lady Tyndall leaned forward to Mrs Palmer and patted her arm. 'What a shame for you, Sylvia,' she said. 'Once this news leaks out you'll be ruined, my dear. Well, I'm sorry but I'm afraid I can't stay to hear any more.'

'She's not the only one who's ruined,' Lavender said sharply before she could rise. He pulled out the warrant from his coat pocket. 'Lady Tyndall, by the power vested in me by His Royal Highness, the Prince Regent, in the name and on behalf of His Majesty King George III, I arrest you on suspicion of murdering David MacAdam.'

'Good grief, Lavender!' Sir Richard leapt to his feet – whether in shock or protest was unclear. Mrs Palmer gasped in horror and Lady Louisa turned pale and pushed her dog to the floor.

A sarcastic smile curled up the corner of Lady Tyndall's mouth. 'Rubbish!' she said. 'What absolute rubbish! How could an old woman like *me* kill a man like MacAdam? Who would believe such nonsense?'

'You were infatuated with the man,' Lavender said firmly.

'You've gone too far this time, Lavender!' she retorted angrily.

'You resented his relationship with Miss Howard,' Lavender's tone hardened to match her own. 'You gave him money, bought him expensive presents and loaned him your carriage. We've two witnesses who heard you arguing with him in the mews on the night of the murder.'

'For God's sake, Lavender!' Sir Richard exclaimed. 'You're wrong – you must be!'

Lavender pulled out the farrier's knife from his coat pocket and held it out towards the surgeon. 'Do you recognise this, Sir Richard?'

'Why, yes – it's the murder weapon. The farrier's knife we found in MacAdam's coffin.'

'We've another witness, Lady Tyndall's former maid, Harriet. She claims they went to Bow Street morgue the day after the murder and she watched Lady Tyndall place something in MacAdam's coffin.'

'She's lying. Who would believe a girl like that over *me*?' Lady Tyndall screamed.

'She says you placed it there as you leaned over the dead man to kiss him goodbye.'

'You kissed him?' Lady Louisa stared at her friend in disgust.

'Did you go to the Bow Street morgue, Clarissa?' Sir Richard asked.

'Did you kiss him?' Lady Louisa asked again, her voice rising in disbelief.

'Oh, she were always touchin' and strokin' MacAdam, according to the maid,' Woods interjected.

Lady Tyndall rose angrily to her feet. 'It was nothing – just a good-bye kiss to a dear friend – that's all.'

'So you admit you *were* at the Bow Street morgue,' Lavender said in triumph.

'I was,' she spat back at him. 'But I've never seen that – that thing – before.'

'Yes, you have,' Lavender said. 'It's the missing knife from the forge next to your carriage house. You grabbed it in fury and stabbed David MacAdam with it while you were arguing with him about his relationship with Miss Howard. Then you hid it where you thought no one would look.'

'Is Lavender right, Clarissa?' Lady Louisa asked. 'Did your jealousy finally get the better of you? Did you stab MacAdam to death because of the girl?'

Lady Tyndall glared back into her face, tight-lipped.

'You damned fool,' Lady Louisa said. 'It was only ever supposed to be a bit of amusing distraction with those men. You weren't supposed to fall in love with one of them!'

'So what happened, Lady Tyndall?' Lavender asked. 'Did MacAdam's deception remind you of your late husband's betrayal? Did you imagine MacAdam and that sweet young girl with the flawless skin and the glossy hair cuddled up together? She was so young and so tender, wasn't she? You couldn't compete with that, could you?'

Sir Richard winced. 'Steady on, Lavender.'

Lavender ignored him and stepped closer to Lady Tyndall. 'Did you picture MacAdam touching Miss Howard like you touched him? Did you imagine him stroking her arm, pushing back her hair and tenderly kissing her soft lips?'

'Lavender!'

She spun round on him like a tiger, her face contorted with rage. 'He deserved it! He wouldn't listen to reason. I gave him everything he needed – the money, the love – but he still threw it back in my face and deceived me with that chit of a girl – that dirty little chee-chee!'

'Good God!' Sir Richard exclaimed. Mrs Palmer looked like she was about to faint.

'You're mad!' Lady Louisa was frozen with horror in the centre of the room. 'Stark raving mad!'

Lady Tyndall shrugged. Her voice dropped. 'He deserved to die. He knew I loved him – yet he still deceived me.'

'Whom did you plan to kill next?' Lady Louisa stumbled over her words. 'I enjoyed MacAdam's company. Did you plan to murder me too?'

'Why don't you understand, Louisa?' Lady Tyndall screamed in the face of her former friend. 'He got what he deserved! A man like that – from his background – rejecting a lady like me! Why can't you see it? I've no regrets – no one can blame me for what I did.'

'Constable.' Lavender gave the signal. Woods pulled out his handcuffs and moved towards Lady Tyndall.

'No!' she screamed. 'No! Get your grubby little hands off me!' She fought like a cat when Woods tried to restrain her. Lavender had to assist and she resisted them with the strength of a woman half her age. In the pandemonium that followed, a chair was knocked over and someone stood on the whippet. It yelped, adding its squeals to the cries of the horrified women and Sir Richard's desperate calls for calm.

Finally, they clapped the irons on the woman's wrists and dragged her sobbing outside to the prison wagon. Young Will watched them wide-eyed with shock from beside the horses. 'You've arrested the old trot?' he asked in awe.

Lavender tossed him a coin and sent him on his way as Woods slammed the door of the wagon shut and bolted it.

'Gawd's teeth!' Woods laughed. 'She's a lively old tabby, I'll say that for her.'

Lavender leaned back against the vehicle and let the relief flood through him.

Woods turned his head and looked at Lavender. 'That was well done, sir, you got a confession – in front of witnesses, too.'

'We'll need it if Magistrate Read is right about the furore her trial will cause.'

Woods grinned. 'It's in the hands of the courts now, sir. You've done your job and hauled another murderer off the streets of London. No one can ask any more of you.'

'*We've* done our job,' Lavender corrected him.

'Yes, we have, haven't we?' Woods stood up taller and puffed out his chest with pride. 'We've done well. We've solved the mysterious murder of a lothario – and uncovered and solved another ghastly crime as well. They've had two for the price of one out of us this week.'

Lavender smiled. 'Yes, we've done well, Ned.'

But Woods hadn't finished congratulating himself yet. 'I said right from day one that this murderer might be a woman, didn't I?'

'Yes, you did – and Magdalena warned me that even sweet little old ladies are capable of great passion.'

'Huh! There isn't anythin' "sweet" about this one. But you should have listened closer to me, sir.'

Lavender grinned when they climbed up to the driver's seat on the wagon. 'Of course, I should have done. Come on, let's get back to Bow Street and release Ike Rawlings – that poor *man* you encouraged me arrest.'

Epilogue

M agdalena sat on the stool in their bedchamber in front of the
mirror while Teresa pinned up her hair. Lavender sat in the
armchair watching them. In his arms lay seven-week-old Miss Alice
Sofía Lavender, who looked very cute and dainty in her white lace
christening gown. Fully satisfied after a good feed from her mother,
little Miss Lavender had burped politely and delivered a small posset
of milk, which Lavender had managed to catch before it soiled his new
gold waistcoat. Now, rather than fall asleep, she lay wide awake, staring
up curiously into her father's face.

Lavender stared back, still unable to believe in the perfection of
his beautiful daughter. She had a lovely head of wavy, dark brown hair,
similar in colour but softer than his own. She'd inherited her mother's
olive complexion and long black eyelashes. Lavender hated to see those
tiny eyes wet with tears, but fortunately, she rarely cried. His little girl
had slipped into the world in late February without much fuss and had
barely murmured since. Magdalena recovered quickly from the birth
and suffered no ill effects apart from the inevitable exhaustion. She
claimed the placid nature of their child was due to the fact that little

Alice had very little to complain about. She had constant attention from everyone in the household and their family and friends were forever calling round to coo over the child.

They'd decided to postpone her baptism until her half-brother, Sebastián, returned home from school at Easter and they'd turned the event into a party. All of their friends and Lavender's extensive family had been invited. Mouthwatering smells of baking and roasting had filled the house for the last two days and twelve-year-old Sebastián had haunted the basement kitchen, begging Mrs Hobart for samples of the food. Lavender had bought Magdalena a new dress for the occasion and had ordered himself the pale gold striped waistcoat he'd admired in the window of Drake's Tailors in Chelmsford.

Yet even at this moment of joy, when his heart swelled with paternal pride and satisfaction, nagging doubt crept into his mind. 'Is there something wrong with her eyes?' he asked.

Teresa paused in her ministrations of her mistress's thick, glossy hair as Magdalena half turned her head towards him. 'What do you mean?'

'She's looking at me in a strange manner. Is everything all right with her eyes?'

Magdalena turned back to her mirror. 'Betsy reminded me this week that this is the age when they start to see things clearly for the first time.'

'So what is she doing? Why is she looking at me this way?'

'*Dios mío!*' Magdalena stood up and flounced across the room, trailing a shower of hair pins behind her. She paused with her hands on her ample hips and observed her husband and daughter. 'There's nothing wrong with her eyes, Stephen. Stop imagining things.'

'But what's this funny expression on her face? Why is she looking at me like that?'

'She looks at you like that because she's *your* daughter and has *your* eyes. That's how *you* look at people.'

'I do?'

'Yes. She's examining your face for clues.' As Magdalena flounced back to her stool, little Alice followed her mother's irritated movements and her tiny rosebud mouth curled into a smile.

Stephen sat silently for a while, reassured about his daughter but unsure whether he'd just been insulted or complimented by his wife. Sometimes it was wisest to say nothing. At thirty-two years of age, Magdalena found this second round of motherhood quite tiring and she could be a little testy at times.

Teresa finished Magdalena's hair and helped her mistress into her gown. Magdalena chose the black silk and lace dress with the intricate beading that he'd bought her for Christmas several years ago, when they'd first met.

'Aren't you going to wear your new gown?' he asked.

She shook her head, walked to the full-length mirror and smoothed the material over her flat stomach. 'I've always loved this one and I wanted to see if I could fit into it again, so soon after the birth.'

'It fits perfectly,' he said, 'you look wonderful. You've regained your figure.'

'That's exactly the right thing to say, Stephen,' she said, smiling.

'You're not the only one to regain their figure this year,' Lavender added. 'You should see Ned Woods now. Betsy has done a fine job restricting his food and ale. His waistcoat doesn't strain over his stomach any more.'

Magdalena smiled. 'Teresa? Pass me the pearls, please.'

Lavender had bought Magdalena a present of an expensive string of pearls with matching earrings after the birth of little Alice. Teresa brought out the box and fastened the necklace round her mistress's throat. They glowed luminously against the flawless olive skin of her neck and breast and were a perfect match for the glistening beads of the gown.

Magdalena fixed the earrings on to her lobes and stroked the necklace gently. 'It's lovely,' she said.

Suddenly the door burst open and Sebastián Garcia de Aviles Morales del Castillo, known to his school friends simply as Garcia, flew into the room.

'I've told you before, Sebastián,' Magdalena said calmly, her eyes still on her mirrored reflection. 'You must learn to knock at this door.'

'Oh! Sorry, Mamá!' Sebastián walked backwards out of the room with great ceremony, closed the door and knocked loudly and pointedly from the other side.

Lavender and Magdalena exchanged an amused glance.

'Shall we just leave him out there on the landing?' Stephen suggested.

Magdalena giggled. 'Enter,' she said loudly.

The door flew open again and Sebastián rushed back. He went straight to their full-length mirror and edged Magdalena out of the way to see his own reflection. 'I just wanted to say, sir – thank you for this topping waistcoat.'

Magdalena sat down on her stool, watching her son fondly. Teresa left the room to get herself ready for the baptism.

'It's my pleasure, Sebastián,' Lavender said. 'I'm glad you like it.' When he'd ordered his own waistcoat from Drake's Tailors, he'd sent in an additional order for a dark blue silk waistcoat for Sebastián.

The boy preened like a peacock in front of the mirror, admiring the garment. 'I feel quite the swell wearing it,' he said, 'and I'm sure Jasper and the others will agree.'

'Remind me again, please,' Magdalena said, 'which one of your school friends is Jasper?'

'Oh, he's not a friend as such – he's in the form above mine – but everyone knows he's an expert on men's fashion. His uncle is a friend to Beau Brummell.'

The corners of Lavender's mouth turned up into a smile. 'I can see how that makes him an authority on the subject.'

'Yes, he's a real swell, is Jasper. A proper – what did you call it? – *authority* on breeches, coats, cravats and waistcoats. Will there be cricket at this baptism?'

'That's not traditional,' Magdalena said. They were both used to Sebastián's mercurial mind and his rapid changes of subject. 'However, once we return to the house, I'm sure Eddie and Dan Woods will be happy to join you in a game outside in the square.'

'Well, as long as they don't let their sister play.'

Lavender saw Magdalena take a sharp intake of breath and knew the cause. Sebastián had been aloof with his own sister since her birth and generally ignored the child.

'Would it hurt to let Rachel join in the game?' Magdalena asked gently.

'Of course it would hurt, Mamá!' Sebastián looked stunned by his mother's ignorance. 'Rachel's a tartar at cricket. She bats far better than Dan – and belts between the stumps like a runner at Ascot.'

This surprised Lavender. Both of Ned's sons were natural athletes. It was strange to think of their little sister bettering them. 'Well, in that case, you'd better not let Rachel play,' he said. 'You can't let a mere girl show you how it's done, can you?'

Sebastián stared at him thoughtfully. Lavender recognised the look in his dark eyes. Magdalena had the same look when she was hatching a plan. 'I suppose I *could* let Rachel be on my team . . .'

'That might work,' Lavender said.

Sebastián walked across and stared down at little Alice in his arms. 'When will Baby Alice be able to play cricket?'

'It may be a while yet,' Magdalena said gently, hiding her smile.

'By the way, I've been talking with Lewis minor.'

'Is he the authority on men's waistcoats?'

'No, I told you before that's Jasper. Lewis minor knows a lot about families.'

'Really?'

'Yes, he has ten brothers and sisters so there's not much he doesn't know.'

'Of course,' said Lavender, 'another authority. So, what has Lewis minor said about us?'

Sebastián fixed him with his frank gaze. 'Well, Lewis minor thinks that now I've got a sister – and we're a proper family – that I should stop calling you "sir" and call you *Papí* instead.' He shrugged as another thought came to him. 'Or I could call you *padre*, if you'd prefer?'

Lavender was speechless. The boy had taken the wind out of his sails.

'The anglicised version, *Papa*, might be better,' Magdalena said.

'Very well, *Papa* it shall be.' Sebastián flew out of the room as quickly as he'd entered it.

Lavender swallowed hard, trying to overcome the emotion surging through him. 'I never expected that. It seems I've gained two children this year instead of the one.'

Magdalena came across and kissed him on the top of his head. 'He adores you, Stephen,' she said. 'He always has.'

The baptism went smoothly. Apart from their family and closest friends, Magistrate and Mrs Charity Read and Sir Richard and Lady Allison were also present. In a kind gesture, Magdalena had included Sylvia Palmer in their invitation. She'd been living with her brother and his wife for some months now. Lavender studied Mrs Palmer during the service. She looked older and more drawn than he remembered. But living with Sir Richard would age anyone, he reasoned.

Lady Caroline Clare and Ned and Betsy Woods were the proud godparents. Miss Alice Sofía Lavender stayed wide awake while she was blessed by the vicar of St Saviour and St Mary Overie and given the names of her two grandmothers. She didn't even flinch when the vicar wet her head, preferring instead to stare up into his face, looking for clues.

Everyone returned to the house after the service and Lavender and Magdalena spent an enjoyable two hours drifting between their dining room and drawing room, entertaining their guests. Magdalena always flowered when they had company but after a couple of hours, Lavender felt himself wilting. Their baby girl was passed from the arms of one adoring adult to another, her progress around the room followed jealously by four-year-old Tabitha Woods, who declared loudly that little Alice was 'my baby'.

The cold collation of beef, ham, larded oysters and small savoury pastries, prepared by Mrs Hobart and Teresa, vanished quickly into the mouths of their hungry guests. And the youngsters, led by a ravenous Sebastián, made short work of the large selection of desserts, especially the quivering blancmange, the sweetmeats and the marzipans. Shortly afterwards, Sebastián, Eddie and Dan Woods found the cricket bats and stumps and led several of Lavender's nieces and nephews out into the lawned area in the centre of the square. Lavender was pleased to see the freckled face of nine-year-old Rachel Woods amongst them.

Feeling rather stifled and hot by the sheer number of people in his house, Lavender found Woods and suggested they went outside to watch the game for a while. 'I want to see your Rachel play,' he said. 'I understand she's a bit of a tartar when it comes to cricket.'

Woods puffed out his chest with pride and followed him out of the front door to the railings that edged the park. 'Yes, she's better than the lads were at that age – and she can outrun most of the boys in her class too. Besides which, she rides better than Eddie.'

'I find that hard to believe,' Lavender said, smiling. 'You forget I've seen your son ride.'

Woods shrugged the shoulders of his Sunday-best coat. 'She's a natural in the saddle.'

Lavender frowned and brushed a lock of hair away from his eyes. A light breeze had sprung up and gently rustled the leaves in the trees above their head. It was refreshing after the stuffiness of the house. 'But where does it lead, Ned?' he asked. 'Where do our daughters' talents take them – apart from to marriage and motherhood?'

Woods gave him a sidelong glance. 'You've been thinkin' too much again, sir.'

'I'm serious, Ned. I never gave it much thought before Alice was born but now I worry about her future. I'd hate to think of any child of mine unable to exercise her brain or find happiness in her God-given talents. The life of a woman seems very restricted.'

'Well, worryin' don't serve no purpose as far as I can see. Besides which, they'll all make their own way in the world – with or without us worryin' and interferin' – especially the gals.'

'You think so?'

'Yes. Look at your wife. She speaks Latin like one of them Romans and sits and chats to you in the lingo by the fireside.'

'Well, we don't just discuss Latin,' Lavender protested hastily. 'Little Alice is proof of that.'

'Quite. And Doña Magdalena is also a crack shot. She used her skill at shootin' to get her and her son out of Spain – and has saved your life with her marksmanship.'

'So, you're saying I should stand back and let little Alice pursue her talents and find her own happiness in life?'

'It strikes me, sir, that we parents don't have much choice – especially where the gals are concerned. All we can do with the little nippers is watch them from the sidelines like we are now, and drop them the odd pearl of wisdom to help them on their way.'

The children had formed into two teams on the grassy centre of the square. Sebastián's team waited to bat. His black hair and dark colouring meant he stood out in the group of fairer, freckled English children. Lavender's nieces had been sent out to field, but he was pleased to see little Rachel standing behind Sebastián in the queue. He was chatting animatedly to the young girl.

'I like your fancy new waistcoat, by the way, sir,' Woods said. 'It's from Drake's in Chelmsford, isn't it?'

Lavender smiled. 'You miss nothing, Ned.'

'Funny case that,' Woods added, frowning. 'It were a pity that woman were never hanged for what she did. And it were a shame they never looked again at her husband's death. I still think there may have been more to that than a simple suicide.'

Lavender nodded. Lady Tyndall's case had never come to court. Following her arrest, her strong-minded, wealthy and influential nephew had stormed into Bow Street. He'd no intention of letting his aristocratic aunt swing on the gallows for the murder of David MacAdam. Once he learned that Lady Tyndall had confessed to being in love with a much younger man from a totally unsuitable background, he'd instructed her lawyers to have her declared insane. Lady Tyndall was whisked away, to live out her days in a remote but comfortable lunatic asylum.

'It were like everyone thought her biggest crime weren't the killin' of MacAdam – but the lovin' of him instead.'

'It's the world we live in,' Lavender said sharply. 'The justice system is designed to protect the wealthy and influential from the rest of us – not to punish them.'

'You're thinkin' too much again, sir. It'll end badly.'

Lavender shrugged. 'Mind you, most of the witnesses for the case disappeared once the scandal erupted in the news-sheets. Mr Howard shut up his house in Bruton Street and took his granddaughters back to India. Even Lady Louisa Fitzgerald grabbed her hounds and retreated to the family estates in Ireland until the fuss died down. The only witnesses to Lady Tyndall's confession who were left in London were Sir Richard and Mrs Palmer. The attention on them at a trial would have been intense and devastating. It was probably for the best she went to a secure asylum.'

'Oh, a bit of pressure wouldn't have done that wheedlin' sawbones any harm,' Woods said darkly. 'What happened to that Bentley chap?'

'He was transported to Botany Bay just after Christmas.'

'Well, at least he got his just deserts.'

'Yes. Ike Rawlings gave evidence at his trial. He recognised Bentley as the young man who'd brought that coffin to Chelmsford. Mrs MacAdam was with him in court – but she's Mrs Rawlings now. She married him in the end.'

'So that's one happy endin', at least.'

'So it would seem.'

Young Rachel stepped forward to bat. Lavender noted with surprise that she was left-handed. She seemed so tiny next to the stumps with her eldest brother towering behind her at the wicket. Woods' younger son, Dan, bowled – slightly softer than normal, Lavender thought. Rachel swung the bat with all her might and cracked it towards the far railings.

The ball flew like a pistol shot – and went straight through a ground-floor window of one of the houses opposite.

For a moment, the children froze like statues at the sound of the shattering glass. Then, as one, they turned on their heels and stampeded back across the grass towards Lavender, Woods and the house.

Woods held up his arms to stop them and hollered, 'Whoa! Stop runnin', you young scamps!'

The fleeing children braked to a halt just in front of them.

Woods lowered his voice. 'It seems to me that a crime's just been committed against the property of one of the neighbours.' He nodded at Eddie and added quietly: 'You should know better than to run, son.'

Eddie blushed.

Little Rachel's freckled face puckered in anguish. 'Will I go to gaol, Da?' she asked.

Sebastián stepped forward and took the bat out of her hand. 'I'll take the blame,' he announced.

Eddie scowled and blushed harder. 'No, you won't, you daft saphead.' He took the bat from Sebastián. 'She's my sister. I'll go and apologise and say I did it.'

'Why don't you all go?' Woods suggested.

The children looked a bit alarmed but they turned and trooped back round to the other side of the square, dragging the bats and the stumps behind them. Lavender and Woods watched them with satisfaction. Sebastián ran alongside Eddie, still arguing about who was to take the blame for Rachel's mishap.

'See what I mean?' Woods said. 'All it takes is a word now and then and they work it out for themselves. Mind you, I hope you've got some money left in your pocketbook after payin' for this fancy party. Since our sons are fightin' amongst themselves for the privilege of havin' their heads bitten off by your angry neighbour, I expect you to pay half for their new window.'

Lavender smiled. *Our sons.* He liked that. 'Of course.'

'And that's another thing – don't expect to retire from work a wealthy man. In fact, don't expect to retire at all. The nippers cost us a fortune.'

'I don't know what I'd do without your pearls of wisdom, Ned.'

Woods gave him another sideways glance and grinned. 'And I don't either.'

Author's Notes

I first came across the unusual effect corsets can have on stab victims while researching the assassination of Empress Elisabeth of Austria in 1898. This poor lady was stabbed to death by an Italian anarchist while she walked with her lady-in-waiting to catch a steamboat on Lake Geneva. The Empress collapsed, was helped to her feet and walked another one hundred yards to the gangplank, where she boarded the steamer. Due to the pressure from her tight corseting, the haemorrhage of blood was slowed to mere drops. This confused her attendants, who didn't realise she was fatally injured and were slow to seek medical help. The steamer left port and was part way across the lake before she lost consciousness and they realised that they needed to turn back.

When I read about Empress Elisabeth's tragic death, I knew I'd discovered an unusual device I could use in my fiction. Fat Regency gentlemen (including the Prince Regent) often used male corsets so it didn't take me long to change Empress Elisabeth into a man for the purposes of my plot.

As for the bigamy – well, I've had an unhealthy interest in the subject ever since I was accused of being a bigamist by my vicar.

Yes, you read that correctly.

Organising a wedding is a nerve-wracking business at the best of times. I was particularly nervous when Chris and I approached the vicar of my childhood church. I'd moved away from the family home and was no longer a member of the congregation but I wanted to get married there, surrounded by family and childhood friends. I expected a lot of questions from the vicar – but the last thing I expected was his outlandish accusation of bigamy.

Apparently, the vicar had recently married a young woman with the same surname as mine. She forgot to mention that she was already married to someone else. The vicar suffered several strained visits from the police after her crime came to light and he was determined never to go through that again. He was convinced I was the same woman – and that I'd brazenly returned with a different man to do it all over again.

To say I was distressed is an understatement. To say that this probably wasn't the vicar's finest moment either is also an understatement. Fortunately, after a phone call from my furious and indignant little mother, the situation was resolved. Chris and I eventually, and somewhat nervously, had our wedding in my childhood church on 23 May 1993.

It was an early indication that my own life would always be stranger than fiction.

I laugh about it now. But it's not the kind of incident a girl easily forgets and it led to my lifelong fascination with bigamists. I read everything I could find about the subject.

Bigamy and marital desertion were rife in England during the nineteenth century. In one month alone in County Durham, half of all the court cases involved bigamists or men (and women) charged with abandoning their families. Both crimes were imprisonable offences but this didn't deter desperate spouses trying to escape from an unhappy marriage. The historical past is not always a romantic place when we dig beneath the surface.

I made David MacAdam into a commercial traveller because his roaming made it easier for him to lead a double life. As most lovers of Regency fiction will be aware, women's fashion of this era was highly ornate and dependent on a precise fit, so ready-to-wear garments for women weren't widely available. However, the relatively simple, flattering cuts and muted tones of men's fashion made proportionate sizing possible in mass production. By the late 1700s, Bristol, England was home to over 200 businesses that exported hats, gloves, drawers, pants, stockings, shirts, jackets, and footwear, mostly to the United States. My fictional character Saul Drachmann, with his catalogues, commercial travellers and ready-to-wear menswear, is an entrepreneur in an industry that rapidly expanded in Britain in the early years of the nineteenth century.

The excellent BBC TV series *Taboo* reignited my interest in the notorious East India Company and led to the creation of the exotic Howard family.

Unlike my last two novels, this book is not based on a true crime solved by the real-life Stephen Lavender; it's all fiction.

Apart from Lavender and Magistrate Read, the only other real historical figure I alluded to in the novel was Doctor Willis, the famous physician of 'Mad' King George III. However, please note there's no record of Willis ever having had a daughter; Lady Allison is also fictitious.

I would like to acknowledge the love, help and support given to me by The Historical (hysterical) Fictionnaires during the months I spent in my writing cave. I'm especially grateful to Jean Gill for her wonderful help with the 'dog' scene and Jane Harlond for her expert assistance with all things horsey and Spanish. I also value the help I received from Kristin Gleeson, Claire Stibbe and Babs Morton. Thanks, ladies.

Thanks must also go to the people of Puerto Rico in Gran Canaria, who for the second year on the trot provided me with a supportive and sunny writing retreat during the dreadful British winter. I would like to pay tribute to my wonderful cover designer, Lisa Horton, and the excellent editorial team at Thomas & Mercer.

Finally, to you, the reader, thank you for following this series to book five. I hope you enjoyed reading *Murder in Park Lane* as much as I enjoyed writing it. This linear structure, where Lavender and Woods move from one set of clues to another, made it far quicker and easier to write than my last two novels, with their complicated multi-stranded plots. The words flowed across the page like silk. I feel this book bears more in common with *The Heiress of Linn Hagh* than any of the others.

If you enjoyed it, please leave a review on Amazon.

Karen Charlton
www.karencharlton.com
14th October 2018
Marske-by-the Sea,
North Yorkshire

About the Author

Karen Charlton writes historical mysteries and is also the author of a non-fiction genealogy book, *Seeking Our Eagle*. She has published short stories and numerous articles and reviews in newspapers and magazines. An English graduate and former teacher, Karen has led writing workshops and has spoken at a number of literary events across the north of England, where she lives. Karen now writes full-time.

A stalwart of the village pub quiz and a member of a winning team on the BBC quiz show *Eggheads*, Karen also enjoys the theatre and won a Yorkshire Tourist Board award for her Murder Mystery Weekends.

Find out more about Karen's work at www.karencharlton.com.